MW00414305

Books by Vaughn Heppner:

INVASION AMERICA SERIES
Invasion: Alaska
Invasion: California
Invasion: Colorado
Invasion: New York
Invasion: China

LOST STARSHIP SERIES
The Lost Starship
The Lost Command
The Lost Destroyer
The Lost Colony

EXTINCTION WARS SERIES
Assault Troopers
Planet Strike
Star Viking
Fortress Earth

OTHER SF NOVELS
Accelerated
Strotium-90
I, Weapon

Visit www.Vaughnheppner.com for more
information.

Artifact

by Vaughn Heppner
and Logan White

ISBN-13: 978-1532982392
ISBN-10: 1532982399
BISAC: Fiction / Science Fiction / Adventure

-Prologue-

"Do you hear that?" Claire whispered.

Andy, her assistant, shook his head.

Claire heard it, all right. It was a persistent hum, a maddening background noise. She was among the two percent of humanity that could hear a low frequency humming, rumbling or droning when everything else was quiet. No one knew the reason why a few could hear and most could not. Hums had bothered Claire ever since she could remember as a child growing up in Houston.

She heard a hum now on the grounds of Angkor Wat, the ancient Buddhist temple in Cambodia. The orange-robed monks observed their customary moment of silence, having bid everyone else to do likewise. Out of respect for this ritual, nearly every human-generated noise had stopped. Along with the other tourists in the courtyard, Claire stood quietly. Many of the tourists held up their cellphones, recording the ancient ceremony.

I must be the only one hearing this, Claire thought, watching the others.

She'd come to Angkor Wat because of persistent reports of some tourists complaining about a hum. Claire belonged to the University of Hawaii's Geology Department. She had one of the two experimental TR-1010 devices specially made to locate the epicenter of the event causing the hum. Well, theoretically anyway.

The so-called "mad scientist" Nikola Tesla had inspired Claire's friend to invent the TR-1010. Tesla had known about the Earth's vibrations long before anyone else had. Now it was true that some natural phenomena caused some hums: mating fish near coastal cities or hidden mining equipment for example. After eliminating those possibilities, there were still unexplained hums, such as the one here at Angkor Wat. Two of the most famous were the Bristol Hum in England and the Taos Hum in New Mexico.

As unobtrusively as possible, Claire turned on her TR-1010, a twenty-pound piece of equipment hanging from her neck by a strap. She slowly extended a long antenna, getting a dirty look from a large German woman in front of her.

The TR-1010 recorded and calibrated many separate phenomena. One of these was ELF waves, Extremely Low Frequency radio waves. Lightning and natural disturbances in the Earth's magnetic field often generated those. Interestingly, ELF waves could penetrate seawater, making them useful for communicating with submarines. The TR-1010 was also an EMF meter, reading electromagnetic fields. It could also detect an ambient wavefield known as seismic noise, the generic name for a relatively persistent vibration of the ground.

As quietly as possible, Claire clicked on the device, adjusting it with several taps to the control screen. The TR-1010 vibrated with power. She rotated the device, keeping the antenna up so it wouldn't bump against anyone else.

Andy gave her an anxious glance. He'd been against doing this during the grand silence ceremony because it might upset the monks.

Claire's heart began to pound with excitement as she saw a pulse on the screen. This was amazing. She hadn't even been able to get a blip in Taos, New Mexico. She made a few quick manipulations, trying to fix the source.

At that moment, the hum intensified in Claire's ears. She winced, never having heard it this loudly before. In the past, it had always been a background noise, stealing her peaceful moments, often waking her at night, making it impossible to get back to sleep.

She glanced around. No tourist showed the slightest sign of annoyance of hearing anything disturbing. None of the shaved-headed monks changed their serene expressions.

Claire studied the TR-1010, and she almost cursed aloud. The signal had spiked while she'd looked away. She tapped the screen too forcefully and elicited another ugly stare from the German woman.

Frowning, Claire shoved the device toward Andy. He glanced at her with confusion.

"Do you see it?" she whispered.

Andy got a frightened look. The head monk had explained in patient detail the importance of the five-minute silence, that no one make a sound during the ceremony.

Claire pointed at the indicator screen.

Andy shrugged, acting as if he didn't understand.

Claire understood the significance, however. An extremely low frequency radio wave was riding a magnetic crest, coming from underground directly beneath Angkor Wat. What would cause—?

The German woman dropped her cellphone. The courtyard began to fill with clicking sounds as the other tourists began releasing their phones and other devices, letting them hit the ancient bricks.

A few of the monks must have heard that. Two of them lost their peaceful gazes, turning toward the tourists.

Claire no longer touched the TR-1010, but it still hung from her neck. She began to feel heat from it through her blouse. She noticed the German woman blowing on her hand as if it was hot. What could have caused all this?

"Do you see that, love?" a tourist asked in a low voice.

Claire looked over at an English tourist, a tall man in his fifties. He spoke to a small woman, his wife, no doubt. She was shaking her head.

"There's another," the Englishman said, pointing.

Claire followed the gesture in time to see a sparrow slam against the nearest wall of Angkor Wat. That was weird. Another sparrow did the same thing a moment later, crashing against the wall full tilt. The little creatures tumbled to the ground, not moving. Claire wasn't sure if they were dead or had simply knocked themselves out.

"What's going on?" Andy asked her.

Other tourists began to speak, a few shouting. Several pointed at the sky, the rule of keeping quiet during the ceremony apparently forgotten.

Claire noticed the head monk opening his mouth. She wondered what he was going to say, but instead of waiting for it, she tore her gaze from him to see what everyone was shouting about.

She sucked in her breath. Birds swirled in the sky, not just a few birds either but lots of them. Even freakier, more birds flew in clumps, flocks, to join the circling ones.

"Why are they doing that?" Andy asked.

Claire shook her head. She had no idea.

"Have you ever heard of such a thing?" he asked.

Claire frowned, realizing she had. There was a place in India...a town in Assam Province by the name of Jatinga. There, birds sometimes committed mass suicide for reasons no one had been able to figure out.

Could the reason have anything to do with hums? Claire wondered. *Some birds use magnetic fields to help them know where to fly.*

"This is extraordinary," the Englishman said. "First our cellphones became hot and now those birds act preposterously."

Claire tore the strap from her neck, lowering the TR-1010 onto the courtyard bricks. She wondered if magnetics could have made their various devices hot.

The large German woman screamed.

Claire glanced at the lady and then up at the darkening sky where the German stared.

Other tourists began to scream. A few ran for cover.

Claire watched, horrified and fascinated. She was horrified because the birds flew down, with one part of the horde coming straight for them. Yet, as a scientist, she was fascinated to witness this exotic event and wished to understand what caused the phenomenon.

"Run!" Andy shouted at her. "Get inside!"

Claire tore her arm free from his grip. Andy could be such a puss at times.

The birds—sparrows, herons, black bittern—began to smash against Angkor Wat. Other birds crashed against the courtyard bricks, the monks and the running tourists.

"No!" Claire shouted. "Help me stop them!" She waved her arms at the descending birds, wanting to save the poor creatures from suicide.

A few of the monks followed Claire's example, waving and shouting, trying to frighten the birds so they would fly away and save themselves.

The rest of the crowd ran, covering their heads as best they could.

A bird struck Claire against the chest. It flopped onto the bricks, opening its beak, chirping. It tried to fly, but must have been too dazed. Claire bent lower to look at it.

Another bird, a bigger one, hit her in the back of the head. That startled her. She staggered. Then two birds at once slammed against Claire. After being struck several more times, it proved too much. She stumbled, tripped over crawling birds and fell onto her hands and knees.

It was dark now, and the sky was getting blacker as if a storm brewed. Claire looked around, seeing the last of the monks and tourists dash into Angkor Wat. The last one slammed the door behind him.

Like rain, birds continued to strike the huge temple and tumble to the ground. There must have been tens of thousands of them. They kept raining, killing themselves.

Fear finally squeezed Claire's heart. She shot to her feet, and twenty birds slammed against her. One smashed against her face with its beak thrusting like a knife, slashing into her left eye.

Claire screamed and clutched her face. Blood dripped. Had the bird blinded her? Beginning to sob, Claire staggered in the direction she hoped Angkor Wat stood. She had to get inside.

Birds kept crashing against Claire, disorienting her. Finally, she stumbled and fell down. As she lay on the bricks, birds continued to thud against her body and head, hitting harder than she believed small creatures like this should be able to manage.

Is this what it felt like being stoned to death in the old days?

It was Claire's last conscious thought.

***

Several minutes after the mass of birds had stopped killing themselves—only a few here and there kept suiciding—a man opened a hidden cellar door by the foot of Angkor Wat. Thirty dead birds slid off the metal. Two flopped onto the stone steps where the man stood. He reached down, grabbing the dead creatures by their legs and flinging them outside.

For just a moment, an intense blue light glowed from deep in the cellar. The man hurried up, closing and locking the metal door.

He did not wear the orange robe of the monks, nor was he Cambodian. He looked Russian, being extremely white as only Canadians and Russians seemed able to achieve. He was medium-sized and unusually compact and strong. He wore coveralls like those worn by mechanics.

Taking a small, flat device from a pocket, he checked it. Then, he hurried across the field of dead birds. He crunched across some with his work boots, breaking bones and feathers. Some people might have tripped making such a walk, but the man seemed to have extraordinary balance. As he neared Claire, a syringe with a yellow solution appeared in his right hand.

The woman moaned painfully, stirring underneath a blanket of birds.

First brushing aside the feathered creatures, the man put a knee on her back to pin her in place. His free hand held down Claire's head.

"What's going on?" she slurred.

He inserted the needle into her neck, causing her to lurch and cry out. His short but thick thumb pushed the stopper, injecting the yellow solution into her.

Removing the needle, putting it in a pocket, the man stood and glanced around. He was aware that Claire sat up, rubbing

6

her neck, staring at him in a bewildered fashion. He seemed unconcerned with her, emotionless. Spying the TR-1010, the man went to it, grabbing the strap, lifting it from the carpet of dead birds.

Claire had already slumped onto the bricks, beginning to shiver uncontrollably.

The man sensed that he had little time left for his foray topside. He strode fast, reaching the cellar door as one in the temple cracked open. A moment later, a monk flung the door all the way open and stepped outside. Behind him stumbled the woman's assistant.

The man in the coveralls removed his thumb from the thumbprint scanner on the cellar entrance, yanking the trap door open. He descended the first few steps. Andy had not spotted him. That was good. The man closed the metal door, clicking the lock behind him.

As the man descended the stone steps, he knew it was time to call Mother. He had one of the TR-1010s and had eliminated the university troublemaker. Claire would be dead in another minute. He would also tell Mother that Angkor Wat Station had become operational. He did not believe anyone suspected them, certainly not the monks or any of the tourists.

The compact man rubbed his hands together. What Mother had always referred to as The Day was almost upon them.

PART ONE:
A TEAR IN THE VEIL

-1-

ARDENNES FOREST
FRANCE

Two men crept through the Ardennes Forest. This particular area of the woods was where General Heinz Guderian had broken through in 1940. It had given the Germans a fantastic blitzkrieg victory against the Allied British and French at the beginning of World War II.

Each of the present intruders wore black garments and hoods with night vision goggles. The leader was medium-sized and moved with economical stealth. His name was Jack Elliot, a veteran D17 case officer with grizzled blond hair and an inability to smile. His facial muscles had frozen in youth when a raving speed freak had broken into their house.

The freak had been like a comic book character, his clothes in tattered shreds as if he grew to vast size when he became angry. The stick-man striding through the broken front door hanging from its hinges—he'd just smashed through—had been in his shrunken state, but he hadn't lost any of his terrible strength. The freak had foamed at the mouth, his eyes glazed like some savage beast.

Jack remembered that terrible night with extreme clarity. The TV had been on. They'd been watching an old movie about gladiators. The young Jack Elliot had turned in his Lazy-Boy chair, gazing into the freak's eyes. The orbs had been

9

devoid of anything human. Instead, it had been like a window into Hell, a terrifying and body-freezing experience.

The speed freak had roared insane words after that with spittle flying from his mouth.

Jack hadn't been able to tear his gaze free from those eyes. He did remember his dad getting up with a shout and his mother pleading with her husband to be careful.

What a joke.

The speed freak had acted exactly like what one would have expected from an escaped convict from Hell. He pounced on Jack's father, bearing him onto the rug. The freak roared, leaning down like a dog, biting his dad in the face.

Jack's mother had screamed crazily then, bounding up from her chair.

Jack remembered the moments like jerkily thumbed-through picture frames. He still dreamed about it some nights.

Sitting on his father's chest, the freak grabbed his dad's head with those skeletal hands and twisted as a hero did in the movies when he easily snapped a sentry's head. The muscles had stood up like steel cables on the maniac's arms and neck. An awful snapping sound and a gurgle from his father started the sickening drumming of his dad's heels against the carpet.

Seeing the freak kill his dad flipped a switch inside Jack's fifteen-year-old heart that had never been reset.

His mother seemed unable to stop screaming.

Jack never knew how he knew, but his mother was as good as dead then. The ache was so terrible his heart seemed to burst into fire. Jack wanted to howl with her, but he buried the feeling. Someone had to save his little sister. That's all he could do, but he had to act at once if he hoped to succeed and he'd have to do it with a minimum of fuss.

As the foaming madman rushed his mother, Jack slid off the Lazy-Boy.

"No!" mother shouted. "Don't you dare touch me!"

Jack didn't look to see what was happening. He couldn't risk the freak spying him and killing him too. *I have to do this slowly or Penny dies.*

As his mother thudded onto the carpet, Jack walked out of the living room and into the hall. Now, he moved. He ran pell-mell for his parents' bedroom. The sounds from the living room—

Jack blotted those out from his conscious mind. They seeped into his subconscious and lodged there deeper than he knew. He couldn't help it, though. He was just a fifteen-year-old kid catapulted into a horror show with his family murdered and his life changed forever in one grim moment of drugged insanity.

Jack burst into his parents' bedroom, diving onto the wooden floor. He reached under the king-sized bed, his left hand falling onto the pump shotgun his dad kept there.

Jack slid it to him. A shell was already in the chamber with four more in the tube—it was a home defense shotgun. Fortunately, there was no trigger lock to slow him down. His dad had always said that was a stupid law. When a man needed his shotgun to defend his family, he didn't have time to fool with a lock and key.

Turning back to the hall, Jack gripped the shotgun. He didn't know that his eyes had become slits and his mouth a fierce line of determination.

His mother had stopped screaming. His little sister cried out from her bedroom, asking what was happening.

Just then, the demon bounded into the hallway. Jack stood on one side of the evil creature, his sister's bedroom door on the other. The door opened, and a sleepy-eyed seven-year-old girl stood there rubbing her nose.

"Hey," Jack said, the only word he could get past his constricted throat.

That didn't do the trick. The freak roared and Penny burst into tears.

"*You*," Jack said, and there was something menacing in his voice now.

The speed freak whirled around with tiger-like speed. Blood stained his mouth, and those eyes—

They might have frozen Jack if this had been the first time he looked into them. But it wasn't. Even so, a psychic shock blossomed against the back of Jack's brain. The creature leaped at him.

11

Jack held the shotgun with rocklike steadiness. He pulled the trigger, knowing that his little sister stood behind the madman. He could not afford to miss. The weapon boomed with a thunderous noise. The buckshot tore into the freak's chest, stopping his forward momentum.

Jack pumped the weapon, ejecting a smoking cartridge that struck the wall, putting a new shell into the chamber.

BOOM!

The round staggered the skinny freak.

Jack pumped the shotgun again.

BOOM!

He knocked the freak onto the floor, bleeding badly, splashing red onto the walls. A streak crossed Penny's left check.

Pumping another shell into the chamber, Jack walked up to the staring animal on the floor. He lowered the barrel, touching the freak's forehead. He didn't want to miss.

BOOM! BOOM! BOOM! Click, click, click, click, click.

Jack finally realized he was out of shells. He stood over the thing, poking it with the shotgun barrel. Only once he realized the freak wasn't going to come back to life and murder his little sister did he drop the shotgun and go to her.

That night forever altered their lives. They went to live with their aunt and uncle across the country. As anyone could imagine, Penny had problems after that. She'd become a psychiatrist, trying to work through her trauma, finally marrying a good man and having two children.

Jack had become a cop. He'd done his job a little too well for the new United States of America. More than once, his superiors had told him he wasn't the caped crusader. That kind of thinking would land him in prison sooner rather than later.

Luckily, D17 had found him in time. The mental fuse that burned out at fifteen had stayed that way. Jack had uncommon presence of mind and a fierce determination. The episode had turned him upside-down. He had a hard time living a normal life, doing the stuff that everyone else found easy like hosting barbecues or lounging in front of the TV. Instead, what normal people found extraordinarily difficult, like staying cool in a firefight or knowing what to do during a blazing fire, he could do like he'd been born to it.

It made for a hard life. In order to compensate, Jack lived by a strict code of honor. He was afraid that if he went by his gut, he would go so far off the reservation that the rest of humanity would have to hunt him down and put a slug in his brain.

So far, in his struggle to live right, Jack had stayed on the good side of the law.

Tonight, he stalked through the Ardennes Forest with Simon Green. The rest of the D17 team was in a van a mile away, monitoring their progress.

Their cover was perfect: industrial spies working for a Russian consortium—IZENOV—known for their heavy-handed theft. D'erlon Enterprises was the target, the experimental industrial site deep in the forest far away from prying eyes.

Something odd went on inside the plant. At least, that was Jack's suspicion. Why otherwise did his orders call for this clandestine search? Simon and he were particularly in search of anything magnetic, a specialty of D'erlon Enterprises. The company was one of the major suppliers of magnetic containers for the giant CERN collider in Switzerland.

Jack was the protection and movement specialist. Simon knew how to use a gun, of course. More importantly, Simon had trained with DARPA people, making him the scientist on the op, the magnetic-everything specialist.

Motioning sharply with his left arm, Jack advanced. He scanned the forest as he cradled a suppressed rifle. Simon and he climbed a hill one slow step at a time. They crested the top, starting down into dark foliage.

"Trouble," Phelps said in Jack's earbud.

She was in the van, monitoring Jack and Simon's body sensors. Elliot had optics in his goggles slaved to her screen. There was an infrared sensor clipped to his chest and a high-frequency chip in the headband of his hood. The same held true for Simon.

"To your left," Phelps said.

Jack raised his left arm with his fist clenched to halt Simon. Slowly, he turned to his left.

"I see it," Phelps said. "I think it's an emitter. Just a second…okay, you can go closer."

Jack had been crouching. He stood, moving a couple of steps closer.

"Stop," she said in his ear.

He froze.

"Give me a sec to figure this out," Phelps said.

Jack waited, scanning the darkness. There were millions of leaves. A section of the forest down there rustled as the wind moaned, bending a few of the highest branches. Then the wind eased and the leaves stilled.

Something felt…wrong. Jack didn't know what, but something waited for them. Maybe it was time to abort.

-2-

ARDENNES FOREST
FRANCE

The wolfish beast trotted through the forest, whining eerily to itself. It was big like an Irish wolfhound with a shaggy coat, but it had a wider chest and extra-powerful jaws. The braincase was also larger than seemed natural. The eyes glittered with an intelligence that was higher on the Benson-Harris Cogitative Scale than a chimpanzee.

A bulky, black-matted collar buzzed gently around its neck. The beast knew the meaning of that. Through painful trial and error, the beast knew to the exact millimeter the length and breadth of its range. It had explored every rock and tree, seeking a way to extend its territory.

The masters brought it food. At other times, they induced lesser humans to engage it in battle. The beast had proven victorious four out of six times. Each loss had brought electrical agony from the collar. As if the jolts could exceed the pain of its wounded vanity. The beast detested every defeat with an unquenchable pride.

Twice, it had attempted to escape the boundary limits of its territory. Each of those times had brought debilitating pain.

The beast felt constricted by its narrow band of territory. It was intensely curious about what went on inside the forbidden zone. Often, it lay in the shadows, watching the humans enter and exit the block buildings. They did things down there that made its hackles rise. Sometimes, the high-pitched sounds from there drove it away to the edge of the outer fence.

The beast knew its role. It was a guardian, but it refused to bark at anything. It had seen dogs before, pack creatures of low cunning and high instinct. Dogs were more cunning than rabbits and deer. They looked like the beast, but growled and barked with savage stupidity.

Oh yes, the beast knew it was greater than a dog. Three times, the masters had let a pack into its territory. Once, the dogs had been the subspecies known as German shepherd. The beast had heard humans speak the words. The last time, Great Danes had roamed through its territory, pissing on everything.

The beast had slaughtered the dull-witted German shepherds and another, tougher breed. The Great Danes had chased it, finally cornering it by the creek. Using their instinctual mentality against them, the beast had whined in submission, cowering, finally turning onto its back for them.

The Great Danes had sniffed it at great length, growling menacingly. Finally, the pack had let it live. For a week afterward, it trailed the Great Danes like an outcast. They suffered its existence and the beast watched and cataloged everything they did. Finally, the beast began an insidious campaign, making its first kill by the creek, trying to wash away its former humiliation with their blood. After the second kill, the giant dogs hunted it again, which was exactly what the beast wanted. It turned at bay each time the fastest Great Dane reached it. The beast knew a cunning move, knocking the opponent onto its back, lunging in and ripping out the throat in an instant. The instinctual creatures had wished to dominate its narrow strip of territory. That night, they paid the ultimate price for their error of judgment.

The beast recalled the episode as it trotted in the darkness, plotting its escape. It cataloged the restrictions surrounding its territory as it had the movements of the Great Danes. The humans acted as if they were the highest species. The beast thought otherwise, having a feral hatred of the two-legged creatures.

The beast halted then and cocked its head.

Why did it hate humans with such ferocity? Why had it needed to slaughter the larger but lesser dogs? It had observed the other animals in its territory. No other creature had its murderous nature.

As it stood there in the darkness, the beast wondered about that. It wasn't an instinctual animal, but a thinking creature of high reasoning power. Why then should it hate so unreasonably?

The beast whined, scratching the leaves and dirt with its front paws. It did not hate now. The ferocious desires only leapt into existence when it saw other higher forms in its territory.

It growled while thinking of dogs and humans wandering in its zone.

The beast shook its head. It must think this through. Might this hatred have an unnatural cause? By unnatural, it meant...a human causation.

The beast had seen young animals before. They always acted stupidly. It had come to see that young creatures learned. That held true for rabbits, squirrels, robins, any animal really.

As it stood in the dark, the beast tried to recall its puppyhood. Dimly, it recalled harsh-sounding humans poking shock rods at it. They had tormented it. Then, handlers had slipped crazed dogs with dense necks and wide jowls into its cage. Each of those fighting dogs had always attacked and proven difficult to kill.

The beast was shocked to realize that humans—the masters—had taught it to hate as it did.

Why would the masters have done such a thing?

The beast resumed its trot. It must reason this out. Was it destined to attack every higher form? What kind of existence was that?

It would seem a lonely and hatful existence. Was it possible there was more to life?

The beast whined eerily. It needed to think this through carefully.

-3-

THE *CALYPSO*
87 MILES OFF THE COAST OF SUMATRA

Dr. Selene Khan sat in her cabin, studying the latest radar readings concerning the sea floor. In her shorts and half-buttoned shirt, she didn't look like an underwater geology professor for the University of Hawaii. Selene was thirty-two, had long, dark hair and could have posed in a Calvin Klein ad. Although she pretended otherwise with others, Selene still grieved over her broken relationship with Dr. Daniel Ferguson, the former chair of the Geology Department.

Selene slapped a folder onto the chart table. She should be happy that she was finally free from the manipulative Danny Ferguson. The man had been twice her age when they'd begun dating. Selene had realized that she had issues in this area. Her foster parents had adopted her when she'd been three. They'd divorced two years later, and her foster mother had been too bitter to remarry, wanting nothing more to do with men.

Danny had swept Selene up her first year of college. She'd truly felt loved for the first time in her life, and the wining, dining and "cultured" existence had been intoxicating. What had finally broken the relationship after all this time was Selene's realization that Danny had been taking credit for her work from the beginning. It reminded her how Edison had used the brilliant Nikola Tesla, promising him a staggering amount of money if he could redesign Edison's inefficient electric motors and generators. Tesla had done just that and then asked for his promised money. Edison had laughed it off, telling Tesla that he didn't understand American humor. That sounded like something Danny could have said.

Danny had been more cunning than brilliant. She wondered these days if he'd zeroed in on her for her brains rather than her body, as she'd believed at first.

Selene glanced at the TR-1010 she had invented and constructed. She wondered how Claire was doing with hers at Angkor Wat. She should have heard from Claire by now.

Shrugging—sometimes Claire was gone for weeks at a time, telling no one—Selene opened the folder. She scanned the radar-mapped sea floor, comparing it to the one before the 2004 Indian Ocean Earthquake. When the India Tectonic Plate had subducted on December 26 beneath the Burma Plate, it had raised the ocean floor in the Indian Ocean to such an extent that there had been a permanent rise in the global sea level by 0.004 inches. In fact, it had—

A loud *bang* sounded from outside, causing Selene's head to snap upright.

What was that?

The *Calypso* lurched—several seconds passed—and went hard to starboard. That threw Selene out of her chair and might have tumbled her onto her side. She'd practiced ballet in junior high and high school—the original instructor had told her foster mother she was very gifted and strong for her age. Selene had worked hard at the art. It was one of the reasons she still had exceptional balance and firm, pleasantly elongated muscles.

The years of training and the natural inner balance allowed Selene to catch herself before she sprawled onto the cabin floor.

She realized the steady thrum of the main diesel engines had stopped. The *Calypso*, a rather small, ocean-going vessel, usually had a steady vibration to it. That had quit as well. Undoubtedly, that had something to do with the bang and the lurch.

Selene hurried to the hatch. She couldn't believe how many accidents had occurred during the voyage out. It had never been this way when Danny ran the research trips.

Selene opened the hatch, stepping into a short corridor. Several quick strides brought her to a ladder. She climbed it, seeing the bare-chested Forrest Dean listening to the chief engineer on deck.

Forrest was a piece of work. He was older, maybe forty-five or so, stocky, not quite six feet with a chest full of white hair. Forrest had a permanently deep tan, rugged features and wore a gold chain around a muscled neck. He was the oldest person aboard ship and had come to them several weeks before they left Honolulu.

Many years ago, Forrest had been in SEAL Delivery Vehicle Team 1, stationed in Pearl Harbor. The man knew diving and underwater vehicles. He would be helping Selene with the T-9 Driver Propulsion Vehicle. Forrest could be gruff, and there was something in his eyes Selene didn't quite trust, a dangerous wildness.

"No," Junior said. The engineer was a big Hawaiian with massive hands who had previously worked on nuclear submarines. Junior towered over Forrest, looking as if he could hammer the ex-SEAL into the deck.

"I don't want to hear that," Forrest told Junior. "You get the engines working or I'm—"

"What's going on?" Selene said.

The two turned to her. Forrest gave her the once over, his gaze going down her bare legs and then back up, pausing at her breasts before he focused on her eyes.

Selene crossed her arms, wishing she'd put on more clothes.

"It's the main engine," Junior said, shaking his head. "We've lost—"

"He's trying to tell you that he wants to go home," Forrest interrupted.

"Is that true?" Selene asked Junior.

The Hawaiian wouldn't look at her now. "This is the third accident so far," Junior said. "Fate is trying to warn us. The voyage is cursed. I can feel it, but I've been trying to tell myself it isn't true. Now—"

"Take a piss on your curse," Forrest said. "Then, fix the engine and let's get going."

Junior scowled down at Forrest. "You're not as tough as you think, you know that?"

Forrest smiled. "Why don't you toss me off the boat then? Show the doctor how tough you are."

Junior glared at Forrest, flexing his thick fingers as if he might try.

"I can deal with this, thank you," Selene told Forrest. Why did some men think all women were helpless?

The shirtless man stared at her. The force of Forrest's gaze made him seem like a wolf ready to lunge at her throat. Then, Forrest blinked, doing something with his eyes. Their force faded back to normal. The man took a deliberate step away from Junior, and he looked elsewhere as if finding something absorbing in the sea.

That was weird.

"I just want to know one thing," Selene said, turning to Junior. "How long until we're on our way again?"

"You don't understand," Junior said.

"How long?" she asked, remembering how Danny had spoken with the crew. The professor had never asked for their opinions on what he should do, but how long it would take them to do what he wanted done.

A guilty look crossed Junior's features. He seemed to be on the verge of telling her something, probably another excuse. She'd had enough of those.

"I don't want to hear about curses or bad luck," Selene said.

"Doctor Khan—" Junior said, going all formal on her. "It will take…hours."

Forrest quit sea gazing to stare at Junior again. He must have amped up the wattage because Junior noticed. Lines appeared in the Hawaiian's forehead.

Junior shrugged, muttering, "Maybe less."

"I want us going again in a *lot* less," Selene said.

21

"It's probably an easy fix," Forrest said, "a simple adjustment and bam, we're on our way again."

"You want to give it a try?" Junior asked, without looking at Forrest.

"If you want," Forrest answered, "I can babysit you and make sure you don't sit on your lard—"

"Please," Selene said. "Let's keep this civil."

"Sure, doc," Forrest said, with what might have been a smirk. "Fifteen minutes," he told Junior.

"I'm not making any promises," Junior told Selene. "You don't know—"

"Junior," Selene said. "Is something the matter? You don't seem yourself lately."

Junior stared at the deck.

"Do you know anything about diesels?" she asked Forrest, deciding to sting Junior's pride.

"As a matter of fact, I do."

"Doctor," Junior said. "You don't know what you're..." His voice faded away.

"What don't I know?" Selene asked.

Junior shook his head.

"I want those diesels running right now," she said. "Or I'll put someone in charge who can keep them running."

Junior looked up, staring through her. "Okay," he said.

To Selene's ears, it sounded like, "Okay, you asked for it." But she told herself it was just her imagination.

With slumped shoulders, Junior headed for the engine room.

Selene headed back for her cabin, wanting to go back to studying her charts. Hopefully, this would be the end of her problems. She never recalled Danny having this many incidents when he'd been in charge of the expedition.

***

A short time later on a large vessel several miles away from the *Calypso*, a man wearing coveralls sat before a screen. He piloted a small drone high in the clouds, watching the university ship. Incredibly, the vessel was on the move again. The captain would not be pleased with the news.

The screen operator clicked an intercom button.

"Yes?" a deep-voiced man asked.

"The *Calypso* is moving, sir."

"So soon? What is its speed?"

The operator studied the screen, saying, "Ten knots and climbing, sir."

"And its heading?" the deep-voiced man asked.

"Two degrees south of the site, sir," the operator said.

"The fool lacked conviction, did he? We'll have to take direct action then. Call the *Blue Angler*. Tell them it is a Code 7 situation. They are to proceed at once on an intercept course."

"Did you say Code 7, sir?"

"Exactly. Mother doesn't want any interference for the coming test."

-4-

ARDENNES FOREST
FRANCE

"Well?" Jack asked.

"It's a perimeter fence," Simon whispered, as he studied a small device with an extended antenna gripped in his hands.

Jack crouched with the suppressed rifle cradled in his arms, located a trifle higher than Simon. He didn't look at Simon or at the odd post with a satellite dish on top. He kept scanning the forest.

"The post emits a high frequency," Phelps said into their earbuds. "I think it will emit something else if you cross an invisible line."

"Why do you say that?" Simon asked through his throat microphone.

"I believe I'm beginning to understand the emitter's function," Phelps answered. "If you cross the invisible boundary, a sonic pulse will either kill or incapacitate you two."

"Clever," Simon said. "Do you think if I broadcast a feedback loop we can safely cross the boundary?"

"I'm checking on the probabilities of success," Phelps said. "Okay. Here it is. You have a seventy-eight percent chance of surviving."

"What do you say, Jack?" Simon asked. "Do we go through?"

Elliot heard the words but did not really process them. He was too intent on studying the darkness.

"Jack?"

Elliot blinked, glancing at Simon hunched near the satellite-dish post. He replayed the words in his memory. Seventy-eight percent...life or death...go or stay. He felt something out there. He trusted his gut, but the code said he had a mission to perform. He couldn't back down because of unnamed and possibly unwarranted sensations.

"We go," Jack said, "but not before we set up an explosive against the post that will take one of us to defuse in twenty seconds, say. If the emitter goes off and incapacitates us, the explosive will destroy it, saving our lives."

"Destroying the emitter would mean scrubbing the mission," Phelps said. "D'erlon Enterprises will have an alarm rigged to any of the posts' destruction."

"I prefer a scrubbed mission to dying," Jack said.

"Sounds reasonable," Phelps said, after a moment.

"Roger that," Simon said, studying Jack in the darkness.

Ignoring the scrutiny, Jack said, "I'll get started rigging the explosive."

-5-

ARDENNES FOREST
FRANCE

For a fraction of a second, the softly buzzing collar around the beast's neck stopped.

The beast's head snapped up. It had been reasoning out its hatred, finding premises for peaceful coexistence with other higher forms. As long as it could find sustenance, it could endure the presence of supposedly vile creatures. In other words, it could conceivably retrain itself, altering the automatic hatred.

The beast found the idea intoxicating.

The abrupt cessation of the buzzing caused anger to jolt its thinking. When the collar-vibration returned, the anger blossomed into rage.

The masters had let someone or something into its territory. The beast found that odd. The last test had occurred only a short time ago.

No! This made logical sense. The masters no doubt understood its intellect. They wished to keep it alert. Thus, they sprang a new test unexpectedly.

The beast set off in a hurried lope, heading for the inner perimeter where each of the test subjects had entered before.

How dare the masters do this as it tried to reason its way to peaceful coexistence. Given enough time, it might have restrained the savage impulses.

After traveling only a short distance, the beast froze. Slowly, it turned its unusual head in the direction of the outer perimeter. Noise—humans blundered through its forest.

A low growl emanated from its throat. It wanted to rend these two-legs into bloody chunks. It would feed on their flesh. It would rip out—

The growl deepened, but it didn't indicate greater rage. Rather, the beast laughed at its own stupidity, its own instinctive behavior.

The beast prided itself on its intellect. Yet, here it wanted to race off to murder because of an instinctive response. That did not seem mature. That was part of its brutish nature. Yet, it was better than the dull dogs.

The beast forced itself to lower its snout. Then, it closed its eyes and breathed deeply. It would control the rage. It would watch the intruders and learn whatever it could.

The masters ruled because they outthought and out-tricked everyone else. If it desired mastery, the beast realized it must learn to do the same thing.

-6-

INNER ZONE
ARDENNES FOREST

Jack wiped the back of his left gloved hand against his
eyebrows. Perspiration dotted his face. He wasn't sweating
from exertion. He could run all day. As crazy as it sounded, the
forest felt even more haunted than before.

Simon and he had come several miles since the satellite-
dish emitter. Each step had stirred Jack's nape hairs more. He
could feel eyes watching him. He could swear he felt
something's vicious desire to rip him and his partner to shreds.

"You okay?"

Simon had asked that seven times during their trek. Jack
had simply nodded for an answer. This time Jack told his
partner to leave it alone already.

Instead of relieving Simon, the man glanced at him
worriedly again. Jack was getting sick of it.

Don't sweat it, Elliot. It's good if we're tense. It kept one
extra-alert. He had a feeling they were going to need that. Later
over beers, they could laugh about the "haunted" op, but now
was not the time for that kind of thinking.

Jack picked his way across dead leaves, his boots crunching
over a few and pushing aside others. Every few steps, he had to
force his fingers to relax. He reached a knoll, crouching,
peering at the lit buildings down there.

A moment later, Simon crouched beside him.

D'erlon Enterprises was located in a small valley of the Ardennes Forest. Jack counted seven large buildings bigger than airplane hangars. The entire complex was fifty acres with administrative buildings and tract housing along two sides. A road wound down a hill, coming to a brightly lit guardhouse.

There was one way in by road and one out. A regular fence with razor-wire coils on top surrounded the giant complex, but Jack didn't envision any problems with that. They'd accounted for the fence before the op and had brought the needed equipment to secretly breach it. Using his night vision goggles, Jack spotted several hidden SAM pits and a few automated machine gun posts. That was something he would have expected to find in a Latin American country, not a French industrial site. It proved D'erlon Enterprises had military connections.

Jack changed the settings of his night vision equipment. A bewildering array of formerly invisible laser lines showed what would trigger the heavy machine guns. It was interesting to him that every one of the inner sensors was well behind the emitter posts.

After several seconds of silence, Simon asked, "Ready?"

For an answer, Jack rose. He froze then, whirling around, bringing up his rifle. A bush up there rustled the wrong way. His finger tightened against the trigger—and stopped.

He wasn't sure why he didn't pull the trigger. The bad thing was out there, he knew. It had been watching for some time.

It could have rushed us just now. What is it waiting for?

"Jack," Simon whispered, in a way that indicated he'd called his name several times already.

"We should abort," Jack said, the conviction hardening in his heart.

"What?" Simon asked. "Now? Do you have a concrete reason?"

"Yeah," Jack said.

Simon waited, finally asking, "Well? And if you're going to say you don't like the feel—"

"I don't."

"I never do," Simon said. "I vomit before every insertion. This one hasn't been any different."

Jack nodded noncommittally. He didn't vomit. Missions made life easier. Usually, he knew how to deal with these kinds of problems. The only other time he'd felt like this…

"You know," Simon whispered.

Jack only half heard. He was too busy tracking the leaves, the blackest areas of the forest. The overriding presence had just dwindled. Maybe they *should* hurry to the buildings.

Am I scared?

Under his woolen mask, Jack frowned. Yes. It felt as if something had crawled under his skin. He didn't like the sensation. It wasn't like him to let fear get the best of him like this.

"All right," Jack said gruffly, turning back toward the valley complex. "Let's go."

He set a stiff pace, listening to Simon pant behind him. He barely heard his partner's warning in time. At the last moment, Jack stopped, his foot an inch from crossing the invisible line. He'd forgotten about it.

"A post-mounted emitter," Simon whispered.

Jack turned around, peering into the forest the way they had come. Behind him, Simon must have taken out his special device. He could hear his partner extend the antenna.

"Hmm," Simon said.

Jack glanced over his shoulder at his partner.

"This is an emitter all right. It's pointed in our direction."

"So?" Jack asked.

Simon shrugged. "It's like…I don't know."

"I do," Jack said, as it all came together for him. "We're in a wild zone. I remember going to the San Diego Wild Animal Park as a kid. On a whispered dare from my sister, I got out of the car. I don't know. I must have been thirteen at the time. When my dad saw me, you should have heard him shout. I dashed back to the car. As I slammed the door shut, a big old lion with a graying mane stood up from behind the bush I'd been approaching. I'd planned to take a whiz there, impress my little sister with my toughness. In the car, I began shaking realizing the old lion had been watching me. I remember the feeling of walking in the wild area. It made my spine tingle. That's the same feeling I've been getting tonight."

"You're saying lions are on the prowl in the Ardennes?"

"Something is," Jack said.

Simon stared at him, finally asking, "Are you serious?"

"Let's get going. We don't have all night."

Simon gave him a longer study.

Jack had a good idea what his partner was thinking. That Jack had finally lost his nerve. He didn't believe that. He *could* feel something vicious in here with them, and he didn't like it in the slightest.

"Come on," Jack said, with an edge to his voice.

If Simon had been ready to chide him, it died on his partner's lips. "Phelps?" he whispered into his throat microphone.

Jack shook his head. They had lost verbal contact with the van some time ago. Clearly, there was interference.

"All right," Simon said. "Here goes." He manipulated his device, got up and dashed across the invisible line.

Jack was on his tail. They hadn't bothered with the explosive this time. Elliot heard a *click* from Simon's device. He tightened his stomach muscles, expecting the worst.

What he got a second later was a vast sense of relief. The grim feeling evaporated. They were out of the wild zone, although they would have to go back through it on their way out.

Jack shrugged. That didn't matter now. It was time to go into the valley, break into the D'erlon site and see if the snitch's story about weird magnetic experimentation was true or not.

31

-7-

THE *CALYPSO*
91 MILES OFF THE COAST OF SUMATRA

A hard rap against the outer hatch of her cabin caused Selene to jerk around. She hated when that happened, having been absorbed with the data, lost inside her head.

"Who is it?" she asked, sharply.

"Forrest."

"Come in. The hatch is open."

The handle twisted and a shirtless Forrest Dean poked his head inside. "Just thought you should know," he said. "There's a ship heading toward us."

"What?"

"It's a speck right now, but it's coming fast."

"Are you sure it's heading for us?" Selene asked.

"Pretty much," Forrest said.

"Why should that bother me?"

"It bothers *me*," Forrest said.

She recognized what Forrest was trying to do and resented it. Danny would never have let any of the crew or dive-team bully him. She shouldn't let any of them do it either.

"I'll ask you again," Selene said. "Why should it bother me?"

Forrest hesitated answering. He seemed to be looking inside his skull for what he should say. Finally, he grinned, shrugging. "There have been too many accidents this voyage, you know what I mean?"

"I don't think I do."

"I'll try a word on you, see what you think. Sabotage," Forrest said, staring into her eyes.

"Why would anyone sabotage the *Calypso*? That doesn't make sense."

"I suppose not. Still, the word is out there now. The probability of so many accidents happening in a row in so few days…" Forrest shrugged once more.

Selene stared back at him. "No. I'm not buying that. You're hinting at something, but you don't want to come right out a say it. That's fine. I can wait. Is there anything else?"

Forrest hesitated for a fraction of a second longer, shook his head and shut the hatch.

Selene turned back to the papers on the chart table. The *Calypso* headed toward the epicenter of the Indian Ocean Earthquake that had occurred December 26, 2004 off the western coast of Sumatra, Indonesia. The event had been a 9.0 magnitude quake, releasing the energy of 23,000 Hiroshima-type atomic bombs. The violent movement of the Earth's tectonic plates had displaced an enormous amount of water, sending powerful shock waves in every direction. The tsunami had killed nearly 230,000 people in 14 different countries that touched the Indian Ocean. The rupture had been more than 600 miles long, displacing the seafloor by 10 yards horizontally and several yards vertically. It had caused the entire planet to vibrate 0.4 inches.

Selene had a theory about the earthquake that involved the hum, which she believed involved magnetic waves as well as ELF radio waves.

She'd found an odd reading in a seismic chart taken a month ago by a U.S. monitoring station. Selene had convinced the University Geology chair to fund an expedition so she could check it out. The woman might not have agreed with the theory, but she'd wanted to get back at Dr. Danny Ferguson. That had been Selene's reading of the chairwoman, anyway. Using what Danny had taught her, Selene had manipulated the crack of resentment into a wide open door into getting the expedition funded.

There was too much riding on this for Selene to back down because of engine trouble, Junior's fear of curses or Forrest's enigmatic allusions. She wanted to prove the utility of her TR-1010 and that the various hums throughout the world had something do to with magnetic waves.

Selene got up, went to her computer and tapped the screen several times. She enlarged an underwater image taken several weeks ago until the object badly blurred. She couldn't tell what it was—a new smooth ridge, a budding volcano in a place it shouldn't be or a wrecked submarine. She was almost certain about one thing. The thing hadn't been there before December 26, 2004. How could it have been?

The object was deeper than a free diver could easily go. Divers would have to use a mixed gas descent, meaning they would only have a few minutes at the bottom of the dive. That's how she'd convinced the Geology chairwoman to purchase the T-9 DPV.

This was more than exciting; it was her chance to prove her theory. Afterward—if she were right—she would write a paper, get it published and start nudging the right people toward getting her a Nobel Prize in Physics.

Selene kept staring at the blurry image. Could the anomaly be the reason the *Calypso* had been having such bad luck this trip? Would that imply Junior had been sabotaging the engines?

That seemed crazy, right? Who would care if she went down there?

Selene tapped the screen, shrinking the image. What was the object, anyway? Did it make any difference it was near the epicenter of the 2004 quake? Soon, now, she would know the answer.

***

Forrest waited for Selene on the bridge, at least, that was his excuse. The first mate conned the *Calypso* while Lulu, one of the university divers, chattered merrily with the man,

34

keeping his attention occupied with her tiny shorts and bikini top.

"I'll be right back," Lulu finally said. She got up and scampered to the hatch, disappearing.

The first mate glanced at Forrest.

"She's got a fantastic rack," Forrest said with a grin. "That's for damn sure."

The first mate reddened, turning away.

That's what Forrest had been waiting for. He picked up the satellite phone, turned so the first mate wouldn't see that if he looked back and stepped through the hatch.

Using a tiny screwdriver and working fast, he opened the back of the phone and inserted a special chip. Before anyone saw him, he raised the phone and punched in a number. Three rings later, a woman answered through a scrambler.

"One, seventeen, three, forty-six," Forrest said.

"Roger that," the woman said.

Forrest waited, wishing the woman could make her decision faster. Some things, though, one just couldn't rush.

"Stick to the plan," the woman finally said.

"Affirmative," Forrest said. He saw Lulu skipping back to the bridge, coming fast. "I have to go."

Forrest pressed the "off" button. He'd resealed the phone before calling and put the tiny screws in halfway. He wasn't going to have time to remove the chip now. Lulu would turn the corner any minute.

I'll have to do this later. Forrest twisted the screws in deeper and palmed the tiny screwdriver as he stepped back onto the bridge, with the phone behind his back.

The first mate glanced at him. Forrest gave the man a dead-eyed stare. The first mate turned away as Forrest had figured he'd do. Quickly, he put the satellite phone back into its holder.

A second later, Lulu entered the bridge, picking up her chatter exactly where she had left off.

Thirty seconds after that, Selene shouted for Forrest.

Damn, the doc had come quicker than Forrest had expected. He headed out the hatch, hoping no one would find the chip he'd put in the satellite phone.

-8-

WASHINGTON DC

Mrs. King put a hand over her heart as her face twisted with pain. There, it felt—

The throbbing abruptly subsided. She began breathing again, massaging her chest. Several minutes later, she relaxed enough to sit back in her chair.

At sixty-three, Secretary Carroll King still had smooth features and glossy, brunette hair thanks to the marvels of modern medicine and an excellent stylist. She had won Miss. Rhode Island thirty-nine years ago. These days, Mrs. King ran Detachment 17, an ultra-secret activities group that worked closely with DARPA.

The Defense Advanced Research Projects Agency, or DARPA, belonged to the U.S. Department of Defense. They were primarily concerned with emerging technologies.

Detachment 17 was also interested in high tech, primarily of a biological, chemical or nuclear nature. Their task was to hinder or halt such advancements among the enemies of the United States. Mrs. King's best agents worked in the cold, meaning Detachment 17 and thereby the United States of America had perfect deniability concerning them. Few people knew that the American Intelligence Community now had *eighteen* agencies instead of the advertised seventeen.

Secretary King frowned as she sat forward, putting her white-gloved hands on either side of a sheet of paper. She was self-conscious of her arthritic fingers, seeing them as twisted and disfigured witch's hands. It was much better to view the delicate gloves, remembering the smooth hands of youth.

The paper contained a hodge-podge of corporate names in her spiky, almost indecipherable handwriting. Mrs. King picked up a pen and drew another line from one name to the next. A spider-web of lines connected many although not all of the corporations.

Sitting back once more, Mrs. King tapped the end of the pen against the desk. She'd run Detachment 17 since its inception, coming over from the CIA. Since that time, she'd cut all connections with the Agency. D17 was America's ghost, going where no one else could to fix the "unsolvable" problems.

Unfortunately, a year and a half ago, the failed number of activity operations had grown. There had been agent deaths, too many of them for mere probabilities. Morale had begun to drop as word of these deaths leaked out.

The pen tapped quicker with greater force. Then, the motion stopped as Mrs. King stared straight ahead. Her gaze took in but didn't really *see* the drawn curtains of her office window.

A new tinge of pain—like a woman bouncing up and down on a high dive, getting ready to leap—threatened her heart. After a pregnant moment, the threatened attack faded away.

Did the possibility of a heart attack accelerate Mrs. King's thinking? The thought was half-formed in her mind enough so she recognized it. Then, the primary idea expanded, pushing the half-formed notion into oblivion. The greater idea—

It must have bubbled up from my subconscious. I must have known this for some time now. No wonder I'm feeling queasy.

Mrs. King set aside the pen, standing, walking to the curtains. She put her gloved fingers to the edge of the curtain as if she was about to peer outside into the city. Slowly, she lowered her hand, turning around, returning to her desk.

She sat on the edge of the chair, her back hunched and her brow furrowed. Normally, she refused to frown, and if she did, she hurriedly pressed her index finger against the skin crease to smooth it out.

She clasped her white-gloved hands in her lap, the frown battling the Botox-frozen skin.

The reason why too many agents had died the last year and a half was obvious to her now. Inadvertently, D17 must have stumbled upon...

I've found a master puppeteer. What is their goal? I can't see it, but I can feel the strings stirring, moving the various puppets.

Mrs. King sat up. She believed that she'd stumbled onto something big. It was insidious and secret beyond her understanding.

Conspiracy theorists aside, it was extremely difficult keeping large and long-term secrets. Eventually, human stupidity or laziness revealed the darkest and deepest mysteries. Something this big and insidious...it implied— *what?*

Mrs. King swiveled her chair, facing her desk. She stared at the corporate names on the paper, willing the secret to reveal itself to her.

Abruptly, she stood again, heading for the door. It was time to talk to Deputy Secretary Smith. Although many considered him the quintessential nerd, the man had a ruthlessness that had left her breathless on occasion. That didn't happen often. People stepped lightly around Mrs. King for a reason.

She wanted to study each of the ongoing operations. Given the year-and-a-half trend, there would be another failure soon, maybe even another death. When it happened, she wanted to be ready to pounce.

-9-

THE *CALYPSO*
96 MILES OFF THE COAST OF SUMATRA

Selene couldn't believe it. Forrest had been right. A small ship had headed straight for them—a 110-foot Indonesian cutter. The patrol boat belonged to the KRI, *Kapal Republik Indonesia*.

The cutter was off the port bow, dead in the water, just as the *Calypso* rode a giant ocean swell with the engines idling. The crew over there aimed a .50-caliber machine gun at them. An Indonesian officer, a lieutenant, held a loudspeaker.

"You must leave the area immediately," the lieutenant said in exceptionally good English.

With a shaky hand, Selene raised her own loudspeaker. She clicked the trigger. "Why should we leave?"

Everyone on the *Calypso* had come up to watch the exchange. They'd see if she backed down, something Selene had no intention of doing.

"This is not a question for debate," the Indonesian said.

How dare he try to just brush her aside? "Tell me the reason," Selene said.

"We should leave," Junior told her. "This is the final straw, don't you see?"

The Navy lieutenant spoke to another officer. Forrest had told her here were two on the cutter with fourteen enlisted personnel.

"We are staging a special training session in the area," the lieutenant said. "Return here in a week, if you must."

Selene pulled the trigger of her loudspeaker. "I don't think so."

"Dr. Khan," Junior pleaded. "You can't argue against a heavy machine gun. They'll sink us, kill everyone."

She lowered the loudspeaker to stare at Junior. "That's seems unlikely."

"Please, Dr. Khan," Junior said with strain. "I think it's very likely."

Selene gave her chief engineer a careful scrutiny. This fear wasn't like him. "What aren't you telling me?" she demanded again.

Junior opened his mouth as if to say something. Then, he looked away.

"I am coming with a boarding party," the lieutenant said. "Do not resist in any way or I shall be forced to confiscate your vessel."

"He can't do that," Selene said.

Junior turned to stare at her as if she'd said something stupid.

The next few minutes frustrated Selene. She watched enlisted personnel lower a motor launch. The English-speaking lieutenant climbed aboard along with several sailors carrying assault rifles.

The minutes ticked away as the launch crossed the distance to the *Calypso*. During that time, Selene paced one way and then another. Finally, she ran to the bridge, picking up the satellite phone. She punched in a sequence of numbers, putting the receiver to her ear.

There was a strange buzzing sound on the other end. Was the phone going to fail her? Several clicks were added to the unusual noise. She was ready to shake the phone, maybe open it up to see if there was anything wrong with it. Then the connection went through.

Selene began talking fast, going up a short chain of command until she explained the situation to Danny Ferguson's closest friend, a U.S. Navy commander stationed in the Philippines on a U.S.N. cruiser.

40

"You're quite right," the commander told her. "This is highly unusual. Did you say the lieutenant has come onto your vessel?"

"Yes, sir," Selene said.

"Let me talk to him."

"Yes, sir," she said. "Give me a few minutes to get down there."

"I'll hold on," the commander said.

Selene grinned, taking the satellite phone with her as she hurried from the bridge.

It was already tense by the time she reached the main deck. The lieutenant with his boarding party had just climbed aboard the *Calypso*. They looked like a tough bunch, holding the assault rifles as if they meant to use them. The really weird thing was that the lieutenant didn't look Indonesian in the slightest, more Dutch than anything, while his boarding party was composed of some of the whitest men that Selene had ever seen. They didn't look like individuals who had spent much time at sea in the sun.

"You will put down your rifle," the lieutenant told Forrest.

The ex-SEAL had a deer rifle aimed at the lieutenant's chest. Forrest grinned as he said, "If any of your boarding party starts swinging their rifles toward me, I'll kill you."

The words shocked Selene. The look on Forrest's face indicated he meant to do exactly what he said. The grimness of the boarding party showed they didn't care.

"Wait!" Selene shouted.

The lieutenant glanced at her.

She raised the phone, saying, "I have a U.S. naval commander on the line."

Several of the boarding party laughed in a mocking way. The lieutenant smirked.

Selene squared her shoulders, walking toward the lieutenant, speaking to the commander, telling him the "Indonesians" thought she was bluffing.

"I'll take care of that," the commander said.

A few seconds later, Selene handed the satellite phone to the lieutenant.

With a superior smile, the lieutenant accepted the phone. The shocked expression on his face caused Selene to wonder about the lieutenant's former certainty.

"Yes," the man finally said into the phone. "I understand." He handed it back to Selene. "I am sorry, Dr. Khan," he said. "There has been a misunderstanding. I have decided to give you a pass on the matter. You may proceed to your destination."

The lieutenant turned toward the boarding party, gesturing sharply.

They looked equally startled and then baffled. Slowly, the men shouldered their assault rifles. Crestfallen, they followed the lieutenant to the ladder, climbing down to the launch.

"What did you say to him?" Selene asked the commander.

"Nothing much," the commander said. "I asked for his orders, telling him I would check immediately with the Indonesian Admiralty. He didn't seem to like that. What he liked even less is that I told him I have you and him on satellite intelligence."

"You do?" Selene asked.

"Surprisingly, yes," the commander said. "I received a strange call—well, never mind about that. I think what's going on is a bit of smuggling of some kind. Be careful, Dr. Khan. I know how much Danny loves you. I would hate for anything bad to happen to you."

Selene wasn't sure she wanted to hear that. She asked the commander, "You don't think the lieutenant has genuine orders to stop us?"

"Not in the least," the commander said. "I hope you keep me informed of the situation."

"I will, and thank you again. You're a lifesaver."

"It's been my pleasure. Good day, Doctor. Please give my regards to Danny once you're back in Honolulu."

"Yes, I will."

The line clicked off. On the water, the launch was halfway back to the Indonesian cutter.

That was close, Selene thought, *but maybe that will be the end of our troubles.*

***

"I don't understand," a deep-voiced man said over a scrambled radio. "How was she able to call through your jamming? Or did you fail to do even that correctly?"

"I assure you we jammed their communications on all levels and at full strength," the man who had pretended to be a KRI lieutenant said.

"The fact of her call going through means you are incorrect."

"That's just it," the pseudo-lieutenant said. "I can't explain what happened."

"I can. It's called incompetence, a sin of the highest order, as I'm sure you are aware."

"I take full responsibility."

"That's a splendid eulogy. I shall remember to announce it at your funeral."

"Respectfully," the pseudo-lieutenant said. "I should point out that I discovered the commander had us under satellite surveillance. I could have taken out the target, but brought the U.S. Navy into this."

"Yes," the deep-voiced man said grudgingly. "In retreating you did the right thing. You defused what could have been— well, that doesn't matter to you. I want you to leave the area. Change your markings and head toward Australia."

"I could slip back under cover of darkness, release a scuba team and destroy their vessel with a—"

"I have given you your orders because you failed in your attempt. Now, I will do this myself."

"The American satellite surveillance—"

"Bah!" the deep-voiced man said. "What is that to me? I will eliminate the target and leave a mystery no one will ever puzzle out. If I leave this to you, I'm sure you'll simply find another way to fail."

"Please, you will tell Mother I had no choice in my decision? I—"

"Enough! Obey me by leaving the area and getting off the line. It's out of your hands now. Do you understand?"

"I do," the pseudo-lieutenant said. "I hear and obey."

43

"Good, because I have much to do before this twit shows up…"

10

D'ERLON ENTERPRISES
ARDENNES FOREST

Jack stuffed his hood, dark garments and boots into a bag. He had a lean frame with puckered scars dotting his nearly naked body. Two of the scars had come from bullets, one a nine millimeter and the other a .22 from an Israeli assassin. Two more were knife scars. The fifth was on his right shoulder where a German contract killer in Bangkok had pummeled his flesh with brass knuckles. His shoulder muscles were sore every morning, forcing him to stretch before he began his day.

Donning D'erlon Enterprises attire—a dark pair of coveralls like ones from a bad 60's science fiction show—he clipped a stolen badge to his chest and quickly tied his shoelaces.

Simon did likewise.

They stood in the dark behind a metal shed within the perimeter fence. Jack hung a pair of ordinary goggles from his neck and screwed a square-shaped cap onto his head. Then he picked up a clipboard with a magnetic pen attached. He lacked a gun or even a knife.

The snitch—the one who had stolen the badges for what he thought was IZENOV consortium hoodlums—had been clear. D'erlon Security would quickly discover any weapons on their persons. They had to go the final lap unarmed.

"Ready?" Simon asked.

Jack saw that his partner was. The man had dark hair, wore glasses, stood three inches taller and outweighed him by fifty pounds, his biceps straining against the fabric of his coveralls. Simon was the scientist, but he was also one of the strongest men Jack knew.

Peering around a corner, Jack spied several D'erlon workers riding a long electric cart.

"Let's go," Elliot said, stepping into view, striding purposefully toward a large hangar door beyond the moving cart.

Simon hurried, catching up in an instant. The two of them walked together. Jack watched his partner in his peripheral vision. Simon seemed okay except he held his neck and shoulders a bit too rigidly.

The cart driver—who wore a black hat with a holstered gun at his side—glanced at them. Jack increased his pace a trifle so he stood in front of Simon in relation to the driver. Whatever the driver saw must have seemed ordinary enough. The long cart passed them, heading elsewhere in the giant complex.

Under his breath, Simon muttered an oath.

Jack glanced at his clipboard. It had a layout of the huge plant. He'd memorized the complex route to their destination, but the map helped. He would have told his partner to relax, but it wouldn't have helped Simon any. This was the rough part for many people. The two of them were exposed. There was no doubt about it. One simply had to act normally. Yet, it was one thing to know what to do. It was another to actually do it.

They passed through the first hangar bay door. The snitch had told them sensors lined the opening. The sensors sent a signal to the badges, which were set for various times of the day and night. If the badge didn't send the right response back, D'erlon Security would appear fast.

The inside of the building was huge, with various exposed levels and steel catwalks. Huge humming machines carried out an assortment of tasks Jack didn't have time to figure out. Men and women in coveralls, wearing color-coded caps monitored various consoles.

Jack checked his clipboard. The two D17 agents turned left. Soon, they exited the giant building. A vast manicured lawn set in a circle had cement paths crisscrossing it. Five people in coveralls used the paths, striding from one place to the next. The sixth person—

Simon gawked at the man before quickly lowering his gaze.

Jack felt his curiosity stir at the sight.

The sixth person on the walkway was huge like a power lifter, standing six-six at least. An ox would have had smaller shoulders. The man wore an open gray jacket with a hand cannon strapped under his left arm. The gun was bigger than a .44 Magnum, more like a .55 caliber weapon. He appeared to be some type of soldier.

Using his peripheral vision, Jack caught the dense, pit bull-like neck and the arrogant features. It was the eyes, though, that truly were remarkable. They burned with intensity.

"I'm surprised the snitch didn't say anything about the soldier," Jack whispered. "The man's unusual."

Simon nodded too quickly, once again revealing his nervousness.

Like a wave of pressure, Jack felt the soldier focus on him, making his nape hairs rustle again. A desire to draw his gun—

I don't have a gun, remember?

Jack's eyes narrowed. It took concentration to keep walking normally.

"You," the big man said in a dreadfully deep voice. He spoke English.

Simon halted.

Jack stopped too. The big man with the jacket had presence. He faced the soldier, looking up, meeting the gaze.

The intensity was like a shock in the back of his brain. Jack's fingers balled into fists. Consciously, he flexed his fingers, willing them straight. Time seemed to slow down for Jack.

The big man moved toward them, walking smoothly like an athlete. The soldier's muscles weren't like Simon's weightlifting lumps, but long, flat and dense-seeming.

I bet he weighs four hundred pounds at least. He's massive.

The slightest frown appeared on the big man's square features. Did he suspect them? If he did, if the man drew his hand cannon, the op would be blown no matter if Jack and

47

Simon survived this particular encounter or not. It was possible the soldier's frown was due to Jack's reaction—Elliot realized that with a start. The big man almost seemed...

He doesn't like me staring back at him. He likes to intimidate others.

Realizing that, Jack dropped his gaze. He doubted he could fake trembling. Here was the thing. If the op was blown, it was blown. That would be game-over for Jack Elliot. So, the only possibility with the big man was to carry through the pretense to the end.

The soldier loomed before them.

Jack took a step back as if frightened, and he studiously kept his head down.

"Let me see your manifest," the soldier rumbled.

Jack held up his clipboard.

The big man plucked it from him. "It's a map," he said in an overload voice.

Jack nodded.

"Are you new here?" the heavy voice asked.

Jack nodded again, forcing himself to shuffle his feet as if terrified.

"Didn't *think* I've ever seen your face before," the soldier said. "You think you're tough?"

Jack shook his head.

"You sure?"

Jack almost nodded before inspiration struck. He shook his head again instead of nodding, trying for the feel of being too scared to think straight.

The big man made a rumbling sound. It took Jack a second to realize it was a chuckle.

"Better hurry, newbie," the soldier said. He shoved the clipboard into Jack's hands, making Elliot stumble against Simon.

Jack clutched the clipboard against his chest. He'd seen a frightened man do that once.

"I said *go*."

Simon stumbled away. Jack copied the move.

Simon began to look back.

"Don't do it," Jack whispered.

Simon glanced at him. The scientist's features were pale.

"We're not going to be here long," Jack purred. "In to see what they're doing and out we go to radio HQ. This will be a breeze."

Simon's features stiffened as nodded. "The bigger they are, the harder they fall," his partner muttered.

"Yeah," Jack said, wondering why the NFL didn't believe that. *The bigger they are, the less they fall.* But that didn't matter. They'd passed the toughest hurdle. Everything should be easy now.

-11-

D'ERLON ENTERPRISES
ARDENNES FOREST

Marcus cracked his knuckles as he watched the two workers scurry away. For just a moment there, it had seemed as if the leaner of the two had some balls. The man had actually met his gaze, holding it for several seconds. In fact, the man had seemed ready to fight.

Marcus cocked his head, grinning at the idea. Imagine one of these lesser men fighting him. One solid blow would shatter the man's skull like a shell. A kick could snap the man's spine. It wouldn't even be sporting.

The worms—the people—in this facility sickened Marcus. A few on the security team had a flicker of fire in their belly. They always dropped their gazes too, though, when he approached. Marcus had begun to long for a challenge.

He still worked on cracking Mother's long-term scheme. That was a matter of a slow gathering of data and piecing the puzzle together. That took his intellect. He wanted something to challenge his strength, his fighting prowess.

Swiftly, Marcus un-snapped his holster and drew the snub-nosed Knocker, as he called the .55 caliber weapon. He aimed it into the darkness, knowing the experimental hound roamed up there. That would be a test worthy of his fighting skills. Well, in several years maybe, after the hound finished its advanced training. The beast was still too primitive to truly challenge Marcus. According to Frederick—

Marcus scowled, sliding the Knocker back into its holster. Something nagged at him and he couldn't place what exactly. He hated when that happened. He had the feeling it had something to do with the man who had dared to meet his gaze for several seconds on the lawn.

Why would the man bother him? So a worker had some balls. A few of the lesser humans did after a fashion. It shouldn't mean anything.

Marcus cracked his knuckles. He doubted the bold worker was the problem. Maybe it was just the importance of the moment. Frederick was coming to take more of the *fuel*. Yet, this had become routine. Sure, the shipments could theoretically cause trouble, but they never had so far.

Putting his hands behind his back, Marcus increased his pace. He passed workers at their stations. They cowered, lowered their eyes and trembled if his gaze happened to fall on them. He'd found that staring steadily at a person could break their will in short order.

It was always the same with women as well. If he lingered on her beauty, any woman would begin to tremble and likely weep. Therefore, he had to find a way to hood his greatness. Lately, he had begun practicing dimming the intensity of his gaze.

"What am I not seeing?"

The idea nagged him, and he disliked that.

Marcus craned his neck, looking up at the highest tower. His subconscious must have drawn him here. Putting his hands to a steel rung, he began to climb the central ladder. It relaxed him doing this.

Quickly, the fifty-acre complex spread out below him. If Marcus could have one wish, it would be to fly like an eagle. Soaring in the thermals, looking down at the crawling people below—

Marcus grunted, scowling. The nagging doubt wouldn't leave him. He halted his ascent and peered into the dark forest. Imagine if this was olden times and he was a knight. He would rule the Ardennes. None would have been able to challenge him sword to sword. Perhaps he would have carved out a kingdom as Charlemagne had in the Dark Ages.

I would have been the champion of the time, invincible in combat. They would have composed ballads about my greatness.

Marcus grinned at the thought. Then, he shouted angrily, his fingers gripping the steel rung. He remembered where he'd seen the man on the lawn before. It had seemed like artifice when the man had dropped his gaze. For a moment, Marcus had the impression the man would fight him. Now, he realized his first instinct had been correct. He remembered seeing the man in a manifest of Detachment 17 case officers. The agent's name was Jack Elliot.

Marcus had unclipped his walkie-talkie before starting the climb. He didn't like it catching on the steel webbing around the ladder as he climbed.

Marcus slid down the ladder, picking up speed as he descended. He had to raise the alarm. D17 agents were inside one of Mother's most important complexes.

-12-

THE *CALYPSO*
100 MILES OFF THE COAST OF SUMATRA

As Selene stood on the *Calypso's* bow deck, she extended the antenna of her TR-1010. She turned it on and immediately found a signal. It came from under the ship. She checked the screen, did a quick calibration—

The signal came from much deeper than the object, which was several hundred feet below the surface. The combined ELF-EMF wave was unique to her theory. The critical idea had come after her breakup with Danny. It had reminded her of Tesla's statement: "Inventors don't have time for married life." She hadn't been married exactly...but the spirit of Tesla's statement had proven true nevertheless.

In any case, this was amazing. The extremely low frequency radio wave originated well below the object by an appreciable distance. Yet, it meant something important that both the object and the deeper emitter lined up like this.

"Selene!" Lulu called. "You should start getting ready."

Pushing the antenna down, Selene shut off the device and hurried to her cabin. She stowed the TR-1010 and climbed down to the stern deck.

The crane operator lowered the T-9 Driver Propulsion Vehicle into the water.

The T-9 was torpedo-shaped, made of ceramic-plate so it had a negligible radar signature, and ran off the latest in

53

underwater batteries. There was a cage around the propeller so no user could accidentally cut his hand or arm. Hydroplanes guided the vehicle, while a small motorcycle-style screen protected the controls.

The DPV would give them more time at the bottom of the dive. This would be a technical dive or tec dive for short. They would be using mixed gas, allowing them to go deeper than an ordinary free dive. That meant it was a much more dangerous dive, however.

At 160 feet, the water would have a pressure of six bars. That meant a diver would breathe six times as much as on the surface (one bar). The trouble with that kind of dive was that once one reached the deepest descent, the diver would only have a few minutes before she would have to begin the slow ascent, stopping along the way to allow the gasses in the blood stream to normalize so one didn't get the bends.

"Look at all the sharks," Lulu said. "There haven't been that many prowling around us before this."

Selene noticed the triangular fins cutting the surface and the long, torpedo shapes gliding underwater. There did seem to be an abnormal amount of the marine predators. Was that weird it should happen now? No doubt, Junior would call this another aspect of the curse.

Selene wasn't crazy about swimming with all those sharks. On the other hand, she couldn't back down now. It would look cowardly. Danny would have still dived: showing everyone how tough he was. She couldn't do any less.

"That's the reason I brought the bang sticks," Selene said, pointing at the sharks.

"That's crazy," Lulu said, "No way would I get in the water today. Don't go, Selene."

The doctor shrugged. Sharks seldom attacked suited divers. The crew could help keep the predators away as Forrest and she boarded the T-9. They'd be heading deeper than the sharks normally liked to cruise. This was just a matter of keeping her head.

With that decided, Selene went to her pile of diving gear and began putting it on. After she was done, Lulu handed her two bang sticks.

In open air, a regular bullet could travel a mile or more from the barrel of a gun. Underwater, with a density 800 times greater than air, the same bullet would only travel a few feet.

A bang stick solved the problem in an elementary but elegant manner. The stick had two parts: an eighteen-foot fiberglass pole with a hollow tube on the end. One aggressively shoved the end of the tube against any offending fish. That caused an internal firing pin to discharge the round inside the tube. In Selene's case, that would be a .44 Magnum shell. The bullet didn't travel through water, but went directly into the sea creature. Interestingly, the bullet did less damage than the pressurized blast. Because of that, blank rounds could prove just as deadly if one used enough gunpowder. In either case, the placement of the shot was critical for immediate success: in this instance, the death of a shark.

During the trip, Selene had carefully applied a thin layer of nail polish to the rim of each round. Too much polish could gum up the tube. The nail polish sealed the small gap between bullet and shell, making it useable underwater.

With the bang sticks in hand, Selene allowed Lulu to help her to the scuba platform. From there, Selene jumped backward into the water. After the bubbles cleared, she saw the first shark swim into view.

It was different thinking about this in their element. Could the combination ELF-EMF waves have anything to do with the shark behavior? The marine predators often used electro-location to pinpoint their prey.

Sharks possessed the *ampullae of Lorenzini*, special sensing organs called electroreceptors. Such organs were primarily found in cartilaginous fish—sharks, rays and others. In essence, the electroreceptors could sense temperature gradients and electromagnetic fields. Sharks were the most sensitive to these fields in other animals. Living creatures produced said electrical fields through muscle contractions. Thus, the sharks could sense Selene through electro-location.

She studied the creatures through her full-face mask. A beautiful tiger shark—it must have been eighteen feet long— glided on a parallel course with her. Instead of waiting for it to turn at her, she swam at the predator with a bang stick extended for a thrust.

The tiger shark turned its head, regarding her.

Selene felt it staring with its black eyes. She felt a momentary chill. Sharks had dead eyes like hard knobs of plastic. If the thing attacked— but she needn't have worried. With a flash of its fins, the tiger darted away. Its swiftness was incredible. Like great whites, a tiger shark could reach speeds of twenty-five miles per hour for short bursts.

The torpedo-shaped predator disappeared, fleeing into the gloom of the ocean.

With a conscious effort, Selene loosened her fist. She was surprised at how hard she gripped the end of the bang stick. She forced herself to grin inside the diving mask. It was bigger than an ordinary sport mask, covering her entire face, leaving her lips free so she could talk to Forrest while underwater. They were using modulated ultrasound comm-units.

The doctor propelled herself like a mermaid, her outsized fins sending her knifing through the water. Soon, she reached the T-9, securing herself onto the forward saddle-seat. She switched on power. The color liquid displays came on, as did the color digital charts. The DPV also boasted a GPS and Doppler velocity log.

Soon, Forrest climbed onto the rider's seat behind her. He tapped her on the shoulder to indicate he was ready.

"You have the ultrasound," Selene said.

"Oh, right," Forrest said. "I forgot."

That seemed like a strange comment coming from him.

With a small shrug, Selene fed power to the propeller and adjusted the T-9's hydroplanes. She moved away from the *Calypso* and the circling sharks, diving into the depths. The DPV's vibration was slight as water rushed against her. The forward screen only partially protected her.

"Doc," Forrest said. Incredibly, he sounded worried. "Look behind and to your left."

Selene glanced that way. She saw the tiger shark from earlier. Beside it was a monstrous great white, a creature at least twenty-five feet long. The two sharks burst into high speed, coming toward them.

They're moving at attack speed, Selene thought.

Both the tiger and the great white were man-eaters. Both could also attain speeds faster than the T-9.

"They're gaining on us!" Forrest shouted.

Why are they attacking? Selene wondered. *What's making them so crazy?* She increased speed. A look over her shoulder showed it wasn't going to be enough.

"Use your bang stick!" she shouted.

The great white moved ahead of the tiger shark. The giant predator just loomed behind Forrest, already opening its cavernous jaws.

-13-

D'ERLON ENTERPRISES
ARDENNES FOREST

Jack shook out his sore knuckles as Simon lowered the unconscious worker onto the floor. The scientist then dragged the worker Elliot had hit around a corner, returning with the man's badge.

They had watched the worker come out of a special door. The worker had hurried to close the door as the two of them had approached. It was at that point Jack hit the worker's "glass" jaw.

The two agents were in the central building with its maze of corridors and giant humming accelerators. Simon had checked his device constantly, shaking his head at each new discovery.

Jack used the unconscious worker's badge, holding it before a scanner. A heavy lock clicked. Jack yanked the thick steel door. Even so, it opened slowly.

The two agents peered into a vast sunken chamber the size of a football field. If they passed through the entrance, they would be on a catwalk one hundred meters higher than the majority of the cyclers and faintly shimmering fields down there. Jack counted approximately thirty people at work.

"What do you think is going on down there?" Jack asked.

From the doorway beside Elliot, Simon's brown eyes widened with amazement. He adjusted his device, elongating the antenna. Then, he began to manipulate the controls with his thumbs.

"I don't want to keep the door open too long," Jack said.

Simon nodded absently, obviously absorbed in his task.

"The shimmering fields are…?" Jack said.

"Magnetic containment barriers, I believe," Simon said in a clipped voice.

"What do you mean?"

"Force fields," Simon said. "You know, like for a starship."

"Come again?"

"Like the old science fiction TV shows."

"We can make those?"

Simon shook his head. "No. We cannot. What I'm seeing is too incredible to believe. Yet, there it is."

Jack peered down, watching some of the giant machines, making little sense of them.

"Close the door," Simon said in a rush. The scientist stepped back, shoving the antenna shorter.

Obediently, Jack pushed until the door locked.

"We have to get out of here," Simon said.

"Why the sudden rush?"

Simon faced him. There was moisture on his upper lip. In a strained voice, he said, "We've stumbled onto the biggest secret on the planet."

"Which is…?" Jack asked, raising an eyebrow.

"If my readings are correct—and I believe they are—they're making antimatter down there."

Jack shrugged.

Simon laughed raggedly. "You don't understand. They make microscopic amounts of antimatter at the CERN collider. Making even a few grams of antimatter costs trillions of dollars."

"You mean billions," Jack said.

"No. I said *trillions*."

Jack raised his eyebrows.

"According to my readings, they almost have 900 grams of antimatter down there."

"And that's illegal?"

"You're not tracking me," Simon said. "What I'm seeing, humanity can't do yet. The Swiss have big magnetic containers to hold the microscopic amounts of antimatter at the CERN facility in Switzerland. To make this antimatter and to hold it…the technology down there is more advanced than anything on Earth. We have to get out of here and report this."

Jack looked up and around as if searching for something. A hint of a frown touched his features. He touched Simon's arm, pointing to the left.

"We came from the other direction," Simon said.

"I know. But it doesn't feel right going that way now."

"Okay," Simon asked. "But what aren't you telling me?"

"Do you hear how quiet it is?" Jack asked.

Simon listened before peering questioningly at him.

"It's subtle," Jack said, "almost under my radar. But it's gotten too quiet the last minute. We must have used the worker's badge wrong and tripped an alarm."

They walked faster in the new direction, covering ground with long strides. Then, sirens began to wail. Red lights flashed in the building.

Jack halted, motioning Simon. They stood in a long row between heavy machinery.

Jack wondered what had gone wrong. If he could figure it out, he'd have a better chance of coming up with the right answer to getting out of here.

They had stumbled onto something *huge*. Simon knew his science cold. If the man said no one on Earth knew how to do what they had seen, Simon meant just that. If making antimatter in big quantities was worth trillions of dollars, their lives were worth less than scrap. That didn't matter this instant except that trust became more of an issue. With trillions, the D'erlon people had plenty for massive bribes that could buy just about anyone. With that kind of backing, one could easily reach into D17.

Something had given them away tonight. Was it the last badge? Could it have been the big man earlier? Maybe someone higher up in D17 had sold them out.

Would the D'erlon people have let Simon and me reach this far then? That was doubtful.

Jack heard tires squeal. He hurried to the edge of the machinery, peering around a metal block corner. One of the long electric carts with benches on the sides slid to a stop. Four security guards jumped out.

Jack glanced up at the ceiling. Had security cameras spotted them? He watched the guards. They fanned out in various directions with handguns drawn. The driver craned around, watching the guards for a moment. Then, he faced his steering apparatus, cranking the wheel as he engaged the electric motor. The tires spun on the smooth floor, catching finally as the cart lurched into motion.

That would be the way to go, traveling by cart. Jack debated it, especially as the machine headed this way.

"Stay put," Jack said.

"What are you—?"

Jack ignored Simon as he stepped briskly from the machinery, holding up his clipboard. He imperiously motioned the driver to stop.

People usually saw what they expected to see. If one acted importantly, most people listened. The driver was no exception. He took his foot off the accelerator and applied the brake.

"Over here," Jack said in a stern voice. "Simon is injured."

"What?" the driver asked, his cart almost to Elliot.

Jack scowled, whipping around. "Do I have to tell you twice during an emergency?"

With these kinds of things, fakery either worked like a charm or it didn't. There were no half measures. The trick was making sure the mark didn't have time to think but acted automatically.

The driver jumped out of his seat, scurrying after Jack.

"What's going on, anyway?" the driver asked. "Why all the commotion?"

Jack moved around the machinery. The driver followed. Jack spun around, already swinging a savage uppercut. His fist caught the driver under the jaw, clicking the man's teeth together and snapping his head up hard. The driver was tougher than the earlier worker had been, however. He stumbled backward, almost into sight of the guards. Jack grabbed the

61

man's coveralls, yanking him close. The driver's hands lifted as he feebly tried to resist. Elliot didn't give him any more time. He drove the driver face-first into a heavy block of metal. The skull thump was audible. As carefully as he could, Jack lowered the seemingly boneless driver onto the floor.

Jack knelt, pulling off the cap and badge. The driver still breathed. He was alive, but he would have a nasty concussion. If it was simply a matter of survival, Jack knew he should kill the driver. But butchering the helpless went against the code.

"Come on," Jack said.

Simon followed him to the cart.

"You're going to sit on the bench," Jack said. "Put your hands in your lap and keep your head down. Don't look up unless you hear me call your name."

"Got it," Simon said, heading for a bench seat.

Putting the new cap on his head, clipping the badge to his coveralls, Jack climbed into the driving seat. He felt Simon sit down. Jack gave him another second before he pushed his foot against the accelerator and cranked the steering wheel. The long cart began to move.

The four security men searched in various directions. This could be going on all over the complex. None of them had heard the little knockdown over the sirens and humming machinery.

Jack took a deep breath, judging the situation. He aimed for the guard nearest the big door. Then, he tromped on the accelerator, picking up speed. Seconds later, he braked, turned a corner and hit the accelerator again as he raced toward the guard.

"Hey!" Jack shouted at the man.

The guard looked over his shoulder. The man had a thick neck but only stood around five-ten, Elliot's height.

"I was supposed to tell you!" Jack shouted.

The guard raised his eyebrows, waiting. He didn't seem nervous that Jack came fast on the cart. Jack kept his features earnest, keeping his machine at high speed. At the last second, when the guard no doubt expected him to brake, Jack cranked the wheel, aiming the front of the cart at him.

The surprise was complete. The guard never expected this. The front of the long cart struck him hard, catapulting the man against a big machine. The guard struck the back of his head with a *bonk* and slid to the floor.

Jack had braked immediately after striking the guard. The jar had thrown Simon off the bench, but Jack didn't have time to worry about that yet. He slid out of the seat and dashed to the unconscious security man.

Blood pooled onto the floor from the back of the man's head. Jack wasn't sure the guard was going to make it. He shoved the thought aside—he could feel guilty for this later, provided he got away.

Working fast, Jack stripped the guard of his gun, holster, and knife, as well as his badge and black cap. The hat had dislodged with the brutal strike and thus wasn't bloody. With the items, he raced back to the cart.

Simon picked himself off the floor, holding a bloody nose. "You could have told me you were going to do that," he said nasally.

Jack hadn't known his own plan until the moment he acted.

"Get in," Jack said. They had run out of time. "The bloody nose should actually help us."

A second after Simon boarded, Jack backed up as he switched caps yet again. He put on the new badge and accelerated out of the middle building. People and carts raced everywhere outside. He observed those nearest him and copied their demeanor. In the distance, he saw the big man striding, shouting orders, holding his hand cannon.

Jack kept his features steady as the minutes passed. They covered ground much faster in the cart. He aimed for the place they had stashed their night vision equipment and black garments. It was—

Jack took his foot off the accelerator, letting the cart slow down naturally.

"What's wrong?" Simon said.

"Nothing," Jack said, his partner's words helping him to shake off the disappointment.

Security people had found their stash, a man running with one of the bags of clothes, another carrying the suppressed rifle.

Simon looked up and saw that. "Now what are we going to do?"

"Yeah," Jack said. "That's a good question."

-14-

UNDERWATER
100 MILES OFF THE COAST OF SUMATRA

It was like something out of a Saturday morning cartoon with an aqua-knight riding a dolphin mount. Selene adjusted the controls, propelling them down at a sharp angle. She glanced over her shoulder just in time to witness a marvel of high-tech lancing.

The great white seemed to be all teeth with a vast underbelly. Forrest twisted around, holding the eighteen-foot fiberglass pole with both hands. He judged it perfectly, barely nudging the tube against the monstrous predator. The great white supplied the needed pressure.

There was a flash of bubbles and then blood. The precision of the great white ended right there. The speed of its attack kept it going, but it hadn't adjusted in time to go down sharply enough. Thus, the huge body passed over them.

Selene had a moment to spy the destruction just under the distinctive snout. The blast had shredded the flesh. More blood poured from the beast. The tiger had veered away at the blast, but it would likely come back to investigate soon enough. Nothing made sharks go berserk with a feeding frenzy like blood in the water. They would cannibalistically devour the giant denizen of the deep.

Selene's adrenaline kicked in all the way now, making her heart hammer and her mouth dry.

"I don't ever want to do that again," Forrest rasped. He let go of the used bang stick. "Hand me yours just in case another shark shows up."

Selene handed Forrest her bang stick with a trembling arm. "Wow," she told him.

"Yeah, I'd love to go back and cut out its teeth. Then, I could string them in a necklace and wear it around my neck instead of the gold chain. I'd wait, you know, for someone to ask. 'What's with the shark teeth?' Then, I'd just causally tell them how I lanced the bastard while riding around the ocean with a long-legged doctor of underwater geology. You know, of course, that no one would ever believe the story. That's what would make it perfect."

Selene shook her head. She thought she'd gotten a read on the man. Now, she wasn't sure again. Why would no one believing the story make it perfect? That didn't make sense.

"You're a strange man," she said.

"True, but I'm loveable. That's the important thing."

"No," she said. "You're definitely not loveable, but you're good at what you do."

"Let's hope so."

"What's that mean?"

"Nothing," he said, "just talking to let out steam."

Selene didn't buy that. The man had to be the coolest, most collected person she'd ever met. He'd pull guns against anyone and had just killed the deadliest murderer of the ocean as if he did it every day.

"How far are we from target?" Forrest asked.

"Target?"

He laughed lightly. "Forgive me the military lingo, doc. Old habits die hard. How far are we from your object?"

"We should be there soon," Selene said.

The T-9 continued to descend, but she brought them down at a lesser angle than before. She wanted to give their bodies' time to adjust to the greater depth and pressure.

The DPV moved through the light zone, or as it was technically called, the euphotic zone. Euphotic meant "well lit" in Greek. That was the upper ocean zone where sunlight penetrated during the day. That could be as little as fifty feet in

66

murky water to the depth of 660 feet with perfect clarity. Fortunately for them, the water was almost crystal clear, allowing the sunlight deeper penetration.

The euphotic zone had all the plant growth due to photosynthesis. The plant growth meant that almost all the fishes in the sea lived near the surface, at least comparatively speaking. The average ocean depth was somewhere around 1400 feet. It would be cold and dark that far down with incredible pressure per square inch.

Selene kept watch of the GPS coordinates, battery power and the Doppler velocity log. They were moving fast, going deeper and deeper.

There was a ridge out here much higher than the regular ocean floor. The object was embedded there. If it had been on the regular sea floor out here, Selene would have needed a bathyscaphe to reach it.

For a time, neither of them spoke. They monitored their mixed air regulators, making adjustments as needed. Bubbles rose every time either of them exhaled. That must have been new for Forrest, who'd used a rebreather as a SEAL. Rebreathers didn't release as many bubbles to give a secret diver away.

"Look," Selene said. "Do you see the ridge?"

"I do. It's a smudge from here."

It was an underwater mountain range. Selene made a course correction and throttled back on speed. She didn't want to descend too fast this deep down.

"Want to make any bets on what the object is going to be?" Forrest asked.

Did he sound strained? Selene wasn't sure. Finally, she decided it must be a trick of the ultrasound. The man was cool under fire. This was his natural environment.

"Could it be an old submarine?" Forrest asked.

"Is that what you think it will be?"

"I have no idea, doc. Just talking to pass the time."

"Or 'cause you're nervous?" she asked.

"Yeah," he said in his callous way. "That's it. You have me pegged, doc."

"I think it will most likely be a beginning volcano, a new type."

"Yeah?"

"We'll see soon enough," she said. It had gotten gloomier with the higher water absorbing much of the sunlight's ambient qualities.

Selene wasn't surprised she could feel her heart thudding in her chest. The GPS monitor told her they were close. Visibility had lessened. They passed over rocks and strange underwater growths. A fish swam lazily in and out of view. Most of the marine creatures were higher in the light zone.

Then she saw the huge object, and it must have been a trick of the dim light. The object seemed metallic, shiny like a steel-plated automatic. She could accept dark metallic of a submarine or sunken ship variety, but not this.

"What are you making of this?" Forrest asked.

"Let's get just a little closer."

After Selene said that, fear boiled in her, and she didn't know why. What was the shiny metal thing? Why would—?"

She gasped, flabbergasted. "Forrest," she whispered.

"I'm seeing it," he whispered back.

Selene could see the object. There was no mistaking the sight. Firstly, it was huge, much bigger than she had realized. Secondly, it wasn't a volcano. It was a dome, a steel dome, the very top of it, anyway. It was embedded in the underwater mountain a little to the left of the peak.

"Forrest," she said, her word choking off because right then, an eerie blue nimbus glowed from the bottom edge of the dome.

-15-

ARDENNES FOREST
FRANCE

From its location behind the inner perimeter fence, the beast listened to the sirens, the shouted commands and the rush of booted feet. It watched the mayhem, reminded of the ants it had once studied from a colony it had dug up with its paws.

This must have come about from the two who had slunk through its territory.

The beast considered that for a time. Then, it noticed a cart with a driver and a rider with a bloody nose. They edged toward the perimeter some distance from here. No one else seemed to pay attention to those two. The driver got out, went to the rider and helped him to his feet. The two men moved to a building, slipping behind it and out of view of the rest of the scurrying population.

The beast trotted in that direction along the inner perimeter.

Out of sight of anyone else, the two men cut through the wire and sprinted for the perimeter fence. They must be trying to escape!

If the beast could have laughed, it would have. The humor of the situation delighted it. The masters wanted it to patrol its territory. The masters counted on its puppy-trained nature to hate everything that entered its range. But it had foiled the vile manipulation.

It noticed the men were doing something with a device. The beast's collar went dead. The men crossed the barrier and the collar resumed its buzz.

Now, that was interesting. The beast hadn't noticed the combination before. It had thought the masters had done that in order to slip test subjects into its territory. Hmm... Maybe it could use the device to cross the barrier itself. That was a very interesting idea. The beast berated itself for not having rushed to where the two-legs came into its territory. It could have observed them manipulating the device from a closer distance, figuring out how it worked.

The beast knew about machines, guns and other manmade tools. It gave the two-legs their incredible mastery. The idea that it might be able to learn to manipulate such tools itself was radical in the extreme.

It must observe these two carefully. Once they reached the outer fence, however, then it would rush in and kill them in order to gain the magical device for itself.

-16-

The blue light coming from the dome deepened in color. At the same time, the T-9's electric motor went out along with the color liquid crystal displays, the digital charts, the GPS and the Doppler velocity log.

"What's going on?" Selene asked.

"No more talking," Forrest said. "Follow me."

"Why shouldn't we talk and where do you plan to go?"

Forrest had already shoved off the T-9, kicking his fins, gliding over Selene. "We're not going to talk because someone over there might be listening to us. We're going over there to inspect the thing." He used the last bang stick to point at the dome.

The dead T-9 and his words gave Selene a profound sense of unreality. This was happening too fast, and it was too weird.

"Who—"

"No," Forrest said, turning in the water, staring at her through his full-face mask. He gave her an intensely significant glance.

She finally got the message. The dome had something to do with their malfunctioning DPV. There could be people inside it. Yet, who could have built such a thing with nobody having heard about it? The idea was crazy.

Sure, old James Bond movies had villains who built elaborate structures on an island with hundreds of workers. It had always been a silly notion. The pouring of goods to the island would have given the game away. Was she supposed to believe a high-tech dome near the epicenter of the 2004 quake had just gone up by magic?

Selene shook her head. She wasn't buying into that kind of nonsense. An old submarine, even a new one, could be explained easily enough. But how did a group go about constructing…?

The thought drifted as she swam after Forrest. She couldn't believe she was doing this. Without the T-9, they weren't going to be able to stay down here very long. They'd have to use a controlled ascent to make sure—

Selene kicked harder, working to catch up with Forrest. The man seemed to be on a mission. Then Selene felt it: heat from her gear. What would cause that?

She began kicking furiously, panicking. At the last second, just before Selene lost it, she realized that her emotions held down the panic button.

I have to control myself or I'm dead.

One of the keys to tec diving was keeping your cool. If you panicked down here at the bottom, it meant you likely weren't coming back up alive.

Selene concentrated on the dome and the mountain. They seemed to have gotten bigger. She focused on them. It seemed to Selene she could see dents in the dome. Had rocks smashed there? Could that have occurred during the earthquake? But that made even less sense.

Am I supposed to believe the structure was here before 2004? How would it have survived the earthquake?

Can this have anything to do with the KRI cutter earlier?

The dome had become huge in comparison to them. The heat still radiated from her gear, she realized, but the water helped cool it.

Forrest swam straight at the blue glow. That meant—

The glow snapped off suddenly as if it realized they'd seen it. The dome seemed darker then, which was simply a trick of light. She'd been staring at the brightness for too long.

As her eyes adjusted to the regular gloom, Selene finally caught up with Forrest. He turned, staring at her with wide eyes.

That made her stomach curl with terror. If Forrest Dean was afraid, she was petrified.

He pointed at the dome. She nodded. He turned back to it, kicking his fins, and she followed. At that moment, she noticed the lip at the bottom of the dome. The structure curved but didn't merge at the bottom into the rock. Some of it went over in a lip. Forrest swam toward that. The glow had come from there.

Twenty seconds later, Selene understood why. There was a large hole under the lip of the dome that was at least thirty feet in diameter.

Forrest swam into the hole. Selene didn't know why he would do that, but she followed. Then, in the murk, she saw what he might have already seen. Maybe he had kept one of his eyes shut before when the blue glow shined. That meant one of Forrest's eyes was used to the darkness.

She saw a latch up there and realized it was a lever to open a hatch. The hatch must lead into an air lock, which would allow them inside the dome.

Forrest didn't hesitate. He swam up, pulled the latch and opened the hatch, swimming inside.

Selene made a silent appeal to God. Then she swam after him, wondering if their lives were ever going to be the same.

-17-

ARDENNES FOREST
FRANCE

Stealthily, Jack led the way through the forest. He felt the thing tracking them. It was like a spotting laser centered on the middle of his back. It waited but he didn't know for what. More than once, Elliot's hand tightened around the stolen gun handle.

"My head hurts," Simon said.

"It's just a little longer," Jack said.

After several steps, Simon asked, "You okay?"

"I'm fine," Jack said as he peered behind them.

"I don't get you, Elliot. Down there in the complex, you acted cooler than anyone had a right to be. Out here in the woods where we're ten times safer than before you act as if your toes are on fire. We did it. We went in and out, and we found something so freaking wild it still doesn't compute."

"Any speculations on the subject?" Jack asked.

"You're still not getting it. The D'erlon people are cooking antimatter as if it's crack. How could something so important, so vast have escaped so many people? How many patents have the French hidden? This has to be the greatest technological power play in history. It's bigger than the Manhattan Project. It's more on the order of being the first to discover fire or the wheel."

Jack hardly heard Simon's words. His gut had tightened like before. If he didn't know better—

"Did you hear that?" Simon asked.

Jack had frozen, peering into the darkness behind them. If only he wore his night-vision goggles. Something out there just stepped on a dry stick. It had cracked like a rifle shot.

"What now?" Simon whispered.

"Keep going," Jack whispered back. He kept his eyes away from the stolen gun because he didn't want to see his hand shake.

Simon's pace increased.

"Slow down," Jack whispered.

Simon did the opposite, his fast walk breaking into a trot. That only made things worse.

"We've got to stick together," Jack whispered. "Slow down."

Simon raced out of sight, rattling leaves and snapping braches. He must have finally felt the thing out there tracking them. It had become ominous.

Jack increased his pace. Then he whipped around, aiming his gun to the left. The thing trailing them moved faster than before. Jack heard it, and he came close to yanking the trigger, firing blindly. That would be stupid on two counts, revealing his position to any humans in the woods and wasting a precious bullet when he couldn't see the thing.

It's hunting Simon. The realization was sharp in his gut.

Jack's eyes narrowed. Then he broke into a run, not a fast sprint or a jog, but a steady run that he could keep up for a time.

The sense of urgency increased as Simon's crashing sounds dwindled. His partner was moving panic-fast.

"Shit," Jack said. Now, he sprinted too, straining to see well enough in the dark to avoid crashing against a tree trunk.

Then the thing he'd been dreading happened. A bloodcurdling scream told him the thing in the woods had found his partner. The scream cut off as if a guillotine had chopped it.

"You bastard," Jack said. He sprinted for another ten seconds before skidding to a halt. *What kind of fool am I?*

Jack's instincts told him his partner was dead. Racing like this would only get him killed the same way. The precious information about D'erlon Enterprises would die with him.

Jack slowed to a careful walk and listened as hard as he could. A feeling of guilt for having failed his partner swept over Elliot.

It's my fault. I should have seen it coming. I was too busy freaking out.

The next words came hard to Jack. "I'm sorry, Simon," he muttered so softly under his breath that even he didn't hear the words.

The fear that had been building in him leaked away. He wasn't really trying to escape now. He wanted a piece of whatever had slain his partner. Elliot no longer gripped the gun with manic strength. He was ready for war.

The beast surprised him, launching from hiding to his left. Jack saw a blur, fired a shot and ducked. Heavy jaws clicked together, missing taking his forearm, hand and gun in one vicious bite. The shaggy creature knocked against the exposed arm, though. A freight train would have hit lighter.

The gun sailed away into the darkness as Jack tumbled backward over leaves. He rolled over an old fallen branch, not a big one, but it hurt his back just the same. He twisted to get off the branch, sinking low behind it. The move saved him from the creature's second rush. The beast must have tripped over the hidden log. Something huge, whining like a dog, tumbled head over heels over and past Elliot.

He got up, remembering he had a knife. He tugged it free of its sheath, holding it parallel against his right leg. A little surprise always helped in a fight to the death.

The thing that climbed to its feet was monstrous. It was as big as an Irish wolfhound but heavier. The braincase appeared too large, but must simply have been caused by the play of moon-shadows. The monster-dog panted, and it seemed to watch him much too carefully as if it actually played out moves in its head.

"What did you do to Simon?"

The beast cocked its shaggy head.

"Can you understand me?"

The thing growled as if angered by the question. That's when Jack noticed the device Simon had carried earlier. It lay beside a tree, shiny in the moonlight. Would Green have dropped that? Jack didn't think so. That left just one other conclusion. The beast-dog had been carrying it in its mouth and had set it down just before it attacked.

"What do you want with that?" Jack asked, pointing at the boxlike device.

The beast-dog actually turned to look at it. Then, it regarded Jack again.

I'm not going to survive if I stay here. Jack began sliding to the side.

The beast-dog leaped without giving any kind of signal that it was going to do so. That was highly unusual for an animal. Even so, the hound didn't catch Elliot completely by surprise.

It rushed in. Jack set himself, still keeping the blade hidden against his leg. At the last second, he dropped to one knee and cut. The knife sliced flesh. The force of it nearly tore the weapon from Jack's grip. He held on, though, just barely.

After passing Elliot, the beast-dog whirled around. A bloody line along its side showed open skin.

Jack stood, the knife held in front of him. "Now we know, huh? You want to kill me you're going to have to pay the butcher's bill first."

Once more, the thing cocked its grotesque head. Then, it began to move sideways in a most unusual manner.

Jack turned with it, always keeping the blade between him and the monster. The beast's maneuver was so strange he didn't understand its purpose until it was too late. At that point, Jack charged.

The beast turned away, raced to Simon's device and scooped it up with its teeth. Then, it plunged into the forest, disappearing in seconds.

Jack stood blinking in the darkness. Finally, he crouched, wiping the bloody knife on grass. By taking the device, the beast had trapped him in the perimeter. How was he supposed to get past the emitters without the device?

I can't just admit defeat.

A snort of derision escaped Jack's lips. What did it matter what he admitted? Unless he could think of something, D'erlon Security would soon find him trapped in the wild zone.

-18-

THE DOME
100 MILES OFF THE COAST OF SUMATRA

The water drained out of the chamber. Hesitantly, Selene removed her full-face mask. Forrest did likewise. They could breathe the air here.

"What is this place?" Selene whispered.

"Good question," Forrest said. "I suggest we move as quietly as possible. I think this place is filled with hostiles."

Selene searched his face. "Who are you really?"

He stared back hard, finally saying, "I belong to D17."

"Who's that?"

"Not a 'who' but a 'what'," Forrest said. "It's the name for an ultra-secret American intelligence agency."

"You're kidding me, right?"

Forrest spun a wheel, opening the inner hatch. He pulled his feet out of his flippers, picked them up and walked through into another chamber.

Selene followed his example, feeling clumsy with all her tec gear.

"Time to get nimble," Forrest said. He sat on a bench and stripped off the diving gear, struggling out of his wetsuit. He wore swim trunks and that was it. Zipping open a pocket on the wetsuit, he pulled out a small automatic.

"You're kidding me?" Selene asked. "You shoot that thing and puncture a bulkhead and we drown."

"I'm a fantastic shot," he said. "I'll put the bullet in a body if it comes to that. We might run into more of our friends like we did upstairs. That means it's good I came prepared."

"Do you think they were part of this?"

"That's what I'm here to find out," Forrest said.

"Why me? Why join our expedition under false pretenses?"

"Deniability is a priceless asset, doc. It's one of our stocks in trades. Come on, and keep quiet."

He opened the hatch to the next room.

Selene wore a bikini under the wetsuit. She wished she'd put on more clothing. This was embarrassing. Forrest liked to strut around. He'd proven that. She felt exposed and therefore vulnerable following him barefoot in just her bikini. She hated the feeling.

They entered a larger, low-ceiled chamber. Steel tables stood along the sides. They were empty. No, wait.

Selene frowned, walking ahead of Forrest, picking up a Mars bar candy wrapper. She showed Forrest.

He nodded before padding to another hatch.

"Wait," she whispered. "Who built this?"

"Don't know," he said.

"Has your organization ever faced them before?"

"I don't know."

"You shouldn't lie to me down here. We—"

"I don't know," Forrest repeated. "Now, you've got to shut up and let me think. And do exactly as I tell you. This…it could get ugly, doc—Selene."

The turnaround was too sudden. She had led the expedition here. He had been a hired hand, a diver needing a second chance. That had been his story. Now, he was trying to take over and run the show.

"This is my find," she said.

Forrest had already started for the next hatch. He stopped, stood straighter and turned around to look at her. Intensity swirled in his eyes.

"You're a smart woman. This is your find, and I'm sorry to have co-opted it. Actually, that was the Secretary's decision. You did find it. Detachment 17 learned about it and gave you me. We're here, and it should be a great day of discovery for you. Well, it still is a huge discovery, but not like you think. These people—"

"Who are they?"

"The enemy," Forrest said. "Why or who—" He shrugged. "That's one of the things we're trying to figure out. *Kapeesh*?"

"Yes. I understand."

Forrest grinned boyishly.

That more than anything he'd said so far helped Selene. He was having fun. He was worried, true enough, but Forrest intended to find out what this place was.

Good, because I want to know too, Selene decided.

Forrest reached the next hatch. Slowly, he moved the bar, opening it. Just as slowly, he cracked it open, peering through with one eye. He opened the hatch wider, still searching. Finally, he stepped through.

Selene came hard on his heels. The sight made her gasp. *This can't be real.*

The next chamber was vast and cavernous with a dome shape. On one part of the walls were blinking, moving and shining lights. Different areas had screens showing heat signatures, she supposed, and ultraviolet light images. There was something weird going on here, as this wasn't modern technology, not the way the T-9's displays had been. It felt—

"Alien," Selene said. "This place feels alien."

"What do you mean?" Forrest whispered.

"Not like us, I guess."

He nodded as if trying to ingest the idea.

"What's that over there?" Selene whispered.

He looked around.

She dared to scurry ahead of him. A device sat on a stand. It had what looked like a tuning fork connected to a longish control panel. She picked it up, noting its lightness.

"Is it metal?" Forrest asked.

She clicked a fingernail against the "fork." It felt metallic. The box didn't seem to be, though.

A louder sound came from across the room. Selene looked there. Out of the corner of her eye, she realized Forrest swung around to look as well.

A man stepped through a hatch. He wore red coveralls and was abnormally thin and bald. From here, he looked Chinese.

The man halted, staring at them in obvious surprise.

"Don't move," Forrest said, training his trinket gun on the man.

The man dug a hand into a pocket, coming up with a flat device. He aimed it at Forrest.

The D17 agent grunted in pain as the skin on a pectoral darkened fast.

"Stop it!" Selene shouted.

Three sharp retorts from Forrest's gun put three slugs into Mr. Red Coveralls. The flat device dropped from his hands. Blood spurted from his chest and throat as he staggered backward. He crashed against a display of lights and pitched forward onto his face, twitching and bleeding onto the stainless steel floor.

It was worse for Forrest. Trickles of smoke rose from a tiny charred hole over his heart. The D17 agent groaned, sinking to his knees. He looked up at Selene, his face drained of color.

"Listen to me," Forrest whispered hoarsely.

Selene nodded dumbly as tears leaked from her eyes.

"Take that thing…" Forrest began to pant. "Leave here… Don't go back to the *Calypso*. Call—"

Forrest Dean groaned, swaying, falling onto his back.

Selene rushed to him, kneeling beside the man. "Yes, yes," she said.

He looked at her with glazed eyes, tried to breathe and made a horrible rattling sound in his throat.

"What do I do?" she cried.

He strained, the skin tightening on his face. "Listen," he whispered.

She'd put an ear by his mouth to hear the words.

"You're smart," Forrest wheezed. "You're tough. I'm…I'm counting on you… Stay alive. Fight…"

After the last word, Forrest deflated, his chest never rising upward again.

He's dead.

With the realization came a frightening need to scream. Selene was afraid that if she did scream, she wouldn't be able to stop for quite some time. Instead, she stood and woodenly headed back the way she had come.

She focused on Forrest's words. She had to stay alive.

Once she reached the changing room, she realized that she still held the tuning fork. Forrest had wanted her to take it as evidence. That's how she'd fight back.

Selene moaned in dread. She had to get out of here before it was too late.

-19-

ARDENNES FOREST
FRANCE

The beast wanted to crush the metal device in its jaws. It would go back and rend the human into itty-bitty pieces of flesh and bones.

The human had cut it. The wound hurt, dripping blood. Instead of obeying its bloody instincts, the beast reached the outer perimeter fence. Slowly, it walked toward a post. The buzz in its collar increased. Jolts of pain began.

The beast whined, backing up a bit. It would appear the metal thing itself didn't have the power to cross the barrier. Dropping the device, the beast examined it, recognizing the controls. As a puppy, it had seen humans turn on TVs and other electrical devices.

With its right front paw, the beast delicately pressed controls. Afterward, it approached the barrier. The same jolts caused it to retreat.

For several minutes, the beast attempted to figure out the device's functions. Nothing worked. Time after time, it tried to cross the barrier and failed.

The sense of defeat loomed.

The beast cocked its head. Security forces were in its territory. Was one of the masters coming? It seemed likely. They must be hunting the one who had cut its side.

What if a master found it like this, trying to escape its prison? That would be bad.

The beast lay down, ignoring the wound as best as it could. It needed a plan. If it couldn't escape in time...then it must go for a secondary prize. That meant—

The beast rose, whining at the pain of the nasty cut. The last human had been cunning. That one knew how to fight. It had lacked fear there at the end. Before that, the beast had smelled its fright. Something had given the human courage. The first one...it had died quickly with a bite to the back of its neck.

Picking up the metal device, the beast turned away from the outer perimeter. It loped through the forest, heading toward the security group. It would show the masters that it had done its duty. The beast realized it needed to play for time. It must make the masters believe it was loyal.

Next time—

The beast's eyes shined with murderous thoughts. It wanted to meet the knife-man again. It had a reason to hate that one. The beast would never forget the man's scent. Someday, somewhere, it hoped for another opportunity to kill the annoying human and piss on its cooling flesh.

-20-

UNDERWATER
100 MILES OFF THE COAST OF SUMATRA

Selene swam out of the hole, propelling herself away from the dome. She held the tuning-fork device in one hand and a bang stick in another. Forrest had put the last stick under the lip of the dome before going in.

I can't believe Forrest is dead. What kind of weapon did the Chinese man use on him?

Could it have been a laser? In science fiction movies, lasers were red lines or energy bolts. In reality, most lasers were invisible to the naked eye. Yet, how could the little flat thing the Chinese man had used have packed such a punch? No military she'd ever heard of had handheld lasers yet.

Selene searched for the T-9, hoping the electric motor would be working again. Unfortunately, the DPV was nowhere in sight. Maybe once the motor had quit its neutral buoyancy had been disrupted. Neutral buoyancy meant the object wouldn't float up or sink on its own, but remain where it was. Selene peered into the greater depths but didn't see the machine. A long scan upward did not reveal it either. She was going to have to rely on her muscles.

That meant it was time to begin a controlled ascent. Should she return to the *Calypso*? Forrest had warned her against it.

She decided she had to return to the *Calypso*. She had to warn the others and then they had to leave the area. Besides, she was one hundred miles from Sumatra. Simeulue Island was a little closer. She could swim there maybe if she had to.

Selene kicked her fins, leaving the mysterious dome behind. She checked her ascent monitor and began to make the timed rises to avoid decompression sickness, or the bends, as it was commonly known.

***

She neared the surface what seemed like a lifetime later. She'd had too much time to think and felt strung out and limp. If she…

Selene frowned, seeing something strange near the surface. It…it looked like an inky, octopus cloud, only much larger. It looked like—

Selene's stomach tightened sickly. The cloud was reddish colored. She spied long torpedo shapes darting through it. Worse, there were bodies, as in human bodies, some of them were half-eaten. She counted—

Selene grinded her molars together to keep from screaming. The conclusion was obvious. That was blood and those were feeding sharks. The bodies were in the spot where the *Calypso* had been. She recognized Lulu's bikini colors. Her best friend was dead.

Forrest had been right. Someone had boarded the research vessel and murdered her team.

Selene moaned as her stomach heaved. Vomit threatened. Lulu, Junior—Selene veered away from the dead and from the sharks. She gripped her bang stick with manic strength.

What am I going to do?

Before Selene could decide, a terrible chill grew between her shoulder blades. She looked back.

A tiger shark followed her at a lazy pace.

Every instinct screamed at Selene to "Go, go. Get the hell out of here!" If she did that, though—

I'm dead if I panic.

Selene's head pounded and her breaths became shorter. Feeling as if she was outside her body, watching this, Selene forced herself to turn and face the beast. The approaching

87

predator felt like incarnate death. Yes, she was about to die, but she was going to make the killer pay with its own blood.

Yet, the intense desire to live beat strongly in Selene. She had irrational hope causing her to make one of the most difficult decisions of her existence. Possibly, it would be her last choice in life. Should she let go of the tuning fork device she'd stolen inside the dome? She was going to need two hands to kill the tiger shark, right?

Stubbornly, Selene shook her head. Forrest had told her to take it. The science fiction thing could be important. Bringing it to the world's attention was worth risking her existence. Clutching the tuning fork device harder against her chest, she readied the bang stick, aiming it at the oncoming monster.

The tiger was huge and oh so menacing. Instinctively, Selene began to sing an old song, trying to bolster her courage. The beast came straight for her, grinning in its monstrous desire to kill.

Suddenly, the shark swerved hard and fast, going down into the depths.

Selene laughed in a voice she didn't recognize. She repositioned herself to watch the depths. The tiger was going to make its attack at high speed. Sharks liked to attack seals from the bottom. To it, she must be like a seal. Selene would have one moment to make the counterstrike—

Selene almost missed it. The tiger zoomed upward. Its speed was fantastic like a missile. She readied the bang stick. It all happened with split second timing. She shoved the tube at its snout, hoping for a killing blow.

Then something happened that Selene found hard to understand. The tiger dodged the tube with a slick and well executed move for such a big beast. Like a kung-fu expert, the tiger dodged the thrust that would have killed it.

Selene tensed her body, wondering if she would go into shock or if the teeth puncturing her flesh would sear with agony.

The tiger amazed her again. Instead of completing the kill and slashing into her body with those razor-sharp teeth, the shark closed its jaws on the middle of the bang stick. The beast

88

snapped the stick in half while swimming past her at great speed.

Then the shark was above Selene. She looked in shock at the broken bang stick in her hand. Was the tiger toying with her?

With sudden understanding, Selene realized what she had to do. Releasing the worthless half of the stick, she bent at the waist, aiming down, kicking her fins to reach the other half with the tube and .44 Magnum shell. She had to get it. She could still do this.

Something big and incredibly powerful bumped against her back. The blow sent her summersaulting in the water. It took several seconds for her to stop. Then, Selene found herself face-to-face with the tiger shark. Maybe seven feet separated them. It was uncanny.

The beast watched her with its black eyes. It regarded her as if judging her quality.

For a moment, it seemed to Selene that the tiger was quizzical of her. There seemed to be intelligence in those dead eyes. Yet that was preposterous. Sharks were creatures of habit millions of years in the making. They did not think and judge. They did not—

The tiger moved toward her, closing the gap, opening those wicked jaws.

Selene thrust the tuning fork device at it, pressing with manic strength. She must have pressed one of the controls. Selene heard the hum of the tuning fork.

The tiger shark must have heard it too. It twisted as if shocked and fled from the device, jerking and twisting with incredible speed.

Selene looked around. She didn't see a shark anywhere now. She studied the tuning fork controls. There were several of them. She debated pressing others, yet she wondered. If this thing could make sharks vanish, could it also make them come?

It was a heady thought. Carefully, hesitantly, she clicked the same button as before. The humming quit.

What is this thing? What's it supposed to do?

89

Selene didn't know. She found herself exhausted by the ordeal. Slowly, she began swimming, thinking of all that had happened. Soon, water dripped onto her lips. Full-face masks were harder to clear of water than an ordinary sport mask. What was she going to do about this?

As Selene asked herself that, she tasted saltiness on her lips.

My mask isn't leaking. Those are tears.

Lulu was dead, slain by sharks. Her friend wouldn't ever laugh with her again, drink wine or go to the movies. Lulu was gone, just like that, snapped out of existence.

Realizing the grim truth filled Selene's chest with a terrible ache.

"Don't cry," she whispered. "Avenge her, avenge all of them and find out what happened to the *Calypso*."

A new determination mingled with the pain of losing Lulu, Forrest and the others. Without the budding emotion, Selene might have succumbed to a terrible feeling of loneliness and futility. Instead, she focused on her new purpose, making vows to see this through to the finish.

I have to survive this. I have to figure out the meaning of the dome and the tuning fork.

Selene dwelled on this new idea rather than her grief. Yet, in the back of her mind, she wondered just how she was going to achieve the first and possibly the hardest of these things, surviving in the ocean one hundred miles from shore.

-21-

THE BARRIER
ARDENNES FOREST

Jack stood with indecision before a satellite-disk post. If he crossed the invisible barrier—

Simon had never said exactly what would happen. There was an emitter of some kind. Would a sonic blast incapacitate him, kill him by turning his brain to mush? Did it have a directional finder, a locator to zero in on him?

Jack bit his lower lip as he peered back in the direction of D'erlon Enterprises. He could hear motorcycles and see distant spears of headlights. The security forces were likely already scouring the woods for him.

The dog-beast killed Simon.

Elliot shook his head. He couldn't worry about that now. He had to get out. He had to tell the others about the antimatter. Jack didn't get Simon's excitement, but he trusted the scientist's understanding.

Several times, Jack felt himself ready to lurch forward. He wanted to dash across the invisible barrier but didn't quite have the nerve.

Maybe I can climb over it somehow.

He studied the trees, but none had overhanging branches at the right spot. Besides, he didn't think that was going to work. What would get him across then? Was he just going to stand here waiting to be captured?

"No," he whispered.

Jack backed up, beginning to breathe more heavily. Maybe if he just sprinted across—

Squeezing his eyes shut, growling as he used to do in high school football, Jack charged toward the barrier. This might be the end, but he couldn't think of anything else.

His eyes flew open. He pumped his arms, and his heart rate accelerated into heavy thumps. Then, shivering with dread, Jack Elliot lowered his head and crossed the invisible barrier.

His feet thudded across the leafy ground. He kept waiting for it to begin. His head was hunched as he continued running. He strained to hear the first sound of a sonic blast, or maybe it would start as an almost inaudible hum. None of those things happened. In fact, nothing did. Jack heard the sound of his own harsh breathing, the rustling of his stupid coveralls and the thud of his shoes on the ground.

At that point, he halted, spinning around, with the knife clutched in his right hand. Slowly, he forced his fingers from their death-grip.

Using starlight—a cloud had moved before the moon—he stared at the post with its satellite dish.

Why am I alive? Why am I unhurt?

If Simon's device had made a mistake regarding the post's emitter—

Jack blinked in surprise as the answer slammed home. The posts with their emitters hadn't been meant for them, had they? How many wild animals would the fence have fried by now if that were the case? No. The fence was meant for the beast-dog that had slain Simon.

Simon's device had correctly gauged the emitter.

Jack shook his head. He was out. Now, he had to get the antimatter information to the others so they could relay it to headquarters.

With a lurch, Jack briskly set out for the van.

***

Jack panted as he ran upslope. He'd been running for a while, believing his time was limited. He still couldn't believe it about the emitters.

"That's far enough," a hidden woman said.

"Phelps," Jack said, halting. She might not have recognized him in the coveralls.

"How do you know who I am—Jack, is that you?"

He nodded in the darkness.

"Speak up," Phelps said.

"Yeah, it's me."

"Don't move."

He didn't plan to just yet as he breathed deeply, the sweat beginning to pour off him now that he'd stopped moving.

"Oh," she said, no doubt looking at him more closely with her night vision equipment. Before, she'd have just seen a D'erlon worker. "Where's Simon?" she asked.

"Dead," Jack said in a monotone.

A lean woman in dark garments and a hood appeared from behind a tree. She holstered a suppressed pistol, coming closer, saying, "You look bushed. Why don't you lean on me? I'll help you to the van."

Jack ignored the suggestion as he climbed the last, steepest distance, reaching a level dirt road. On the other side of the road was a camouflaged van sprouting a host of antenna on top.

He crunched over gravel, banging on the side of the van with a fist. "Open up," he said.

A door slid open on rollers. It revealed massed equipment with computer screens and two agents on chairs, a big, bald black man and a half-White Mountain Apache.

Jack climbed into the van, ignoring the other two as he slid onto a chair at a third screen.

"Must be big," he heard the black man tell the half-Indian.

Jack's screen flickered into life with an old-fashioned TV test pattern showing. A blinking green light in the top of the screen told him he was live.

"Daniel Boone was a man," Jack said. "Yes, a big man."

"Just a minute," a scrambled-voiced person told him from the other end. "You're claiming this is a national emergency?"

"That's what I just said," Jack told her, having used a coded phrase for the highest-level disaster possible.

"Jack?" a scrambled-voiced person asked.

There was no difference to the voice, but Jack knew he had Mrs. King, the Secretary of Detachment 17 on the line.

"This is Jack."

"Talk to me," the other said.

Jack took a breath before he spoke in a fast monotone. "Simon Green is dead. Before he died, Green found the targeted people making antimatter. They weren't just producing particles or hundredths of grams. They're making anti-atoms and already have 900 grams. They also have a way of storing the antimatter long-term in much smaller magnetic containers than Green believed should be possible."

"Wait? Simon is dead?"

"Yes. Now listen. The targeted people have produced at least 900 grams of antimatter."

"That's impossible."

"No. It isn't. We saw it."

There was silence from the other end. Then, "This is incredible. I want to see the raw data. We're going to risk sending it through immediately."

"I can't do that," Jack said. "I lost the device that did the analyzing and recording."

There was a longer moment of silence. Finally, the scrambled voice said, "This is no good. I have to verify your analysis."

"No doubt," Jack said. "There's one other thing. The targeted facility is on high alert. Something gave us away."

"Did you notice anything else unusual?"

That seemed like a strange question to ask now. "Like what?" Jack said.

"Anything at all."

"Yeah, there's something else. They had a giant dog guarding the outer perimeter of the facility. It was like a bear, and it struck me as smart, if that makes any sense." Jack wondered if the big man counted. He supposed the man might. "And there was a giant security officer inside the complex. He seemed..."

"He seemed what?" the scrambled voice asked.

Jack stared at the old TV test pattern. Did the voice sound overeager?

94

"The security man was huge and unnaturally strong," Jack said.

"Is that all?"

"No. He had a presence like I've never felt before. It radiated off him. It was strange now that I think about it."

The Secretary didn't say anything for a time. Finally, she asked, "You're sure about the antimatter and its amount?"

"No. I'm not sure but Simon was. He kept raving how nothing on Earth was like this. He said they had advanced technology like no one should have."

"Bingo," the scrambled voice said softly. "Get out of the area. Head for Rome and stay on alert. That means sleep in shifts."

"Got it," Jack said. "You want to tell me what is going on?"

"Do as ordered, and stay alert. This is the break—never mind. Go now. I don't want them finding you." A moment later, the connection cut off.

Jack stared at the TV test pattern. With a start, he swiveled around. "We're packing up, people," he said. "So let's go. The Secretary wants us in Rome."

"Why there?"

"I have no idea, but she wants us to stay on alert. I have a suspicion we're not finished with the D'erlon people." As Jack stood, he hoped he was right. They'd killed his partner.

Jack's eyes narrowed. He wanted to mourn Simon but he wasn't going to do it now. That wasn't Jack's way. He had a job to do first. When everything was over...he could mourn Simon then.

Elliot knew that was lie. He hadn't mourned his parents properly, and he'd never done that for any of the friends he'd lost. He bottled everything inside. That wasn't good, he knew. But Jack Elliot was who he was.

He found himself clenching a fist so tightly his hand shook. One of these days—

Jack opened the fist, shaking his hand, and exhaled sharply. It was time to get on with it.

-22-

100 MILES OFF THE COAST OF SUMATRA

Selene was on the surface. She'd been studying the endless horizons for some time. Now, far in the distance, she believed that she'd discovered the *Calypso*. It appeared as a dot on the southern horizon.

She had been diving for years, spending more time in and on the water than inside a classroom or research center. Others might have questioned her ability to know that dot was her vessel, but she knew.

While bobbing in the salt water, it became clear to her that the ship was leaving at high speed. Someone had slipped aboard, murdered her team and then taken over the ship. Didn't they fear the U.S. Navy commander using a satellite to see what they were doing? How hard was it to track a ship in the ocean? Maybe the enemy had simply set the *Calypso* on a course and left it to its own devices.

One thing was clear. She was all alone out here. Wait a minute. Selene frowned, spying movement closer to home. It looked like a large speedboat. The machine went fast, slapping across the water.

Selene kicked harder, trying to lift herself higher as she readied to wave. At the last second, she let herself sink without doing so.

Selene had a read a book once about the gift of fear. One of the key premises was that a person often knew a thing in her subconscious before her conscious mind reasoned it out. The mind took in hundreds possibly thousands of cues a day, too many to think about every hour. But the subconscious mind, now that was a tricky tool doing wacky and imaginative things.

The *Calypso* was leaving. Sharks had devoured Lulu and the others while some bum in a speedboat roared around. He had to have come from another ship. Yet, that wasn't all. A deep underwater dome with a Chinese man in it had killed Forrest Dean with a super-science invisible ray gun. Earlier, a fake Indonesian naval lieutenant had tried to scare them away.

A sinking feeling filled Selene. This was much bigger than she realized. She would not hail the speedboat. It had to belong to whomever the secret American intelligence agency was fighting.

At that moment, Selene knew she was going to die. It was the logical outcome of the situation. The speedboat indicated the secret group wasn't done with her yet. She had to hide, starting out here in the middle of the sea.

With practiced skill, she shrugged off the scuba equipment and pulled off the full-face mask. Letting go, she let both items sink into the depths. They weren't going to help her now, as she was almost out of air.

Fortunately, she had always been paranoid when it came to diving, at least in terms of surviving accidents. She had a normal sport mask and snorkel in a bag attached to her belt.

Selene dug them out. Soon, she floated face down in the sea, sucking air through the tube. She unbuckled her weight belt, letting it sink too, so that she would be more buoyant.

The best long-distance swimmers could travel sixty miles at a stretch, and that was without a wetsuit, mask, snorkel and fins. The better ones could do this in approximately thirty hours. Such swimmers lost ten pounds or more, trained for many months beforehand and had a trailing boat to lower a shark tank if needed. Well, she had several advantages...

Selene smiled tightly. Once again, her subconscious had already come to the obvious conclusion. She was going to have to swim one hundred miles or more to reach Sumatra. Simeulue Island was closer, but it would be easier for the hidden ones to find her there and harder for her to escape off

Simeulue unnoticed. Sumatra gave her more options, meaning she might leave Indonesia alive.

Death frightened Selene. Was there a God or not? Part of her wished there was. If not, she was nothing after this life. She didn't want to be nothing. She wanted to exist for as long as possible.

Studying the sun, she figured out which direction to go. Then, she began to kick her fins, starting the journey.

Before long, a great sense of futility welled up from her gut, freezing her for a moment. She couldn't swim one hundred miles without any drinking water. That was crazy. That was—

Think of something else!

She gripped the tuning fork device and thought about the underwater dome.

"Who could build that without anyone else knowing about it?"

Asking the question aloud let water slip into her mouth. She coughed, choking on the saltiness. Finally, she raised her head above water, spitting out the mouthpiece. She coughed more, breathing deeply, bobbing in the sea. Looking around—

The endless horizons proved too much for her. Selene chewed the rubber back into her mouth and put her head underwater. That felt...better, not so alone and desolate.

She had to survive. Then, she had to return to the underwater site with others.

This was an endurance run now. Thus, Selene forced thoughts of sharks, dead friends, runaway vessels, underwater domes and secret ray guns, everything but swimming, from her mind. Until she walked on dry land again, nothing else mattered.

-23-

WASHINGTON DC

Mrs. King paced inside her office as indecision boiled inside her. This was a hard call, maybe the most difficult one of her life.

Despite her age, she walked three miles a day and trained with weights. Her legs weren't as good as the day she'd won Miss Rhode Island, but they didn't embarrass her when she wore nylons. The fabric helped to hide the imperfections of age.

Mrs. King sighed. She didn't know what to do. Pausing by the curtains, she peered outside as bright sunlight glinted off the Potomac River. It was morning in DC but still night in France. The heaviest traffic had dwindled as office workers and others slaved at their appointed tasks for the day.

She released the curtain, striding to her desk. Pressing an intercom button, she said, "Smith."

A moment later, the door opened. The Deputy Secretary stepped inside, closing the door behind him.

The man was medium-sized with a doughy face, pudgy hands and the faintest of mustaches. Fifteen-year-old boys could grow them thicker. It didn't help that Smith wore wireless spectacles. She had spoken to him in the past about his rumpled, slept-in looking clothes. Today, he wore an expensive black suit and tie, although the sleeves were a little too short. Still, it was a good beginning.

"Jack Elliot claims D'erlon Enterprises has manufactured 900 grams of antimatter at the Ardennes complex," Mrs. King said. "D'erlon didn't just produce antimatter particles either but anti-atoms."

"That's incredible," Smith said. Many might have shown surprise at this news, but not the Deputy Secretary. He appeared as calm as ever. "Does Agent Green confirm this?"

"I'm afraid Simon Green is dead."

Behind the lenses of his glasses, Smith blinked several times, the full extent of his emotions. "I'm sorry to hear this. Simon...was a good man and an excellent scientist. We'll miss him."

Mrs. King nodded.

"Yes, this is a tragedy, an outrage, one could say. There have been too many casualties lately."

"Agreed," Mrs. King said.

"But we must deal with the issue at hand. 900 grams of antimatter..." Smith said, shaking his head. "How does Elliot know this to be true? He's not noted for his scientific acumen."

"I understand Agent Green informed Elliot before he died."

Smith stared into space before saying, "This is a difficult one. Making vast amounts of antimatter isn't against the law, but it's so unbelievable that it must mean something portentous."

"It means France has technology far beyond that of the United States. It means they will eclipse us in short order."

"Yes, of course," Smith said. "Yet...

"This is such an outrageous allegation that I'm having trouble believing Elliot," Smith said.

"Don't be. This fits."

Deputy Secretary Smith studied Mrs. King. "Ah," he said, shortly, "You think this has something to do with your *master puppeteer* hypothesis."

Mrs. King shifted uncomfortably. It felt to her as if the hidden strings were pulling tighter. Yet, the idea of someone so powerful... Could she be wrong about this? She could feel the manipulations out there. She was still waiting to hear from Forrest Dean.

She concentrated on Smith, hoping his intellect could help her make the right choice regarding the Ardennes plant.

"I had a suspicion about D'erlon Enterprises," she said. "It's why I sent Jack and Simon to investigate. I never expected anything like this, though. It confirms my feelings about…about the puppeteer."

"Sometimes feelings are all we can go on," Smith said.

He was being polite; she knew that. "Feelings are also very subjective," she said, "which is a danger in our line of work. But let's forget about that for a moment. Why does anyone need so much antimatter?"

"Given the D'erlon people can manufacture such an incredible amount," Smith said.

"Let us suppose Elliot is right."

Smith nodded before looking up at the ceiling. Mrs. King felt as if she could see the wheels turning inside his head.

Smith regarded her. "Perhaps the D'erlon people are making a doomsday bomb."

Mrs. King grew pale at the idea. That seemed like a logical conclusion.

"That would be of grave concern to the French political leaders," Smith said. "Given the leadership knows nothing about the antimatter, I would think the French military could be convinced to storm the Ardennes complex."

Mrs. King stared hard at Smith. What was he thinking?

"Of course," Smith said. "In suggesting this to others, we must be certain of our facts."

"Do you doubt Simon Green?" Mrs. King asked.

"He was a first rate case officer and a better scientist. DARPA always spoke well of him. I would not doubt him, although this is an unbelievable claim. We should remember that Jack Elliot doesn't have Green's scientific knowledge. I realize Detachment 17 employs some of the most ruthless people in the United States chosen precisely because they get things done. Without such agents as Jack Elliot—"

"Please, Mr. Smith, what is your point?"

"I believe we should convince the President to call the French, which seems to be your plan," Smith said. "You just want my confirmation to make such a bold decision."

She hated it when he was right.

"Yet attempting to convince the President without the raw data and going off the word of someone without direct scientific knowledge—that will make this a hard sell, Mrs. Secretary. In fact, being wrong here could mean the end of D17. Barring that, it could bring about your dismissal, likely mine as well as the political entities clean house to cover themselves."

Mrs. King sighed. "Yes, those are all distinct possibilities. But don't we have a responsibility to do the right thing?"

"If D'erlon Enterprises is truly making antimatter and using improved magnetic containment devices to hold the grams... The extent of their advanced technology is mind numbing. If you are correct about a master puppeteer—then we cannot afford any delay."

Mrs. King looked stricken. "As always, Mr. Smith, you are succinct. I would now like you to answer me this. How do I explain this to the President of the United States without direct evidence?"

"In my opinion, it's madness to try," Smith said. "Instead, we should send another team to inspect the D'erlon premises."

"We don't dare if we're dealing with the master puppeteer, and I think the evidence of 900 grams of antimatter clinches it."

"If the data is correct, it is startling indeed."

"This has been my nightmare for some time," Mrs. King said. "We've come up against something huge and menacing, but I don't have the foggiest notion as to what it is. This is our first real break regarding them. I mean to exploit this even at great personal risk."

"Maybe there is another way to do this," Smith said.

"I'm open to suggestions."

"Let me gather everything I can on D'erlon Enterprises, particularly this complex in the Ardennes."

"How long would it take?"

"Twenty-five minutes," Smith said.

"No! You have ten to gather a data packet. Use everyone. This is an emergency."

Smith whirled around, heading for the door.

***

Twelve minutes later Smith was back. Mrs. King watched him march to her desk, slapping down a thin folder.

"There it is," he said. "It's most remarkable. I'm much more inclined to think Elliot's data is factual."

Mrs. King opened the folder with her gloved fingers. Speed-reading, she absorbed three pages of information. Tapping the third sheet, she said, "This is a giveaway here."

Smith nodded, saying, "D'erlon Enterprises has been trying to hide their massive energy use."

"One could even call the usage staggering."

"I'd agree to that," Smith said.

Mrs. King became thoughtful. "It doesn't prove anything, though, does it?"

"Not directly," Smith said, "but it is compelling."

"These past few minutes I've been thinking about what I'm supposed to say to the President. I doubt I could move him with one dead agent's belief."

"That wouldn't be the only way to move the French," Smith said. "If you continue reading the third page, you'll find that D'erlon Enterprises has connections with Iran."

"Go on," Mrs. King said.

"What sort of clandestine endeavors are D'erlon Enterprises and Iran involved in?" Smith asked. "Why this secrecy in hiding their energy usage? Perhaps there wouldn't even be a need to mention the antimatter."

"So...?

"So instead of speaking to the National Intelligence Director to give you an appointment with the President," Smith said, "you could have a private chat with the head of French Intelligence. Given some of these salient facts concerning D'erlon Enterprises, the French might want to make a snap inspection of the Ardennes plant."

"Ah. You sly devil," Mrs. King said. "The Iranian connection means a possible nuclear link. That would interest the French and motivate them to go to the plant, possibly tonight. I like it."

She pressed a switch on her desk. A section on it opened and a computer screen rose into view.

Smith turned to go.

"No," Mrs. King said. "I'd like you to stay. I may need your expertise."

Deputy Secretary Smith sat down before the desk.

Mrs. King glanced at the folder again, took a deep breath and began to open a channel.

-24-

UNDERWATER
OFF THE COAST OF SUMATRA

Selene heard a *burbling* speedboat before she saw it. Raising her head, she spied the sleek machine. It didn't fly across the waters as she'd seen before with the front lifted. Instead, it trawled along.

She watched it for a time. Finally, barely, she could make out a standing man with binoculars. He appeared to be scanning the ocean.

A cold knot tightened in her stomach. *He must be looking for me. They must have found Forrest's body and the dead Chinese man in the dome. Now they're going to—*

With a start, Selene realized the tip of her snorkel was orange-colored. She ripped the rubber tube from her mouth and mask from her face, holding them underwater.

She watched him, growing more terrified by the minute. A premonition touched her. Could her staring create a psychic energy he could sense? Surely, that was ridiculous. Nevertheless, Selene no longer started directly at the speedboat, but watched with her peripheral vision.

Time passed slowly. The man seemed thorough. With the engine barely above idling, the boat crept through the sea. Finally, he dwindled, becoming no more than a speck.

At that point, Selene slid the mask onto her face and put the rubber mouthpiece against her teeth. She used her legs, propelling the extra-large fins in a languid manner.

There was no sense hurrying this. The fins were designed for long swims underwater. They worked just as well near the surface. This was a long-distance contest, not a sprint.

The wetsuit made her buoyant and the snorkel allowed her to keep her head down, saving energy. She only looked up to check the sun. Its journey across the sky helped her navigate toward the western coast of Sumatra.

I can do this. I don't have any choice if I want to live.

Her resolve firmed. Nothing was going to stop her.

-25-

D'ERLON ENTERPRISES
ARDENNES FOREST

Marcus set the D17 device on a table. Beside it were the dead agent's other items, the ones found in the two bags. An assortment of black garments, night vision equipment, suppressed weapons, knives, boots and various paraphernalia littered the large table. He had already inspected the dead case officer.

A woman wearing a D'erlon Security cap poked her head through the door. "The superior is ready," she said.

Marcus looked at the woman. She quailed, making no pretense of being able to withstand his gaze. Without a word, he stalked from the room, passing the trembling woman.

A few minutes later, Marcus sat down before a blank computer screen. He had to do this to Mother's specifications.

"Well," the robotic voice asked from the seemingly blank screen. "Is the report correct?"

Marcus expanded his broad chest before answering. "I have checked carefully. The device recorded the antimatter and the magnetic fields."

"Did the agents communicate with someone outside the site?"

"I don't have concrete evidence but I think we must conclude that they did."

"You failed me, Marcus."

The words bit into his heart. He hated them, and he refused to accept them. "I did not fail. I gave the warning because my excellent memory recalled the D17 agent. Because of me, we know why the French military is racing here for a snap inspection. Otherwise, we would be in the dark as to why this is happening."

"That's only partly true. I have received word of the event from a…mole in the French government. Still, perhaps you have a point."

He had more than a point. Marcus made a fist and banged it on the desk, making the screen jump. "It would be easy to stop the convoy. We must have more than enough antimatter now—"

"Marcus," the robotic voice said.

He stopped talking.

"You must learn patience," the robotic voice said. "I have. It is one of my greatest powers.

"I thought we were close."

"We are, my darling boy, closer than you realize. I want those 900 grams. You are to send the trucks immediately. Afterward, you will initiate a slowdown procedure. Because The Day is almost upon us, I want all the technicians down there. No one will spoil the event I've waited—listen to me. I'm more excited than you can realize. Do you understand about the technicians?"

"That seems so wasteful."

"Don't question me, my hero. I will not leave the inquisitive a trail to follow. By the way, who does the dead man belong to?"

"He tried to pass himself off as a Russian from IZENOV."

"And?"

"The dead man is an American. I've run an analysis. He belonged to Detachment 17."

"Again D17 creates trouble for me," the robotic voice said, "twice in one day."

"Will you finally let me destroy them?"

"Marcus, Marcus, Marcus, you have such a murderous and wasteful rage. That is not how I maneuver. It isn't needed."

"You said this is the second time—"

"Marcus," the robotic voice said, sharply. "You have talents. I am quite aware of them. However, we will always do this my way. Do you understand me?"

He wanted to spit or even to refuse to answer like a petulant child. But that would be a waste because Mother would find a way to discipline him for his insolence. No. He must continue to obey her.

"I understand," he rumbled.

"Then go, do as I have instructed."

"What should I do about the hound?" he asked, realizing he was hesitating to commit the foul deed.

"Explain your question."

"Your experimental creature sought to trick me," Marcus said. "The hound let the D17 agents into the complex."

"It is my understanding the hound destroyed one of them and brought the device to you."

Marcus would have liked to know which of his security people had already reported to Mother. "The beast did that," he admitted.

"Listen to me, my child. Of course, the hound attempts trickery. It is part of the process. You will of course take the hound with you when you leave. I have plans for it."

For just a moment then, Marcus wondered if Mother treated him in the same way she did the experimental hound. Did she realize he—Marcus—had ulterior plans? The idea frightened him, something he hated beyond death.

"You must hurry, my boy. The convoy rushes to the site, hoping to catch us by surprise. I want everything in order by the time they arrive."

"It will be so," Marcus said. "The first trucks have already departed with the antimatter."

"Yes, you are a good boy. I trust you, Marcus. Do not let me down."

The connection cut, leaving him to wonder if she toyed with him. More than ever, he yearned to know her final objective. Why was Mother so secretive? How could he win her trust the way Frederick and a few of the others appeared to have achieved?

109

He stood. First, he had a hard task to perform. Then, he had to leave before the French military convoy arrived.

* * *

Marcus scanned the throng of scientists and technicians down there in the basement chamber. He used the same door Jack and Simon had used earlier.

The people worked although not as efficiently as usual. A woman looked up at Marcus. She stared for a moment before looking down. She must have whispered because soon others looked up at him. Within seconds, everyone in the antimatter production chamber peered up at him.

Marcus sighed, closing the heavy steel door. He walked to a portable screen. No one else was with him for this grim task. The scientists and technicians did not go back to work down there. Instead, they turned to each other, no doubt asking why they had stayed for an extra shift. That hadn't ever happened before.

This was distasteful. Marcus didn't want to do it. He didn't sweat, though, nor did his heart hammer.

I will make a name for myself. The world will know that Marcus has walked the Earth.

The central conviction of his existence brought calm, smoothing the icy trickle in his gut. He could perform the hard tasks. Mother trusted him, he believed, because he could do the difficult chores without complaining or becoming a drunk who drowned out a soft conscience.

The trick was to do this without taking delight in it. That way laid sadism and other harmful psychoses. He must remain the soldier, a warrior with valor and superior élan. A butcher lacked heart. That would never be his problem. He had to admit, though, that to date he'd hadn't found a worthy opponent. That troubled him. How was a warrior supposed to prove himself without worthy foes?

Marcus raised a ham-like hand, pointing a blunt-tipped index finger. Time was wasting. The military vehicles and French Secret Service agents would be here soon.

"The hell with this," he muttered. Marcus pressed a red button.

110

Before him, on the viewing screen, grams of antimatter joined an equal amount of matter. It was like a nuclear explosion, which would have destroyed the entire complex with Marcus included if he hadn't used a special dampener, unknown to anyone else on Earth.

Down there in the basement behind magnetic containment fields was a terrific and annihilating explosion. The floor under Marcus shook, as did the walls. Everyone and everything on the screen vaporized except for the magnetic force field that contained the dampened antimatter blast. All the scientists, the technicians, their clothes, bones, shoes, hair and all the equipment had ceased to exist.

Now, all Marcus had to do was take down the magnetic generators. He still had enough time to hide those. The French Intelligence people weren't going to find anything in the complex.

-26-

UNDERWATER
OFF THE COAST OF SUMATRA

In time, the sun sank into the western horizon. The stars
began to appear and then the moon. The dark waters frightened
Selene. For the first hour, she peered intently into the inky
depths. She expected a shark to appear any second. They loved
to hunt at night.

After a tense hour of watching, she finally told herself, "I
can't keep going like this." If a shark was going to bite her, it
was all over anyway.

The next hour proved much easier, the third even more so.
Then, she saw a gliding shape, a huge monster.

Every muscle tightened in her. Selene gasped for air as her
heart began hammering. The creature glided toward her, no
doubt to inspect the prey.

Yes, she had the tuning fork thing. But what if she pressed
the wrong button? What if those hunting for her could tune in
on its frequency it if she turned it back on? Thus, she'd first try
this the old-fashioned way.

Selene knew the hunters of the sea usually made several
passes of inspection before they actually used those teeth. All
bets were off with blood in the water—the reason for the
frenzy earlier.

Get a grip, Selene.

She forced herself to breathe normally as she kept watch. The shark, an eight-foot creature, swam close the first pass and even closer the second. At the third, Selene pivoted in the water and kicked with her heel, connecting with the sandpaper skin.

The shark flashed its tail, heading down.

The next few minutes Selene swam as slowly as she could manage, watching everywhere. The minutes continued to tick by with agonizing slowness. Finally, she realized the shark was gone. She'd frightened it away.

Selene journeyed throughout the night. It rained once. She bobbed in the sea with her mouth open, catching drops. She also held her mask up, sipping when it collected enough water. Finally, the rain stopped and she continued swimming.

In the middle of the next morning, she spied a smudge of land on the horizon. She laughed with exhaustion. She had traveled one hundred miles in record time.

I'm going to make it. I've survived this part of the ordeal, at least.

She had done much soul-searching during the lonely hours. Someone had built the underwater dome and gone to murderous lengths to hide the fact. That meant several things. These people must have money, as in billions at least. They also had incredible reach and deadly intent. Would they stop coming after her if they knew she was alive?

Selene didn't think so. What did that mean to her? She would need to take precautions obviously. Until she knew more, she was going to keep a low profile. Her friends had become shark food. She could be next on the list.

This could be the greatest mystery on Earth.

Selene thought about that as she neared shore. She had begun life as a loner, an orphan. She could go that route again if she had to. She had a hefty sum of money saved. Before she raised her head, as it were, telling authorities what she knew, she wanted to have something concrete to show them besides just the tuning fork thing.

This must have something to do with the hum. Maybe that's why she hadn't heard from Claire. What had happened at Angkor Wat?

113

Should I go there and find out?

Maybe Claire had found something terrifying at Angkor Wat just as she had here. If that were true, what would Claire do next? She wouldn't just come running home. Claire had an insatiable curiosity. She would want more data. Thus, Claire would go to the next site on the list.

Selene knew her friend. They had stayed up many long nights discussing extremely low frequencies combined with magnetic waves and geological oddities. One of the more interesting and perplexing hums had begun at the Siwa Oasis in Egypt. Study had shown it was a recent phenomenon. Claire had almost gone there instead of Angkor Wat.

Claire had talked about the Old Man, a conspiracy theorist of the first order. She'd been in contact with him for some time. The Old Man had weird ideas, but he heard the Siwa Hum all the time. Claire had planned to investigate the oasis after Angkor Wat.

As she swam toward shore, Selene realized she'd already been thinking about Philip Khios subconsciously. He'd worked with her in the past. She might have dated him if she hadn't already been involved with Danny. Philip was in Athens, Greece, his hometown. She was sure he would be willing to help her. Philip had made several trips to Egypt.

Selene was beginning to feel better. If anyone knew what to do with the stolen tuning fork device and underwater dome, it would be Claire. Before Selene went public with her knowledge, she would first go to Egypt. Maybe Claire was on the run from these secret people too.

With renewed confidence, Selene began working on what she would say to Philip Khios.

-27-

SOMEWHERE ON EARTH

"D17 has become too intrusive," Mother said.

"We have—"

Mother glowered at the speaker. The other hastily fell silent.

"The Day approaches," Mother whispered. "After all this time... There are loose ends. You know I do not approve of loose ends."

"I know."

"This Dr. Selene Khan entered Station Thirteen and stole a hummer. The D17 agent, Jack Elliot, saw too much in the Ardennes. No, no, I do not approve. The worst is that spider in Washington. Secretary King has become too meddlesome. It is time to remove her from the board."

"Then..."

"Send Mouse to Washington. It is time the head of D17 had an accident. At this late date, we will keep everything simple. Afterward...well, it won't matter what any of them knows then."

PART TWO:
RUNNING WITH THE HORSEMEN

-28-

"You're never going to believe this, sir."

"With that smirk on your face, I'm not sure I want to hear it."

"It's about Dr. Selene Khan."

"You've found her? Where is she hiding, in the middle of a Sumatra jungle?"

"She's in Africa, sir."

"Impossible!"

"She's been clever, but she slipped up as we knew she would."

"No! Don't be arrogant. She's proven more elusive than anyone thought possible. In Africa, you say? The woman is remarkable. She's slipped through our fingers several times already. It is unwise to underestimate her."

"This time, she's ours, sir."

"Go ahead. Give me the report. The last two days searching the net, every Southeast Asian airport manifest—"

"She's given us a chase, sir, that's true. Now, she's in the Siwa Oasis."

"The Hell you say?"

"I thought you'd be ecstatic to hear it, sir."

117

There were several moments of silence. "Yes, I suppose this should work to our advantage."

"She's delivered herself into our hands, sir."

"Can that be blind luck or is something more nefarious going on?"

"Sir?"

"I'll have to call Mother. We could have a situation on our hands."

* * *

Selene walked briskly down a dusty street. She was nervous, heading to a meeting with the Old Man. He had agreed to see her, although he'd sounded nutty on the phone. He'd given her absurd procedures to follow—"safety steps," he'd called them.

The Old Man had refused to say anything about Claire except that she had missed their scheduled appointment. Selene had heard some strange news about birds at Angkor Wat, but she hadn't been able to contact either Claire or Andy.

Had they gone to ground?

Luckily, Selene had used throwaway cell phones each call, trashing them afterward. That had been Philip's idea. He had done a stint in the Greek Army, working in Intelligence as a lowly private and later a corporal. Still, he knew a few tricks.

As Selene hurried down the street, she glanced over her shoulder. An older Egyptian in a dirty robe and headdress pedaled an ancient bicycle. It had a plastic carton fixed to the back. In it, he carried several squashed chickens. They clucked in complaint as the squeaking contraption passed Selene on the street.

Selene took a deep breath and held it for a count of ten. It felt strange to realize that just a little over thirty-six hours ago, she had been swimming in the middle of the Indian Ocean. Slowly, she let out the air.

She wore a tan business suit, and because she was in a Muslim country, she wore a scarf over her head. Dark sunglasses shielded her eyes from the sun while a snub-nosed .38—from Philip—weighed down her right suit pocket. She might have felt strange carrying a gun, but Danny had taught

118

her to shoot one of her first years in college. "The places we'll be traveling, a gun will be handy." She'd learned enough throughout the years to know she'd have to be very close to hit anything more than fifty percent of the time.

Checking her recently purchased cell phone, Selene realized she was going to be late for the first stage of the appointment. The Old Man had insisted on precision or he would cancel.

Where did Claire find these people?

Selene lengthened her stride, passing sleepy, rundown shops and the strong smell of coffee.

This was the Siwa Oasis, one of the most isolated settlements in Egypt. It was near the Libyan border, bracketed in the west by the Egyptian Sand Desert and in the east by the Qattara Depression. The oasis was just fifty miles long and twenty wide. It boasted a salt lake, tens of thousands of trees— palms and olives, mainly—and lay in a depression nineteen meters below sea level. Twenty-three thousand Berbers—non-Arabs—lived at Siwa. The oasis's great claim to fame was the ancient oracle of Ammon, which Alexander the Great had once trekked to consult after his conquest of the country.

Across the narrow street, a man sat outside a coffee shop reading a newspaper with only his fingers visible. Cigar smoke trickled into view. The hidden man was Philip Khios. Selene felt a hundred times better knowing he was there.

She hadn't told him everything that had happened in the Indian Ocean. She'd even kept the tuning fork hidden from him. Selene first wanted to compare notes with Claire. Philip had a greedy side. Selene wanted him here, but she wasn't sure how much she could trust him with everything.

Taking out her cellphone, she pressed *send*.

The left side of Philip's spread-out newspaper folded inward. She could see the cigar clamped between his teeth. He was ready.

Selene turned to her right, pushing through a door into an antique shop. A bell tinkled above her head. The smell of Turkish coffee and wet air struck her. The shop must have a swamp cooler instead of an air conditioner.

Selene moved past rows of clay figurines, glass trinkets and old wooden plaques with Arabic sayings on them.

An older man in his late forties or well-preserved fifties stood behind a wooden counter, watching her. He had creased skin and a large hooked nose. His hair was shiny black instead of its likely natural gray. Most unusual, he had a gaudy ring on each of his fingers.

"It is apparent to me that you do not speak Arabic," the older man said with a heavy accent. He wore a red vest over what seemed like 1930's-era clothing.

Selene shook her head. She only knew a few words of Arabic.

He studied her as he rested his ringed hands against the countertop. Finally, the fingers of his left hand began to tap the wood impatiently.

"Oh." Selene dug out a roll of Egyptian pounds. She peeled off several high denominational notes and set them beside the man's tapping fingers.

He spread out the bills, shaking his head.

"I thought the Old Man said—"

The clerk raised an admonitory finger, waggling it back and forth. "Please permit me to point out that you have a gunman within call. That breaks the spirit of the agreement we—"

How could he have known about Phillip? Selene thought fast. "I need protection," she protested. "Surely, you can understand that."

The clerk's gaze flickered over her form. "Please," he said. "It is obvious you are able to protect yourself. You don't need a lazy Greek to help you do that. In point of fact—"

"I wasn't sure about you. I thought this shop might be a front for kidnappers." That sounded legitimate, didn't it?

"Go," the man said, sweeping the bills off the counter so they fluttered toward the floor.

Selene watched the money as a sinking feeling grew. She concentrated on the clerk, willing him to understand. "Don't you see why I might bring the—?"

He put a spread-fingered hand against his chest. "*You* must understand. The one I represent will not permit himself to fall into an obvious trap."

"Please—"

"You must leave. You offend the spirit of Siwa with your presence."

Selene retrieved the bills from the floor, using the time to ponder her next step. Standing, she doubled the rejected money with fresh notes, putting the combination onto the counter.

"I made a mistake," she said. "Maybe this will cover it."

The man wet his lower lip with the tip of his tongue. He studied the money, finally looking up and shaking his head.

Was he really worried about Philip?

"I'm here about the hum," Selene said.

"Go!" he said, fluttering the fingers of his right hand.

Selene breathed deeply and let out the air slowly. She observed the storekeeper more carefully. In this new light, she could see that he was tense. The black ceiling glass must hide a camera, maybe several of them.

A prickle in her neck told Selene that someone moved behind her. She didn't turn around but used the reflection in a glass display case farther away.

A man was in the store with them, someone who hadn't rung the bell. The man studied her intently, and he had a gun holstered on his hip.

This is a setup.

She spun around, and the new man looked up in surprise. He wore a policeman's hat with a badge on a uniform.

I'm not falling for that.

Selene shouted, stepping at the supposed policeman. Danny had taught her self-defense. She twisted her torso and lashed out with her right palm, striking him against the chin. There was a crack. His head shifted sharply to the right.

To Selene's surprise, the man crumpled, sprawling onto the floor, unmoving.

The clerk gasped, speaking rapidly in Arabic.

Selene turned back to him.

The clerk was trembling. When he realized she stared at him, he flinched, stepping back from the counter.

Selene scooped up her money. "So this was a trick all along."

Shock widened his eyes. "Do you know who that is? That is Captain Nasser, the chief of police. Why did you attack him?"

"I don't believe you."

The clerk stared at her as if she was mad.

Selene felt a moment of doubt until she remembered the bell. "Look. How did he get inside the shop without ringing the bell?"

"That is easily answered. The captain despises the tinkling sound. He says it reminds him of his cow of a wife. He always opens the door slowly to make sure the bell does not ring. Now, you have assaulted a police officer, the chief of police. You are in terrible danger."

Selene looked at the prone man. Was he really the Siwa captain of police? If that was true—

She pushed away from the counter, stepping over the policeman.

"Where are you going?" the clerk shouted. "You must stay for your arrest."

"I don't think so."

"No," the clerk said, racing behind the counter, lifting a board. "I will not let you leave."

Selene made a swift calculation. She hated to do this, but she pulled out the .38, aiming it at the clerk's stomach.

The man stopped as his mouth opened and closed.

"We're going into the back," she told him. "You're going to erase the video of me hitting the police captain."

"Never," he said.

"Fine!" she said. "Then I'm going to shoot you right here." Selene couldn't believe she was saying this. Making the one hundred mile swim, seeing all those dead bodies in the ocean must have done something to her.

The clerk searched her eyes, nodding fast. "Yes. I will show you the computer. Then you must—"

"Get moving," Selene said, waving the .38 toward the back.

"What are you planning?"

"You're going to find out."

"If you try to rob me—"

Selene laughed, the sound coming out wildly even to her ears.

It made the clerk's mouth snap shut.

"Move," Selene told him.

He nodded, turning around. Together, they moved behind the counter into the back area. There, the clerk showed her the heart of the security system. Then, he showed how to erase video. Finally, he did just that, getting rid of the past few minutes.

"Please," he said, afterward. "Leave my shop and never return."

Selene had a pained smile. "We're both leaving."

"What? No. I cannot leave my business. Thieves—"

"You're taking me to see the Old Man."

The clerk appeared as if he wanted to plead. Instead, after a second, he became calm, studying her.

It made Selene suspicious again. Had the clerk been faking his fear?

"Give me the money," he said, holding out his left hand.

Selene poked his side with the .38. "You'll get your money once I'm face-to-face with the one I came to Egypt to see."

"I cannot leave my store at this time of day."

"You're leaving it. First, we're going to bind and gag the police captain."

The clerk blinked several times. "No. That would be foolish. Yes. I will go with you, but we must leave at once and out the back door."

"Why's that?" Selene asked.

"I will not take you to… *him* if your Greek is going to follow us. Heading out the back will foil his surveillance."

Selene weighed her options. It was a dangerous request. Yet something in her gut said she should go. She decided to trust her instincts.

"Agreed," she said.

The clerk headed for the exit, opening it, making a bell tinkle up top.

Selene glanced at the bell and promptly ignored it as she followed the clerk into a dusty alleyway. The bell rang one more time as the door closed.

There was a motor scooter on a kickstand waiting. The clerk went to the scooter, inserting a key and pressing the ignition switch. The man straddled the bike, revving the throttle, making the small machine sound like an out-of-control lawnmower.

As he did all that, Selene pressed *send* again. It was Philip's signal to head back to the hotel. Afterward, she climbed on back of the scooter, putting an arm around the clerk's waist, swaying a little as he gunned the scooter, heading out of the alley onto a street.

***

At the second chime of the bell, the police captain opened his eyes and sat up. He did not appear woozy, nor were his eyes particularly red, although his neck was sore where the woman had popped it.

Selene hadn't really knocked him out, although she had hit with uncommon strength. Instead of fighting with her— something forbidden by his instructions—the captain had feigned unconsciousness, hoping to hear something he could tell the other. Silently, he now congratulated himself on his cunning.

Taking a walkie-talkie from his belt, the captain of police spoke softly. "She left with Souk the antique shop clerk." He listened to a question. "I believe they're headed to see someone called the *Old Man*." The silence on the other end frightened the captain. Finally, thankfully, the speaker asked another question. "Yes, I'm certain," the captain said, glad that he could be.

There was further silence. Then, the captain listened once more. Relief filled him at his new instructions.

"I will do as you say."

The captain hooked the walkie-talkie onto his belt, hurrying for the front door. He had one more task to perform. He was to arrest the Greek sitting across the street. He would make up something. Then, he would forget that the tall beauty had ever existed. She was out of his hands, now and forever. May Allah save her immortal soul.

-29-

It was tight inside the stationary Chief Cherokee with the three D17 agents at their consoles.

Last night in Rome, Jack had received his instructions from Secretary King over a secure line. She had sounded winded, maybe even uncertain. That was unlike the Secretary. Jack had asked about the Ardennes, if she had received further information about the D'erlon Plant.

Jack was still in the dark about the rest of the mission. Whatever had happened afterward in the Ardennes had become extremely hush-hush. Jack wanted to know how Simon's information had gone over without the actual raw data. Not knowing bothered him more than he cared to admit.

The Secretary had hesitated before brushing aside his question. Jack still wondered about that. Something had been off during the conversation. D17 was still after the antimatter, although King had sounded evasive when he'd asked for further details about that.

From Rome last night, the team skimmed the Mediterranean all the way to Libya. The cargo plane had landed on a lonely stretch of road a half hour later. The team had gunned the modified Chief Cherokee down the ramp, roaring without headlights for a bumpy 116 miles to the Libyan-Egyptian border. That's when the operation had become tricky. For fifty miles, they skirted saltpans and negotiated sand dunes, almost dumping the vehicle twice. Finally, just before dawn, they parked thirteen miles from the Siwa Oasis.

Hours later, the engine still idled, powering the air conditioner. It hummed less for their comfort than for the expensive equipment inside.

The fourth member of the team squatted six miles away outside a mud-brick hut on the lone tarmac road from Cairo. David Carter had trekked on foot from the jeep earlier this morning. He was Simon Green's replacement. Carter waited for three trucks supposedly belonging to Abu Hammond, the notorious Iranian arms smuggler.

Jack missed Simon, but he forced himself to bury his feelings. He was on an op. That meant full concentration. His agents deserved his best. He had to bring his people out alive, not leave them dead in the field as had happened to Simon.

Get a grip, Elliot. The others are counting on you.

Jack tapped his computer screen. He focused on the image from David Carter six miles away. The lenses from the man's sunglasses sent a signal to the jeep. The optics showed rocks and gravel that could have been from Mars.

"We're right on target, boss."

Jack glanced over his shoulder at another screen. From a small drone's vantage, it showed more of the rocky desolation of the Qattara Depression, made famous a little over 70 years ago. The depression had flanked El Alamein to the south, the place where Montgomery had stopped Rommel's Africa Korps in 1943, changing the course of WWII.

As seen from the drone, a ribbon of road snaked through the barren landscape. Three big trucks moved along the route. They'd been traveling all night from Cairo, 348 miles away.

Terrell Williams, a big black man, piloted the drone. Terrell shifted the joystick and tapped a computer key. The trucks zoomed bigger on the screen. With the drone's adjustable camera, he tried to peer past windshields into the cabs. Unfortunately, the visors were down. The occupants of the trucks remained in the shadows. Jack couldn't tell if there were any D'erlon people among the passengers.

"Are you picking up any radiation signatures?" Jack asked.

Terrell manipulated his screen, soon shaking his head. "Could this be a false trail, boss?"

"Maybe," Jack said, "or maybe they're shielding the antimatter better since unloading it in the harbor." He drummed his fingers on the console. "How soon until the trucks pass Carter's position?"

"At their present speed," Terrell said, checking, "eleven minutes, thirty-two seconds."

Jack pressed a computer key, sending a signal to Carter six miles away.

As he did, a distinctive buzz startled them. Terrell, Phelps and Jack whipped around to stare as satellite phone buzzed a second time.

Jack picked up the phone and clicked the switch. "Jack Elliot here," he said.

-30-

SIWA OASIS
EGYPT

Selene felt exposed on the back of the scooter, and it was difficult to find proper purchase for her feet. The heat against her ankles reminded her that one wrong placement could burn her skin.

She looked around, noticing a Berber woman watching them pass. Wet clothes hung from a line. The woman wore a burqa, staring with disapproval.

For a Muslim country, Egypt was a cosmopolitan place in the large cities along the Nile. Siwa was an isolated oasis, however. Despite being a tourist attraction during part of the year, it remained very old-fashioned. Selene could imagine how immodest she appeared on the back of this strange man's scooter.

She bit her lower lip. Maybe it had been a mistake leaving Philip behind. The desire to meet the Old Man—

Wait a minute. When had the antique shop clerk phoned the Old Man? He had not. The clerk had rejected her money, only agreeing to take her to *him* after she'd knocked out the police captain. There hadn't been any phone calls to affirm the meeting or the location. Did that mean the clerk had intended to take her to the Old Man all along?

This feels like a trap.

Selene's gaze narrowed. While keeping her one-arm hold around the clerk's waist, she put her other hand in her suit pocket. She almost shoved the snub-nosed revolver against the man's lower back. Instead, she simply shouted in his ear.

"I need you to stop a minute."

"There's no time," he shouted over his shoulder.

"Stop!"

He shrugged fatalistically. A second later, the scooter winded down, finally idling as the clerk put his feet onto the blacktop, balancing them on the scooter.

"We have a schedule to keep. *He* said—"

"I'm changing the schedule," Selene told the man.

The clerk twisted around. She expected to see surprise. Instead, there was calculation in his gaze.

"Why did you pay the police captain to act as he did?" the clerk asked.

"What are you talking about?"

The leathery-faced clerk searched her eyes more deeply. "You pretend to act like a tourist. But I sense strength in you. You are not what you seem."

"If you have a point to any of this," Selene said, "I'd appreciate hearing it."

The clerk frowned. "You did not pay the police captain?"

"Pay him to do what?"

"Pretend to slump unconscious," the clerk said. "Did you not realize he faked his fall?"

"I doubt that. My palm where I hit him still hurts."

The clerk studied her.

Could the man be telling her the truth? That didn't make sense. "We're going to take a slight detour," Selene said.

"Do you say this in hopes of avoiding the shadowy ones?"

His words shocked her, making Selene's stomach twist. "What do you mean *shadowy ones*?"

Instead of answering, he said, "Yes, I will take a detour. Perhaps it is wise."

Selene nodded, more unsure of the clerk than ever. Who was he anyway? He acted like a fool at times. At others, he seemed dangerous.

Despite her misgivings, she said, "Let's go then. The sun is getting hot."

The clerk faced forward, twisting the throttle, making the scooter rev. Then he caused the small machine to lurch as he set out once more.

-31-

QATTARA DESERT
EGYPT

"Jack," the voice said on the other end of the satellite phone. "This is Deputy Secretary Smith."

Jack frowned. Why would Smith be calling in the middle of an op? That was strange.

"There's been an accident," Smith said.

Jack said nothing, but a bad feeling radiated outward from his sternum.

Smith hesitated before he said, "Secretary King is on life support."

Jack closed his eyes. He couldn't believe it.

"She's had a heart attack," Smith continued.

"That's confirmed?" Jack whispered, not knowing what else to say.

"I wouldn't have called otherwise. The Secretary was unconscious by the time I spoke to the doctor at Memorial. Mrs. King is in critical condition. It's highly unlikely she will live through the night."

Simon Green and now Mrs. King—

"D17 protocol required that I immediately brief the advisor on any ongoing ops," Smith said. "I have to report..."

Jack opened his eyes. This was going to be bad. It felt as if strings were tightening around him. How could Mrs. King have a heart attack at this precise moment?

"Did the doctor find any marks or abrasions on Mrs. King?" Jack asked.

"That was my immediate concern," Smith said. "The answer is no. This was a natural disaster."

Jack didn't believe that. He wondered if Smith really did, either. Who else listened to the call? It must be the advisor, put in place at the inception of D17. They were America's ghost, but someone had to have watch over them to make sure they stayed within governmental control.

"The advisor does not believe this is a wise operation given Egyptian hostility to former American involvement in their country," Smith said.

Jack realized he'd guessed right. "The antimatter—" he said.

"I'm only going to say this once," Smith said in a rush, interrupting Jack. "French security forces raided the D'erlon Plant several nights ago. The Secretary risked her career convincing them to do so. The French didn't find any evidence of antimatter in the plant."

"The D'erlon people destroyed the antimatter before the security forces got there," Jack said. "Or they got it away before—"

"Agent Elliot," Smith said. "Listen to me carefully. One doesn't just destroy antimatter. It would be like destroying nuclear bombs by exploding them. People would notice. This is important for you to understand. There was no antimatter at the D'erlon Plant nor was there any equipment that could have conceivably produced it. Thus, that ends the matter."

"But Simon Green's readings—"

"Agent Elliot," Smith said, interrupting once more. "We don't possess Agent Green's data. Secretary King believed you about Simon but we came up empty. The advisor cannot in good conscience continue the Siwa Operation given these parameters."

"But the radiation signature readings in Cairo," Jack said.

"I understand. That was strange. However, on the advisor's direct orders, I am canceling the present op."

"Sir—"

132

"It's out of my hands, Elliot. There was no antimatter in the Ardennes and certainly none in Hammond's trucks. That is the official position. You are to return to Libya at once for extraction."

Jack said nothing.

"Are you there?" Smith asked.

"I'm here," Jack said in a tired voice. He couldn't believe this. Had Simon died for nothing?

"Leave Egypt immediately," Smith said. "Do you understand?"

"Suppose Hammond is transporting plutonium," Jack said, grasping at whatever he could. "We picked up radiation signatures. If it's not antimatter—"

"Hammond cannot possibly have plutonium or antimatter. The advisor has spoken. While I am the acting Secretary, I do not have the authority to dismiss her orders. We're recording you, as you know, so I hope you follow orders exactly."

"We'll leave Egypt, sir," Jack said. Smith had as good as told him the advisor was listening in to the conversation. If he failed to comply, the advisor would likely cashier him on the spot.

"Immediately," Smith added in an ominous tone.

Jack got the message, and he found it strange. Still, orders were orders. "I'll need to collect my team first, sir."

There was a pause on the other end of the satellite phone before Smith said, "Brief me on the present situation."

Jack told him about Carter six miles away, waiting by a cluster of mud brick ruins along the Cairo road.

"I see your problem," Smith said. "You'll have to let Hammond's trucks pass. You are not to engage in any activity concerning them. That means I want Agent Carter to stand down."

Jack ingested the order, gripping the satellite phone harder. "Yes, sir," he said.

"Do you have a drone in the air?"

"I do, sir."

"It has a kill switch?"

"It does, sir."

"Land it immediately and destroy it."

133

Jack said nothing.

"After Hammond's trucks pass Carter's position," Smith said, "you are to pick him up and head for Libya. We will discuss a rendezvous point after you're out of Egypt. Do you understand your orders?"

"Yes, sir," Jack said. "Now, if you'll excuse me, sir, Hammond's trucks are almost to Carter's location."

"I'm sorry, Elliot. I'm... Good luck with the extraction." A *click* sounded afterward as Smith hung up.

In the Chief Cherokee in the Qattara Depression, Jack set down the satellite phone.

"Sounds like trouble," Terrell said.

Jack nodded, giving them a rundown on the situation.

"So we just leave?" Terrell asked. "Simon died for nothing?"

The words were like nails in Jack's heart. "Bring the drone home." He leaned near a microphone, clicking a switch. "David."

"Yeah?" Agent Carter asked.

"Turn off your optics."

A second passed before Carter said, "Are you kidding me?"

"Turn them off."

"But—"

"Now," Jack said.

"This is crazy, but I'm turning them off."

The desert view and approaching trucks on Jack's screen disappeared.

Jack felt a cold knot in his stomach. This was wrong. He knew the advisor was with Smith. She would be studying his files. Why did the advisor insist on this? Didn't they believe Simon?

"I'm disappointed in you," Terrell told him.

Jack didn't reply.

"Letting a suit like the advisor—"

"Hey," Carter said over the comm-line, with worry in his voice. "The trucks are slowing down. I can hear their brakes squeal."

"Trouble?" asked Jack.

"Yeah, there's trouble," Carter said in a low voice. "I think the trucks are going to stop. One of the drivers is staring at me." Carter swore. "Jack, I recognize a driver. You're not going to believe this. It's—"

At that moment, a harsh sound filled the speaker in the Chief Cherokee.

"Carter," Jack said into his microphone. "Carter, can you hear me?"

"Listen to that growl," Terrell said, as he indicated the speaker. "Someone is jamming Carter's signal. If that someone is in those trucks—Hammond could be on to us."

-32-

DESERT ROAD
EGYPT

David Carter squatted on his heels outside the ruins of a mud-brick building. He wore a Bedouin robe that blended in with his White Mountain Apache skin-tone.

Sunlight glinted off the windshield of the lead truck belonging to the arms smuggler. Carter didn't know why, but the moment felt surreal. It sent a chill down his spine. He remembered the last time he'd felt that: it had been seconds before the horrible injury his senior year in college.

At that moment, he noticed that the middle truck was swaying from side to side. Was it carrying a heavier load than the others?

"Hey," Carter said into the microphone pinned on the underside of his robe. "The trucks are slowing down. I can hear their brakes squeal."

"Trouble?" asked Jack, the words coming out of the earbud in Carter's left canal.

"Yeah, there's trouble. I think the trucks are going to stop. One of the drivers is staring at me." Carter swore. "Jack, I recognize a driver. You're not going to believe this. It's—"

Before Carter could give the name, a harsh sound came out of the earbud. Carter said, "Ney," even as he realized someone jammed his device.

Several thoughts jumbled together in a mess. *They're jamming me. They've cut me off. What is Ney doing with Hammond's people?*

Carter spat the stub of a cigarette from between his lips. The orange glow burst apart on the dirt. He hated the cancer sticks, but it seemed as if every Egyptian in the country smoked. Squatting here puffing had helped him to blend in better.

That's not going to work anymore, now is it?

Carter stood, stumbling forward three steps. His legs were stiff from squatting for so long.

Ney Blanc waved to him from the front cab. The Frenchman even had the gall to smile.

Carter didn't have time to show surprise or bother to wonder why an agent of the French DGSE—General Directorate for External Security—was driving for Hammond. Ney was one of the best, a ruthless case officer. Yet, if Ney was undercover, why was the Frenchman waving?

My cover is blown, Carter thought. *I wonder if Jack heard me name Ney.*

Deciding that waiting here would almost certainly result in his death, Carter pivoted. He hiked up his robe and sprinted for the nearest entrance.

The unreality of the moment impinged upon Carter. This was crazy. Incredibly, a jackal poked its pointy-snout through the entranceway. The carrion-eater stared at Carter before its ears lay down on its head. The next second, the animal vanished, likely tucking its tail between its legs as it fled the premises.

Behind Carter, the squeal of brakes increased in length and volume. Old springs groaned. Was that the clack of a machine gun bolt he heard?

Carter's sandaled feet struck the hard-packed dirt as pain blossomed in his right knee. The old injury loved to make itself known at the worst possible moments. Carter ignored the agony, straining to reach the door, wanting to get behind the thick bricks.

Time seemed to slow down for Carter. It felt like the moment he'd that made the runback in overtime. Notre Dame

137

had kicked the football right into his arms. Oh, man, that had been the highlight of his life. No one had been able to touch him. He had juked, faked and outmaneuvered all of them, spiking the football in the end zone and doing his signature war dance with the tomahawk chop.

I'm going to make it.

That's when the first assault rifle opened up. The peculiar *rat-a-tat-tat* told Carter it was the Chinese knockoff version of the Russian AK-47.

Why are they using such an old weapon?

In lieu of an answer, the dirt a little to the left of his feet spit, leaving three ugly divots. Those were bullets, damnit! The firing stopped. Carter faked left. The firing began again as he'd known it would. A bullet seared the skin of his left shoulder, burning away part of the robe and causing a splash of blood to fly. Agent Carter launched off his feet, diving to the right and the door. Out of the corner of his eye, he saw bullets smash against the left part of the doorframe. Then he sailed through the entrance, tucked his shoulder, hit the ground, rolled and launched to his right. Bullets followed him, but they weren't fast enough.

Carter came to a thudding halt in the gloom of the hut as more assault rifles opened up. The bastards were trying to kill him. Ney's wave—*he tried to lull me. The Frenchman's in tight with Hammond.*

"All righty then," Carter said under his breath. A second later, he gripped his Glock. However, only an idiot would try to trade gunfire using a pistol against assault rifles. He felt better holding it, and there might come a moment soon when he could strike back. But under no circumstances did he intend to dart into view and pop off a few rounds.

Carter crawled on his belly for a back window. At this point in the game hitting back wasn't nearly as important as remaining alive. Jack and the others would be coming. The Chief Cherokee had more than pistols. Would Hammond want to stay around and engage in a firefight with the cargo he carried?

Ney's with Hammond. I have to figure out a way to use that.

Carter reached a back window. He darted up, crawled through and tumbled onto the ground outside. Scrambling to his feet, he limped for another of the mud-brick buildings. It was time to play hide and seek for real.

-33-

QATTARA DESERT
EGYPT

The Chief Cherokee's oversized tires spun in the sand. A second later, they bit. The desert-colored jeep jerked forward. Inside, Jack drove with his hands at ten and two o'clock on the steering wheel.

"What do you see?" he asked.

Terrell swayed in his chair in back. "Give me a minute, boss."

"That's too long. Carter's in trouble." Jack wasn't going to lose another agent in the field.

"I can appreciate that," Terrell said, "but trouble or not doesn't change the laws of physics."

"You're right," Jack said. "It's just—Simon—"

Terrell grunted, focusing as he manipulated the drone controls. He still managed to ask, "Does it bother you that Smith ordered us to explode the drone *immediately*?"

"It does," Jack said.

"So that means we're staying on the mission?"

"No. It means we grab Carter and hurry to Libya."

Terrell looked thoughtful. "Think we'll ever make it to Libya?"

Jack glanced back at the big man. "You think the D'erlon people got to the advisor?"

"What did Simon tell you?" Terrell asked. "He said the antimatter was worth trillions. Given enough dough, you can buy just about anyone. Well, anyone but Jack Elliot."

Jack concentrated on driving. If Terrell was right… Why had they stayed so far away from Carter? Six bloody miles was too many.

"I have them in drone sight," Terrell said. "The trucks have stopped. Men with AK-47s are swarming the ruins, hunting for Carter."

"Give me a visual."

Terrell tapped his screen.

The windshield's upper left-hand corner showed Jack what the drone camera saw. This was the latest technology, used on the newest U.S. Air Force fighters.

The three big trucks were parked just off the tarmac road. Seven men wearing combat fatigues and gripping AK-47s advanced on the closest mud-brick ruin. It told Jack that Carter had high-tailed it. Smart man. The agent would be trying to buy time. The thought caused Elliot's facial skin to tighten. He didn't plan on disappointing Carter.

"Phelps," Jack said. "Get an AT4 ready."

"If Hammond has plutonium…you're risking spilling it everywhere. If he has antimatter…"

"Got any other ideas?" Jack asked.

"We have the drone," Terrell said. "Let me buzz them. Let Hammond know we see him."

Jack gripped the steering wheel harder than ever. The advisor would burn him for this, saying he should have left Carter to the wolves. They had protocols for events like this. No one agent was worth saving if it exposed D17—that was the team's golden rule. Besides, he was already supposed to have deactivated the drone.

"Buzz them," Jack said. He wasn't leaving anyone behind. "Once we get in AT4 range," he told Phelps, "fire wide so as not to hit a truck. We don't want the antimatter to spill—if it's onboard. But right now they don't know we know about it and that we're firing to miss."

"You're trying to *scare* them?" Terrell asked.

"No," Jack said. "That's what you're hoping buzzing them will do. I'm warning them, telling them to run away. If they do, I'll pick up Carter and leave."

"And if Hammond decides to stay and fight it out?" Terrell asked.

"We kill him," Jack said, with his eyes shining.

"The advisor isn't going to like that."

"Oh well."

As the jeep crunched onto gravel, Jack punched it so bits of rock flew. The Chief Cherokee picked up speed, creating a cloud of debris behind it.

A sour expression appeared on Elliot's face. "Is the drone almost there?"

"Look at the windshield," Terrell said.

Jack did. What he saw almost brought the hint of a smile to his lips.

-34-

Selene and the clerk had been zipping on side-trails, flashing in and out of shadows underneath thousands of palm and olive trees. Now, the clerk zoomed out of the relative coolness of the groves into the hot sun. He headed toward the ancient Temple of the Oracle of Ammon in the abandoned, mud-brick village of Aghurmi.

The choice intrigued Selene. Claire had gone to Angkor Wat, an old Cambodian temple, although not as old as the one here. Did the hums have anything to do with temple sites?

On the journey to the oasis from the Cairo airport, Selene had read on the internet about Siwa. In ancient times, people had called this place *Ammonium* because of the oracle of Ammon, a ram-horned god originally adopted by the Libyans. Some believed Ammon was a derivative of Baal Hammon of the Carthaginians. Others suggested the god had come from the Egyptian Amun, one of the Old Kingdom deities of creation. The oracle was claimed to have existed since prehistoric times, with believers trekking across the desert to ask it questions.

There were two notable ancient events connected with Ammonium. Each came at the hand of a foreign conqueror.

The first involved Cambyses II, the son of Cyrus of Persia, who conquered Egypt in 525 BC. The legends spoke about Cambyses' arrogance and madness. He sent an army on the road to Ethiopia. Along the way, he detached fifty thousand soldiers. Their task was to destroy Ammonium in the Libyan Desert. The mercenaries and Persians trekked across the bleak sands. Unfortunately for them, they lost their way and died in the desert, buried under a terrible sandstorm.

As Selene pondered the place's history, the scooter headed for the hill of the oracle. The hill had been larger in times past. Throughout the centuries, sections had cracked and sloughed off, shrinking the rocky edifice and threatening the ancient temple with eventual destruction.

The second historical event had happened in 331 BC. Alexander the Great, with a small force of Macedonians, had traveled two hundred and twenty miles across the desert to Ammonium. His force might have lost its way like the earlier Persians, but legend held that two snakes had led them to the oracle, hissing all the way there.

According to the ancient historian Plutarch, the chief priest of Ammon had gone out to greet Alexander. The priest had wished to say, "Oh my son," but being a foreigner, had mispronounced the words so as to say, "Son of Zeus." The mistake had pleased the conqueror. Together, chief priest and Macedonian went to the god, but what Ammon revealed to Alexander was unknown. It was so great a secret that he had not even dared to communicate it to his mother in writing.

The god's revelations had a profound impact on Alexander. From Ammonium, historians could trace two new facets regarding the conqueror. From that time forward, Alexander began to speak about his divine origin, calling himself the son of Zeus-Ammon. The second notion was more beneficial to the world. It was the idea of Ammon-Ra ruling over all humanity. Alexander wished to treat all the conquered peoples as equal, not dealing with humanity as separate tribes or in different camps, such as the Greeks had, calling everyone else barbarians. This had been a radical idea in the ancient world.

The clerk gunned the scooter. The rear tire kicked up dust as the small engine complained at the steepest part. Before Selene could comment, he brought the scooter onto a level area. He made a sharp turn and stopped, shutting off the engine.

144

Selene slid off, noticing the silence and that the place was deserted. Interestingly, she did not hear any humming. There was supposed to be one here.

"Come," said the clerk. "He is growing impatient."

Selene hesitated. The clerk seemed nervous. "Answer me this first," she said. "What did you mean earlier when you spoke about the shadowy ones?"

He stared at her, his manner turning creepy.

Selene pulled out the .38, stepping back. "You're one of them, aren't you? How else could you know about them?"

Instead of making him more nervous, the revolver seemed to calm him. The clerk shook his head.

"There is no Old Man," she said.

"Walk up those stairs and I'll show you otherwise."

Selene couldn't make up her mind. The clerk sounded sincere, but a good conman always did.

"Why do you care what I see?" Selene asked. "Is it the money you're hoping to get from me?"

"He wants to show someone. He would have shown Claire, but she broke her appointment. She betrayed his confidence."

"Claire will still show up."

"If she can," the clerk said, ominously.

"What's that supposed to mean?"

Instead of answering, he said, "You can hear the hum from inside the location. It's most obvious then, and eerie. Maybe you're afraid to hear it."

"You bet I am," Selene said, "and you're starting to frighten me as well."

He lowered his gaze. "I cannot help it. I'm nervous. I've never—he's never shown anyone else before."

So, he was the Old Man. The clerk act was a front. She should be safe as long as she had the gun. Maybe it would be wisest to continue playing along with the act.

"Sure," she said. "Take me to the hum. But if you're playing me false..."

"Come," he said, starting up the ancient stairs.

Selene followed. It didn't surprise her when the clerk produced a key, unlocking a large iron gate. After they passed through the modern barrier, the clerk closed the gate. Afterward, they entered the ruins of the unroofed temple.

"This way," he said.

They stepped into a side passage with stairs leading down into a tunneled corridor. It was cooler here and darker. Instinctively, Selene's grip tightened around the .38.

The clerk fished a penlight out of his red vest, using it to light his path. After another turn, they came to a dead end.

"What trick is this?" Selene asked hoarsely. Was he going to attack her?

He didn't respond. Instead, he crouched low, pushing something heavy so stone scraped against stone.

To Selene's left, a portion of wall swung inward. A waft of cool air blew against her, smelling like a cellar.

"Few know of this passage," he said in a soft voice.

Selene blinked with surprise. She'd studied several brochures regarding the temple. This hadn't been part of the ancient floor plan.

"Shall we proceed?" he asked.

"It can't be safe in there."

"I give you my assurances, it is."

Selene studied the clerk, finally taking several steps away from him. "Go ahead. Lead the way."

He did, shining his penlight before his feet.

Selene listened to their footfalls as they descended into subterranean darkness. Narrow stone steps twisted around, heading deeper into the earth. The farther they walked, the cooler the air became. Finally, Selene shivered. The last thing she'd expected was to be cold today.

"Why is he meeting us down here?" she asked.

"In order to foil the shadowy ones," he said.

"Who are these shadowy ones? What's their objective?"

He kept walking as if he hadn't heard the question. Finally, they reached another dead end. "Would you turn away for a moment please?"

Selene snorted in an unladylike fashion.

He shrugged after a moment, reaching into an alcove, pushing a stone.

146

This section of wall slid inward like a sliding door, revealing a metallic chamber on the other side.

Selene's heart rate quickened. Now she could hear a distinctive, low-grade hum.

"You hear it, yes?"

"I do," she whispered. "What is this place?" Was it linked to the undersea dome in the Indian Ocean?

"You must step through with me," the clerk was explaining. "Otherwise, we shall be separated when the spring slides the wall shut."

On impulse, Selene slipped the .38 into a pocket. Then, she stepped beside him, nodding. Together, they moved through the secret entrance, stepping onto a smooth steel floor. Immediately, the combination doorway slid shut behind them.

The clerk clicked off his penlight and stepped away from her into pitch-blackness. It seemed like a treacherous thing to do. Had he lured her here for nefarious reasons?

Selene crouched in the darkness, making herself a smaller target. Did he have a gun? Would he start firing?

"Who are you?" he asked, sounding more confident now. "It is time you tell me.'

Selene said nothing, deciding to remain as hidden as she could in the darkness. What was his game?

"I will leave you here if you do not answer me," he said.

Selene still said nothing.

"Very well," he said.

There was something menacing in his voice. Was he going to slip away and leave her here? "Wait," Selene said. "I told *him* who I was on the phone. He's the one who told me to go to your shop."

"Let me hear what you said again," the clerk said.

That seemed like an odd thing to say. "You're one of them, aren't you?" Selene asked.

"No. I have nothing to do with *them*."

Selene believed him. The man seemed unhinged, though. Maybe it would be smartest to humor him. She began to tell him what she'd told the Old Man over the phone. "I'm a geologist for the University of Hawaii. I found something in the Indian Ocean like this place. There was a device in there,

147

too, a tuning fork, which must have something to do with the hum."

"Tell me about the tuning fork."

"I don't think so. Not yet, at least."

"You will remain in darkness for the rest of your rather short life if you don't."

"I don't believe you," she said, deciding suddenly to play a hunch.

"That's a pity. The Old Man instructed me to use my discretion regarding you. He said I could leave you here to die."

Selene laughed, deciding to prick his pride. "You're a liar."

"You are a foolish woman," he said in a stung tone. "Why would you say such a thing to me?"

"Because I know who you really are."

"Who is that?"

"You pretend you're just a clerk and messenger, but really you're the Old Man. Why bother with such a flimsy deception? You're not fooling anyone."

Except for the hum, there was silence, which lengthened uncomfortably.

Finally, something clicked audibly. A diffuse glow came from the entire ceiling, increasing brightness. Selene saw that the metallic chamber contained a steel table and chairs. There were three closed hatches on the far side of the room. The clerk sat on a chair at the table. He set what looked like a clicker onto the smooth surface. Afterward, he did something with his hand, a conjurer's trick perhaps. He gripped a small black pistol aimed at her.

"You are one of them," he said. "Why you should pretend otherwise, I have no idea." He smiled in a sinister way. "What did you do to Claire? Why didn't she come? Why did you come instead?"

The gun and the man's ruthless grin made Selene's face go cold.

"If you twitch the wrong way," he said, "I will shoot out one of your kneecaps."

"I'm not one of them," she said. "I want to know what happened to Claire even more than you do."

148

He laughed, shaking his head. "It is so obvious I wonder how you could think to fool me."

"Why don't you admit you're the Old Man?"

"Are you wearing a wire?" he asked.

"I'm Dr. Selene Khan, a Hawaii University geologist who studies magnetic effects and the hum on the side."

"That's the wrong answer," he said, pulling the trigger.

-35-

DESERT ROAD
EGYPT

Sweat dripped from Carter's nose, plinking onto the hot clay of the roof where he lay. He eased toward an edge. An Iranian in camouflage gear holding an assault rifle moved toward his building. The seven Iranians had spread out, each heading to a different ruin.

Carter heard a familiar buzz. He looked up and spied the drone. It dive-bombed almost straight down.

Carter slithered to the middle of the roof where he slid through a dark opening. He hit the dirt floor below, rolling until he lay in the cooler gloom. He had to act fast because Terrell was giving him an opening.

The Iranians must have seen the drone, too. The sound of their firing confirmed it.

Carter hurried to the nearest window. Would you look at that? An idiot had a spread-foot stance. The assault rifle shivered in the Iranian's hands with empty, smoking shells kicking out of the chamber one right after another, striking the sand around him. The fool lacked fire control.

Carter drew his Glock, placing his free hand under his shooting hand.

The Iranian out there yanked the spent magazine from the rifle, dropping it at his feet. He fumbled in a pouch, bringing out another magazine, slamming it into place. That wasn't the way to treat a weapon. Sure, the AK family had been constructed for hardiness, but come on…use a little common sense already. Treat your weapon disrespectfully and it would fail you at the worst possible moment. Mr. Anti-aircraft had other ideas. The Iranian pulled the bolt, putting a new bullet into the chamber, raising the rifle so the butt fit snug against his right shoulder. Then, the Iranian shifted, tracking the drone, putting his back to Carter.

In rapid succession, Carter put three bullets into the middle of the Iranian's back. The man pitched forward, hurling his weapon from him. He staggered for several steps, apparently trying to stay upright. Maybe he attempted to call out a warning to the others, but it didn't matter. The Iranian went down hard.

Carter didn't hear the drone anymore. The six shooters were going crazy, hosing fire at it.

Carter knew this was his moment. He eased through the window as his belly tightened. This was plain insanity, but he had to do something before Hammond's men finished with the drone and hunted him down.

Carter crawled across the hot dirt toward the dead Iranian. It surprised him none of them had hit the drone yet.

Several things happened at once then. Carter reached the dead man's assault rifle. As his fingers caressed the wood, Carter heard several Iranians shout in Allah's name in horrified surprise. A second later, the drone smashed against the middle smuggler, catapulting the man backward as the machine exploded.

Terrell piloted drones the way LeBron James shot hoops.

Carter picked up the assault rifle, put the butt against his shoulder and swiveled around. He flicked the selector switch to single fire, targeted the nearest smuggler and squeezed the trigger. The Iranian collapsed as if he had been a puppet with cut strings. Carter targeted another smuggler, needing two shots to kill him.

An Iranian shouted, aiming at Carter. The White Mountain Apache proved faster, using three bullets to put the man down.

The last three smugglers might have had brain overload. One of them dropped his AK knockoff and ran shouting in panic, with his arms flailing in the air. Carter ignored him. Another smuggler also ran away clutching his weapon against his chest. The last one howled with rage, spraying assault rifle fire. Carter emptied his magazine into that Iranian. Each impacting bullet made the man howl louder but seemed to have no other effect. Finally, Carter's rifle clicked empty.

The crazy man over there staggered at Carter. They were both out of ammo. The smuggler reached into his pouch, stopped as if he'd just thought of the most important thing in the world and gave Carter an amazed expression. Afterward, the Iranian toppled dead onto the dirt.

Agent Carter stared at the dead man. He shivered a second later as if someone had thrown cold water on him. He'd gotten lucky none of the man's shoots had hit.

Carter lurched upright, pitching the AK from him. He drew the Glock, steadied himself as he knelt on one knee, clutched the weapon two-handed and vaguely noticed the shadow of a man mixed in with his own shadow.

Carter was hot, tired, excited and glad the crazy man had missed with the wild firing. As Winston Churchill had once said, "The most exhilarating feeling in the word was being shot at and surviving."

A split-second later, the man-shadow mixed in with his own registered in Carter's thoughts. The sun was up and behind him. That meant—

Carter whipped around just in time to see the blur of a baton. It cracked against his skull just above the left eye, making a hollow-sounding noise. The Glock fell from Carter's nerveless fingers as he pitched sideways onto the hot soil.

Before Carter could get around to shouting in pain, the baton cracked against his head a second time. That overloaded his brain with trauma, rendering the D17 agent unconscious.

-36-

DESERT ROAD
EGYPT

Jack saw the smudge of buildings first as hot desert air blew into the Chief Cherokee. They were moving fast cross-country.

Phelps stood beside him with her head and shoulders sticking through the modified sunroof. She wore zoom goggles against the sand and clutched an AT4. It fired a High Explosive Dual Purpose warhead, which was good against bunkers, personnel and light armor. That would include Hammond's heavy trucks.

"I don't see any vehicles," Phelps shouted through the sunroof.

"They could be behind the buildings waiting for us," Jack said.

"Maybe," Phelps said. "Do you see the ribbon of smoke?"

"Yeah."

"Must be from the crashed drone," Phelps said.

"Just charging in doesn't seem wise," Terrell said from the back. "The Iranians could be lining us up."

Jack had already been thinking that. How did it help Carter if Hammond blew up the jeep with RPGs or anti-material rifles? They had to survive in order to save Carter.

"Hang on," Jack told the others.

One of Phelps' hands appeared as she gripped the inner side of the open sunroof.

Jack cranked the steering wheel. Phelps swayed. She didn't complain at the treatment. Phelps never did.

Jack circled the lonely cluster of ruins from an appreciable distance. If Hammond's people fired an RPG from hiding, he wanted time to swerve and get out of the way. He kept an eye on the ruins, looking for dust, any sign of the three big trucks. So far, no one had locked any radar onto the jeep. He would have heard a *ping* otherwise.

"Still think Hammond's hiding back there?" Terrell asked. "Slowly moving his vehicles as he's watching us circle?"

"I do not," Jack said.

"Neither do I," Terrell said. "Phelps, what you think?"

"I don't get paid to think," she shouted from outside. "Just destroy stuff." She was their demolitions expert. "I let Jack do the thinking for me."

Jack glared at the ruins. There was a time to play it safe and a time for wild chances. He yearned to go in and see if Carter was alive. There were low percentages to just storming in right now, though. A minute, maybe two, of circling wasn't going to change the outcome of this. Thus, he would practice caution.

"Phelps," Jack said. "Bring it in."

"If they're hiding over there—"

"If Egyptian police show up, I don't want you waving your AT4 around."

"Screw the police," she said.

"Phelps!" Jack said.

"All right," she muttered. "I'm disarming the launcher."

Jack kept circling as she began the process of bringing it in.

By the time Phelps sat in her seat, Jack realized Hammond and his trucks had left the premises. If Carter was out there, why hadn't he tried to contact them with his comm-set?

The Chief Cherokee swayed as Jack roared down and then up a steep ditch, climbing onto the road. This part of the Qattara Depression had short but steep canyons to the immediate east of the buildings.

The ride smoothed out on the tarmac road. He increased speed, heading for the ruins.

"Feels deserted," Terrell said from the back.

"You said you hit an Iranian with your drone," Jack said.

"I did," the big man said. "Phelps had it right before. That line of smoke is from the wreckage."

Soon, Jack was braking well before they reached the buildings. The hairs on the back of his neck lifted. He pushed the brake pedal harder, bringing the vehicle to an abrupt stop.

"What's up, boss?" Terrell asked.

"Wait here," Jack said, opening the driver's side door, putting his feet on the baking road.

"What do you think you're doing?" Terrell asked.

"I'm going to reconnoiter on foot," Jack said, getting out.

"Think they buried land mines or some claymores over there?"

"Maybe," Jack said.

"You stay," Phelps said. "I'll go. Booby traps are my specialty."

Jack stared into the Chief Cherokee at her as his neck tingled with unease. Phelps was lean, with a faint scar hidden under her baseball cap. She hated the scar and always wore something to hide it. When Phelps smiled and wore a tight miniskirt, it made every man's heart beat faster with desire. In the field on a mission, she wore baggy clothes and kept her hair tucked under the hat. She had a cunning mind and set the most lethal traps Jack had ever seen. No one was better at finding little trip wires or the odd piece of junk lying in just the wrong place. She had issues, though, just like everyone else in D17.

"Go," Jack told her. He slid back into the driver's seat, slamming the door shut.

She opened hers.

"Turn on your microphone," he said.

She nodded.

"Once you head out there I'm going to back up," Jack told her.

She nodded again.

"Something is definitely off. I can feel it."

Phelps cocked an eyebrow at him. "You want to tell me to be careful?"

"I do. Be careful."

"There. Does that make you feel better?"

Jack stared at the ruins. He had come as fast as he could for Carter. The road to the Siwa Oasis dipped half a mile from here so any vehicles traveling the rest of the way would be out of sight from this location. Could Hammond's trucks have high-tailed it there before the Chief Cherokee came into view? Hammond would have had to gun the big vehicles to hide in time.

"What's bothering you?" Terrell asked.

"Where are the bodies?" Jack asked. "If Hammond left in a hurry, bodies should be lying outside the ruins."

"That's easy," Terrell said. "Hammond took the bodies with him."

"We saw Carter kill one of them. My bet is he killed more after your drone struck. Did they have enough time to load the corpses into the trucks before we showed up?"

Terrell peered at the ruins as if judging time and distances. "It would have been tight."

"Climb back in," Jack told Phelps.

"You were going to check the area but you don't think I can? Forget that." Phelps shut her door, started walking and flicked something on her collar

A speaker in the jeep crackled into life.

"Testing, testing," Phelps said over the comm-link.

"We hear you, love," Terrell told her.

"I told you not to say that," she said.

Terrell looked over at Jack with a smirk. Jack shook his head.

"Roger," Terrell said into the microphone.

Putting the Chief Cherokee into reverse, Jack began backing up.

"You think police are going to show up?" Terrell asked.

"Soon," Jack said. "The Ninth Egyptian Border Regiment is stationed at Siwa. They're sure to send someone."

"That makes sense. Yeah. We'd better hurry."

Jack kept backing up as he watched Phelps jog toward the dismal ruins.

"See anything yet?" Terrell radioed.

"I'll let you know the minute—ah, look at this," Phelps said. "I think there's blood on the ground." She swore softly.

"What now?" Terrell asked.

"The trail of blood leads to a building," Phelps said. "Do you think they stashed the corpses in there?"

Jack's bad feeling solidified though he still wasn't sure what caused it.

"Do you see Carter?" Terrell asked.

Phelps didn't answer right away. When she did, she said, "Maybe he's in the hut with the other corpses? I'm going to check."

Jack found himself backing up faster yet.

"Do you see something, boss?" Terrell asked.

"Tell her…" Jack said.

"Yeah?"

"Tell her to come back."

"Right," Terrell said, "like she's going to listen to that. We have to know about Carter, don't we?"

Jack frowned. The bad feeling was getting worse. A trick in this business—with life in general—was listening to your inner cues. Mugged individuals often told police later that they'd felt something was off but couldn't figure out what. One's subconscious often realized things faster than the conscious, logical mind. The wise man listened to his gut.

"I'm near the building," Phelps said. "The line of blood goes through the doorway.

Jack could see her diminishing figure approach the first ruin.

"Don't see any wires," Phelps said. "Oh-oh."

"What?" Terrell asked. "Speak to us."

"Those look like Carter's sunglasses on the floor," she said.

"Don't touch them," Jack warned.

Terrell repeated that into his microphone.

Phelps snorted softly. "Who do you think you're dealing with? Course I won't touch them."

Jack slowed his retreat as lines furrowed across his forehead. What was he missing? What didn't he—

"Take a look at my monitor," he told Terrell.

157

The big man swiveled around on his chair. "Your screen is blank."

"I know that. I turned it off. I want you to turn it on."

"Don't make any sudden shifts while I'm doing it," Terrell said. He moved to Jack's console, clicking it on, sitting in the new seat. "It'll take a second to power up."

Phelps cursed over the comm-link. "I see bodies, gentlemen, freshly dead and heaped on top of each other. Looks like Carter did a number on the Iranians."

"This is weird," Terrell said. "I see her boots on your monitor. I thought Carter turned the optics off in the sunglasses."

"Get out of there, Phelps!" Jack shouted. "Run!"

Terrell looked over at Elliot.

"Tell her to run," Jack said.

"This is strange," Phelps said over the speaker.

At that moment, an explosion flashed on the computer screen. The brightness lit up Terrell's face.

Then, from the ruins, a titanic blast erupted. It demolished the hut and continued to blow skyward at an alarming rate. In seconds, a small mushroom cloud appeared.

Jack understood its significance. He floored the pedal to the metal. The tires squealed as smoke billowed around them. Then the tires bit into the tarmac moving the jeep. Cranking the steering wheel, Jack spun around, aiming the Chief Cherokee away from the blast as he put the vehicle into drive.

"Hang on!" Jack shouted. "Throw yourself onto the floor!"

The contradictory advice failed to penetrate Terrell's mind. He stared mesmerized at the growing blast.

At the same moment, the Chief Cherokee sailed off the road. It flew through the air, the front end tipping toward the bottom of a mini-canyon.

"We're going to hit hard!" Jack shouted. "Hang on!"

The Chief Cherokee flew down a steep embankment. The ground rushed up as the fireball's blast reached the embankment, blowing over them. At the same time, the front end of the jeep smashed against the rocky hardpan.

Seatbelt straps dug into Jack's flesh, keeping him from hurling against the windshield. Air bags popped into existence,

158

smashing against him. All around Jack metal crumbled and twisted, screeching horribly.

The wreck of the Chief Cherokee groaned metallically as it flipped onto its top in slow motion. Then, blast wind howled over them. The heat became intense.

Jack closed his eyes, enduring. An antimatter blast was in the process of killing them with radiation. Maybe Terrell and he had survived the heat for the moment, but they were too close to ground zero. Radiation poisoning would kill them soon enough. They were dead men. It was just going to take a little longer to die.

-37-

MINI-CANYON
EGYPT

After the airbags deflated, Jack cut himself free of the straps and crawled to the rear. "Terrell," he said. "Are you all right?"

Elliot reached the big man a second later. Blood pumped from the black man's forehead. He must have gashed it against one of the consoles during the crash. Terrell hadn't strapped in.

Jack moved fast. He grabbed Williams's jacket from a back seat and gently applied it to the terrible wound. If the man had injured his spine, Jack didn't want to paralyze Terrell for good by moving him while there was still hope.

"Terrell," he said. "You have to wake up."

Elliot knew the radiation poisoning was going to kill them sooner rather than later, but it wasn't in him to give up. The blow to the head would have caused a terrible concussion. He had to wake Terrell and keep the man awake.

Jack crawled closer. The big man just lay there. On impulse, Jack took a wrist, using his fingers to feel the pulse. There was nothing.

For the first time, it occurred to Jack that the blow to the forehead might have killed Williams. That seemed impossible, though. They had survived so much together. Phelps was certainly gone. There was no way she could have survived the blast.

"Terrell, are you hearing me?"

The man's brown eyes were open and staring, lifeless.

Jack froze as he stared back at them. Then, Elliot squeezed his eyes closed. His jaw muscles bunched tight. No sound came from Jack. No tear leaked from his eyes. He wanted to rave, but he refused to let himself do that. Instead, he silently grieved for Terrell Williams.

I killed him. My stunt murdered another of my friends.

The enemy had murdered Phelps, but Jack couldn't escape the truth that she had been his responsibility. He had failed her and Terrell just as he'd failed Simon Green.

"*Damnit,*" Jack whispered, the word torn from his soul. He was a lousy team leader. This proved it beyond a doubt.

Jack opened his eyes. The sorrow was stark because such an emotion was so rare for him.

Finally, the sorrow drained away as something else took its place. Jack didn't want to return to old wounds. The new one was bad enough. While he lived, he would do his job. He did that one thing well—usually.

"I'm sorry," Jack whispered to Terrell's corpse.

He was getting tired of having to say that to his comrades. The desire to wallow in his agony nearly drove Jack to bow his head. Instead, he crawled deeper into the wreckage.

Jack came to his smashed computer. He'd hoped to download the file and replay what the optics had seen the last few seconds in the hut of the dead.

Someone had turned on the optics and set the sunglasses to watch the corpses. Obviously, the person who had placed several grams of antimatter had put the sunglasses there, knowing how the tech operated, to wait for the D17 agents to investigate.

Why did they use the precious antimatter to cover their presence? It seems like wild overkill.

Setting off antimatter was going to bring the Egyptian border personnel here in a hurry. They would likely think it had been a nuclear explosion.

I have to get out of here.

Jack made a sour sound a second later. None of this mattered because he was a walking dead man from the radiation exposure.

Egyptian Army personnel would be coming from the Siwa Oasis. Jack would have to move away from the road, which meant walking in the desert for at least ten miles. The sooner he got started the sooner he'd reach the oasis. If he waited too long, he'd be dead anyway.

Hardening his resolve—refusing to look at Terrell's corpse—Jack began rummaging through the wreckage. He wouldn't be able to take much. Hiking through the desert would be an ordeal.

In three minutes, Jack crawled out of the smashed Chief Cherokee. He didn't know if Carter was dead or alive. That was why he'd wanted to study the last video from the sunglasses' optics: to see if Carter's corpse had been in the heap of dead or not.

Jack stared at the wrecked jeep. He knew what he had to do next. D17 protocols demanded it. He had the satellite phone and—

Jack hefted the phone. Mrs. King's supposed heart attack, the antimatter in Hammond's trucks, Smith telling them to destroy the surveillance drone immediately—

Jack pitched the satellite phone into the wreckage. If his instincts were correct, someone had compromised the operation. The jamming earlier from Hammond, the timing of all this—

Jack mumbled softly, saying a prayer for the first time in years. That's what one was supposed to do at a funeral, right? Ask God to let the deceased into heaven. Jack sighed, turning away, studying the escarpment.

He had purposefully aimed the Chief Cherokee for this spot, hoping to shield them from the antimatter's blast. If he'd known the plunge would have slain his best friend—

"Time's up," he whispered.

Jack began to walk away from the wreckage, away from the sudden drop and the epicenter of the blast, the former cluster of ruins. He would have to go around for two reasons:

to get away from the coming investigators and to stay as far away as he could from more radiation poisoning.

If Carter still lived, he planned to rescue the agent. Nothing else mattered now.

After circling a rocky area, Elliot took out a switch and pressed it with his thumb.

A moment later, another explosion sent fire shooting into the air. Metal screamed and flames roared. He had to hide the presence of D17, leaving debris instead of computer files, a modified Chief Cherokee and a distinguishable corpse.

Jack tightened the straps of his pack, lengthening his stride. The sun beat down on him. He had water, reasonable stamina and a core of stubbornness few could match. Ten miles through the desert—except for the radiation poisoning, he had no doubt that he could make it.

How long until the radiation begins to wither my cells?

After climbing up a rise, Jack stared at the blast zone in the distance. There was a crater with smoke lazily drifting into the sky. He was still far too close. This—

Jack's features tightened as he raised his right wrist, tapping the screen of what looked like a bulky watch. He readied himself for the worst of the report.

What the—this wasn't right.

Jack shook the wrist-monitor, raising it to his ear, listening. He heard the soft clicking. It seemed to be fully functional. Lowering the watch, he ran through a quick diagnostic as he continued to trudge across the hot sand.

The device worked. It told him something amazing. There were no traces of radiation at the blast site. It hadn't been an antimatter blast or a nuclear chain reaction. He'd seen the mushroom cloud, though. That meant...

Jack began to tap the screen of the monitor. He stopped, facing ground zero. The tips of his fingers tapped faster as he ran through an analysis. According to these readings, it had been a regular explosion heightened in some manner.

Jack blinked in shock at the readings on the device. This meant—

I'm not going to die from radiation poisoning.

163

Instead of laughter or any other sign of relief, Jack's features hardened with resolve. He had to leave the area before anyone came to inspect the blast. Clutching the straps of his pack, he walked away.

Why did the advisor order us to destroy the surveillance drone and deactivate Carter's optics?

Jack took a deep breath of hot desert air. Then, he increased the pace and length of his stride. He had to reach the oasis. He had to figure out how an Iranian arms dealer was connected with D'erlon Enterprises in France. More than ever, he believed Hammond carried antimatter. Why would anyone take possibly the greatest treasure on the planet to an Egyptian hellhole?

-38-

UNDERGROUND CHAMBER
SIWA OASIS

Selene jerked her head because of an awful smell. She felt woozy and disoriented, not knowing where she was or what had happened to her.

She sat up groggily, rubbing the bottom of her nose and making a face. Had someone put smelling salts under her nose? Frowning, she tried to remember what had happened to her.

A gun, she told herself, slowly recollecting. *He pointed it at me and—*

Selene squeezed her eyelids together, realizing something was wrong with her vision. The clerk, who was actually the Old Man she'd talked to on the phone, had shot her with his gun. Only, the gun hadn't contained bullets but a dart. She recalled looking down at her blouse, at the feathered dart sticking out of her.

The man had jumped up, stepping around the table as she'd slumped unconscious. Now, Selene felt discomfort. Her panties were bunched wrong and her blouse—

I'm not wearing my suit jacket anymore.

Selene opened her eyes, willing away the blurriness. Her head hurt. She felt groggy—

"What did you do to me?" she slurred, her words making her wince.

"Try to relax," he told her. "If you'll notice, there's a glass of water and a pill on the table in front of you."

She swept her forearm over the table in one fluid motion, knocking something flying. A second later, glass shattered against a wall as shards tinkled onto the steel floor.

"That was foolish," he said. "The pill would have helped you recover quicker."

Selene wasn't sure if that was true. The bastard had drugged her, though, and removed her clothing. She didn't feel as if he had done anything to further violate her, though.

"I drugged you because I had to check to make sure you were safe. I asked if you wore a wire, testing your reaction. It was also possible that *they* had put a bug on you. I had to know before I could proceed, although I apologize for any inconvenience."

"You took off my clothes!"

"It was a repugnant chore, believe me. I took no joy in it."

Selene rubbed her eyes. She could vaguely make him out sitting across the table from her.

"How about returning my jacket and gun," she said.

He made a *tsking* sound. "Our time is limited. While you were unconscious, an explosion occurred in the desert. It must have been a powerful blast for me to hear it down here. It is my belief they are nearing something so important that they are willing to move more openly than they have for ages."

"I want my gun," Selene said.

"Don't you realize I could have left you here in this chamber? You would have soon died of thirst."

Selene rubbed her eyes. She needed to use her wits. The reality of this chamber under the Temple of Ammon was fantastic. Where did the three hatches lead? What did this place's existence mean anyway? Who was this mysterious man to have access to all this?

"Why did you bring me here?" Selene asked.

"Good. You're thinking again. I expected nothing less of you."

"Don't patronize me."

"Very well," he said. "I am a direct descendent of the priests of Ammon. Not in a literal blood relationship, mind

166

you. That would be impossible. The priests did not engage in animal rutting. The mere idea would have made any acolyte nauseous. Alas, I am the last of that illustrious line for reasons I do not wish to relate to you, a meat-eater and a practitioner of sexual relations. The point is that I remember the old legends, the ancient stories of the truth as told to those of Ammon."

"Wait, wait, wait," Selene said. "I don't want to hear about ancient whatever. That's immaterial to this place. Look around you. We're in metallic chamber with working lights, or a form of lighting."

"I realize that."

"Where do those hatches lead? What's causing the hum? We should investigate."

He shook his head.

"Have you gone through those hatches before?" Selene wished she'd explored the dome when she'd had the opportunity. Could these be similar places?

"I have brought you here to lend credence to my story." The clerk drummed his fingers on the table.

Selene's vision came into greater focus. Her .38 was near his hand with her jacket folded on the floor.

"Have you ever heard the tale of Cambyses?" he asked.

"Cambyses, son of Cyrus the Conqueror?" she asked.

"Exactly," he said. "Cambyses invaded Egypt long ago, and he sent an army fifty thousand strong to destroy the oracle. She appeared then just as the oldest tales said she would in times of trouble."

"What do you mean 'she'? Who is this she?"

"Ah," he said. "That is the right question."

Selene was beginning to wonder if the clerk was nuts. If it weren't for this chamber, she'd think him a lunatic.

"As the Persian army marched to Ammonium, she told the priests of Ammon to pray for her. Then, she went into the desert, meeting the army. As she had done many times before, she bewitched the commander. Her advice led the man and thus his army astray. The legends tell of her wisdom, her capacity to know the weather well in advance of others. She led the army into a colossal sandstorm that devoured the host. She slipped away during the storm's height, her task completed.

Her ability to survive where others died was and is among her most fantastic powers."

"That's quite the tale," Selene said, her patience growing thin. "You should write it in a book and put it on Amazon."

He scowled. "The story doesn't end there. She went to Egypt and insinuated herself with Cambyses. There, she slipped maddening drugs into the Persian's wine. Her whispered words drove him insane so he stabbed the Apsis bull, turning Egypt against him. Because of her, Cambyses lost the Persian throne. It was her punishment for his daring to threaten her oracle."

"Okay," Selene said. "That's a story, all right. But first, who is she and second, what does any of this have to do with now?"

The clerk no longer looked at Selene, but sat with a faraway stare in his eyes.

"Almost two hundred years later," he said in a soft voice, "Alexander the Great came to the oracle."

"I don't see what that has to do with—?"

"She appeared at the oracle then, too," the clerk said, slapping the table, staring at Selene. "She took the high priest's place, going out to meet the great conqueror. She spoke the words that turned Alexander's mind. I imagine it served her purposes to bring a new mode of thought to the ancient world, one of universal brotherhood. She did it through the arrogant Macedonian, using his amazing conquests for her own ends."

"Wait a minute," Selene said. "There's a problem with your story. According to the legend, a priest, a man, spoke to Alexander, not a woman."

"You speak of trifles," the clerk said, snapping his fingers. "She disguised herself as a man, don't you see?"

"No, I don't see. Cambyses sent his army in 525 BC and Alexander came in 331. That's a difference of 193 years. I hope you're not suggesting this woman lived over 200 years."

The clerk laughed bleakly, shaking his head. "How small your mind is that you fail to perceive what I've been suggesting. In some fashion, and for reasons beyond my understanding, Ammon touched her in the beginning. Our god granted her eternal life. She has passed through history as a

168

shadow, affecting the affairs of men for reasons of her own. Once, I thought she must be doing Ammon's bidding…" The clerk shook his head. "I no longer believe that. I think she tricked Ammon, using the god. Why otherwise did the oracle fade away? Why hasn't she restored the temple to its former glory? It must be within her power to do so."

Selene stared at the man. Claire could dig up the craziest people sometimes. The man had more than a screw loose. He thought Ammon was real and granted eternal life like an Arabian Night's genie granting wishes to one who rubbed his lamp.

There had to be a reasonable explanation for the metal walls and the lights. This didn't have anything to do with the underwater dome. Sure, there was a hum here, but the clerk was a lunatic. He happened to be a dangerous one, and he had her down here in a hidden vault with her senses dulled from his dart.

What's the best way to play this?

"Can you prove any of what you're saying?" Selene asked.

"No! I can't prove a thing." The clerk worried his lower lip with his teeth. "I'll tell you this, though. In the old days, a few of the priests of Ammon began to suspect her of disloyalty to the god. The few initiated into the mystery chronicled her actions across the centuries, one carefully chosen priest after another. The last of them to do so buried a scroll in a hidden place. I found the manuscript twenty years ago. At first, I was like you, scoffing at the possibility. Oh yes, you're not fooling me in the slightest. I can read the disbelief in your eyes. You think I'm mad to say these things."

The clerk shrugged. "That is the way of small-minded people. I understand all too well. I hoped since you were Claire's friend that you would be different." He shrugged again. "When I first found the scroll, I mulled it over for many months. My laughter concerning its tale died when a strange dream began to plague me. After I accepted her existence and the reality of her immortality, I began to piece together other legend. Finally, I went to the Mountain of Alamut in what is now a part of Iran. What I found in the ruins of the Assassins opened my eyes to the existence of a shadowy organization moving through time, attempting a purpose I do not begin to understand. I also spoke to the Old Man of the Mountains there. His words were revealing and uplifting. It is why I began calling myself the Old Man once I returned home to Siwa."

The man smiled sadly. "I have continued to search for understanding, but carefully so I didn't alert *them* or much worse, *her*. What you hinted at over the phone—I wondered if you could give me another clue to the greater puzzle. Perhaps once you tell me your story, the truth will shine more brightly on her, revealing just a little more."

"I don't see how—"

"Listen to me," he said. His face was shiny with perspiration and his eyes had become like burning coals.

Selene sat very still.

The clerk touched the .38 with the palm of his left hand. At the same time, his sad smile trembled.

"We have little time left," he said.

Selene nodded, wondering what to do.

Before she could decide, an explosion interrupted her thoughts. Metal crumpled and tore, and stone from the other side blasted into the chamber. One of the bigger pieces struck the clerk's head, catapulting the man off the chair onto the floor.

Selene sat across from the clerk, out of the direct-line-of-blast and killing stones. She saw the clerk skid across the floor. Stone fragments ricocheted against the far wall, sprinkling against the dead clerk and the floor. Smoke billowed. Then, a massive man walked through the smoke.

He was huge like a power lifter, standing at least six-six. The soldier wore goggles, a helmet and body armor. He reminded her of the man in the speedboat in the Indian Ocean who had been searching for her.

Selene didn't scream, but she realized she had to act now, this very moment, or—

She lunged across the table for the .38, grabbed it, aimed and pulled the trigger. The shock to her hand and the loud sound startled her.

The bullet struck his vest, slowing him just enough so Selene got off a second shot. This one ploughed through his throat. Before she could pull the trigger a third time, he swung his right arm. The gloved hand dealt her a savage buffet across the side of the head, knocking her off the chair as the .38 tumbled from her hand. He stood hunched over, panting, with blood pouring down his neck, soaking the body armor. Selene lay on the floor, dizzy from his blow.

"Stupid, bitch," he said, in an impossibly deep voice.

Selene willed her body to move. Dazed numbness had stolen her strength. She had the desire but not the ability.

"If the old priest hadn't bought it—" The soldier's eyelids fluttered. One of his knees gave out, but he caught himself on the edge of the table. It had been secured to the floor in some manner.

While Selene watched from the floor, the soldier lost his grip. He toppled in what seemed like slow motion, hitting with a clatter of body armor.

I have to get up now.

Although her head throbbed, Selene concentrated on dragging herself to a sitting position. With a slow but steady effort, she managed to stand. With her head pounding worse than ever, she staggered until she clutched the table. Carefully, she stepped over the soldier's prone body. She panted as perspiration soaked her garments.

Think fast, Selene.

She staggered to the wall, retrieving her gun and suit jacket. Then, as she passed the table, she picked up the clerk's notebook. Maybe he hadn't been totally mad after all. His shadowy people must be the same as those from the Indian Ocean. This was horrible. They had found her.

Taking what she hoped was a calming breath, Selene stepped through the jagged opening. She had to escape before the soldier recovered and captured her.

-39-

SIWA DESERT
EGYPT

Jack stopped, cocking his head. He heard sirens wail in the far distance.

It's about bloody time.

He staggered several more steps, coming within the shadows of a large boulder. He crouched, leaning against the large stone.

Sweat soaked his clothes, drying almost as fast as it oozed from his pores. He'd been drinking bottled water for the last half hour. By the watch's count, he'd already made four miles, having a mere six more to go.

He shook his final water bottle, deciding to save it for later.

At that point, his watch buzzed. Jack raised and tapped it. What he saw almost made him grin. Carter was alive. The man had turned on his tracker, a piece of hardware injected into each D17 agent's body.

"Let's see where you are," Jack whispered.

He tapped the watch a bit more, nodding. Carter was at the Siwa Oasis. For several seconds, Jack studied the signal. It had stopped moving. He waited longer. There wasn't any more movement whatsoever. Could Hammond have reached a safe house or some other secure location at the oasis?

Jack scanned the horizon. In the far distance dots of vehicles roared along the lonely road. The trucks, jeeps or cars were impossible to make out as exact models, but he had no doubt they belonged to the Ninth Egyptian Border Regiment.

Could the border regiment have any linkage with Hammond or the D'erlon people? *Where are you going with the antimatter, you bastard?*

Jack shuffled around so the boulder hid him from the army vehicles on the road. He stood with a grunt. The sun was hotter than before and getting worse by the minute. He hesitated reentering the sunlight.

Part of him debated staying here until nightfall. A six-mile hike in this heat was going to exhaust him. He wasn't as young as he used to be.

Then Jack thought about Terrell, Phelps and Mrs. King. He put his baseball cap onto his sweaty head and walked into the sunlight.

Sand shifted under his boots. The heat bounced off the ground to bake him. It was like walking in an oven. He yearned for the air-conditioned comfort of the Chief Cherokee. He wanted to close his gritty eyes. Just a few hours of sleep, a cool pool, some watermelon—

Jack pushed the thoughts aside. He needed to plan. He had a gun, his wrist-monitor, a knife, cash, compass, an AT4 and enough food concentrates to last him for days.

What would he do once he reached the oasis? How likely could he rent a car? Stealing one might be dangerous. Possibly, he could pick up a bicycle or motorcycle. Then what would he do? The enemy had stayed a step ahead of him all along the line.

He had to get Carter. If the advisor was compromised... Jack had to get Carter and leave Egypt, maybe get back to Rome. If he did that, though, the antimatter would disappear.

Jack used the sleeve of his shirt, wiping his forehead. He looked up, seeing a vulture soar up there, pacing him. Did the—

Jack shaded his eyes from the sun. Farther away in the distance was a helicopter. Did it belong to the Ninth Border Regiment, to Hammond's people or to the people using the Iranian—D'erlon Enterprises?

That had to be the answer. Hammond was obviously a front. Okay. What should he do about the helo?

Jack watched it, finally deciding he needed an edge. The only way he could get one was to trick them. That was assuming it belonged to the opposition, which he was going to assume all right.

This would be a long shot.

Jack dropped to his knees. Before he completed the illusion, he took out the last water bottle. He poured the cool liquid over his head and soaked the front of his shirt. Only then did he fall onto the burning sand.

Now came the hard part. Jack waited. Several minutes later, he heard the machine. The heat baked him as the helicopter got louder and louder. Now, it was a roar of sound.

Would they land? Yeah, they had to land. That was the whole point. If he could get a free ride to the oasis—

A cold spot grew in the middle of Jack's back. He realized the helicopter had sounded the same for the last five seconds. It had to be hovering in place. The iciness in his back became worse. Finally, ever so slowly, Jack raised his head.

He heard the rifle shot and saw the discharge of smoke from the barrel. A second later, sand kicked up in front of his face, particles striking his cheek. The helicopter hovered two hundred feet above him. The shooter leaned out of the bubble canopy with his left foot on the landing frame, aiming down. The vehicle was a small two-seater, the kind crop-dusters used in the States.

The marksman aimed and fired again. Jack was already moving, lunging to the side. The bullet plowed where he'd just been, kicking up sand by his shoulder.

The unreality of the attack might have slowed down another person's reflexes. Jack Elliot was seldom worried about how things should be. He dealt with the here and now. Did it matter who owned the helo? The shooter up there was trying to kill him. That was enough.

Jack carried a .45 automatic in his shoulder holster. It was possible he could hit something on the helicopter but unlikely.

The shooter turned his head into the bubble canopy, likely telling the pilot to drop a little lower. A helicopter was an uneasy firing platform. Maybe if the man had a fifty-caliber machine gun, he could have hosed enough bullets to hit Jack eventually. Ideally, the shooter should have had a grenade launcher.

As the shooter spoke to the pilot, Jack slid the AT4 from his shoulder. It was a single-shot, disposable rocket launcher firing a HEDP 502.

Jack readied it for firing. A Stinger would have been much better, but Stingers weighed over twice as much as an AT4. The AT4 had already been questionable at fifteen pounds. He'd taken it along as a bunker buster or to blow open a way into a building. Hitting the helicopter up there would be a gamble.

Jack raised the AT4, using the iron sights, aiming practically straight up. The pilot saw him through the bubble.

The two-man machine jerked sharply to the side, no doubt the pilot trying to throw off Jack's aim. The motion caught the shooter by surprise. It appeared he had taken off his seatbelt earlier, maybe in order to get into a better shooting position. That had been ballsy, but what a good shooter often did.

That was costing the man now, though. The helicopter tipped in the shooter's direction. The chopper wobbled before beginning to straighten out.

Clearly, the pilot had reacted badly to Jack's AT4. Jack hesitated firing his weapon. He would only get the one shot and he had to make it count. A miss wouldn't help him any.

Then, the shooter let go of the rifle, likely as he tried to save his balance. The heavy rifle dropped. A moment later, the shooter's foot slipped from the landing frame. The man yelled a second before he began to fall from the machine.

Jack watched the man plummet. The former shooter yelled the entire way down, flailing and finally holding his hands palm outward as if he could stave off the coming impact. The man struck the sand with a heavy sound twenty-five feet from Jack. The man bounced up, flopping in the air and hit again. There was no thrashing about, no crying out. The man just lay there with his head tucked awkwardly under his body, the neck obviously broken.

Carefully, Jack set down the activated AT4. Once he let go of it, Elliot sprinted across the sand, reaching the man's rifle, a bolt action. It still looked good. He picked it up and sighted through the scope.

The helicopter was lifting. It began to juke.

Jack pulled the trigger, sending a slug after the machine. This thing kicked like a son of a bitch. A spark up there in the metal frame told Jack he'd hit something.

The helicopter rotated, juked once more and started back in the direction of the oasis.

Jack knelt on the sand, aiming carefully, firing shot after shot. He was certain he hit the machine several more times.

More smoke began to pour from the helicopter. The machine kept going, though.

Jack lowered the rifle, examining the dead man on the sand. That had to be the whitest man Jack had ever seen.

With a grunt, Jack climbed to his feet. It was time to see if the corpse carried anything that could help him figure out what in the heck was going to happen next.

-40-

TEMPLE OF AMMON
SIWA OASIS

The locked gate blocking Selene from leaving the ancient temple might have worried someone else, but not her. She grabbed the iron bars as high as she could and pressed her feet against them. Then, with a soft grunt, she first grasped one hand higher and then the other. Afterward, she heaved, pulling herself to the top. Carefully, she negotiated the iron points, working herself onto the other side. Finally, she slid down the bars, outside of the gate.

She wanted to sprint away. She didn't know how long the soldier would remain unconscious or if he would bleed to death. It had taken her far too long to figure out how to move the secret wall, reentering the normal ruin.

Moving slowly, she strained to hear voices, more of the shadowy people. If others had been here, wouldn't they have coming running after the gunshots? It was hard to know. She peered around a corner, spying a new Volkswagen beetle parked near the scooter. That seemed like the wrong sort of vehicle for the massive soldier. She didn't see anyone else, nor did she spy another vehicle. The bug had to be his then.

Move, Selene, get the heck out of here. It's time to leave the oasis, leave Egypt as fast as you can. You have to find Claire. She'll know what to do.

Selene pushed away from the wall and hurried to the beetle, trying the driver's side door. It was locked. Racing around to the other side, she found that door was locked as well.

Okay. She couldn't use the Volkswagen. What about the scooter?

She silently berated herself for failing to search the clerk for his keys. Philip wouldn't have forgotten such a fundamental thing.

Should I have shot the soldier, made sure he was dead?

Selene shuddered, wondering how she could think such bloodthirsty thoughts.

A well of panic began to churn in her stomach. Standing around wasn't going to help her any. She ran to the scooter, pushing it off the kickstand. Maybe she couldn't turn it on, but she could use it for a little while. She kept pushing, moving the small machine to the steeply sloped path.

Hopping onto the scooter, Selene steered as it picked up speed. At the bottom of the slope, the speedometer said fifty kilometers per hour. She rode the two-wheeler as it slowed down, willing the scooter to reach the trees. It didn't, stopping a quarter mile short.

Selene hopped off, letting the scooter drop as she paused, thinking. She picked it up, wheeling it to a ditch, and lying it down in the bottom. Selene hurried along the bottom of the ditch, finally climbing onto the road. It was hot. She lacked water—

Selene heard gears grind. Twisting around, she spied the beetle at the top of the hill. Was the soldier inside? Who else could have made the noise?

Selene sprinted for the grove of palm trees. She didn't know how reaching them was going to help her, but having any plan was better than having none.

Glancing back, she saw the beetle picking up speed. The soldier had to be inside. She couldn't see anything distinct past the windshield except for bright red.

I bet that's blood—his!

That meant the soldier had made it inside the Volkswagen. He would be coming for her, if for no other reason than vengeance.

As Selene ran, a vehicle appeared within the grove, coming up the dirt path. It was a white Toyota pickup.

"Hey!" she shouted, waving her arms.

Selene put on a burst of speed. Behind her, the Volkswagen grinded gears. The soldier must be groggy, having trouble driving. He could still run her down or worse, pull out a rifle and shoot her. She'd gotten lucky with the .38. How good would she do a second time? The soldier wore body armor. She just had a suit jacket.

"Hey!" she yelled, waving her arms harder, hoping the driver was a normal person.

The Toyota took the fork, turning toward her instead of continuing through the grove.

Behind her, the beetle swerved back and forth on the road, kicking up dust and making the tires crunch gravel. Selene turned around in time to see the beetle skid off the road and plow into the ditch. The passenger's side lifted up so its front and rear tires gained about three feet of separation from the ground.

Come on, flip, Selene thought.

That didn't happen. Instead, the Volkswagen came down normally, the fall making the car bounce on its springs as it came to a stop. The driver's side door opened. The soldier with his bloody neck and blood-soaked armor staggered out. He had a small, ugly-looking machine gun in his grip. The soldier pulled back the bolt, letting it snap forward. Unsteadily, he aimed at her.

Terror welled in Selene. This was like a zombie movie. She almost froze in fear. At the last moment, she hit the ground. Bullets struck around her. She moaned, watching him, unable to look away.

The soldier sank to his knees. Thank goodness, the little machine gun slipped from his fingers, falling to the ground a second before he crashed atop it.

Selene exhaled, finding herself shaking. She was still alive. He'd missed. This was a miracle. *I have to leave before more show up*—she climbed to her feet.

The Toyota pickup braked beside her. At last, she was getting some luck. The Good Samaritan would surely give her a lift back to the hotel. Dusting her clothes, trying to smile but finding that impossible, Selene turned to the Toyota.

The driver's door opened and the Siwa police captain climbed out. His eyes widened with surprise.

"You," Captain Nasser said, the man she'd hit earlier in the antique store.

Selene felt surreal, as if she was floating. Her mind moved slowly but surely, seeing what she must do. As casually as possible, she put a hand into her jacket pocket, the one with the .38. Before she could do more, the captain unsnapped his holster and drew his pistol.

He aimed the gun her. "Hands up," Nasser said. "You're under arrest for assaulting a Siwa police officer."

-41-

STORAGE SHED
SIWA OASIS

The beast raised its snout as the door closed. The human had left. The creature heard the lock click. That meant the human would be away for some time. Likely, the man would drink more of the substance that caused a stink to exude from his pores and his breath.

The beast rose from where it had pretended to sleep. Since the intruders in the woods, the masters hadn't let it roam free, but had put it in a cage.

The dark eyes shined in the shadows of the storage chamber. It had been traveling in the back of a large vehicle in its cage. At the end of the journey, a woman with a machine with two metal prongs had lifted the cage from the truck and deposited it into this stuffy chamber.

Once again, the beast inspected the padlock of its cage. Each time a human had opened its iron-barred quarters, the creature had watched in a fervent manner. It understood that a *key* opened the padlock and it marveled at the utility of a human hand.

Lifting a front paw, the beast studied it. The paw would never wield a key the way a human could. Perhaps it could grip the end of a key with its teeth. How could it insert the key into the padlock from within the cage, though?

For some time, the beast worried the idea as if it were a mental bone. It could not see an answer. To open the padlock, it would have to be *outside* the cage. If the beast were outside, opening the padlock would no longer matter.

With an eerie whine, the beast lay down. It would continue to wait for an opportunity to escape. It hated the cage.

The beast closed its eyes. Now that the human was gone, it could sleep. When humans were around, it watched. Oh yes, it studied the two-legs, planning and thinking...always thinking about what it would do once free of the hated confinement.

-42-

TEMPLE OF AMMON
SIWA OASIS

Selene held onto the .38 inside her pocket. It was like an anchor to her sanity. All she had to do was squeeze the trigger to shoot Captain Nasser. She had to do that, right? She had to get out of here while she could. More of these people were going to show up. She knew that now.

"You will put your hands *up*," Nasser said in heavily accented English. "Do it this instant or I shall shoot."

Selene hesitated just a moment longer. Coldblooded murder, especially of a police captain—she released the .38 and raised her hands. What had she been thinking?

"Officer," she said in a hoarse voice. Selene was surprised she could think at a time like this. "The antique store clerk is dead. The monster—the man lying by the Volkswagen killed him."

Nasser frowned severely. "Souk is dead?" he asked.

Her mind raced and Selene felt the fear boiling in her, but the world seemed to be moving normally again.

The captain looked to be fifty or so with brown skin like a Pakistani. He was short and slight. It was one of the reasons Selene had believed earlier she'd knocked him out with a single punch. The uniform was pressed and spotless, his tie looked new. His black-polished shoes could have doubled as mirrors.

183

"Why are you driving around in an unmarked pickup?" Selene asked.

"I will do the questioning," Nasser said. He appeared quizzical, troubled.

"Are you taking me to jail?" she asked, trying to hurry this up, to get out of here.

Nasser glanced out at the desert, becoming even more thoughtful. "You are trouble," he said. "Souk is dead and the—" He peered at the Volkswagen before eyeing the fallen soldier.

"Do you know who that is?"

"Proceed," Nasser told her, motioning toward the man with his gun.

Selene wanted to scream. They had to leave. Instead, she forced herself to act calmly. "What are you asking?" she said.

"Walk ahead of me to him," Nasser said. "Before I decide what to—let us see if the man is dead or alive."

Selene couldn't see any way around this. It seemed wisest to play along for the moment.

I have to figure out the cop's angle. He might be one of them.

"Why did you fake being unconscious in the antique shop after I hit you—which was a terrible mistake, by the way."

"You are trouble," Nasser said, as if speaking to himself.

Selene almost lost her balance sliding down the ditch. It forced her to think about what she was doing physically. A copious amount of blood had pooled around the soldier's throat. The man must have lost quite a bit already. It was a wonder he was still alive.

"Oh, this is bad," Nasser said, as he looked at the soldier. "Stand on the other side of him."

Selene obeyed while keeping her hands in the air.

Nasser knelt on a pristine trouser knee, peering at the soldier's throat. The police captain sighed as if this was a great inconvenience.

"Did Souk shoot him?" Nasser asked.

Selene nodded.

Nasser looked up into the sky.

"Do you know who he is?" Selene repeated.

184

As Nasser regarded her, the indecision left his face. "Go to his vehicle. There should be a first aid kit inside. Get it and return here."

It took Selene an extra second before she nodded. She was going to get a second chance. She still had the gun in her pocket.

"Ah, but before you do that, though," Nasser said, as if reading her mind, "please be so good as to remove the pistol from your jacket."

Nasser raised his gun, aiming it at her head.

The strength to resist drained away. Carefully, Selene used her thumb and forefinger to grip the revolver by the barrel. She removed the .38 from her jacket and set the weapon on the ground.

"Excellent," Nasser said. "Now, get the kit."

Selene found it easily enough. As she brought it back, she noticed Nasser speaking into a walkie-talkie. He pointed at the soldier. She nodded.

The police captain watched her as she bandaged the soldier's throat. The wound was raw and ugly, the blood coming out thickly like lava. It was a wonder the soldier had managed to walk out of the temple and make it into his car.

"I'm not sure how long this bandage will hold," she said.

"Souk did not shoot him," Nasser said.

Selene looked up.

"You did it," Nasser said.

Selene said nothing. Everything seemed to be going wrong.

"If it is any consolation," the captain said, "I doubt it will make any difference. But I wish you to understand that I know what you did." He studied her, soon tilting his head.

"What is it now?"

"I have formed an opinion about you," Nasser said. "I will keep this opinion to myself, if you don't mind. Speaking it might shorten my time on Earth."

"Why are we just standing here?" Selene asked. "Are we waiting for someone?"

Nasser didn't bother answering.

That made Selene quail inwardly. The police captain had been in the antique shop and he'd come out here. Did Nasser

185

know that the clerk had believed himself a priest of Ammon? It was possible the cop didn't belong to the Indian Ocean people. How could she convince him about the danger they were all in? Maybe if the captain saw the metal chamber down there he would believe her about other things.

Selene cleared her throat. "What if I told you Souk showed me a modern chamber under the Temple of Ammon with hatches leading even farther into the Earth?"

The captain's lips tightened.

"That's impossible, right?"

"Utterly," Nasser said in a deadpan voice.

"Yet what if I showed you—?"

"You will remain silent," Nasser said. "I am uninterested in your revelations concerning the ancient ground."

That didn't sound good. She needed to know which way the captain leaned. "Who is this man?"

Nasser stared at her for several seconds. He finally nodded, opening his mouth, maybe to tell her.

A heavy engine took that moment to cough in the distance. Nasser took several steps away from the soldier and Selene. He raised the pistol again, gripping it with both hands. He spread his feet in a shooter's stance. Then, he concentrated on her.

A big truck appeared from behind the hill. It looked new and heavy duty. A smiling man with black hair drove it.

Selene's fear redoubled. This had to be more of them. She was trapped. She should have shot the police captain when she had had the chance.

Soon, the big truck parked on the road beside them, releasing its air brakes with a blast of noise. The tailgate came down. Several men in brown fatigues jumped out. One went to the Volkswagen, climbing inside and starting it. The others went to the downed soldier, squatting around him, inspecting the wound and bandage.

As Selene watched helplessly, the one drove the beetle out of the ditch to behind the big truck. Two men slid out long steel ramps. The driver revved the engine and took a running start, driving onto the ramps into the truck bed. Afterward, others laid the soldier onto a stretcher, carrying him up the ditch to the truck and sliding him in the back as well. Those men shoved in the ramps, closed the tailgate and climbed inside, disappearing from view.

"You will come with me," the driver told Selene. He had an obvious French accent.

"Where are we going?" she whispered.

"Questions are forbidden," the Frenchman said.

Selene had one last hope. Maybe she could force the police captain to take her away from them.

She turned to Nasser. "Am I under arrest, Officer?"

The police captain clicked his heels, bowing his head to the Frenchman. "Please, tell her—"

"I assure you this isn't personal," the Frenchman told Nasser, interrupting the policeman. The Frenchman raised a machine pistol, aiming it at the well-pressed uniform.

Nasser tried to speak. Bullets from the machine pistol cut him down before he could say anything. Nasser toppled backward, riddled with slugs.

"*Mon dieu!*" the Frenchman exclaimed, as if surprised. "My gun went off. I'm terribly sorry, Captain. You have my deepest regrets." The smile evaporated as he turned to two others. "Put him in the truck with Marcus. Then check under the temple. Souk is supposed to be down. Bring him up. We'll feed him to the pets with the others."

Selene watched in renewed horror. This was the worst. The cold-bloodedness of the murder—

"Mademoiselle," the Frenchman said, smiling again, "you will ride up front with me, yes?"

Selene was too numbed to nod or speak. One of the others pushed her from behind. Woodenly, she headed for the truck cab.

-43-

SIWA OASIS
EGYPT

Jack trudged across the hot sands. He kept debating shedding something to lighten his load. He carried the heavy rifle with its five bullets. That was the extent of the extra ammo he'd found on the dead man.

The shooter hadn't carried any ID or tags, although he'd had a strange tattoo on the bottom of his left foot.

Jack had thoroughly searched the fallen corpse. He'd not only taken off the boots and socks, but the pants and shirt as well. He'd gone through the garments, using his knife to shred them into ribbons. It had taken time and energy, but he'd needed to find positive information in order to make a wise decision.

Nothing about the shooter had linked him to Hammond. The corpse had smacked of D'erlon Enterprises. The shooter had been big, six-five. He must have weighed over 300 pounds, too, with those muscles. The man had reminded Jack of the big soldier in the Ardennes. The knuckle scars had told Elliot the shooter had fought hand-to-hand before. The act of loosening his seat belt and perching his foot outside the helo told Jack the man had been cocky, probably more than a little reckless.

The heavy sniper rifle was Russian. The AK-47s the Iranians had used against Carter had been Chinese knockoffs. The two-seater had been American.

Jack had no doubt the shooter belonged to the antimatter people. He believed the advisor had taken bribes or could belong to the conspiracy.

Jack halted, took off his baseball cap and wiped his forehead with a shirtsleeve. The oasis had grown from a smudge to the point where he could make out individual trees.

He tugged the cap back onto his sweaty head. He had a raging thirst. But it would be a little while before he was dehydrated. Jack lowered his head as he began to trudge for the trees.

As he strode across the sand, Jack checked his wrist-monitor. Carter's signal had moved a half mile from its last location, but now it was stationary again.

What did the strange tattoo on the bottom of the shooter's left foot mean? It hadn't been a rune. Jack closed his eyes, recalling it. It had been distinctive. After fifteen steps, Jack's eyes flew open. He'd seen the symbol before. His sweaty features hardened with concentration, trying to place it.

He listened to the crunch of his boots. He felt the baking heat. Every once in a while, a faint wind stirred. It would have felt good if it had been a cooling breeze. Instead, it blew the desert heat against his face.

Five minutes later, he heard a faint cry.

Jack stopped, took off his cap, wiped his forehead and looked straight up. A vulture soared in the thermals. Was that the same carrion bird that had circled before the helicopter had showed up?

Screwing the cap onto his head, Jack continued trudging. He still cudgeled his memories, trying to place the tattoo on the bottom of shooter's foot.

Jack's eyebrows rose. He remembered where he'd seen the symbol before. It had been in high school, in a history textbook on ancient Egypt. The symbol had been a hieroglyphic in a pharaoh's tomb.

Why would a starkly white man have a tattoo like that on the bottom of his foot? People didn't get tattoos there. One might mark a prisoner that way, though.

Did it mean something the tattoo had an Egyptian significance?

He was in Egypt. The tattoo was a hieroglyphic. Hammond had brought antimatter to the Siwa Oasis. That all had to mean something, but he had no idea what.

Jack halted abruptly, thinking of something else. The enemy should have sent another helo, sent someone to finish him. They knew he'd survived the first helo. What were they waiting for? Hmm…maybe they knew he was coming to them. How would they know that?

"Of course," Jack muttered.

They'd found the tracking device in Carter. The D'erlon people had already shown they had the most advanced technology on Earth. They might have figured out how to track the chip embedded in him.

Jack took off his baseball cap, wiped his forehead and took out his knife. He was going to have to dig out his own bug.

D17's tech chief had told him no one could track the latest bug. That it was state-of-the-art.

That told Jack he was going up against a better-than-state-of-the-art foe. He was going to have to use his chip to his advantage—that the enemy knew he was coming and Jack knew they knew. What other advantage did he have against them?

Tightening his grip of the knife handle, Jack loosened his belt. Digging this out was going to hurt like a son of a gun…

-44-

STORAGE SHED
SIWA OASIS

Selene was terrified. She was beyond her depth, finding it impossible to stop trembling. The amount of killing she'd witnessed, the causal brutality and murder—

She was a prisoner, sitting on an old wooden chair inside a huge warehouse. Plastic wrist-ties secured her hands behind her back to the chair. Giant wooden crates piled four high created a cul-de-sac around her. She could still see most of the warehouse, bigger than a football field in area. Huge air conditioners hummed, keeping it cool in here. Men hustled, working fast and efficiently.

Two forklifts moved giant wooden crates out of the last of the heavy-duty trucks. There were three of the large trucks parked in here. The forklifts brought each crate to the middle of the building. There, men pried apart the wood with crowbars, revealing a shiny metal container in each one. Obviously, those containers held something critical. A woman in a white lab coat checked each container, studying a screen, tapping keys and reading the screen again.

A leaner man but much like the soldier Selene had throat-shot paced around the metal containers. He wore a black leather jacket and seemed hyper-competent.

Selene bent her head while lifting her right shoulder. She rubbed a cheek against the shoulder because it itched horribly.

The ride to the warehouse had been uneventful. She'd tried to talk to the Frenchman. He'd finally told her to seal her lips or he'd staple them together. After watching him murder Captain Nasser, she had not felt that to be an idle threat.

The warehouse stood in the middle of a palm grove. A fierce-looking guard had walked up to their idling truck, glanced at the Frenchman and pressed a switch. A huge warehouse door rolled up and the Frenchman drove in. He'd hustled Selene to this chair, from where she had watched the activities.

A half hour ago, the Frenchman had instructed a group of Iranian-looking men to sit down on the floor. Several of them had seemed as if they'd wanted to protest. The lean, scary man with the black leather jacket had turned their way.

Without further protest, the Iranians sat on the floor. Afterward, the Frenchman came by with a needle. Roll up the sleeve, swab the skin, jab and inject. The Frenchman had been efficient.

Selene had assumed it must have been a vaccine. She imagined the Iranians had believed the same thing. One by one, they'd lain on the floor. Soon, they twitched and jerked horribly. Now, each had begun to stiffen with rigor mortis.

Now, the Frenchman strode toward her.

Selene's trembling increased. Would he inject her next? She wouldn't beg for life. She would—

"Please," she said, the words spilling out of her despite her best attempt to remain stoic. "Why are you doing these horrible things?"

The Frenchman halted, blinking with surprise. He grinned a moment later. He was lean with dark hair and a hatchet face. The ready smile and the cheery delight in his eyes proclaimed him a sadist.

"Mademoiselle, permit me to introduce myself. I am Monsieur Blanc, although most people call me Ney. My mother," he said with a shrug, "loved the Napoleonic era, naming me for that ass Ney. The bravest of the brave, they called him, but he was a stupid lout of a general. The one time he shined was in Russia during the rout. Ah! What can I say?"

"You killed those men." With her head, Selene pointed out the Iranians.

"Abu Hammond and his smugglers, bah," Ney said. "The world is better off without them. I have committed a noble deed. The chief of the DGSE would pin a medal on me if he could."

"Who?"

"The French CIA, one could say."

"You belong to this DGSE?" Selene asked.

"*Wei.*"

"You're combating terrorists?"

Ney smiled. "Mademoiselle, I am a hero of the human race. I am doing much more than squashing a few mosquitoes. I am liberating us from our petty squabbles and setting humanity on a path to the stars."

Selene stared at him as her trembling increased.

"Why should that upset you?" Ney asked.

"You..." Selene licked her lips. "Were you in the Indian Ocean a few days ago?"

Ney stared at her with conflicting emotions playing across his face. It was a strange performance. Finally, he settled on a grin and spoke in a conspiratorial whisper:

"As a matter of fact, I was there, yes."

Selene wasn't sure whether she believed him or not, but she asked, "You know about the underwater dome?"

He winked at her. "*Wei,* I most certainly do."

Selene swallowed. "Who are you really? What's going on here?"

Ney leaned closer so he hovered over her, whispering, "Tell me about this dome. Tell me what you remember."

She frowned. "Are you testing me?"

He gave a Gallic shrug.

Selene still wondered about his sincerity, but what did it matter anyway. "I...I went down to study an anomaly near the 2004 Indian Ocean quake's epicenter—" she began.

"Ney!" shouted the scary man with the black leather jacket. "Why are you talking to her?"

Ney grew pale as he turned to the man. The French DGSE agent smiled nonetheless. "I'm making sure she's secure, monsieur."

"Stay away from her," the man said, "or I'll be injecting you next."

"As you wish," Ney said. He didn't turn back to Selene, but headed to the twisted corpses on the floor.

Selene stopped trembling. What had just happened? Ney said he'd been in the Indian Ocean a few days ago. But the lean man—he must be in charge here—he'd just told Ney to stay away from her.

Why?

Had Ney been lying? Had he been trying to gleam information from her? Was he really a DGSE agent or had he lied about that too?

I don't know enough to make any judgments. This is bewildering.

Selene squeezed her eyes shut and then opened them wide. If she was going to figure things out, she had to start thinking. It would help to catalog what went on around her.

One of the forklift drivers drove his machine close enough for her to smell the propane energizing it. He didn't even glance at her, but wheeled the forklift so the prongs slid under a wooden slat. With the rev of his engine, he raised a giant wooden crate. Cranking the steering wheel, he turned his forklift and raced for one of the heavy-duty trucks.

He's reloading the vehicles, putting these crates in lieu of the ones he took out.

Selene nodded, filing that away. Across the warehouse, there were several rooms along the other side. She counted three doors, making probably three separate chambers. She had no idea if they were kitchens, restrooms or rest areas.

She spied a white tarp covering something the size of a large truck. She had no idea if it was another vehicle or not. Finally, she noticed a few more large crates on the other end of the warehouse.

Selene's head swayed back. A large electric motor whirled. Then, a section of flooring slid open near the middle of the warehouse. It appeared this place boasted a basement. A vehicle engine revved and a Land Rover drove up. More appeared, twelve altogether.

If it had been busy before, now men scrambled. They loaded ten Land Rovers with the metal containers taken from the heavy-duty trucks. The eleventh vehicle received the throat-shot man on a stretcher. A forklift entered one of the rooms through a larger opening. It returned with a cage. Inside the cage was a large, shaggy hound.

Something about the creature caused Selene to shiver. The dog seemed too self-possessed, if that was possible.

The forklift driver set down the cage. Several men cautiously approached it and the hound. They used poles to lift the cage, working it into the back of the twelfth Land Rover.

Each of the rovers had outsized tires, which indicated desert terrain vehicles.

Soon thereafter, the Land Rovers headed for the front of the warehouse. A large door rolled up. One after another, the vehicles roared away. As soon as the last one departed, the opening closed.

Approximately fifteen minutes later, seven men walked among the Iranian corpses. They knelt or squatted, undressing the dead, and then stripped out of their own clothing, putting on the dead men's clothes. Once finished, the seven dispersed, each going to a heavy-duty truck.

The trucks coughed into life and gears grinded. The big machines inched or jerked toward the main entrance. The opening rose as before and the trucks headed out.

This time, the garage-like door remained open.

The man in the black leather jacket called Ney to him. He pointed at Selene. Ney nodded. The man spoke sharply. Ney nodded once more.

Three men in camouflage gear appeared and strode to one of the separate rooms. They reappeared, helping a stumbling man. He blinked constantly as if his eyes hurt, and he had a thick bandage on the side of his head.

Ney approached her. "It is time," the Frenchmen said.

"Time for what?" Selene asked.

Ney smiled without any warmth. "You are about to learn a secret, mademoiselle. I had to absorb this secret myself. It is a

195

painful process, I assure you. In the end, however, you will find it liberating."

Selene didn't like the sound of this. "Can you be more specific?" she asked.

"Naturally, I could, but I won't, as that would spoil the surprise. Are you ready?"

"No!"

Ney laughed in what appeared to be a good-natured manner. "We will go to a different part of the compound."

"Do you—"

"No more questions, mademoiselle. Stand up. We're taking a ride."

"You'll have to undo this tie. My wrists are connected to the chair."

"Of course," Ney said, coming around, opening a jackknife and cutting the plastic. He put a new tie on her wrists, one free of the old chair.

Selene stood. It amazed her that she no longer trembled. Maybe the anticipation of danger was worse than having to do something. Selene followed the Frenchman to a large SUV.

The three camouflaged soldiers sat inside with the head-bandaged man. Selene scooted in and the woman with the white lab coat forced her to scoot into the middle so she could enter.

There were three rows so there was more than enough room for them. Ney climbed into the driver's seat. He turned the ignition so the engine purred smoothly.

Using the rearview mirror, Ney waited until Selene's gaze met his. "Soon you will be just like me," he said.

"What?" Selene asked, the word coming out like a hoarse cough.

"Quiet," the white-coated woman said. She spoke with a heavy accent and with authority. "We must hurry now. The last agent has almost reached the oasis."

"One of them is still alive?" the head-bandaged man asked.

"Keep him quiet," the woman said.

"Listen, woman," the bandaged man said. It was all he had time to say before one of the soldiers pressed a stun rod against him. The head-bandaged man groaned painfully.

"Easy," the woman told the soldier. "We don't want to damage him."

The soldier removed the rod, although he held it ready for another touch. Maybe for the good of everyone in the SUV, the head-bandaged man didn't give the soldier another reason to shock him.

Through the rearview mirror, Selene noticed Ney giving her a significant glance. Then the Frenchman chuckled as he put his foot on the accelerator, heading for the warehouse's exit.

-45-

SIWA OASIS

Jack rested in the shade of an olive tree. He'd made it to the oasis. He was thirsty, hot and tired. On his monitor, he noticed that they were moving Carter again.

Wherever they're taking him, I bet that's where they mean to trap me.

He watched until they stopped. The process took another ten minutes, which was fine with him, as Jack needed the rest. The spot...was three miles from here.

Wearily, Jack climbed to his feet, slung the Russian rifle onto his shoulder and limped toward the destination. Underneath his pants, he wore a bandage on his left hip and had dried blood on his fingertips. He'd dug out the bug and wrapped it in a piece of cloth, which he had shoved into one of his pockets. After several steps, his pace smoothed out, the self-inflicted wound no longer bothering him as much.

Because of the rifle and the AT4, he risked someone spotting him and calling the Siwa police. Thus, he stayed in the shadows, keeping in the groves when he could. Twice, he passed irrigation water. He wanted to drink, but he didn't trust it. Better to wait until he could find drinkable water. Otherwise, he risked stomach cramps or worse.

This was a gamble all right. The enemy was quite possibly better than he was, certainly better prepared and held every tactical advantage. So be it.

As Elliot trekked, he ate some food, hummed an old rock song to build up his morale and thought about drinking an ice-cold, American restaurant glass of water, the kind with big ice cubes and condensation on the sides. He looked around constantly. The Siwa Oasis was a pretty bleak place. It was too hot and had too much sand. He wondered when the enemy would try to spring their trap against him.

One thing kept troubling Elliot. Why bring antimatter way out here? Was this the destination or was this the safest place D'erlon could think of to store antimatter?

How had they escaped the French inspection? They couldn't have torn down the antimatter-making equipment fast enough, could they?

Jack shrugged. How they had done it didn't matter, not out here anyway. Instead, he needed to figure out a way of rescuing Carter with five rifle bullets, twenty .45 shots and an AT4.

Talk about improvising.

Jack checked his watch. He had a little over two and a half miles to show time, if he was right about their springing the trap at that location. Whichever way he sliced it, soon now, the enemy was going to make his move.

-46-

MASTER BUILDING
SIWA OASIS

The brick structure looked out of place in the oasis. It was a squat, two-story monstrosity with an attached garage. The SUV didn't go into the garage, but stopped in front of the main building.

At the woman's orders, everyone climbed out.

Selene studied the ugly modern structure. It could have belonged in any American professional park. It didn't have any windows, although it had a two-door entrance with a sidewalk leading up to it. On either side of the sidewalk were well-watered flowers.

"What is this place?" Selene asked Ney. "Why am I here?"

"I like her curiosity," Ney told the lab-coated woman.

The tall woman with blond hair shook her head. She was pretty in a severe way, like a Nordic dominatrix, with her hair pulled back in a way that accentuated her eyebrows.

The soldiers helped the brown-skinned American.

The group headed up the sidewalk, Ney walked behind Selene with the Nordic woman in front. The woman produced a key, unlocking a glass door.

"Is anyone else here?" Selene asked.

Ney prodded a knuckle against her back. "No more talking for now, mademoiselle. It will all become clear soon enough. Then, we shall be asking you all manner of questions."

The Nordic woman turned around, staring at Ney.

The Frenchman grew quiet.

They entered a stifling hot main lobby. The woman strode to a set of wall controls, her fingers playing upon them. In seconds, a powerful generator roared into life powering a massive conditioning system that blew cool air into the lobby.

"Ney," the woman said.

The Frenchman went to the American.

"You know what to do," the woman told the three soldiers.

The sergeant nodded, taking out a flat device that looked like a tablet. The other two pulled out long-barreled pistols with silencers.

The Nordic woman checked her watch. "One hour," she said. "Then we need to be on the road."

Ney pushed the head-bandaged American ahead of him. The blond woman marched behind Selene, shoving her in the back, propelling her after the two men.

The group moved to an elevator, Ney pressing a button. It pinged shortly, opening. All four of them moved inside. They rode the elevator up a floor, entering a huge, spacious area that looked like a cross between a science lab and vast dentist's office.

"Sit there," the blond woman told Selene.

Dutifully, Selene sat down on an end chair. There were two rows with six chairs in each.

The woman regarded Selene. "There is no escape for you. If you resist, I will make the process more painful than it has to be."

"How about giving me some idea about what's going on?" Selene asked.

"Questions are a form of resistance," the Nordic woman said. "Do I make myself clear?"

Selene didn't like the woman, but she nodded.

"We'll start with the agent," the woman said.

Ney pushed the American toward a dentist-like chair. Even with his hands tied behind his back, the American resisted. Ney pulled out a buzzer, pressing it against the man's neck.

The American shouted with agony.

"Shall I do it again?" Ney asked cheerfully.

201

The American tried to turn around. Ney pressed the buzzer against him again. This time, the American cried out, collapsing onto the floor.

The woman gave Ney a withering glance.

Ney tried to lift the American back onto his feet. The man was obviously too heavy. The woman strode near. She grabbed an arm and gave Ney a look. The Frenchman grabbed the other arm. They hauled the American to his feet, dragging him toward the chair.

After they had deposited him in it, Ney took out a small blade and cut the hand-ties. The two worked fast, locking thick restraints around the man's ankles, thighs, wrists, biceps and chest, securing him to the chair.

Selene swallowed in a dry throat. She watched carefully, knowing it would be her turn next.

The woman selected a long, rolling, waist-high machine from a group of medical equipment stored in the room and pushed it near the chair. She spread her fingers, rotated her shoulders and began to manipulate the controls as if she was a pianist, clicking switches and pressing buttons.

Several things began to happen at once. A large circler device lowered from the ceiling until it was in front of the unconscious American's face. Other large parabolic dishes surrounded him on all sides.

By craning her neck from her location, Selene could still see the agent behind the man-sized dishes.

"Give him the injection," the woman said.

Ney went to a table, selecting a syringe full of blue substance. The drug he'd injected into the Iranians earlier had been yellow. He marched to the American, swabbed the man's neck, pushing the needle in far too deeply it seemed to Selene.

The American's eyes snapped open. He struggled to move.

"No!" the woman said.

The American didn't listen to her but struggled harder.

She hurried from around her console, grabbing the American's head, holding him immobile. Ney shoved the needle's plunger, putting the blue substance into the man.

"What are you doing to me?" the American shouted.

202

"Calm yourself," the woman said sternly. "It will soon be over."

The American swore at her. She merely observed him. The brown-skinned man began to rave, spitting at the Nordic woman, shouting obscenities.

The woman turned to Ney, smiling. For once, Ney didn't seem amused.

"No jokes or quips for the occasion?" the woman asked.

The Frenchman said nothing.

The woman shrugged, going back to her console.

The American's curses had dwindled and then turned slurry. His eyelids fluttered, and he moaned.

"Does it matter if he has a concussion?" Ney asked with seeming worry.

"It will help speed the process," the woman said. "Now, make sure the geologist doesn't interfere."

Ney strode to Selene, standing guard.

It shocked Selene that the woman knew she was a geologist. That's when she knew beyond a doubt. These had to be the same people who had been in the Indian Ocean, the same who ran the underwater dome. The mystery of the dome tickled her curiosity even here."

What would the underwater dome reveal to her? Would it be magnificent or diabolical?

"It is time," the woman said. She manipulated her console. A painful whine began from the parabolic dishes surrounding the American. The noise rose until it was like a toothache to Selene's ears. Bright colored lights appeared on the dish before the American's face.

His curses cut off altogether. He sat slackly in his prison chair, staring glaze-eyed at the lights.

"Is she trying to hypnotize him?" Selene whispered.

Ney gave Selene a sharp look.

At that point, the American screamed. It was loud and drawn out.

"What is she doing to him?" Selene shouted over the noise.

"Nothing that isn't going to happen to you in a few minutes," Ney said in the oiliest voice that Selene had ever heard.

The American screamed again as if he was getting his mind torn out by the roots. It was vile.

The colored lights swirled faster. Then they flashed in bizarre patterns. It hurt Selene's eyes from here. She couldn't imagine what it would be like right in front of her face.

The American thrashed in his chair and howled like a lost soul.

Tears sprang to Selene's eyes. This was madness. She had to get out of here but couldn't. She was trapped, next in line to lose her mind, it seemed.

-47-

OLIVE GROVE
SIWA OASIS

Jack saw a man in camouflage gear working through the olive tree shadows toward him. Jack spied the long-barreled pistol with a sound suppresser screwed onto the end.

This was interesting. How many of them were there? That would be the biggest determinate to the outcome. If the enemy had a platoon of soldiers, Jack knew he didn't have a chance.

Jack's mouth was bone dry. He was already tired and he was very much alone.

"Okay," he whispered.

Elliot dug the bloody cloth with the tracking chip from his pocket. He shoved it against the base of this tree. This was an excellent spot from which to fight, so they would believe he'd hide here. It also had enough of a shallow area that one of them would have to crawl here to see the cloth.

Jack backed away, his trap baited with their technological advantage. As carefully as possible, he crept through the shadows, taking up a position fifty yards away with a clear field of fire at the baited spot.

Then, Jack waited.

Seven minutes later, he saw one of them again. The camouflaged man crawled through the dirt with his suppressed pistol held in front of him. They must have decided he wasn't coming in the rest of the way. Did they speak to each other?

Yes. Jack saw the man's mouth move. Likely, the commando had a throat-microphone and earbuds.

Lying down, Jack slowly worked the bolt action, sliding one of the precious bullets into the chamber. He had five, all of them in the magazine and now with one in the chamber. He lacked a sound suppresser. This rifle would make a loud noise and they would know exactly where he was once he fired.

He had five shots to take out the enemy commandos. Once he was down to the .45, he wouldn't have any range advantages.

Ah. He saw enemy number two. Neither of them appeared to have a monitor to spy his bug. That meant—

Okay. There was a commando with a monitor. The man stood, peering from around a tree. Elliot kept searching, but he didn't see anyone else. Three against one, those were hard odds but within the realm of the possible.

Jack only had iron sights. He would have liked a scope. Then again, the drop from the helo would have jarred a scope. He'd fired several rounds at the helicopter. That hadn't been enough for him to get used to the Russian rifle, but it was enough to give him a good idea of the weapon's capabilities.

One more time, give me one more—

The commando with the monitor leaned around the tree again, peering at the baited spot.

Jack aimed the rifle and squeezed the trigger—the rifle went off with a loud retort. The butt kicked against his shoulder as the leader stumbled behind the tree. Jack reached up, moved the bolt action, retargeted and fired at a prone commando staring in his direction. The man relaxed as if going to sleep. The problem for the man was he would never wake up again, not with that hole in his head.

Jack repeated the bolt-action motion.

The remaining commando fired at him. The front of the long-barreled pistol rose, came down, rose, came down, rose— slugs whined past Jack's head. One thudded against a tree trunk, another knocked Elliot's cap off his head.

Jack returned fire twice. The commando scrambled up and dove to the side. A Russian round spat debris from an exposed tree root. The other slug had missed.

Four shots are gone. This is my last one. Got make it count.
Jack slithered from his position to a new one.

The commando reappeared from behind the exposed tree root, snapping off several rounds before ducking back behind it. The man's slugs spit dirt from where Jack had been.

The commando came up again.

Jack's rifle cracked, and a hole appeared in the commando's forehead. The man disappeared from view behind the root.

I'm out, Elliot thought. He set down the rifle. He was thirstier than ever, his tongue beginning to feel swollen. Even so, his heart pounded. He knew what he had to do. Five bullets were far too few to take out three trained soldiers. If he thought about this too long—

Elliot scrambled to his feet and sprinted as fast as he could toward the commando with the monitor. As Jack ran, he drew his .45, flipping off the safety. He didn't think he had much time. He—

The other commando reappeared. Blood poured from the side of his head. Jack had hit him all right, but not put him down. The commando had already been raising his weapon when he appeared. Jack watched the trigger finger. It pulled back, and Elliot knew this was it. The commando had him dead to rights.

Only nothing happened. No fire spewed from the barrel. No slug tore into Jack.

The commando had a dud. God did me a favor.

That gave Jack enough time to line up his .45. The first shot tore bark out of the tree. The second slammed into the man's side, throwing him away from the tree, staggering him out of shadow and into the sunlight. Two more trigger pulls put two slugs into the commando's head. Jack had wondered if they wore combat vests, that was why he hadn't been trying for body shots. The commando catapulted onto the soil.

Jack hid behind a tree, waiting. His gun was loud. If others were around, they knew exactly where he was. Lowering himself to his knees and then his belly, Jack crawled to a new position. He scanned the shadows, straining to see or hear the enemy.

Nothing moved. What did that mean?

Jack waited several more minutes. Could he have already slain the squad sent to take him down?

He had a feeling this was it for the moment. No more commandos were out here with him. He'd beaten the helo and now these soldiers. He had to consider round three with the enemy.

Checking his watch, Jack saw that Carter was in the same location, which was very close.

Cursing softy, Jack crawled for the nearest dead commando. He found the corpse in the shadows and figured they were almost the same size. As quick as he could, Jack stripped the dead man of the camouflage gear. He worked fast, taking off his own shirt, shoes and pants.

Elliot hated having to get dressed fast like this. It reminded him when he used to play hockey in his youth. His dad had always been late getting him to the games. That meant Jack had to don his equipment with everyone else waiting on him. Tying the shakes' laces used to make his fingers tingle with anticipation. It was like that now with the camouflage gear.

He knotted his boots' laces. He liked having a suppressed weapon.

Jack went to each commando to make sure he was really dead and to arm himself with extra ammo. He moved swiftly and surely, having done this sort of thing many times before.

Finally, Elliot set out for Carter, trotting along the grove. He saw the brick building and the SUV parked in front. He heard the generator from the garage. According to his watch, Carter was inside the main building.

How many people were in there? Did the SUV indicate the total possibility? Jack had no way of knowing.

What was the right move? Should he go inside? Maybe there were enough enemy gunmen in there to easily take him down. Maybe the place was rigged with traps.

They sent three commandos to kill me. Are they that confident in themselves?

Jack hated indecision. He had to get Carter. It was that simple. He couldn't lose another agent. But if he was playing for the highest stakes with people using super-technology to produce antimatter...

"No," Jack said. He slipped the AT4 off his shoulder. One man against many needed chaos in order to win.

He aimed at the garage and fired the HEDP 502 round. The AT4 operated on the principle of a recoilless rifle. A powerful blast billowed behind him as the hot round hissed out of the tube, speeding at the target. The 502 hit and exploded. Debris blew against the sand and near the building, taking out a swath of flowers.

As the smoke cleared, Jack was up and charging. He had to do this fast, as he was sure enemy reinforcements would be coming soon enough. Before they arrived, he had to grab Carter and—the SUV looked like a good first-stage escape vehicle.

Jack ran into the garage, the .45 aiming in one direction and then another. No one was in here, although a powerful generator made a mind-numbing racket, as a turbine whined at high speed.

Elliot went to the controls. He saw the cutoff switch but hesitated pulling it. He had no advantage other than surprise. To win, he had to maximize his tactical edge because he was just one person against an unknown many.

Jack wasn't Phelps. She could have rigged this—

He shook his head. Phelps was dead. He didn't want to think about her now. The—

"No," he said. Without further ado, he studied the board. He could shut down power or he could give them a high-level energy pulse. He wanted to make things blow up in there and make smoke, carnage—chaos. Logic said they had more people in the building than Carter. Yeah, this was a risk to David, but Jack didn't see how he could win this round without taking crazy risks. That he had made it this far was amazing, but now it was time to take it to the next level.

"How do I do this?"

Jack scowled. Well, if he pressed this switch and added the energy sequence here—

"Just do it, Elliot."

Jack nodded, pressing switches and throwing levers. Then, he grabbed his .45 from where he'd set it down and sprinted out of the garage. He ran with his head down straight for the SUV.

Time was his enemy.

As the generator whined louder and louder, Jack used the handle of his .45, first starring and then smashing the window. He reached in, unlocking the vehicle, opening the door. It had a tricky, anti-theft ignition system.

"No problem there," Jack said from the driver's seat. He knew all about hotwiring.

As Elliot went to work, the generator howled in the garage, the air beginning to vibrate with the noise. Seconds later, the SUV's engine turned over. Jack put it in reverse and stomped on the accelerator, backing up fast, steering, wanting to get around the corner. Just before he did—

Interior explosions shook the two-story building. A moment later, the garage went KA-BOOM! The out-of-control generator blasted itself into annihilation in one titanic fiery detonation, obliterating the garage and hurling debris everywhere.

The SUV swerved around the corner, escaping the main mass of shrapnel. Glass shattered somewhere, although not in the vehicle. The edge of the building that Elliot could see exploded with burst bricks, sending shards flying. A few peppered the car, one starring the front windshield.

Jack slammed on the brakes and ducked. He heard secondary explosions, but the worst of it was over.

How long did he have now?

He opened the driver's side door. Then he sprinted for the front of the building. *Now* it was time to go in and see what he could do for Carter.

-48-

MASTER BUILDING
SIWA OASIS

Selene raised her head from where she lay on the floor. Sparks lit up the cavernous second-story floor with fleeting, horrific images.

The American was still strapped to the dentist-like torture chair. It lay on its side, at least one of the explosions having blown it down. Blood pumped from the American's head. Each sparking flash showed him stock-still, but Selene couldn't tell if he was still alive.

She groaned as she moved her left leg. It hurt. She looked back. In one of the flashes, she saw that the pant leg was torn and she saw bloody flesh. Willing her hand to move, she brushed her fingers over the wound. It wasn't deep, just a bad gash.

Selene laughed quietly, relieved. She couldn't see any sign of Ney or the Nordic woman. Had the blasts slain them? She hoped so.

I have to get out of here.

She realized the plastic ties no longer bound her wrists. When had that happened? She couldn't remember and that bothered her. Had she been knocked unconscious?

Selene touched her forehead and winced in pain. Something had struck her all right. She wondered how long she'd been unconscious.

Move, you idiot. Don't lay here woolgathering.

Selene shoved up to her hands and knees. She crawled for the elevator. Then she stopped, turned around and crawled back to the knocked over chairs. A fire had started by the console of the Nordic woman's machine. It burned enough to give Selene flickering illumination. The book she'd stolen from Souk lay on the floor. The woman had taken the book and set it there before torturing the American.

The tuning fork was still in her hotel room. Maybe Philip had it. What had happened to him?

Selene began crawling again. She didn't trust herself to stand up just yet. What had happened? The deafening whine of the torture devices meant none of them had heard a thing until everything began blowing up.

Why had the machines done that? Either luck had jumped in or the man the three soldiers had been sent to kill had failed. Could the man be from D17 like Forrest Dean?

Reaching the elevator, using the wall to lever to her feet, Selene pressed the button. Nothing happened, so she pressed it again. Finally, it dawned on her that the power was out.

She exhaled with frustration.

Leaning against the wall—she was dizzy—Selene worked around the huge chamber until she came to a door. Pushing the bar, she staggered into a pitch-black stairwell. The air conditioning system hadn't reached here, and it was stuffy hot.

Dare I try to walk down the stairs?

Grabbing a rail, she started down one scary step at a time. She found it difficult to tear her fingers off the railing each time. The dizziness worsened in the heat. She felt like vomiting. She just wanted to close her eyes and go to sleep.

No! Stay awake. Otherwise, you're going to be sitting in that dentist chair soon with these monsters hypnotizing you.

It occurred to her in the hot darkness that would explain Ney Blanc of the DGSE, the French CIA. They had hypnotized him, but sometimes he showed glimpses of the agent he'd been. He tried to figure out what he could for his country.

The mind machine must not always work perfectly, Selene decided. It—

Her foot slid out from under her. She cried out, falling, gripping the railing but sliding down so it hit her underarm hard.

"No, please," she moaned.

She lost her grip, felt herself falling back and worried about hitting her head. She managed to lunge forward, teetering on a stair with her toes. She heard something in front of her then. She shouted in panic, lost her balance and plunged face-first.

In the darkness, a man shouted. A gun boomed just in front of her. She saw the gun's flame. Something hot flashed past her. Was that a bullet? Then she crashed against a person. They both catapulted down the stairs in a tangled mess, tumbling, striking and coming to a landing.

Selene panted in the darkness. She was prone, breathing and very conscious. What had just happened?

Then she realized she lay on a person, a breathing someone. Who was this? She felt a face, and moving down, realized this was a man.

He groaned.

Oh no, she realized what must have happened. This was the person the three soldiers were supposed to kill. He'd won, caused the explosions upstairs—how had he done that? Selene had no idea.

"I'm Dr. Selene Khan," she said.

There was no response.

"Are you okay?" she asked.

The man groaned.

"Who are you?" she asked.

"Elliot," he slurred.

"Are you one of them or a good guy?" As soon as Selene asked it, she thought it a stupid question.

"Carter," he muttered.

"You're Elliot Carter?" she asked.

"No. Up there, Carter, they took David Carter."

"Do you mean the brown-skinned man?"

"Yes." Elliot's voice strengthened just a bit. "Is Carter okay?"

"I think he's dead."

Silence greeted her words.

"Are there others up there?" he asked.

"There was an explosion. I think I'm the only one who lived through it. They had me captive. Please, help me get away from them."

"Why did they capture you?"

Selene blinked. "I know too much. They're some kind of secret society."

"Help me up," the man said, speaking with authority now.

"What are you going to do?"

"Go up there and check on Carter."

"You can't," Selene said. "Others are coming. I think they control the entire oasis. We have to get out of here."

"I can't leave my friend."

"He's dead."

"I have to see that for myself."

"Don't be so stubborn," Selene said. "We have to leave before it's too late."

She pulled away from him. He must have sensed that and grabbed one of her arms. Savagely, she twisted free, pushed up and swayed in the darkness.

"Wait," he gasped.

"Get up," she said.

"My head," he said. "You have to help me up the stairs."

"I'm leaving this madhouse. Are you coming?"

Elliot said nothing.

"Your friend is dead," Selene said again, not sure it was true but wanting help getting away from these people. If this man knew what was in store for them if they were captured, he'd want to get away too.

"I'm hurt," Elliot said.

"You and everyone else," she said.

"Help me stand."

"I'm not going back up there."

"I know. I think you're right. We have to regroup before the reinforcements show up. I got close. Why did you have to fall on me?"

"Why were you sneaking around in the dark? You must have heard me."

"Yeah," he said.

214

"That's no answer."

"Help me stand. We'd better leave while we still can."

Selene agreed with that. She bent down, grabbed him and struggled to help him stand. "How far away is the door? Are there more steps?"

He panted for several seconds. Finally, he said, "Just a few steps away. Go slow. We don't want another spill. We're too badly off as it is."

Selene put one of his arms over her shoulder. Then, she clutched his torso. It was a harrowing few steps down. With too much fumbling, she found the door handle and opened it. Together, they staggered into the lobby. Smoke poured from somewhere. She could see Elliot now. Blood ran down his face. His eyes were unfocused.

"Can you do this?" she asked.

"Keep going," he said in a grim voice. "I have an SUV."

Selene didn't nod or say anything else. She negotiated the lobby for them, eased past the shattered glass door and helped him around the corner to the running SUV.

She deposited him in the passenger side. It was almost cold in the car; the air conditioner had been running long enough. She hurried around, climbed in and slammed the driver's side door shut.

"Which way?" she asked.

Elliot sat with his bloody head pushed back against the backrest. "We need a different vehicle. They're going to know this one. I'm sure they have a GPS device in it."

Selene nodded, frowning. "I know where there's a white pickup. I'm not sure if they did anything with it after murdering the police captain. I don't have the truck keys, though. Can you do anything to start it without a key?"

"Hotwire it, yeah, I can do that."

Selene glanced around, trying to place the Temple of Ammon, which way she should drive. "Right," she said, knowing where to go. "Hang on."

He gripped an armrest. Then, Selene's foot tromped on the accelerator. She wanted to get the heck out of the Siwa Oasis and back to civilization. She didn't ever want to meet these deadly people again—but she wanted to know more than ever the point to all of this. What did a metal, underground room beneath the Temple of Ammon have to do with an underwater dome in the Indian Ocean and these mind-screwing bastards?

PART THREE:
STATION EIGHT

-49-

SAHARA DESERT

The beast lay in its cage in the back of a Land Rover, plotting its escape.

It had traveled with the two men in front throughout the night across bleak terrain. Starlight had shown rocks, scrub and shifting sand and gravel.

Now, the sun glared onto an even grimmer scene: giant sand dunes. The caravan of gasoline-stinking vehicles toiled through the hellish desert-scape.

It was cool in the Land Rover with the air blowing from vents. The men adjusted controls, shifting the flow as they spoke. Each man wore dark sunglasses and camouflage gear.

Twice, the men had stopped the machine. The entire caravan had halted. Under guard, men had opened the back. With dart rifles aimed at it, men had opened the cage, letting it out to urinate and defecate.

The two had shouted at it the one time it had defecated in the back of the Land Rover. It had done so as a test. Normally, the beast would never have soiled its own quarters. It had gauged their reactions, wondering if that could help it in some way to escape.

Despite the coolness in the vehicle, the sun beat down outside. The Land Rover climbed a dune, the balloon tires churning at times across the soft substance.

The beast cocked its head. The men spoke to each other, growing animated. The beast listened more carefully. It had learned much of their speech. From the words, it would seem the caravan neared headquarters.

The beast puzzled that out. This was a desolate, deserted region. Would the two-legs practice more of their hideous experiments on it?

The beast did not care for more needles, more taunting, more games with giant creatures like the Great Danes. It wanted to return to the cool forests. The beast disliked this hot land. Yet...maybe this was the place to try for freedom. It hadn't seen the special posts that would make the noises that caused its collar to give it pain. It seemed that nothing lived in this place. Would the two-legs expect it to try to escape here?

The beast did not think so.

For days, ever since the forest event, it had practiced acting stupidly before humans. The big one, the master from the Forest Land, was hurt. The beast had seen him in one of the other Land Rovers. If ever there was a time to practice deception, it was now. The beast was certain of it.

The two in his vehicle had been afraid of it at first. He had smelled their fear. The beast had cowered before them, especially when they shouted at it. Once, it had even tucked its tail between its hind legs. That had made the leaner of the two laugh at him.

The beast remembered the laughter all right. He'd wanted to sink its teeth into that one's throat. How dare the two-legs laugh? Yet, the beast had come to realize the mockery was good. Because they believed it stupid and frightened, they would likely drop their guard.

An inner voice told the beast now was the time to make its move.

The Land Rover crested the latest dune. The front vehicles in the caravan were already at the bottom of the giant dune, beginning to climb the next one.

The beast rose so its back struck the ceiling of its cage. Then, it began to whine, pacing around in a tight circle.

219

The passenger-side two-legs noticed. The man called out, "Hey, you stupid mutt, sit down. You're making Hans nervous."

The beast wasn't sure of every word, but he had them agitated. Good, maybe this could work.

It whined louder, circling faster.

"What's its problem?" the driver complained.

"Been cooped up too long," the other said.

"We'll be there soon enough."

"It doesn't know that. Maybe it thinks—"

The beast squatted in its cage.

"Hey!" the driver shouted, who looked back through the rearview mirror. "Stop that. Don't stink up the Land Rover, you idiot."

The beast whined, hesitating, wondering if this could possibly work.

"I'm going to stop," the driver said.

"This is a bad spot. We've fallen behind again."

"Doesn't matter," the driver said. "I don't want to have to smell his shit the rest of the way in."

The Land Rover stopped on top of the dune.

"Radio ahead," Hans said.

As the passenger-side man did so, the driver opened a compartment, taking out a long-barreled pistol.

The beast knew about dart guns. They shot a dart that put it to sleep. There were other deadlier guns. For some reason, these two did not want to kill it, but put it to sleep if it tried to escape.

The beast began to pant, unable to hide its excitement. This was the chance it had been waiting for.

"Frederick said we have to hurry," the passenger-side human said.

"Tell that to the animal," Hans said. "Let's do this."

They opened the doors, letting in hot, desert air. Each man walked alongside a different part of the vehicle. Hans opened the back.

"Listen to me, you miserable hound. If you try to run, we're going to shoot you. Then, when the time comes, I'll kick you like you wouldn't believe. So make this quick."

220

"I don't care what the others say," the lean man said. "This beast isn't that smart. It craps in its own cage. You tell me how smart that is."

"Let it out," Hans said. He stepped back, raising the dart gun.

The leaner man unlocked the cage before he too raised his dart pistol.

The beast nosed the cage door, pushing it open. It wagged its tail to show the two how harmless he was.

"I think he's thanking us," the leaner man said.

"Maybe," Hans said.

The beast jumped down onto the sand. It was hot, and the heat gave it an idea. The beast whimpered, jumping back up into the Land Rover.

"Oh, give me a break," Hans said. "Drag it out of there."

"You drag it out."

The beast let its ears droop as it looked at the two men, wagging its tail so it thumped against the cage.

"Stupid bugger," Hans said. He stepped near, grabbing the hound's collar as he lowered his dart pistol.

As quick as a snake, the beast lunged, biting the soft throat. Hans gurgled with terror, bringing up the dart gun reflexively.

The beast leaped, shoving Hans before him while keeping hold of the throat. They rolled onto the sand as its jaws crushed flesh and bones. Even better, the beast heard the leaner man fire his dart. It sank into the sand. The beast shook Hans savagely, tearing out flesh. Then, it whirled around.

"No!" the leaner man shouted, as he worked the pistol. "Please. I never hurt you."

The beast wasn't fooled. It leaped again, crashing against the man, bearing him onto the sand. The man let go of the gun and grabbed for a sheathed knife. The beast killed the man then as it had once slain a Great Dane.

It all happened fast with perfect surprise. Even so, it left the giant hound panting. It peered at the men twitching on the sand. Blood still ran from one torn throat, sinking into the hot desert ground.

Where was it going to find meat and water out here? The beast decided not to worry about it for the moment. It was time to flee, time to—

No, no, it must use its greater reasoning power. It needed to calculate this cleverly.

It slunk to the other side of the Land Rover, glancing down the giant dune. None of the other vehicles had stopped yet. The humans in them didn't seem to realize yet what had happened.

That meant it had a few precious moments.

The beast went around to the driver's side, jumping into the vehicle. It found water bottles. Carefully, it tore one open, drinking. Then, one by one, it took the other bottles outside, burying them for later use.

The beast went back to look at the caravan. Two of the Land Rovers had stopped. The rest continued to travel.

The beast went to the lean corpse. It picked up the knife with its teeth by the handle. Then, laying in the shade of the vehicle, it wedged the handle between its held-together paws.

This was the trick. The beast's collar had always betrayed it. Many times, it had tried to rub off the collar. That had never worked.

Carefully, with the sharp knife held between its paws, the beast sawed at the collar. Once, the knife blade cut its skin. The beast whined, concentrating. Soon, a miracle occurred. The hated collar parted from its throat. The beast stood, shaking itself. The collar flew off, falling onto the sand.

With great care, the beast once more slunk to the Land Rover, studying the other vehicles. Two of them climbed the dune, coming back.

It was time to go. The beast hesitated for a moment. This was a new beginning. It would have to fend for itself now.

Although the beast wanted to bark with joy, it refrained. Instead, it trotted down the opposite side of the dune as the others climbing it. It would have raced away, but it would save its strength in this new and hideous land of blistering sand.

-50-

UNDERGROUND ROOM
LIBYA

Marcus's eyelids fluttered. He lay on his back in a sterile white room that smelled of disinfectants.

I'm in a hospital.

He frowned. Why would he be in a hospital? Why would—

Marcus ground his molars together. He remembered the woman with the .38. He had toyed with Dr. Selene Khan, but she had been made of sterner stuff than he'd realized. She'd moved like greased death in the outer chamber under the Temple of Ammon. Where had she received superior genetics like that? Only a few people could have beaten him as she did. Those few all served Mother.

Inhaling through his nostrils, Marcus gathered his resolve. Dr. Khan had shot him in the throat. It would have killed an ordinary person. He had no doubt of that.

But I'm far from ordinary.

He remembered now. He'd endured the horrible wound, falling, getting up, falling and finally reaching the Volkswagen. He had bled far too much by that point. He'd driven down the site but crashed the vehicle in a ditch. That was the last thing he remembered.

Sitting on the edge of the bed, Marcus examined the room more closely. It had white-painted cabinets and a closet. He noticed that he was nude. Even more startling, there wasn't a scar on his person.

His eyebrows rose. He checked his left thigh. There was no pucker scar from a .357 slug. With his fingertips, he felt the smooth skin. The scar had been seven years old and rough to the touch. Now the wound was gone.

"Mother," Marcus whispered.

Had he finally advanced to the next level? Frederick and that Valkyrie bitch Hela were two of Mother's chosen ones. They'd advanced to a higher level many years ago. Marcus hadn't because—

A lock tumbled in the door.

Am I a prisoner?

The heavy door to his room opened. Hela in her white lab coat walked inside. As always, she'd tied her blond hair back. She acted like an ice goddess, believing herself superior to everyone but Mother.

"Put some clothes on," Hela said, indicating the closet.

Marcus sat where he was, regarding her.

She shrugged after a moment, putting her hands in the lab coat pockets. "There's no need to stretch this out. You're here because you took a life-threatening wound to the throat."

Marcus touched his throat. The skin there was as smooth as the rest of his flesh.

"Mother decided you could still be useful," Hela explained. "But you were dying. Thus, she realized nothing short of the rehabilitator could fix the damage."

"That's a machine?" Marcus asked, having never heard of this *rehabilitator*.

"Your mental acuity is astounding as always," Hela said sarcastically. "Yes, the rehabilitator rebuilds cellular damage, among other things. In order for it to work, we first had to submerge you in a chemical solution for a day. It was a second birth, you could say."

Marcus caught the hint. "What are the side-benefits?"

"Since you were unsurprised just now by the lack of a scar on your throat, you must have surmised that *all* your wounds have finally healed properly. Actually, they re-healed. You must still be tired from the ordeal. Entering the rehabilitator is an exhausting process. Soon, though, you shall feel more invigorated than ever before."

"Why is that?"

"You should have already figured that out," Hela said. She paused as if waiting for him. Finally, she said, "You now have perfect health."

Marcus considered that, his lips spreading into a grin.

"It appears you have surmised a few of the benefits to perfect health," Hela said. "Everyone else's bodies on this mud-ball are always sick. It's a matter of degree, of course. Some are ninety percent well. That's as good as they will ever be, with all sorts of bacteria and germs crawling on and through their person. When they drop to seventy percent well, then they think of themselves as sick. It's all relative. Along with perfect health, you will also be stronger and faster than ever before. Let us hope you will also be smarter and wiser."

If Marcus hadn't felt so weak, he might have been tempted to slide off the bed and slap Hela's smart-aleck mouth. Then he reconsidered the situation. It didn't make sense. Mother operated by two simple formulas, at least regarding them. Success brought reward and failure brought punishment.

The words galled, but Marcus forced them out. "I failed under the Temple of Ammon. Why then has Mother rewarded me with this healing treatment?"

Hela shook her head. "Entering the rehabilitator wasn't a reward."

"You're wrong."

Hela sneered. "You're so literal, so direct. You fail to realize that Mother desires to rub your nose in your failure. She can't do that if you're dead. You must be alive so she can make you understand your inferiority."

Marcus's eyes narrowed as the good feeling evaporated.

"Can you rise above your mediocrity to join the elect, brother? That is the question. That is what you must strive to achieve. You don't even understand the glories just beyond your reach. You have no idea what the New Order will mean to Earth and to those like us."

Through an act of will, Marcus held his tongue.

Hela smiled without warmth. "The damned must toil without reward. You are nearing that state with your repeated failures. Mother has decreed that you have one more chance to redeem yourself."

"I didn't fail in the Ardennes. My wit helped to save the situation."

"Keep telling yourself that, brother. I'm sure it will gladden your heart during your years of bitter slavery."

"Speak plainly," Marcus snapped.

Hela scowled. "I am here to give you a charge. In this, I am Mother's representative. Or do you wish to speak directly with her?"

"I do," Marcus said.

"Then you are a *fool*," Hela said with heat. "Thus, I will saddle you with fools to help you with what could be your final mission in the highest of services."

Once more, Marcus managed to hold his tongue. He was alive because Mother was invincible. She had access to unbelievable technology. And like the mythical Loch Ness Monster, she remained hidden until striking at her time and for her purposes. What did Mother strive to achieve with her technology? It tore at Marcus that he remained in the dark. Why had Mother trusted Hela and Frederick over him? They were smarter in terms of IQ…

There was the answer, and it galled Marcus. But sometimes the race did not go to the quick or the strong—or in this case, to the smart. He would win Mother's good graces. He would show her that he was more useful than this arrogant ice goddess.

"What is my task?" Marcus asked.

"Look at that wall," Hela said, pointing at one.

Marcus turned his head.

On the wall appeared a photo of Jack Elliot. A second later, another appeared of Doctor Selene Khan.

"Your two failures have joined forces," Hela said. "They escaped from the Siwa Oasis."

Marcus understood in a flash. "We captured the woman, didn't we?"

Hela's nostrils pinched together.

"Did she escape from you?" Marcus asked.

Hela removed one of her hands from a pocket. It held a clicker, which she aimed at Marcus.

"I wouldn't do that," Marcus said in a silky tone. "You failed Mother, I'm thinking. That is why she put me in the rehabilitator. She must realize my worth at least in relation to you. Thank you, sister. I'm beginning to think—"

Hela hurled the clicker against a wall, shattering the plastic device.

Marcus raised an eyebrow.

"I'm too tempted to torment you after listening to your smug arrogance."

"Me?" Marcus asked. "What about your arrogance?"

"I pride myself on being coldly logical—"

"That's false pride, sister, as you are far too emotional."

Hela's lips thinned angrily.

Her discomfort gladdened Marcus, and that helped him feel better. He slid off the bed, stretching his arms. "Tell me about Elliot and Khan."

It took a moment before Hela said, "They are together. Mother finds that troubling. We swept Mrs. King of D17 from the board. The Secretary appeared far too curious about us. She also made too many shrewd guesses. No one has done as well...for a long time. It is possible Mrs. King communicated with Elliot before her heart attack. Now Elliot is with Dr. Khan. We had lost track of her. Khan's surfacing in the oasis..."

"You want me to kill them?" Marcus asked.

"Yes, the sooner you do so the better."

"You spoke of fools," Marcus said.

"Ney Blanc of DGSE will assist you, along with David Carter of D17."

"Carter went under the mind scrambler?"

"If he hadn't," Hela said, "he wouldn't be helping you, now would he?"

Marcus ignored the sarcasm, nodding before striding to the closet. He flung it open, taking a pair of briefs, putting them on. Turning to Hela, he asked, "Is Elliot cut off from D17?"

"We're seeing to that."

227

"It would be unwise to make it a broadband situation."

"That's obvious. We don't want the world hunting him, or it's possible they'll capture Elliot, allowing him to talk. No. This is a delicate operation. We are working on convincing D17 to send assassins to take him down. That would be the easiest solution."

"And if D17 decides to capture Elliot and bring him in from the cold?"

"Yes, yes," Hela said, "that's one of the many reasons *you* must find and kill them. By the way, for this assignment, you will have full access to Mother's data net."

Marcus had been reaching for a pair of pants. He froze, turning his head, staring at Hela. Could this be true?

"This is a priority *one* situation," Hela said.

Marcus had a good idea what that meant. Whatever Mother had been working toward all these years must be very close to completion. This was getting more interesting by the second.

He grabbed the pants, putting them on. "When do I start?" Marcus asked.

"You already have."

"Right," he said, as he buckled the belt, reaching for his .55 Knocker next.

-51-

TEHRAN
IRAN

Jack opened his eyes, disoriented and confused. Where was he and how had he gotten here? The last thing he remembered...

Jack groaned. He remembered hours maybe a day of blurry motion and a strong-willed woman helping him. He had vomited several times. When he drank water, he'd vomited that up too. The woman had wanted to take him to a doctor. Instinctively, Jack had refused. The amazing thing was that he'd gotten the woman to agree with him.

An airplane, they had flown on a commercial jet. From where to where, though?

Jack wasn't ready to sit up just yet. He lay on the bed. There was no pillow under his head. He had removed pillows from his existence a long time ago. It helped an old injury in his back if he slept without one.

How long had he slept in this room?

From his prone position, he looked around. The wallpaper in this dump had peeled in places. He noticed a cockroach scurrying up a wall. That's when he saw the single harsh light bulb in the ceiling. A urine stench penetrated his senses then as well.

Instead of making him feel worse, the rundown room made him feel better. He didn't like cockroaches or piss stenches, but he appreciated the woman's intelligence in taking them to a rundown hotel. In this sort of place, people didn't ask questions as quickly. Eventually, everyone got curious. They would have to leave before that happened here.

That still didn't answer the question of where he was.

Jack frowned. What did he remember? They'd left the Siwa Oasis in a white Toyota pickup. That's right. He'd hotwired the machine. In places—like just before they reached an Egyptian army barricade—they went off-road. That had been a risk driving in the desert. The Toyota had lacked an air-conditioner. It had been hot, bumpy and almost over when the woman drove into a saltpan. Jack had climbed out and pushed far too long. He'd passed out somewhere during that time.

The next thing he remembered was noise, lots of shouting, pushing people. Someone, the woman— Selene Khan—had helped him walk in a semi-conscious state through a crowded bazaar. Money exchanged hands. Right, right, the woman pocketed the Egyptian pounds. They no longer had a white pickup because they'd just sold it. They lacked guns, having sold them, too, although Jack had retained a knife. With the money—

"Airplane," Jack whispered. The woman—Selene—bought tickets to—

"Tehran," Jack whispered. "I'm in Tehran."

He vaguely remembered Selene paying custom bribes. They lacked solid IDs. He would have to repair that. Selene had taken a big risk flashing the money. If the wrong airport security official—

Jack shook his head. He remembered enough now. They'd taken a taxi to a crappy part of Tehran. He'd stumbled up the stairs. The elevator must have stopped working years ago. This was a fly-spotted hole in the wall.

Jack smacked his lips. His mouth tasted awful. He tried to rise and fell back. His muscles felt slack. Was this a concussion or had he become ill?

I have to get up.

He tried, but found himself laying back. Soon, his eyes closed. He fell into yet another troubled slumber...

***

When Jack opened his eyes next, the light bulb no longer glared down at him. Someone had pulled a dirty curtain to the side. Sunlight slanted into the room, showing the dust particles in the air. It was hot in here. There must not be any air-conditioning.

How long did I sleep?

However long it had been, he felt better. His head didn't ache like before and his mouth seemed normal.

Slowly, Jack worked up to his elbows. There was a noise to his left. He looked there.

Selene Khan sat in the room's only chair, a patchwork stuffed thing. Her feet were up on the bottom cushion with a book before her face so he couldn't see it. She couldn't see him either. She wore panties, revealing her smooth, long legs. She must have taken off her pants because of the heat.

Whatever the reason, sight of her legs brought a hint of a grin to Elliot's face.

Did she feel his gaze? She lowered the book and caught him grinning. She made a soft sound, closing the book with a snap, putting her feet down and putting the book over her lap.

"Please don't leer at me," she said.

Jack looked down to show he appreciated her. She'd kept them both alive and free when he'd been a mental and physical wreck. Carefully, he swung his legs off the bed, putting his feet on a filthy rug.

"Feeling better?" she asked.

"Some. Thanks, by the way."

"For what?" she asked.

He raised a hand, indicting the room. "For getting us out of Egypt and into Iran," he said.

"You did most of that."

"I did?"

"Don't you remember?"

"No."

"I simply followed your instructions," she said. "They were quite shifty and manipulative. Once, you pared your fingernails with the knife. It convinced the fence, as you called him, to add

231

several hundred pounds to the final price. I'd never have gotten us out of Cairo on my own. What kind of work did you do again?"

"American Intelligence," he said.

"The CIA?"

"No. D17."

"I've...I've never heard of it."

He noticed her hesitation saying that. It seemed as if she had heard about Detachment 17 before, but he let it pass. "Good," he said. "That's partly the point. We're ghosts."

"Ghosts?"

"Only a few people think they've seen us, and no one else believes them."

"Ah," Selene said.

"I could use some water."

Selene reached down, and almost pitched him a water bottle. She stopped herself. "Can you catch?"

"Maybe in another day," he said.

She stood, making Elliot glad he'd said what he had. She looked good. She crossed to him, and this woman knew how to walk in panties.

She shoved the water against his chest, almost knocking him back.

"I told you not to leer at me," she said.

"I know it's hot, but you might want to put some pants on then, because you're definitely worth leering at."

"Is that supposed to be a compliment?"

"Yes," he said. He unscrewed the cap and began to guzzle, draining the bottle before pulling the plastic away.

She took that time to follow his advice, pulling on a pair of wrinkled pants. "I haven't had time to find a Laundromat yet," she said.

"We'll buy new clothes. That will be easier."

"Our money supply is running low."

"You don't have access to more?"

"Actually, I do," Selene said. "Don't you remember telling me it would be a mistake using my ATM card?"

"I don't but I was right."

"What have I gotten mixed up in?" Selene asked.

232

"I don't know. I was hoping you'd know."

"Great!" she said. "I'm more baffled than ever. Even this book hasn't been much help."

"What book?" Elliot asked.

She lifted the notebook she'd been reading.

"What's it about?" he asked.

Selene sat in the stuffed chair, staring at him. "Are you feeling well enough to hear a story?"

"Let me drink more water and go to the rest room. I'll wait a while before eating."

"Sure," she said.

Jack drank another bottle and went to the restroom. When he returned, Selene Khan was standing by the window, staring outside. He wore a shirt and pants, both of them wrinkled from constant wearing.

The bed creaked as he sat on it, leaning against the headboard.

She turned around, the first few buttons undone on her blouse, the skin there shiny from the heat. Selene was beautiful but there was fear in her eyes. It wasn't the frightened doe kind of fear. She had too much inner strength for that. Jack recognized that in her. Besides, despite her telling him he'd done most of the thinking that had gotten them here, she'd been the one who actually did the deeds. That took nerve.

"I don't know whether I can trust you or not," she said.

He nodded, liking that. She was cautious.

"The little I know about these people, maybe this is all an elaborate setup."

"If it is a setup," he said, "why would it matter if you told me what's been happening to you so far? I'd already know."

She considered that, studying him more carefully afterward. "You say you belong to...?"

"D17," he said. "We're strictly hush-hush and we...liquidate more than most."

"You mean kill, don't you?"

"I do."

She nodded. "I can believe that. You scared a few people along the way. Do you remember the thug who tried to rob us?"

233

Jack shook his head.

"Look at your left hand, the knuckles."

He did. The hand was a touch puffy. He fingered the knuckles. They were sore.

"I think the Cairo fence that underpaid us sent the thug after us," Selene said. "In an alleyway, the thug clicked a switchblade and rushed me. You had told me to carry the money and the fence might have heard that. I've never seen someone hit so hard. You vomited on the thug afterward. It was disgusting."

"How about that," Jack said.

"I don't think you're faking any of this. But I've been through a lot. Especially after the underwater dome—" Her scrutiny of him intensified.

"I'd like hear about that," he said.

She walked to the stuffed chair, sitting down. Her fingers intertwined and she bit her lower lip.

"It happened just before Egypt. I lost...I lost most of my friends that day. I saw things that shouldn't exist. Sometimes I wonder if I was hallucinating. It's just too weird, too...impossible."

"That's a good word," Jack said.

"Why?"

"Before I tell you, I want you to tell me what they were doing to you and Carter in that building."

Selene shuddered. "I don't know exactly. They strapped your friend into a dentist chair."

"What?"

Selene explained what had happened on the second floor with the chair, swirling color patterns and the parabolic dishes. She suggested they had been trying to hypnotize Carter.

"What led you to that conclusion?" Jack asked.

She told him about Ney Blanc the DGSE Frenchman and her theory concerning him. That he was under their control but still tried to act like a French secret service agent at times.

"Interesting," Jack said. "Yes. I could see how turning an agent would be critical. That might help explain the Ardennes too."

"What happened it the Ardennes?" she asked.

234

Jack said nothing.

"Is that classified?" she asked.

Jack continued to remain silent as the seconds stretched. Finally, he said, "Your theory about hypnosis seems believable because these people produce antimatter by the gram."

Selene's eyes widened.

"You realize how impossible that is with modern technology?" Jack asked.

"I've read about CERN. They make miniscule particles of antimatter."

"That's right," Jack said. "But D'erlon Enterprises' science is light years ahead of what it should be. I think they also experiment with animals, making them more intelligent."

The strength seemed to go out of her legs. Selene slumped into the stuffed chair, staring straight ahead.

"It seems I touched a nerve," he said.

She nodded slowly.

"We should compare notes," Jack said.

She stared at him.

"If I'm right, I'm cut off from D17."

Selene frowned. "That doesn't sound good. Why would you think that?"

"Mrs. King's heart attack came at precisely the wrong moment. Smith gave us odd instructions on the satellite phone. Ney Blanc is helping them. Throw in mass antimatter production and a genetically altered dog..." Jack frowned. "When you fit it all together it feels as if the Illuminati are real."

"You mean the Illuminati as in a secret conspiracy group?" Selene asked.

"Yes."

"You're making my story seem more believable."

He waited.

Her stomach growled, which seemed to embarrass her. "Let's eat before I tell you about the Indian Ocean."

Jack felt a faint stirring of hunger, so he agreed.

They ate food Selene had bought at an Iranian market: rice with slivers of chicken, along with dried apricots.

Afterward, she told him about the fake Indonesian Navy cutter, Forrest Dean, the fantastic underwater dome and the gun firing an invisible ray that had smoked Forrest's heart, killing him. She told Jack about the tuning fork, how it had stopped a tiger shark from killing her. Selene finished the tale with the man in the speedboat searching for her.

"Interesting," Jack said. "I think—"

Before he could finish, someone outside the room rapped against the door, shouting at them in Farsi.

-52-

TEHRAN
IRAN

"What should we do?" Selene asked.

Jack rubbed his forehead. He felt crappy, but at least he wasn't woozy anymore.

"They sound Iranian," he said. "Make the bed, button your blouse all the way and sit demurely in the stuffed chair."

Someone now banged a fist against the door. The shouting was more insistent.

"Hurry," Jack said over his shoulder. He moved toward the door.

He didn't make it in time. One last shout sounded and another fist-bang. Then, a boot smashed against the door. It tore the lock apart and sent the flimsy door flying inward. Jack had almost reached it, barely halting in time as the swinging door fanned him.

A burly Iranian in an army jacket staggered into the room. He had a baton in his fist.

One look at the man caused Jack to back up. The man was fleshy faced with the arrogant stamp of someone used to pushing people around. He had thick shoulders and strong-looking hands. Another one just like him followed the first into the hotel room. The third man was thinner, older, with a gray beard, wearing robes and a turban.

Jack guessed the older man to be an imam, a Muslim holy man. These men must belong to the ruling government that first came into power during President Carter's time. The Ayatollah Khomeini had started the Muslim Revolution that had ripped Iran from the Shah's grip. Maybe these men were *Basij*, morality police. Wasn't their main goal making sure Iranian women wore the *higab*?

The first burly thug shouted in Farsi.

"I'm sorry," Jack said, trying to sound contrite. "I don't speak Iranian."

The imam spoke a quiet word. The two thugs glanced at him. He blinked in a meaningful manner. Like angry Doberman pinchers, the two baton-wielders stepped back, flanking the older man.

"You are American?" the imam asked in decent English.

"We are, sir," Jack said.

The imam didn't frown or smile. He stared at Jack and then glanced at Selene. "She is wearing a head covering. That is wise."

"We wish to respect Iran's laws," Jack said.

"Your papers are in order?"

Jack licked his lips. He couldn't remember anything about papers.

"Yes," Selene said. "I have our passports."

The imam scowled, perhaps because Selene had spoken without anyone asking her a question first.

Jack turned around. She had risen, taking two passports from her purse. He didn't remember buying these. Had they done that in the Cairo bazaar?

Taking them from her, Jack approached the imam. The first Basiji stepped in front of Jack, blocking the way.

Jack handed the passports to the thug. He turned and gave them to the imam.

The gray-bearded man had been watching Jack the entire time. The imam now opened the first passport. He glanced at it and looked at Selene. Then he opened the second passport and glanced at Jack.

"Hers says Dr. Selene Khan," the imam told Jack. "Yours is Henry Ford."

238

"Yes, sir," Jack said as politely as he could.

"You are not brother and sister," the imam said.

Jack understood his error. This was Iran, ruled by the Shia mullahs under Sharia law, the Muslim ideals as propounded in the ninth century.

The imam spoke a few words in Farsi. The two Basij listened intently. The first one's face twisted into a hard smile.

"She is my niece on my mother's side," Jack said. "I am escorting—"

The imam held up his right hand. "Please, do not lie. That will only compound your sins. You have obviously had sexual relations in this room. The woman has that distinctive flush to her skin and you appear winded. You foreigners with your lustful degeneracy believe you can flout the Prophet's ways. No. I will have to teach you—"

"Please," Jack said, his face twisting into a mask of fear. He made his lower lip tremble. "I-I didn't know... I-I..."

Elliot dropped to his knees and hung his head as if with shame. He shuffled forward, making his body shake as if weeping, his head hanging lower and lower. As he approached the imam, he focused on the feet of the two baton-wielders.

The first Basiji laughed fiercely, muttering in Farsi.

Jack made himself blubber as he bent lower, clutching the imam's knees. The gray-bearded man touched Jack's head, speaking sharply.

Elliot concentrated, tightening his grip, getting his feet under him and thrusting forward, catapulting the older man backward, keeping the legs pinned. The imam fell hard, hitting his head on the way down, thudding onto the carpet.

Jack let go. He was on his stomach now. Rolling onto his back, he saw the first Basiji stare in disbelief at the imam and then Jack.

Elliot waited, needing them to react.

The first Basiji shouted with rage, lifting his baton, charging Jack on the floor. The second also charged. Jack spun on his back, leg whipping the second Basiji. The man cried out, falling forward, taking the brunt of the first thug's baton swing.

Jack scrambled to his feet, tearing the baton from the second Basiji's weakened grip. He thrust the baton like a rapier into the first man's gut, catching him by surprise. The Basiji grunted painfully. Jack swung fast and hard, clubbing the man on the head once, twice, three times. The thug thudded unconscious onto the carpet.

Elliot felt nauseous from the exertion. He didn't have much strength left. With it, he clubbed the second Basiji on the back of the head. The thug struggling to rise thudded onto the carpet. Jack stumbled from him, becoming dizzy. Even so, he hit the imam two times with the baton. The oldster wore a turban, cushioning the blows. Jack wanted to make sure none of them would wake up too soon.

Finally, Jack let the baton hit the carpet. His chest heaved, but he held back the vomit by sheer force of will.

"What have you done?" Selene gasped, who stared at him wild-eyed.

"We're going to check their pockets for money," Jack whispered. "If you find keys, take them. We might have gotten ourselves a vehicle as well. The old man will have the gun. I need it."

"Are you crazy?" Selene asked.

"No. Desperate. There's a difference. Now, hurry." Jack staggered for the bathroom. "I'm going to be sick for a minute. Then I'll help you. We have to get out of here as fast as we can."

-53-

CAIRO
EGYPT

Marcus shook his head as he sat outside at a café, sipping exceptionally potent coffee. What he really would have liked was a glass of red wine. Unfortunately, the Koran frowned on alcohol, and this was Egypt.

The street swarmed with humanity, a mass of sweating bodies surging this way and that. There were too many people in this country. An ant colony would have felt more relaxing than this.

Marcus picked up the cup. Despite the crowding, he'd never felt better physically. Hela had told the truth. Perfect health was astounding. He felt sharp, alive to a vital degree. He was going to find Jack Elliot and Selene Khan. Marcus owed the woman for shooting him in the throat.

He sipped, thinking about that. If she hadn't shot him in the throat, would he have entered the rehabilitator? And if he hadn't entered the rehabilitator, would he be experiencing perfect health right now? Did that mean he owed the woman a favor for shooting him instead of retribution? That was a philosophical quandary. Her attack had forced Mother's hand. Because of the reaction, his mind now purred at high velocity.

I wouldn't have looked at a situation like that before. This is new.

That was interesting, and that—

Marcus lowered the cup onto its saucer. He frowned. Was it possible Mother had...*fiddled* with his mind? How would he know? He might not. He would have to examine his thoughts carefully, comparing and contrasting before and after the rehabilitator.

Marcus didn't like people messing with what was his or having authority over him. That was one of the greatest things about working for Mother. Normally, he was a law onto himself. He did not follow the herd. He was above the herd, moving among them to do as he willed.

I am Marcus.

He self—

A cellphone buzzed, interrupting his thoughts. With a flash of irritation, Marcus withdrew the cell from a coat pocket. The smug Frenchman was calling.

"Yes?" Marcus said.

"I have a lead, monsieur."

"Let's hear it."

"I have uncovered a white Toyota pickup, the one formerly belonging to Captain Nasser."

"And?"

"The owner is proving reluctant to tell me who sold it to him."

"What do I care about that?" Marcus asked.

"Of course, I can pry the information from him. My new friend David Carter is proving a helpful addition to our party."

"Get to the point."

"Monsieur, we jackals have sniffed out the scent. If I am not mistaken, we will need the lion to... to *persuade* the seller to give us what we seek."

Once, Marcus would have looked forward to the task. Now, the idea bored him. He realized, in that instant, that for years he had delved into trivia. With The Day approaching, he needed to sharpen his focus into a laser, aimed at the one thing that mattered.

A chill touched his spine. Marcus glanced to the right and to the left. Then, he looked behind him. He could see nothing troublesome. Yet, the chill persisted.

It dawned on Marcus that he sensed something metaphysical, rather than a physical threat. Why had Mother kept the purpose of The Day from him? Was it her innate love of secrecy or was there something more nefarious going on?

"I want the name," he told Ney.

A pressure was building in Marcus. He could feel it expanding against his consciousness. He sensed…a need for expediency. Yes. He had been dawdling. That was going to stop right here and now.

"*Wei*, monsieur," Ney said. "Do you want—?"

Marcus stood. "I'm coming," he told the Frenchman. "I'll home in on your signal. Be ready to move fast."

***

Marcus sat cross-legged before a Cairo fence. The other wore robes and a turban with puffy-fat features and wisps of a moustache and beard. Several hard-eyed gunmen in Western garb stood against the walls. A large ceiling fan rotated above, mixing the stenches that radiated from their bodies.

The others bathed. That wasn't the problem. The smell of their diseased bodies was what offended Marcus. Was this an aftereffect of perfect health? Did it make normal people odious? Marcus thought that a distinct possibility. Everything had hidden costs—why not perfect health as well?

Ney and Carter stood behind him, having supplied him with the fence's name.

"How can I help you, my friend," the fence, a man by the name of Abdullah Bey, was saying.

Marcus stared at the man, who wouldn't look at him directly. Marcus glanced at the thugs. A few tried to stare him down. Each failed, looking away. They couldn't help the reaction, as much as they fought against it. It was instinctive. He could literally smell their fear of him.

No wonder dogs lunged at frightened people. The beasts knew the person or persons would flee in terror. The old Marcus might have intensified his gaze to watch them squirm. There would have been a slight possibility one of the thugs would have had the courage to draw a gun. But the man's hand would have shaken so badly—

243

"Please," Abdullah said in English. "I am here to help others. How can I be of service to you?"

Marcus nodded and even forced himself to smile. For some reason, that didn't put Abdullah at ease. Producing two photos, Marcus set them on the table between them.

Abdullah leaned forward, looking at the pictures without touching them. For just a moment, he looked up at Marcus before dropping his gaze.

"You are searching for them?" Abdullah Bey asked.

Marcus nodded.

"I am beholden to my patrons, sir. As a man of honor, I am sure you realize this."

Marcus stared at the fence. Prickles of sweat appeared on the man's oily skin. Marcus sighed, tired of the old game. He wanted to get this over with.

Letting his voice drop to a lower level, Marcus said, "Let's make this easy. You and I, we are men of the world. We understand business."

Abdullah Bey nodded a trifle too hastily.

"I have no interest in haggling. Nor do I desire to kill any of you. I wish you peace and long life." Marcus reached into his jacket and took out a bundle of Egyptian pounds, dropping it beside the photos.

Abdullah's eyes widened. "These two...they must be important to you to pay this sum."

"Yes," Marcus said.

A little more sweat oozed onto Abdullah's features. He produced a rag, dabbing his lips. He looked up again at Marcus. The man made a swift appraisal before looking away.

"I sold them passports," the fence said. "The man seemed ill, but he was dangerous."

"Where were they going?" Marcus asked.

"To the airport," Abdullah said. "I'm afraid that is the extent of my knowledge."

"What names did the passports have?"

Abdullah Bey told him.

Marcus breathed deeply, and he wished he hadn't. The stench of fear was strong in the room. Normally, in this kind of hunt, he would now kill everyone in range of the ceiling fan.

244

Today, he decided to practice something different. It wasn't mercy, strictly speaking. It was rather...protocol of his own devising.

I am Marcus.

"Good doing business with you, Abdullah." Marcus stood, turned around and motioned with his head to Ney and Carter.

The Frenchman looked perplexed. He knew what should happen now.

Marcus didn't bother to explain. He marched between his two aides, forcing them apart as he headed for the exit.

Jack Elliot and Selene Khan had fled by plane. Now that he had the passport names, it would simply be a matter of using Mother's data net to see where they had gone.

I'm better than I was. My old ways were sloppy. It's time to become the most efficient man in the world.

-54-

TEHRAN
IRAN

Selene gripped the steering wheel with both hands, telling
herself she could do this. She wore Elliot's baseball cap with
her hair tucked under it and a dark pair of sunglasses.

Jack was slouched in the seat, leaning against the passenger
side door. He had his eyes closed and shivered now and again.
He'd vomited in the hotel room just as he'd said he'd do. He'd
done so again in the car, barely managing to get his head out of
the opened door, vomiting on the street as she drove. She'd
reached over, grabbing his shirt so he wouldn't tumble out of
the moving vehicle.

The car was old and rundown, some crappy Soviet-era
vehicle. It had taken several tries with the ignition to get it
started. The engine made clunking noises as they drove through
Tehran, giving a loud bang now and again. The only lucky
thing was that the tank was full of gas. How far this jalopy
could go, though... Selene didn't want to make any bets. That
wasn't the worst of it. The traffic had that award. The most
aggressive drivers in Tehran had the right of way. It was that
simple.

Tehran was a huge city, and it seemed like there were
thousands of motorcycles on the road. She'd read somewhere
that motorcycles accounted for fifty percent of Tehran's sound
pollution. She could believe it.

"How are you holding up?" Jack asked.

"Me? How are you doing?"

"Don't worry about my end."

She glanced at him. He still had his eyes closed. "Don't open the door while I'm driving, okay?"

"I had to before. Stains—"

"Car stains I can live with," she said. "You tumbling out and killing yourself... They'd put me in jail for sure. I don't want to end up in an Iranian prison, especially not after what you did to those three."

"They'll live," Jack said with a shrug. "Might have headaches for a while, though." The idea seemed to please him.

A driver honked. Selene looked up, swerved and passed a man shaking his fist at her. She slouched a little lower in the seat after that.

"No," Jack told her.

She noticed him staring at her. His eyes were bloodshot.

"Sit up," he said.

"I know how to drive."

"Sit up," he said, sounding dead tired. "Look confident and you'll start to feel confident. We can't afford any timidity out here."

She sat up, if only so he wouldn't exhaust himself telling her what to do.

"Good," he wheezed. "You can't drive with these maniacs if you're cowering. I like that you tucked hair under my cap. To complete your disguise as a man, shake your fist at one of them every once in a while."

"I don't think so."

When he didn't answer, she glanced at him. He'd closed his eyes again.

She weaved through traffic, enduring honks and shouts, realizing several minutes later that it wasn't personal with these drivers. That's just how they drove in the capital of Iran. When in Rome and all that, right?

Feeling slightly more confident, Selene concentrated on heading north. Their plan was flimsy and ill-conceived, but it was all they had. They were heading to the Alamut Mountain in Qazvin Province. The mountain was part of the central

247

Alborz Mountains. They went there because of Souk and his stupid notebook.

She hadn't been able to figure out much of Souk's coded references. The real reason they were going was due to the existence of the metallic chamber under the Temple of Ammon. That gave credence to Souk's ideas. Where had the three hatches in the back led? Did the underground chamber have any connection with the underwater dome in the Indian Ocean?

Jack had spoken about the Illuminati before. She wanted to look that up on the cellphone, understand the reference better. She didn't believe he meant the actual Illuminati, but some kind of conspiracy group.

Wouldn't that be the kind of people who would build secret underwater domes? Who built underground chambers beneath ancient temples? Did that mean the metal chamber was as old as the Temple of Ammon? That didn't have to be the case. But why build it there in the present day? What was the purpose?

Selene mulled over her questions as she left Tehran, heading north as she followed the signs. Maybe an hour later, Jack snorted, raising his head.

"How are you feeling?" Selene asked.

"Dehydrated and…"

She glanced at him. He touched his forehead, wincing as he did so.

"I need rest," he said, "lots of it. But I don't think I'm going to get any for some time." He shrugged. "It doesn't matter."

"Of course it does."

"I've been going in and out, doing some thinking while I've been half-awake."

"And?" she asked.

"I want to hear the rest of your story, everything. Why did you come to Egypt? Well, how did you get out of the Indian Ocean? Didn't you tell me you were a hundred miles from shore?"

"Yes."

"What did you do?"

"Swam, what else could I do?"

Jack stared at her.

"Did I say something wrong?" she asked.

"You could have surrendered to the man trolling in the speedboat."

"They killed my friends and my crew."

"That's the logical conclusion, yes."

"Forget about the man in the speedboat," Selene said. "I want to know who built the underwater dome."

"Sounds like D'erlon Enterprises might have had a hand in that. The dome sounds difficult to construct, especially in secret. Who better to do that than the same people making antimatter by the gram?"

Selene drove in silence for a time. The little car struggled as it climbed a steep hill. Bigger, better cars and trucks passed them.

Right now, they were on Road 49 to the city of Qazvin. The peaks towered in the distance. The mountainous view was breathtaking.

"Look," she said, indicating one of the gauges. "The engine is heating up. I'm not sure we'll make it."

Jack nodded absently. "Why did you pick Egypt? Why didn't you go home and lock the doors after making it to Sumatra?"

"I was too scared to go home. If these people had killed everyone on the *Calypso*, surely they would have found my Kauai address and sent someone to finish me. Besides, Claire had some leads. I decided to follow her route."

"Who's Claire?" Jack asked.

Selene told him about her best friend and how they both worked in the University of Hawaii's Geology Department. She told him more than she intended, even delving into Danny. Maybe it was Jack's head injury keeping him from interrupting too much; or maybe he was simply a good listener. Many men interrupted her too much when she told a story. After a time, he did throw in a comment or two. Mostly, it was to guide her back to the point.

Selene ended up telling him about hums and her theory how they had something to do with interior movement inside the Earth. She explained how the TR-1010 worked, and how Claire had gone to Angkor Wat to test it.

"Angkor Wat," Jack said. "I've heard of that before. What is it again?"

"An old Buddhist temple," she said. "Actually, it started out as a Hindu temple, but it got converted in the past. The temple complex is in Cambodia."

"How old is it?"

"I don't know the exact date. It's a huge tourist attraction."

"Why does a hum occur there?"

Selene laughed. "That's what Claire went to find out."

"I wonder what happened to her," Jack said.

"I phoned and got some weird news about birds."

"Oh?"

"They went crazy, apparently," Selene said, "smashing themselves against the temple during a ceremony, killing themselves by the thousands."

"Why did they do that?"

Selene shook her head. "You hear wild rumors all the time. I…" She glanced at Jack as a thought struck. "Do you suppose the birds might have really gone crazy?"

"Maybe," he said. "Why did your tuning fork scare off the shark?"

"That's a good question. I figured it had something to do with the creature's electroreceptors."

Jack frowned. "What do you mean?"

Selene explained sharks to him, their sensitivity to electric fields, particularly those generated by muscle activity.

Her eyes got big as she stared at him.

"You thought of something," he said.

"Some birds use magnetic fields to help them navigate. Could…could the story about birds committing mass suicide have anything to do with…with magnetics?"

"The tuning fork would indicate so. By the way, do you still have it?"

Selene nodded, pointing at the back seat, her gym bag of accessories. She had buried it in the desert before entering the Siwa Oasis. On their way out of the oasis, she'd dug it up while Jack had fallen asleep.

250

Jack looked thoughtful.

"Now, *you've* thought of something," she said.

"Your friend Claire went to Angkor Wat, an old temple. You went to Egypt, to the Siwa Oasis. Did you visit the Temple of Ammon by any chance?"

"I did." She told him about Souk and the excursion to the temple, down into it, including the unusual underground chamber.

"The chamber is strange," Jack agreed. "Why did you pick Siwa Oasis?"

She explained about the recent hum that had developed. Claire had talked to Souk before and had planned to go there after Angkor Wat. Selene had hoped to find her friend already there.

"We're seeing a theme," Jack said, "ancient temples. Why did Souk suggest you visit Alamut Mountain?"

"Maybe I'd better tell you everything he told me. It got pretty weird at the end. I'm not sure we should trust what he said."

"Go ahead," Jack said. "I'm listening."

Selene told him about the ancient priestess who was supposed to have lived over 200 years, messing with Cambyses the Persian conqueror and Alexander the Great. Selene added that Souk had told her he realized the existence of the shadowy organization after visiting Alamut Mountain in northwestern Iran.

"Souk does sound as if he was mental," Jack said, "although he was right about a conspiracy."

"You don't believe his stories about Alexander and Cambyses?"

"They're ancient history. This is now. Hundreds of grams of antimatter and underwater domes sound like a conspiracy to me."

"What do you think is under the Temple of Ammon?" Selene asked. "Why did the birds go crazy at Angkor Wat? If there is a global conspiracy, when did it start?"

Jack didn't have an answer for that.

251

Selene drove in silence for a time, thinking. She noticed that Jack had closed his eyes again. When he moved, she spoke up:

"Do you think you can drive for a while?"

He took his time answering, finally saying, "I know you're tired, but I don't think that's a good idea right now. If you need a break, pull over."

She pulled onto the side of the road. They were in rugged terrain. It felt good getting out and stretching. It was hotter here than in Tehran, she noticed. She would have figured it would be cooler in the higher elevation. She walked around the car, finally climbing back in.

Jack had closed his eyes and snored softly.

Instead of starting again or trying to nap, Selene took out her cellphone, soon surfing the internet. She found information about the Old Man and Castle Alamut. It was wild. Back in the day, the place had been home to the Assassins, a medieval Shia cult.

Her interest in reaching Alamut Castle grew. She put away the cell and started the car. Crunching over gravel, she eased back onto the road. The engine began knocking. She gave it more gas. That made it lurch, the engine knock louder and threaten to quit on them. She babied the car for a bit, slowing down. Finally, the old engine decided it still had a few more miles left in it.

Selene noticed Jack was awake. "You're never going to believe what I found on the internet while you napped."

"What did you find?"

"Have you ever heard of the Assassins?"

"Of course," he said. "They're contract killers."

"That's what an assassin is now. Back in the Middle Ages it was a group of Shia Muslims. Back in 1090 A.D. a man by the name of Hasan-i Sabbah captured Alamut Castle, never leaving it again. He started the Nizari Ismaili State."

Jack yawned.

"Stay with me," Selene said. "The Ismaili never had a big country, but a bunch of hilltop castles controlling certain areas. Alamut Castle was the strongest. After a time, it sported one of

252

the biggest libraries around. Scholars and philosophers would go to Alamut. I bet medieval scientists hung out there as well."

"Okay."

"Alamut means 'Eagle's Nest.' Since the Ismaili lacked armies, they did their fighting through assassins, trained men called *fida'i*, which meant self-sacrificing agents. Anyway, the Old Man of the Mountain ran these assassins. Sometimes, to convince others to leave them alone, an assassin would sneak into an enemy leader's bedroom and leave a wavy dagger on the pillow, saying in effect, 'See, we could have killed you if we wanted.'"

"Clever," Jack said. "I like it. Did it work?"

"According to the article I read, it did for a time."

"What happened in the end?" Jack asked.

"Ever hear of Hulagu Khan?"

"One of your relatives?" Jack asked.

"I doubt it. He was a grandson or great-grandson of Genghis Khan. Anyway, he marched through this area in 1256. Hulagu destroyed the Assassins, besieging Alamut Castle until they surrendered. In the process, the great castle library was burned down."

"This is the Alamut Mountain Souk visited?" Jack asked.

Selene nodded.

"The leader of the castle—"

"Of the Ismaili," Selene corrected.

"He was called the Old Man of the Mountain?"

"There's a legend he would drug his best assassins," Selene said. "When they woke up, the assassin found himself in a perfect garden with grapes, wine and nubile women to use. After a time of enjoying paradise, the young man would find himself drugged once more. Upon awaking, the Old Man told him he had tasted paradise, and he could return, but only if he followed the Old Man's instructions to the letter."

"That's dirty," Jack said.

"By what I read, it worked. The Old Man's assassins were fearless, striking terror into the heart of Saladin, for instance. That's the Muslim leader who fought Richard the Lion-Hearted during the Third Crusade."

Jack glanced at her. "For a geologist, you certainly know a lot about history."

Selene felt herself blushing. She was curious about things.

At that moment, a loud *retort* from outside gave Selene a second's warning. Then, the steering wheel spun out of her grip. The car swerved with the tires skidding across the road.

-55-

NORTHWESTERN IRAN

Jack watched as Selene clutched the steering wheel, fighting for control. He knew what had happened. The right front tire had blown. Under normal circumstances that wouldn't have been too much of a problem. This wasn't ordinary.

They were in the hills, the road curving back and forth, now beside a mountain and now near an edge that tumbled down thirty or forty feet. The car skidded toward an edge.

"Hang on!" Selene shouted.

Jack grabbed the dashboard.

The tires skidded as Selene slammed on the brakes. The steering wheel jerked back and forth in her white-knuckled hands. She kept the car from going sideways over the edge. They would have tumbled over and over then. Instead, the front tires went over, the car tipping almost straight down. The rear end followed the front, and Selene fought the steering wheel as they plunged down the side of the hill. It was a wild, jerky, boulder-slamming ride. Metal screeched as she barely avoided crashing head on into a boulder. A sharp turn to the right kept them from a huge divot that would have flipped the car for sure. They rode out the steepest part, gravel crunching and another nearly bald tire exploding. With a sharp jerk that hurled Jack against his shoulder strap, they came to an abrupt stop.

He panted. He was in one piece. Turning, wincing at a pain in his neck, Jack saw Selene pry her fingers from the steering wheel.

"Are you okay?" he asked.

"I don't know."

He studied her. She was pale and trembling.

"We can't stay here," he said.

She brushed hair from her eyes. "That…that was nuts."

Jack unbuckled his seat belt and tried the door handle. It moved, but the door refused to open. It was crushed into place. "We'll have to go out your side," he said.

"You want to give me a minute?" she asked.

"I'd love to," he said. "But we don't have the luxury. We have no idea what the authorities are like in Iran. Once they check the registration…"

"Right," she said. She undid her seat belt, twisted around and grabbed her gym bag from the back seat. Afterward, she opened the door as if nothing was the matter.

He winced climbing over her seat.

"You look stiff," she said, giving him a critical once-over. "Are you okay?"

"I don't have a choice. Let's go."

"Where are we headed?" she asked. "What's the plan now?"

"It hasn't changed," he said. "We're heading to Alamut Mountain."

"Ah…we don't have a car anymore. I screwed up."

"No. You did great. You kept us in one piece. That was fantastic driving."

She gave him a grateful look.

"We'll hitch a ride or steal another car," he said. "The thing is to get moving so nobody links us with this wreck."

"We'll have to hike a long way for that."

Jack eyed the wreck. "At least there's no smoke trickling into the sky. That's in our favor. People on the road aren't going to see this right away either. We might have caught ourselves a break."

Selene said nothing.

"Let's go," he said, trying to sound more confident than he felt. His neck was beginning to hurt and the strap had strained his chest. The worst, though, was his head. It was beginning to throb again. A long hike up and down these hills wasn't going to help it.

"All right," she said, turning away, scampering over some rocks.

Jack picked his path more carefully. It took him longer crossing the rocks, too. Not only did his head throb, he was beginning to feel dizzy and nauseous again. Soon, he was in his own world, climbing, wheezing, pausing and forcing himself to start again.

"Jack."

He heard the word, but it didn't penetrate his fuzzy world of exertion.

"Jack Elliot."

Hmm, this rock would take a bit of work. Something stopped him. He tried to keep going.

"Jack, look at me."

He focused, and he made out a woman staring in his face. She was good looking. He liked the hair.

"You have to sit down," the woman said, sounding as if she was far away.

"Move," he said. "We have to keep moving."

"I hear a car coming. Maybe I can flag it down."

For a moment, his thoughts cleared. "Don't do that," he said.

Selene stared into his eyes. "You can't keep hiking in your condition. You're beat."

"No," he whispered intently. "I am not beat."

She gave him a shrewd study. He hadn't liked her saying that. This man didn't like to lose, ever.

"I think you'd tell me that no matter what shape you were in," Selene said.

"Listen to me," he said. "Let the car pass. We can rest and then climb back up to the road. We'll catch a ride later. You have to trust me."

"I would, but not when your eyes are moving crazily like that. You need some real rest, Jack. If you don't rest, you're not going to be any good to me later when I need you to fight."

She had a point, but he didn't trust this car. "Listen, you're the brains to figuring out this puzzle. I'm counting on you."

"Okay?"

"I'm the muscle. I'm the movement specialist. You have to listen to me when it comes to getting from C to D. Do you understand?"

"We're in deep shit, aren't we, Jack? Sorry. I don't like talking like that. But we are in trouble, right?"

He decided to tell her the truth. "Yes," he said.

"Okay, Jack. I'll listen to you as long as you don't lie to me."

"Deal. Now, let's go."

He moved uphill with her help. Splotches appeared before his eyes, making it harder to see. He ignored those. The worst part of the climb was coming.

"Oh, oh," she said.

"What's wrong?"

"I hear a truck stopping. I think someone spotted the wreck. What do we do now? They're going to know we wrecked the car. I hear a truck door slamming. What do we do?"

As Jack stood there trying to think, he figured that was a damn good question.

-56-

NORTHWESTERN IRAN

The goats kept staring at Selene, bleating from time to time.

Jack and she leaned against the back of a cab, sitting in an ancient truck bed with a dozen goats watching. The machine rattled constantly, swaying from side to side. Old crisscrossed slats kept everyone from falling out of the truck bed. The highway had gotten steeper, and the old truck kept grinding gears as if searching for exactly the right one.

A few times, Selene looked up as the old woman in the cab tapped on the window, smiling encouragingly at them outside. Her husband, an even older person with threadbare garments, drove the truck. They'd been on the highway for twenty minutes already.

The old people didn't speak English and neither Jack nor she spoke Farsi. They had communicated by sign language. Finally, the old man had gestured at the back of his truck. It had been a heck of a time getting Elliot up there. He had groaned, stretching as he climbed, and for a moment, the gun tucked in the back of his pants had been visible. Neither of the old people had seemed to care about it.

Presently, Jack snored softly beside her.

Selene had been watching the terrain, noting the thickening trees. It felt quite a bit hotter than earlier. Was that right for this time of year up in the hills?

Selene studied the clouds. It must have been at least a hundred degrees. At least it wasn't humid.

What would the old people say once they reached a town? Should she wake up Elliot and ask him their plan? No. The man needed rest. He also needed medical attention. He must have a concussion. Clearly, Elliot was one of those tough guys that never quit. He was so deadly serious. What had happened to him to make him like that? She couldn't recall having seen him smile once.

Enough about Elliot, already, I need to figure out a plan.

She had one lead: Souk's notebook. It behooved her to study it until it made sense. Souk had been a nut, all right. He…

"He found a hidden chamber under the Temple of Ammon."

That was the critical fact to remember. How had he found the chamber in the first place? He'd been a priest of Ammon. Okay. That kind of made sense. He'd been part of an ancient fraternity that had passed along ancient and rather harmless secrets. This one secret had involved hidden passages.

Selene zipped open the gym bag, taking out the notebook. She zipped the bag closed so the old woman wouldn't see the tuning fork device inside.

She paged through the notebook, going over every line. She had spent countless hours in her life reading, endless reading. She agreed with Nikola Tesla when he'd said, "Of all things I like books best." The miles slid away as she perused the coded writing. This wasn't making any sense, this—

"Hello," Selene said, softly. This was a diagram, right? She'd been thinking it was of the Temple of Ammon in Siwa. Now, she wasn't so sure. This was on the page…

She flipped back several pages, reading with renewed interest. Yes. These pages concerned Alamut Castle, not the oasis temple. But that meant—

Selene flipped back to the diagram. Yes! It showed another hidden chamber. Was this a metal chamber or an old secret passage the real Old Man of the Mountain had built in his Assassin hideaway?

260

Lines radiated downward from the diagram. Did that indicate some deep underground structure? Would that link it to the underwater dome in the Indian Ocean?

The questions flooded her mind. She knew so little. What if she went with the idea of high technology, assuming these people could do things no one else could on Earth?

"How did they get the knowledge?" she whispered.

Selene glanced at Elliot, wanting to wake him up more than ever. She wasn't sure she wanted to go there in her thinking. People—especially conspiracy theorists—could come up with some wild ideas.

She glared up at the sun.

How about we catch a break for once?

She shifted around Elliot, sliding into the little shade she could. Once properly situated, she studied the diagram in the notebook. It was too bad she couldn't have spent more time with Souk. Could he have discovered the metal chamber under the Temple of Ammon because the Old Man of the Mountain had shown him one at Alamut Castle?

Was that a silly idea?

Selene closed the book. Maybe it was time to toss out the idea of any of this being crazy or too far-fetched. An underwater dome, mass bird suicide, a secret chamber under an ancient temple, new hums and 900 grams of antimatter secretly produced in the Ardennes...

Maybe the only right answers were wild. *What have we stumbled onto anyway?*

Selene glanced at Elliot. He frowned in his sleep. What did he dream about? She bet it wasn't nice.

The truck lurched. A few of the goats bleated in complaint. The old woman tapped on the back glass. Selene looked up at her. For once, the old woman wasn't smiling.

With a bad feeling creeping into her, Selene half rose and peered through the windshield. Several cars blocked the road with military men holding machine guns.

The ancient truck swayed as the brakes squealed. They were coming to a stop. What did the Iranian military men want with the truck?

"Selene," Jack whispered.

She looked down at him.

"Why are we're stopping?" he asked.

She told him about the roadblock and the Iranian soldier.

"Listen to me," he whispered.

She slid down beside him. "What?"

"Listen," he said, with greater urgency.

"What is it? Tell me already."

"If we're separated, don't say anything."

"What?" she asked. Fear began to trickle its oily tendrils into her stomach.

"Tell them I've forbidden you to talk," Jack said. "They'll understand that."

"I don't understand."

She might as well have spoken to a corpse. Elliot was unconscious again. Had he been delirious or did the man actually have a plan? If she kept quiet, it wouldn't spoil anything he made up on the spot. Had that been his idea?

Oh, this was terrible.

-57-

REGION 1 MILITARY DISTRICT
IRAN

Two burly Iranian soldiers deposited Jack on a chair inside a detention cell. A table was before him. On the other side, an officer sat on his chair sideways, with his legs crossed at the knees. The officer smoked a cigarette.

Jack rested his chin on his chest. They hadn't beaten him yet. They wanted answers not just a mewling pile of bruised flesh. He should have ditched the revolver when he had the chance. Jack was certain they had used it to trace his attack against the Basij in the Tehran hotel room.

The officer spoke in Farsi. The two soldiers left the cell, closing the door behind them.

"Well, well, well," the officer said to Jack with a British accent. "What am I to make of you?"

Jack raised his chin, focusing on the man. He wasn't a combat officer, but belonged to the Intelligence Unit of the Islamic Republic of Iran Army. The man was a captain, and he had a shrewd manner about him.

The captain took a drag on his cigarette before removing it from his lips, exhaling smoke.

"I can understand your hesitation to speak," the captain said. "Once our session is over..." He shook his head. "Your next few days will be an ordeal, I assure you."

"Why's that?" Jack asked.

The captain smiled in an urbane manner. "There's little to like about you other than your efficiency. You strike me as a brutal, dishonest man."

"I have my faults."

"Yes, one of them is poor timing. Tell me. How did you acquire your firearm?"

"I took it from a Basiji in Tehran," Jack said. "First, I beat the man into unconsciousness."

The captain's eyebrows rose. "I see. You're hoping to startle me with your honesty. Why did you take it from him?"

"I thought I'd need it."

"Let me rephrase the question. Why did you attack the Basij team, putting two of them in the hospital?"

"They broke into my hotel room. I believed they were getting ready to beat us, maybe jail us."

"I doubt that. Maybe they would have fined you, pushed you around—"

"It hardly matters what they would have done," Jack said. "They never got the chance. Do motives really matter in this?"

"For you, an American, in this situation, I'm afraid not. I doubt you shall ever leave Iran. I'm curious about your reason for coming."

Jack began to recite a litany of numbers.

The Intelligence officer crushed the stub of his cigarette in an ashtray. "What am I to make of those numbers?"

"Punch them into your cellphone. Ask the person who answers what you're supposed to do with Viktor Konev."

The captain frowned. "If I called the number, who would I reach?"

"IZENOV," Jack said.

"Can you elaborate?"

"They're a Russian consortium."

"Please," the captain said. "Do not strain my credulity. You are an American."

"What is an American these days?" Jack asked. "Many Russians have immigrated to North America. I could easily be working for IZENOV."

"I see. You are claiming to be a Russian in the company of an American university professor?"

"Have you taken a good look at her? You bet I'm in her company. I have plans for her, and they don't involve her university degree."

The captain's frown deepened. "Why are you in Iran?"

"I'm taking the long way home."

The captain took out a half-crumpled pack of cigarettes, shaking one out. "Do you smoke?"

"No."

"You are an American for sure, my friend. I've never met a Russian who didn't smoke."

"Just call the number," Jack said. "I think you'll be impressed by the results."

The captain lit the cigarette with a match and sucked on it thoughtfully. "I suspect you of being an American spy. I have a feeling for these things."

"I'm sure you're as clever as Hell, Captain. If you call the number, however, it's possible you will find it an enriching experience."

"You are attempting to bribe me?"

"You think I'm one thing, but I'm not. Is it so terrible if IZENOV reimburses you for your time?

"I am an Iranian Intelligence officer. You have assaulted fellow nationals."

"Have the Basij and the Revolutionary Guard ever treated *you* with respect?"

The captain smiled coldly. He stood, gave Jack a fierce scrutiny, and headed out a different door than the one Jack had entered.

Elliot slouched in his chair, exhausted by the exchange. What had happened to Selene? It seemed he had misjudged the Intelligence captain. This was a fine mess. Maybe it was best the captain hadn't agreed to phone the number. His cover in IZENOV might not bear close inspection.

The minutes passed and no one came to get him. Finally, Jack put his arms on the table and lay his head on them. He closed his eyes, unsure of how long he fell asleep.

"Time to get up, Viktor."

Groggily, Jack raised his head.

"Would you look at that," a thickset Russian said, a large man with a shock of red hair. "He's so sleepy he doesn't even recognize his good friend, Ivan Rodin. It's time to go, Viktor. The boss wants a rundown on your latest activities."

"Of course," Jack said, standing.

"One thing," the Russian said. "We're leaving the girl behind. You weren't supposed to bring her, remember?"

Jack stiffened. "The girl comes, Ivan. The boss said—"

The Russian laughed. "Didn't I tell you he would be stubborn about her?"

The Intelligence captain said nothing, his features deadpan as he watched from the door.

"Let us include the woman," the Russian told the Intelligence captain.

The captain's lips thinned. "I'll see what I can do."

"I'll double the price—"

"Please," the captain said, in a strained voice. "Let us keep this..." The officer glanced right and left.

"I understand," the Russian said, as he brushed the side of his nose.

"You may leave with your friend," the captain told Jack. "Whether you get your woman...that remains to be seen."

LEARJET 85
EASTERN MEDITERRANEAN

Marcus scowled as the private jet began to shake. This was the second time the pilot had hit turbulence.

The intercom came on. The pilot spoke, and he sounded nervous. "Please fasten your seatbelts. This…this could get rough."

Marcus clicked his seatbelt into place. He heard Ney and Carter do likewise.

The jet rose sharply, and it shook, vibrating the entire fuselage. A glance outside the window showed the wing shaking more than Marcus cared to see.

Had Mother given him an inferior pilot?

He endured the ride. Suddenly, the plane plummeted. Marcus clutched the armrests. Fear began as a pin-dot in his chest. He seldom felt such helplessness, finding it a repugnant sensation.

He liked facing problems he could stomp, shoot or cut with a knife. Waiting on others to perform skillfully enough to save his life—

The Learjet evened out. The shaking lessened and then quit altogether.

Marcus unclicked the seatbelt, lurching to his feet, striding toward the cockpit. He yanked open the door, stepping into the cramped quarters. The pilot and navigator each gave him a worried glance.

"You're supposed to be the best," Marcus said, unsure if that was true. It had been in the past. He'd assumed it would be so today.

The pilot was a rugged-looking individual with a five o'clock shadow. "I am the best, sir," he said with an Israeli accent.

"What do you call this latest performance?"

The pilot wouldn't meet Marcus's gaze. The man even hunched his head before shaking it. "I don't understand these weather patterns, sir."

"Then how can you be the best?" Marcus snapped.

The pilot glanced at the navigator. The navigator nodded with encouragement.

"Sir," the pilot told Marcus. "I can't explain this. We're...we're hitting pockets of— Well, I have to call them pockets of superheated air."

"Meaning what?" Marcus asked.

"Exactly that, sir," the pilot said, "a gush of superheated air as from some...giant kettle."

"How is that possible?"

"I don't know. But that isn't all. The weather reports coming out of Athens, Istanbul, Tehran—" He glanced at the navigator before telling Marcus, "Sir, it's hot out there."

"So what?" Marcus said.

"Hotter than it should be," the pilot said. "It's one hundred and ten degrees outside and rising."

"It's always hot in summer."

"Not that hot over the Eastern Mediterranean."

"What are you suggesting?" Marcus asked.

The pilot looked Marcus in the eye. "Sir, I'm suggesting that this is strange, unexplainable weather, particularly with the pockets of superheated air."

"How superheated do you mean?"

"One hundred and thirty degrees Fahrenheit," the pilot said.

Marcus stared at the pilot until the man dropped his gaze, turning forward. The pin-dot of fear reappeared. Marcus disliked it now as much as he had the first time. It was time to squash the fear and take control of the situation. He wanted a confident pilot.

"If you're the best, as you claim, trust your instincts. Figure out the pattern here, even if it seems odd to you. Adjust, and react accordingly."

"Yes, sir, that's good advice. Thank you."

"Inform me if you discover...other anomalies," Marcus ordered.

"Yes, sir," the pilot said. "I'll do that."

Marcus retreated, closing the door behind him. Thoughtfully, he returned to his seat.

Ney and Carter had gone back to watching their respective movies on their iPads, listening to earphones.

Could the hotter-than-normal weather and these pockets of superheated air have anything to do with The Day?

The antimatter they'd manufactured at the D'erlon Plant had been transported to the hidden stations scattered throughout the planet. Marcus had no idea what Mother's technologists did with the antimatter once it arrived.

Mother was the ultimate ghost, compartmentalizing everything. Marcus believed that only Mother knew every aspect of her unseen empire.

Mother used one group here, who had no idea of what that group over there did. Proxies like Abu Hammond, the arms smuggler who moved the larger antimatter shipments, never survived the completion of a mission. The world was full of hungry people eager to take the place of those who'd died.

Mother operated on a simple principle: Dead men told no tales. Ignorant fools couldn't say much either.

Marcus wasn't even sure Mother's great thinkers, such as Hela and Frederick, knew the last intricate steps in Mother's ultimate plan.

Mother had long hinted at The Day. She'd told him The Day would bring peace to the Earth, as if he cared about universal peace. She'd said The Day would unite humanity, rid the planet of disease, stop all war and end poverty. It would also bring him vast rewards, properly ordering society so he and his brothers and sisters would take their rightful place in the scheme of existence.

Mother had a grandiose way of speaking when she referred to The Day and its aftermath.

Marcus took her promises to mean that he would have whatever he wanted once The Day came. Surely, it meant that Mother would take over. She would rule, and he would be one of her chief lieutenants. How The Day would achieve this, he didn't have a clue.

It was going to be spectacular, he knew that much. He was also fairly certain the underground stations dotting the planet would somehow use magnetics to achieve this great event.

Marcus had kept his ears open throughout the years. He knew Mother disliked the Hawaii University geology scientists with their hum theory. They'd undoubtedly brushed too close to some hidden truth for Mother's liking.

The destruction of the antimatter section of the Ardennes plant had been troubling Marcus. Mother's need for antimatter had grown insatiable lately. To destroy the most profitable site…

What does that portend? It has to mean The Day is almost upon us.

Could the pockets of superheated air and changing weather patterns have anything to do with antimatter? Marcus didn't see how, and yet—

His tablet buzzed. Mother must be calling. The pin-dot of fear intensified. He set the tablet into position, clicking it on. Nothing appeared on the screen, a sure sign Mother called.

"Marcus," a robotic voice said.

"I'm in the number seven Learjet," he said.

"My boy, I know exactly where you are. I've found Jack Elliot and Selene Khan."

Marcus waited.

"Your Cairo information allowed Frederick to pinpoint them."

Still, Marcus waited.

"I want you to pick them up and bring them to Libya in the desert."

Marcus sat straighter. He was to bring them to headquarters? That seemed strange. Had he misjudged the situation?

"You're quiet today," the robotic voice said. "Is anything the matter?"

"No," he said. "Where are these two now?"

"On their way to the Caucasus," Mother said. "You're to pick them up in Grozny. I see your confusion. We had a break, my boy. They had an accident. Elements of the Iranian Army picked them up afterward. The D17 agent tried a clever ploy to escape their grasp. It worked after a fashion. He had his friends in IZENOV buy his way free. The Iranians like to keep the Russians happy. It was a smart play."

Marcus worked on keeping his features impassive. He'd never heard Mother this expansive. Could she be excited? That would lend credence to the idea that The Day was here or almost here.

"IZENOV is a front for D17?" Marcus asked.

"IZENOV is a scourge on the planet. They're a front for Russian industries and thus ultimately for Putin, stealing patents and ideas from everywhere. I have a few individuals working within the consortium. Jack Elliot has unknowingly delivered himself and more importantly, Dr. Selene Khan, into the hands of one of my agents. He's taking them to Grozny. You'll pay him in gold certificates."

"It will be done," Marcus said.

"Do not fail me in this. I want the woman."

"And the man?" Marcus asked.

"If the D17 agent becomes troublesome, kill him. Otherwise, yes, bring him, too. It could prove interesting."

With that, Mother abruptly cut the connection.

That felt like her. After a moment, Marcus stood, heading to the cockpit. They were no longer going to Tehran—he'd been waiting for confirmation. Now, they would race to Grozny in the Caucasus.

-59-

NORTHWESTERN IRAN

Selene stared out of the Mercedes, watching the mountainous countryside go by. Jack had fallen asleep again, snoring softly in the back seat.

The Russian had given Jack painkillers, the man's bodyguard helping Elliot into the car. The two Russians, big men in suits, sat up front.

Surprisingly, the Iranians had returned the gym bag, which included the tuning fork device. Jack no longer had a gun or a knife, though.

The Russian hadn't said if he was driving to Alamut Castle or not. Jack had muttered a few slurry words at her before falling asleep. Selene didn't know if she should ask the driver where they were going. Jack was the movement specialist. She still couldn't believe they had gotten out of military custody. What had Elliot told the Iranians?

"Excuse me," Selene said.

The driver, the leader Ivan Rodin, looked at her through the rearview mirror.

"Where are we going?" she asked.

"Grozny," he said.

"Where's that?"

"Not in Iran," he said. "I imagine that's good news, eh?"

Selene didn't know what to say to that so she just gave the driver a slight smile. She wondered about these men.

272

Something felt off about them. Could they belong to the shadowy people? Yet, if that were true, why would Jack have given himself up to them so easily?

Selene nudged him. Jack just kept on snoring. "Jack," she whispered. He didn't respond. First, glancing at the Russians—they didn't seem to be paying her any attention—she pushed him. It didn't make any difference.

"Jack," she said, loudly this time.

"You should let him sleep," the driver said.

She smiled at Ivan Rodin through the rearview mirror. "Jack," she said, pushing his shoulder.

"It won't help," the driver said. "I gave him a sedative earlier."

"Why would you do that?" Selene asked, worried now.

"Do you care for him?" Ivan asked.

"We're friends," she said hesitantly.

The two Russians looked at each other and laughed.

"What's wrong with you two?" she asked.

"Nothing," Ivan said, the humor draining from his voice. "We're headed for Grozny."

It dawned on Selene that maybe the Russians weren't good friends with Jack. Why would the Russian give Jack a sedative, telling him it was a painkiller? Maybe because Jack Elliot was a dangerous man. Better to slip him a Mickey if you planned to double-cross him.

"Did Jack tell you about Alamut Mountain?" Selene asked.

The two Russians glanced at each other.

"No," Ivan said shortly. "What about it?"

"Maybe if you woke Jack up—"

"Listen, *devotchka*," Ivan said. "It is long drive to Grozny. I don't want to hear your clever schemes the entire trip there. Tell us about mountain. Then, you will shut up."

The other Russian grinned at Ivan, as if his boss had said something unusually witty.

"Uh…" Selene said, thinking fast. "We've…well, Jack has found…" What would sway these two? "Jack has found ancient Nizari Ismaili gold."

"Yah?" Ivan asked.

273

"Assassins gold," Selene said. "You've heard of it, I'm sure."

The two Russians burst out laughing, Ivan shaking his head.

"You are a stupid—how do you say? You are a stupid American *bitch*. You shut up now."

"Please," Selene said. "I'm telling you the truth."

Ivan stared at her through the rearview mirror. He had an animal's eyes without remorse or pity.

Selene shrank back in her seat.

Ivan smiled at her nastily. "Maybe it is time to see her breasts. What do you say, Petr?"

The other Russian nodded. "I like to see what our friend Viktor sees in her. Her breasts would be good start."

Ivan glanced over his shoulder at Selene. "Unbutton your shirt. Then take off your bra. I want you to cup your breasts. I want you to lick nipples for us, yah?"

"No," Selene said.

"Devotchka," Ivan said in a softy menacing voice. "I want to see your breasts. If you cannot do this thing for me, then I will stop car. I will take you all the way, as a man should. It is your decision."

Selene remembered the gym bag on the floor. She leaned toward it, put her fingers on the zipper and oh so quietly began to unzip it.

What sounded like a gun cocking caused Selene to look up. Petr had turned around, aiming a heavy semiautomatic at her forehead. The barrel looked huge.

"Sit back," Petr said.

For just a moment, Selene debated grabbing the tuning fork and trying to club them with it. The device had never worked against her as it had the sharks. Otherwise, she would secretly try to turn it on. The gun intimidated her either way. She was certain these men would kill her if the need arose.

With a growing feeling of defeat, she sat back.

Petr licked his lips in anticipation. "Unbutton your shirt," he said in a husky tone.

Selene found that she couldn't move. Did these two animals really plan to rape her? That seemed like a distinct possibility. She—

Selene frowned. Out of the corner of her eye, she saw Jack's index finger move up and down on his knee. The knee was hidden from Petr's view. Then, the index finger began to move from side to side. It seemed very deliberate.

It struck Selene then. Jack hadn't swallowed the two "painkillers." He must have palmed them while pretending to swallow them. Had he suspected these two of double-dealing?

Selene thought she understood. Jack wanted her to distract them. "Why are you making me do this?" Selene whined. "Please, I-I've—"

Petr struck with the gun, clubbing her on the side of the head. That flung her to the side of the door.

Jack exploded into movement. He clutched Petr's extended hand, twisting. The Russian shouted in pain and outrage. The gun boomed, stunning Selene. She lay beside the door, panting in fear as bits of cushion floated in the air.

At the same time, the Mercedes swerved.

Please, Selene thought, *not another accident.*

The Russians were yelling. The slammed brakes hurled Selene forward against the front seat. She looked up. Jack had ripped the semiautomatic out of Petr's grasp. The barrel was pressed against the bodyguard's head. Three booming shots obliterated it, spraying blood and bone everywhere. Ivan swung his arm as he turned in his seat. The heavy fist struck Jack, knocking him back.

Ivan could have done several things then. What he did do was brake harder as he held onto the steering wheel with one hand. With the other, he reached inside his suit, no doubt going for his gun.

Jack was faster. As he lay against the back seat, Elliot pulled the trigger four times. The bullets smashed through the fabric of the front seat, riddling Ivan's beefy frame. The Russian was hurled forward against the steering wheel, gasping in agony.

Jack grabbed the front seat with his free hand, hauling himself forward. He put the barrel of the gun against Ivan's head.

"Slow down to a stop or I'll kill you."

To Selene's surprise, the man obeyed Elliot. A moment later, she realized the desire to live still beat strongly in the man.

The Mercedes pulled off to the side of the road, coming to a complete stop.

"I...listened to you," Ivan panted. "Don't...kill me, yah?"

"You need medical help," Jack told him. "Do as I say and you'll get it."

Slowly, Ivan turned his head. As he wheezed, he mumbled something in Russian. His hands released the steering wheel, reaching down within his jacket. The man struggled with something.

"Down!" Jack shouted.

Elliot grabbed Selene, pushing her onto the back-seat floorboard. She felt him slide on top of her. Then, a sharp explosion sent shrapnel shrieking against metal. The hot smell of gunpowder and blood told her that Ivan Rodin had double-crossed them one last time.

-60-

ALAMUT MOUNTAIN
IRAN

It was hotter than ever as Jack and Selene climbed out of the Mercedes, which was parked at the bottom of the mountain. The journey here since dumping the Russians had taken three and a half hours. Jack had used the men's suits and clothes to wipe away as much blood and gore as he could. Ivan had been particularly gruesome, his body having absorbed the majority of his hand grenade's blast.

Jack theorized Ivan had known he was dying and had wanted to take them with him. The Russian had simply lacked the strength to toss the grenade over his shoulder. Shrapnel had almost knocked out the steering system. The lights and other electrical systems had gone dead, but the grenade hadn't altogether incapacitated the Mercedes.

"Thank God for German engineering," Jack said.

He'd cleaned up the interior as best as he could. They'd sat on towels and had driven with the windows down. Finally, the increasingly hot weather had forced them to roll up the windows and use the air conditioner despite the burnt electrical smell and the wisps of smoke it had trickled into the car.

It was a little after seven p.m., and the winding road up the mountain was blocked off. A large portion of Alamut Castle— at the top of the mountain—had scaffolding around it. It looked

277

as if the Iranians were renovating the castle and the surrounding area.

"Do we try to find Souk's Old Man of the Mountain?" Selene asked.

"How hot do you think it is here?" Jack asked in lieu of an answer.

"We don't have to wonder," Selene said. "I have a temperature app." She took out her cellphone. "It's one hundred and twelve degrees."

"At seven in the evening?" Jack asked.

"It's blistering," Selene agreed. "I feel like I'm breathing inside an oven. Still, what's your point?"

"Birds committing mass suicide, intense heat, tuning forks that make man-eating sharks flee—I'd like to know why," Jack said.

"You think it's all connected?"

"Everything these past few days has been a surprise. Why not?"

"I'd like to find the secret chamber under the castle," she said.

"Souk's notebook is making sense to you now?"

"Enough so I have an idea how to find the secret chamber—if it exists."

Jack peered up at the high castle, at the extensive scaffolding around it. "We'd better get started then. I doubt we'll get there before dark."

They began trudging up the winding road. Forty-five minutes later, with the tip of the bloated sun sinking into the horizon, Jack began to sway from exhaustion. He looked pale and shaky.

"How are you holding up?" Selene asked.

He didn't answer. He had that grim look again, the bitter determination that seemed to be the essence of Jack Elliot.

Before she could worry more, headlights appeared up the road. A car was coming down.

"Jack," she said.

Elliot stopped, staring at the headlights.

"What should we do?" she asked.

Jack glanced around.

278

To Selene's way of thinking, there wasn't anywhere to hide. "We'd better decide what we're going to tell them," she said.

"Start waving," Jack said. He made a single, tired pass with his hand.

The car was getting closer fast. She could hear the tires rolling on the blacktop.

Selene began to wave with both hands, forcing herself to smile. Their clothes had bloodstains. Would that show up in the waning light? Before she could decide, the headlights appeared from around a curve. The car was heading straight for them.

-61-

LEARJET 85
CAUCASUS MOUNTAINS

Marcus peered at the forest below. They were almost to Grozny. The pilot must have been good after all. He said there'd been more superheated air pockets, but his navigator had figured out a way to sense them before they flew through them.

It was hot outside, though, one hundred and eighteen degrees. On a suspicion, Marcus had checked the internet. It was hot all over the planet, much hotter than normal. People all over the world had already begun to speculate on the reasons.

Marcus believed the hot weather was Mother's doing. The Day was almost upon them. The heat had something to do with the underground stations throughout the world.

His tablet beeped.

Marcus positioned it before him, clicking on the connection. The robotic voice and blank slate told him it was Mother checking up on him.

"There's been a change in plans," the robotic voice said. "The IZENOV people never made it to Grozny. Their bodies are in the woods, several hundred feet from the road. One corpse lacks its head. The other has no heart."

"Jack Elliot," Marcus said. He recalled the little man in the Ardennes. He had been right about that one.

"They're headed to Alamut Castle," the robotic voice said.

"You mean Station Eight underneath it," Marcus said.

"An abandoned Station Eight," Mother corrected.

"Oh."

"Your inflection suggests it doesn't matter. You are incorrect. I do not want them inside the abandoned station."

Marcus almost asked why. Instead, he said, "It's getting hotter around the world."

"That it is," Mother said.

Marcus inhaled deeply, staring at the tablet. He suspected that Mother watched him, gauging every reaction. Maybe the tablet even monitored him: breathing speed, heart rate, that sort of thing.

"The Day must be upon us," Marcus said.

"Dear, dear boy, you have always been too curious. It is why you have remained in the lower ranks. That being said, I have no greater killer among my children. Go at once to Alamut Castle. Kill Jack Elliot. Capture Dr. Selene Khan. I want her in the Libyan Desert before…within the next twenty-four hours.

"Act with extreme unction, my boy. This is your most important assignment."

Marcus kept his features impassive. He did not dare ask why.

"Neither of them must leave Station Eight under their own power," the robotic voice said.

"It will be done," Marcus said.

Mother cut the connection.

Three second later, he used the tablet, searching for the nearest airport to Alamut Mountain.

-62-

SAHARA DESERT

The huge beast trotted through the desert, its tongue lolling as it panted in the tremendous heat. Never in its existence had it felt heat like this. Worse, it was unsuited to the alien environment of endlessly shifting sand. Only at night did it know a semblance of peace.

It was free. Free to die of hunger and thirst. Free to be miserable without learning anything it yearned to understand. Why was it unlike any other creature it had ever seen? Why had the humans caged it? What reason could they have for taking it from the cool forest that had been its home?

For a time now, it had searched for meat and water. Without the hidden water bottles, it would have died of thirst already. Fortunately, there were tiny, unwary creatures in this alien place.

The beast had a fantastic sense of smell and hearing. It had used both in order to find and then chew the mousy morsels that had still failed to assuage its eternal hunger.

It had known abundant food as a captive beast. It hadn't realized being free would bring such tremendous issues of life and death to the fore.

The beast trotted into shade, using a towering dune. The hiss of shifting sand day and night had begun to drive it mad.

Maybe it had made a mistake killing the two captors. Would it be better to endure needles, tests and mockery?

No! It was better to die free, to do as it willed. Then why did it rush toward the maddening hum and the growing vibration it felt in the sand?

The beast wagged its tail and put its shaggy head on its paws. The humans had journeyed to that place. It saw the tracks in the sand and sniffed the burnt rubber of the tires. As it followed the track through the endless waste, the hum increased and the vibrations told it a powerful engine thrummed with life.

For quite some time, the beast had debated with itself. Should it seek better land by turning around and trotting for as long as its strength held out? That was one possibility, and in many ways, it seemed like the wiser choice.

The beast hadn't been idle in its cage, however. It had judged the extent of the desert as the vehicle journeyed through it. It had watched and reasoned out the speed of the vehicle. The human machines could travel many times faster than it could run. Therefore, the sandy area was huge. It was possible the extent was greater than its strength.

That was galling. For as long as it could remember the beast had yearned to be free of the humans. It had dreamed of hunting in the wilds on its own. Maybe, it would be able to find a female like itself. He would rut, and they would hunt together and rut some more. That would be the dream life.

Instead, because of the masters and their wicked plans, it was stuck in this hot hell of shifting sand.

Therefore—oh, the beast had thought this through very carefully indeed. Therefore, it would torment the masters and hurt them. What else was left? Surely, it would only be a matter of time before the masters sent hunters to track and slay it. The beast knew the masters would never let it know peace.

If only it could make them suffer as they had made it suffer. Why was it different from every other creature it knew? Where could it find an answer to the terrible dilemma of its existence?

Why did it have to face life alone? Others had mates. Others had creatures just like it. Humans had other humans. Great Danes had Great Danes. The mousy creatures of the desert had others just like them. Only it was alone. Only it had to live apart from every other. That was wrong.

Had the humans marked it in some nefarious manner? That seemed all too possible.

With a groan, the beast stood. The hum raised its pitch again. The beast shook its head. It hated the endless hum. It sought the source so it could stop it forever.

How would it do that?

The beast trotted out of the shade and back under the burning orb of the sky. It would attack while it had strength. Without a collar to harm it, the masters no longer had any source of control over it.

The beast planned to destroy the masters before they sought it out and destroyed it.

The Great Danes had not acted like that—and they had died because it was wiser than they had been. And if it wasn't wisdom but a vicious cunning, the beast accepted that.

It wanted peace. It wanted to know why it was different and why it was alone. It wanted freedom but it also wanted a full belly. If the truth were known, it also wanted green grass, trees and babbling brooks and streams. This was a hell world. The masters would have to pay.

Once it found the source of the hum…then…then it would go to war before its existence ended in this cauldron of blistering heat. It would teach the humans finally that they never should have tormented it in the first place.

-63-

ALAMUT MOUNTAIN
IRAN

Jack was thirsty and tired. The excessive heat combined with his concussion and exhaustion had left him weary, making it difficult to think. He put his hands before his eyes because the headlights were making his head throb.

The lights dimmed, and they seemed to slow their rate of advance. A few seconds later, the vehicle came to a halt. A car door opened. A man spoke to them in Farsi.

"See if he speaks English," Jack whispered.

Selene shouted at the man.

"Yes, English," the man said with a heavy accent. "I speak it. What are you doing here?"

"Tell him we're tourists," Jack whispered. "No. Tell him you're a historian. I'm your bodyguard."

Selene did as bidden.

"You should go back down," the man said. "The castle is closed for renovation. It is not safe here on the road in the dark."

"It's very hot," Selene said.

The man stayed hidden behind the shining lights and said nothing for a bit. "It is beyond hot," he finally said. "I've never experienced weather like this here. You two look tired. Do you have water?"

"I'm afraid we don't," Selene said. "And my companion is dehydrated."

"For a fact, he looks ill," the man said. "Yes. I will give you a ride down to your vehicle."

"Thank you," Selene said. "Now what do we do?" she whispered to Jack.

The car door slammed. The vehicle inched forward. Finally, the headlights passed them. The vehicle stopped. It was an ancient jeep with a canvas top. The man behind the wheel was massive with a shaved scalp, a long black beard and a long-sleeved shirt.

"I am Samson," he said, training two intense eyes on them.

"You look like him, too," Jack said.

Samson's harsh features softened. "You are a man of the Book?" he asked.

"I guess I am," Jack said. "I went to Sunday school as a child."

Samson shook his head.

"It's an old American custom," Jack said. "The adults sent their children to a church class on Sunday. Instead of regular school, they called it Sunday school."

"Ah. Yes. I understand."

"I'm surprised you've read the Bible," Selene told the man.

"I am not a Muslim, if that's what you're implying," Samson said. "I'm an Assyrian. We are Christians living in a Muslim land. Assyrians no longer have a country of their own, but live in Iran and Iraq primarily."

Samson opened the jeep door, sliding out. He was huge, six-six. He held two water bottles, giving one to each of them.

Jack twisted his cap and guzzled.

"Here," Selene said. "You can have mine."

"No, no," Samson said. He pulled another water bottle out of the jeep, handing it to Jack.

Jack drank that one too.

"You are a historian?" Samson asked Selene.

She looked at Jack before saying, "I've studied the Assassins."

Samson rubbed his chin, staring up into the deepening twilight. "I am a foreman. This heat—I decided to check the

286

premises. I was heading back down. The renovation team has a camp several miles from here. Since you are Americans... I will drive you up. I can show you a few of the sights. Then, I will have to take you to your car."

"That's very kind of you," Selene said.

"Yes," Jack said, trying to mask his unease. In his condition, he didn't believe he could incapacitate the man if the need arose. The man's size was a complication.

Selene sat up front with Samson, while Jack climbed into the back. The big man put the jeep into reverse, turning around on the mountain road. A moment later, he put it into first gear and started up the mountain.

***

"I'm curious," Selene said, looking like a child beside the massive Assyrian. "How long have you been working here?"

"Two and a half years," Samson said.

"Did you ever hear of someone called Souk?"

Samson hesitated before saying, "I don't think so. Should I know him?"

"He was an Egyptian antique shop owner. He met someone here called the Old Man of the Mountain."

Samson frowned, and his big fingers tightened around the steering wheel. Selene smiled up at him as the Assyrian's frown deepened.

"I don't think you are a historian," the big man said.

"You're right," Selene said, smoothly. "I'm a geologist. I'm Dr. Selene Khan from the University of Hawaii."

"Geology," he said. "You study volcanos and strata?"

"Sometimes."

"What does any of that have to do with Alamut Castle?" Samson asked.

"I'll answer you with a question," Selene said. "Have you ever heard a hum when everything becomes very quiet?"

"No."

Selene felt as if he said that too quickly. "Have you heard of anyone who's heard of a...a weird hum around here?"

Samson eyed her. His frown no longer seemed quite as severe. "I have," he admitted.

287

A well of excitement bubbled in Selene. "Did they say where the hum originated?"

Samson shook his head.

"There's a similar hum at Siwa Oasis."

"This place, this Siwa, is in a desert?"

"In Egypt," Selene said. "As I said, Souk met the Old Man of the Mountain. The Old Man told Souk many interesting things about the castle. I would like to speak to the Old Man and see if he's heard any of these hums."

Samson glanced at her. "Now, I believe you are speaking the truth. I have an ear for truth and for lies. A foreman has need of such an ear," he added.

Jack listened to Samson closely and watched him too. He would have liked to have the man's ear for the truth. Something about Samson seemed off, and Jack was trying to figure it out.

They drove in silence for a time until Samson slowed down. The castle loomed before them. It was almost night now, with only a little of the ambient light of twilight left.

"Hums, geologists and antique dealers," Samson said. "That is quite a list, each different from the other. Combined with this heat…it makes one wonder."

"Oh," Selene said.

"Do you believe in fate?" Samson asked.

Selene pursed her lips. "No, I guess I don't."

"What do you believe in then?"

"Things I can touch."

"Are you an atheist?"

That seemed like an odd question. "Does it matter what I am?" Selene asked.

Samson didn't answer that.

"No, I'm not an atheist," Selene said. "That would mean I know whether God exists or not. I haven't been everywhere so how could I know. I'm an agnostic, I suppose. Why do you ask?"

"I do believe in fate," Samson said, "actually in Providence. This is a strange night. I have long waited for such an event to show me the beginning."

"What beginning?" Selene asked.

Samson smiled in the darkness. He had white teeth. "I have been driving up and down the mountain this evening. The hot weather is a worldwide phenomenon. Did you know that?"

"We didn't, no," Selene said.

"I believe the globally hot weather is significant. In fact...I have a confession to make."

Jack grew tense, putting his hand on the gun.

"I have heard a hum before," Samson said. "I have heard it more and more often lately. I have also heard of Souk. I remember the Egyptian well."

"What?" Selene asked.

"I am Samson, but I am also known to a few as the Old Man of the Mountain."

-64-

ALAMUT CASTLE
IRAN

Jack didn't trust the big man. There was explosive power in the man's gait. The Assyrian exuded a feeling of hyper-competence and therefore deadliness.

Jack remembered where he'd seen another individual move in a similar fashion. It had been at the D'erlon Plant in the Ardennes.

The three of them left the jeep behind, entering an area of floodlights hooked to the scaffolding. Samson steered them toward a postern gate.

Alamut Castle was part masonry and part of the mountain. What had Selene said earlier? "Alamut" meant "Eagle's Nest." The Qazvin Plains spread out below them. With only swords, spears, arrows and catapults for weapons, the fortress would have nearly been impenetrable. Jack could well understand why the first Assassin had wanted the stronghold. It also made sense why it had taken the all-conquering Mongols to root the Assassins from this vantage.

"If you're the Old Man of the Mountain," Jack said, "it stands to reason you're not the foreman renovating the castle?"

Samson glanced back at Jack. "That doesn't follow. I am indeed the foreman. It's the perfect assignment."

Assignment? Jack thought, that seemed like an odd word choice.

"Why would Muslims allow a Christian such a position of authority?" he asked.

Samson chuckled. "You have an odd idea of how things are run in Iran. I'm a hard worker. Even better, I'm excellent at delegating authority and getting my men to work. I admit, my size helps in this. Few care to disappoint me. That's worth money. It is the same everywhere when people truly want things done. They hire the best they can. Why would it be any different here?"

"That makes sense, I suppose," Jack mumbled.

Selene glanced at him. He gave her the barest of shrugs. She glanced at the giant. Selene was carrying the gym bag by its strap and clutching Souk's notebook in her other hand.

Samson opened the postern door, taking a flashlight sitting in an alcove, clicking it on.

"You really impressed Souk," Selene told Samson.

"I remember."

"Did he ever end up telling you about the priestess of Ammon?"

"Refresh my memory," Samson said.

As they walked the halls, climbing stone staircases, moving through long passageways and finally going down spiral stone steps, Selene told the big man Souk's tale about Cambyses and Alexander the Great.

"If Souk's right," Selene said at the end, "that means the priestess would have to have been over two hundred years old. I simply can't accept that."

Samson turned around with the flashlight held negligently in his left hand. It wasn't as hot down here in the guts of the mountain fortress.

"I have studied the past intently," the Assyrian said. "This was a Shia stronghold once, and I am Christian by heritage. Still, I have discovered...interesting facts concerning Alamut Castle. A marvelous library existed during the time of the Assassins. It drew philosophers and other students. There is a legend that the library originated with the Old Man's mistress. She was a woman of rare talents. The legend tells of her genius, claiming that she taught Hasan-i Sabbah the unique Assassin techniques."

"You mean how Hasan drugged his best assassins, bringing them into a fake paradise?" Selene asked.

"That and other techniques," Samson said. "In truth, her genius allowed the Nizari Ismaili to hold onto power as long as they did."

"Wait a minute," Selene said. "You're not suggesting this woman lived the length of the Assassin kingdom?"

"The legend says she did."

"Hasan captured the castle in 1090, just before the First Crusade. The Assassins held it until 1256." Selene touched her fingers. "That's 166 years."

"Which is similar to Souk's two hundred years," Samson said.

"You can't be serious. People don't live two hundred years. They don't even live 166 years."

"You are not a person of the Book," Samson said. "If you were, you would know that Methuselah lived 969 years. Adam lived 950 years."

Selene glanced at Jack before staring at Samson. "Are you making fun of me?"

"I am giving you data. I'm saying there are records of people living more than two hundred years."

Selene scoffed. "Sure. There are legends of fire-breathing dragons, too. That doesn't mean I believe in them. Unicorns and griffins abounded in ancient tales. Are you going to tell me this woman flew into Alamut Castle on Pegasus?"

"I do not care for your mockery," Samson said.

"And I don't care for your Methuselah reference. I'm dead serious about what I've been telling you."

"As am I," Samson said.

"You believe this legendary woman existed?" Selene asked. "You're saying that she started an oracle at the Siwa Oasis and in later years she migrated here and began the Assassins?"

"Yes," Samson said. "She worked from behind the scenes, has been working in history's background for untold millennia."

"That doesn't hold," Jack said. "It's one thing to say Methuselah lived 969 years. It's another to say a woman has been alive for thousands upon thousands of years."

"Maybe it's not the same woman," Samson said with a shrug. "Maybe it is different women with the same goal, all working to achieve the same purpose."

"What purpose?" Selene asked.

"Ah," Samson said. "That is the question of the ages."

"Let me get this straight," Selene said. "You're saying Souk's woman, the one who supposedly spoke to Cambyses and Alexander the Great, are two different women?"

"No. I think they are the same. I think these women live unnaturally long lives. I do think the priestess of the Siwa Oasis is different from the one who began the Assassins by using Hasan-i Sabbah."

"No self-respecting Shia would want to hear that," Selene said.

"True."

"Why do you believe what you're saying?" Jack asked.

"Yes," Samson said. "That is the right question. How do you know? How do you know the Earth orbits the Sun? How do you know George Washington was the first President of the United States? Have you been on a spaceship watching the Earth orbit the Sun? Did you see George Washington? No. Others tell us these things. Yet, we believe they are facts."

"You've read about this woman?" Jack asked.

"I have," Samson said.

"Your tone implies an 'and'," Selene said.

"I have also seen advanced technology," Samson said. "It is beyond our present technology. That has caused me to wonder if the women in the past had access to the greater technology, allowing each of them extended life."

"Who are you?" Selene asked. "Who are you really?"

The big man expanded his chest. He was indeed huge. He exhaled, nodding slowly. "I am a genetic experiment," Samson said. "I am one of Mother's children."

Jack and Selene traded glances.

"Mother?" Selene asked.

"The present incarnation of the women behind the veil of history," Samson said in a solemn voice.

"You're part of the shadowy organization," Selene said, "the one that's been hunting us."

"I was part of it once, yes."

"What does that mean?" Selene asked.

Samson turned his head, peering at a spot in the shadows. "I am a genetic experiment. I am stronger, faster and smarter than ordinary men. Why and how Mother did this, I don't know. I refused an assignment once. Mother told me she would punish me if I continued in my stubbornness. I still refused her. I cannot murder for her, as she desires. The Book taught me that. Mother sent others like me to hunt me down. In the end, they captured me. I went to a hideous place, and there, genetic surgeons altered me yet again. Now, I am bound to Alamut Castle, to its near environs. We know it more accurately as Station Eight."

"This is Station Eight?" Selene asked with excitement in her voice.

Samson didn't answer.

"What happens if you leave Alamut Castle?" Jack asked.

"I'll melt."

"That means…what?" Jack asked.

"My body will overheat."

Jack frowned. "How is that even possible?"

"My body will heat at the atomic level," Samson said. "The transmitters will focus on my molecules, radiating intense heat through them. Soon, I will literally burn up. I've seen it done to dogs. I can still hear their howls in my nightmares."

"That's horrible," Selene said.

"Yes."

"Why does she let you live?" Jack asked.

"Maybe in the hope I'll change my mind," Samson said, "maybe as an example of how she can turn someone's life into Hell on Earth."

"You've never tried to contact the authorities?" Jack asked.

"I don't care to die in a hideous fashion."

"But you told Souk some of these things," Selene said.

294

"I whispered to him certain truths," Samson said. "I stayed within the rules of the game."

"What game?" Selene asked.

"Mother lives by a strict set of rules. Her children stray from them at their peril."

"What is Station Eight?" Jack asked.

Samson nodded. "I'll show you what I can."

"Why?" Jack asked.

"What do you mean?" the big man asked.

"You don't know who I am," Jack said.

"I do. You're an Intelligence agent. You already admitted you're Americans. That would imply you work for an American Intelligence agency."

"Which means that your telling us this is telling the authorities. You're breaking the rules."

"I realize this," Samson said in a bleak voice.

"Why have you changed your mind?" Jack asked.

For a time, Samson didn't say a thing. Finally, he whispered, "Because I think The Day is almost upon us."

-65-

UNDER ALAMUT CASTLE
IRAN

"What is The Day?" Selene asked.

"It is the culmination of Mother's work," Samson said, "the reason for these stations."

"Which is?" Selene asked.

"I have no idea. I don't think anyone but Mother does."

"What do the stations do?"

"Maybe I can finally find out," Samson said. He faced a blank wall of stone, bent at the knees and reached to the base. His fingers disappeared into the stone. They must have moved a latch. There was a clink.

Heavy, hidden stones ground against each other. Slowly, the wall lifted upward like a castle gate revealing a smooth steel corridor. The wall halted its upward movement. A diffuse glow began to brighten the ceiling of the metal corridor.

Samson ducked under the lifted wall, heading into the corridor.

"Wait a minute," Selene said.

The Assyrian turned around, regarding them.

"Are you suggesting this metal corridor was fashioned in 1090 A.D.?" Selene asked.

Samson laughed. "No. I would never suggest that."

"Okay," Selene exhaled. "Good. When do you think it was built?"

"Long before 1090, maybe in the Fourth or Fifth Millennium B.C," Samson said.

"What?" Selene exploded. "You expect us to believe that? There's no evidence of any kind of high technology in early human history."

"Legends say otherwise," Samson said. "Or have you never heard of Atlantis?"

"You're kidding me, right?" Selene said. "You're going to try to snow me with that?"

"Atlantis, the Antediluvian world, ancient astronauts, our world is rife with legends that speak about high technology in early human history or prehistory. Why can't there be a grain of truth in the various tales?"

"I'm looking at a metal corridor hidden behind a wall of stone down here in the bottom of Alamut Castle," Selene said. "The idea the corridor is older than history... That's preposterous."

Samson shook his head. "There are hundreds of tales throughout the world of hidden ones working at an unimaginable conspiracy. These stories have some truth in them, too. How does one keep such a thing hidden over the centuries, over the millennium? By telling no one."

"I'm not buying this," Selene said. "You knew about the conspiracy. Souk knew. How secret could it be?"

"I knew because I was born into it. Souk knew a tiny portion because I told him. My point is that Mother is the key to understanding the truth behind a thousand whispered tales."

"Okay, sure," Selene said. "But even supposing I believed you, who built this corridor? Who constructed Station Eight in early human history? Who made the underwater dome in the Indian Ocean? And what do the stations *do*? Why is it getting hotter all over the world?"

"Believe me," Samson said. "There is an answer. And there's a reason Mother has remained hidden all this time. I think we have to find the answer and stop it before Mother completes her goal."

"Why does your Mother need antimatter?" Jack asked.

"I don't know."

297

Jack turned to Selene. "We can stand here and ask questions all night. Let's see what he can show us. Let's combine our brainpower and figure out what we can."

Selene felt breathless and then lightheaded. She couldn't accept Samson's premises and yet, this metal corridor existed under Alamut Castle.

"Okay," she said. "Let's do this."

***

Selene watched Samson as he led the way. This hidden area couldn't be ancient. People would have used it to their advantage if that were the case. Could humans hold such a fortress, possess such advanced technology and not use it to change the world? That didn't strike her as psychologically correct.

In time, the metal corridor branched off. Samson took them to the right.

"What's in the other direction?" Selene asked.

"A dead end to us," Samson said.

Soon, he brought them to a hatch. He tapped a sequence onto a panel before twisting a latch. The door opened into a domed chamber with metal tables along the walls. Selene had seen a room just like this before in the underwater dome. She shivered as goosebumps rose on her arms.

The big man strode across the chamber, opening another hatch. Jack and Selene followed him into a large, dark area.

"Keep the door open," Samson said. "It's the only light we'll have other than my flashlight."

Selene felt a shiver of dread course through her. This area was just like the underwater dome, but this larger chamber lacked lights playing along the walls. She spied blank screens and various controls along the walls. Nothing in this room seemed to have power.

"The underwater dome had power," Selene said.

"Remember," Samson said "this is an abandoned station. That's why Mother banished me to it. It has an extremely limited power source."

"Something has been bothering me," Selene said. "I can't accept...Mother using this place during the time of the Assassins in the Middle Ages."

"I never said she did," Samson said.

"What?" Selene asked. "But you said—"

"I said the stations are ancient. I didn't say they've been in use all the time. It's my belief they've come back online only a short while ago, at least in terms of recorded history."

"You're claiming these stations have been idle for what, thousands of years?"

"That's right," Samson said. "Come. I have something else to show you. It's why I believe Mother, or the women who called themselves Mother, have been able to live extended lives."

With the flashlight, he led them through the large, dark chamber. He came to three hatches.

"If you listen carefully at each entrance," Samson said, "you can hear a faint hum."

Selene went to a hatch, putting an ear near it. Yes, she could hear a hum. It was very faint, as he'd said. She did likewise at the other hatches, hearing a similar sound each time.

"I think it is emergency power," Samson said. "It keeps air cycling and certain engines, or whatever you want to call them, operating. Two of these hatches remain closed to my best efforts. I have been able to breach the third. Please, step back."

Selene and Jack did as requested.

Samson withdrew a small device from a pocket. He pressed it against the door, manipulating the device. Finally, a loud sound indicated he'd moved something in the door.

The hatch swung open.

"Oh," Selene said. She'd moved closer. Now, she waved at the foul air before her nose. "Whatever is in there smells bad."

"It's ancient air," Samson said. "The cyclers don't work as well in this section. We're only going to head in a short distance."

"How far do these corridors go?"

"I've never reached an end."

"How far did you reach?" Selene asked.

299

"Half a mile before I had to turn back," Samson said. "It got too hot."

"Who could build something like this at various locations around the world?" Selene said.

"You're sounding like a broken record," Jack told her.

"I'm trying to wrap my mind around all this," Selene said. "I...I expected a logical answer."

"I've been giving you logical answers," Samson said.

"Reasonable answers then," Selene said.

"They're also reasonable. What the answers don't do is comport to your idea of history and technology. You have to expand your thinking."

"I'm trying," Selene said.

"First," Samson said, "let's step away from the hatch. Then, we'll hyperventilate. Soak your lungs with good air. You're going to need it."

Jack, Selene and Samson went into the center of the dark chamber. Each of them began to breathe deeply. Selene remembered doing this during swimming parties as a teenager when they were going to see who could hold their breath underwater the longest. She'd always won those games.

"This is it," Samson said in a strained voice. "Follow me."

Selene hurried after him with Jack bringing up the rear. The D17 agent had been quiet for a while. He had a stoic look. Selene had no idea what Jack thought about all this. His hand never strayed far from the gun he'd taken from Petr though.

The flashlight gave them enough light to show a path for their feet. Their steps echoed in the corridor. The air kept getting staler and warmer.

Finally, the big man led them into a chamber deep underground. Selene had a sense of immense size. Samson played his flashlight on the ceiling. It was almost too far to see.

"Ready?" he asked. His voice seemed deadened in here.

"Show us," Selene said.

The Assyrian shined his light on a huge statue. It was three times Selene's height and fashioned out of gold. It had a muscular, manlike body with the head of a jackal.

"Is that supposed to be the Egyptian god Anubis?" Selene whispered.

300

"Very good," Samson said softly. "Did you know that Anubis was associated with mummification and the afterlife in the ancient Egyptian religion? Could that have been an old memory indicating Anubis had something to do with extended life?"

The big man shined his light on a square stone object cracked open horizontally. Selene realized the crack wasn't jagged, but smooth and straight. Someone had hinged a stone lid onto the object. With his light, Samson showed them thick metallic cords snaking from the stone to a wall. The cords disappeared into the wall.

Selene approached the object, which seemed like a giant coffin. Was there an ancient mummy in there? She heard buzzing from the object, and there were hieroglyphics painted on the stone.

"Do you know what the hieroglyphics say?" Selene asked.

"I do. It says, MODEL 3."

Selene felt lightheaded. The stone object felt extremely old. She had to admit that. Yet, the stone hummed softly with internal power.

"What is it?" Selene asked. "You're not suggesting it's a coffin, are you?"

"Here," Samson told Jack, handing the agent the flashlight. "Keep shining it on the stone."

Jack kept the light there.

Samson approached the object. He pushed against the lid, raising it with a grunt. "Can you see?" he asked.

Selene approached, relieved there wasn't a mummy. Instead, there was a body-shaped cavity in the middle of the stone. Studying the lid, she saw a similar cavity to match the lower one. She also saw more hieroglyphics inside.

"What do they say?" she asked in a soft voice.

"LONGEVITY TREATMENT LOT 3 BETA-9," Samson said.

Selene shook her head. "How...how does it work?"

"Do you see those tiny holes in the cavity areas?"

Selene squinted. Yes, she did see them. They were everywhere around the body cavity both upper and lower.

301

"I have surmised the process," Samson said. "Of course, one must lay a person in there and close the lid. If you'll notice, up there is a tiny nozzle that will spray mist. I believe the mist is a numbing agent. Afterward—here, let me show you."

The big man drew needle-nose pliers from a back pocket. He leaned in, inserting the nose of the pliers into a hole. Carefully, he extended a wicked-looking silver needle.

Selene shivered at the sight. If each of the holes thrust a needle—over one hundred of them would jab into the person lying in the body cavity.

"Notice the needle's length," Samson said. "If a person were trapped in the stone, the needles might well jab into the prisoner's *bones*, into the marrow. I believe they would inject that person with a longevity serum. Maybe the serum would change the person's very nature."

"A horrifying and brutal process," Selene whispered.

"Agreed, but possibly well worth it depending on how long the person would live afterward."

"Why haven't you tried it?" Jack asked. "The stone coffin strikes me as operational."

Samson nodded absently. "I haven't dared to try. I'm afraid Mother has already given me an anti-serum. If I closed the lid on myself, I think I would die in a horrible manner. I'm sure that would delight Mother to no end."

It grew quiet in the chamber. Several seconds later, a distant *boom* caused Samson to look up.

"What is it?" Jack asked. "What just happened?"

Before Samson could answer, a woman spoke, "I auto-closed a hatch, sealing you in this passage."

Samson swung the flashlight around; he'd taken it back from Jack. The huge Assyrian searched for the source of the voice. Jack drew his gun, training it in the darkness from the direction the voice had come.

"Look," Selene whispered in horror.

Samson must have seen it. He aimed the light on the golden statue. The jackal eyes of Anubis glowed brightly. Then, what had first appeared as a giant statue moved in robotic stiffness toward them.

302

-66-

STATION EIGHT
IRAN

Jack fired at the ancient robot. The bullet ricocheted with a spark, hitting a wall, making a secondary spark, a third and a fourth before it lost its energy and tumbled onto the floor.

"Run!" Samson shouted.

"Where will you run?" the Anubis robot asked. "I've sealed the outer access hatch. You're trapped with me, my naughty boy. I must say, however, that I am impressed with your insights. You are correct in thinking you cannot use the longevity treatment. I do so wish you had tried, though."

"You're...*Mother*?" Selene asked. "You're an ancient robot?"

The golden head turned, the glowing Anubis eyes focusing on Selene. "Must you ask such absurd questions? You are—"

Since his first useless shot Jack had been analyzing the robot—if that's what it was. He aimed carefully now, targeting the left eye. A flash of fire blazed from the barrel of the gun. The Anubis head swayed as something metallic broke and shattered on it. The glow from the left eye-port flickered wildly before dying out.

The jackal-head swiveled toward Elliot. "You are a resourceful agent, aren't you? I can see why Secretary King delighted in you."

303

Jack fired again. He sparked the forehead as the bullet ricocheted off, missing the right eye-port, bouncing around the room.

The robot accelerated in its stiff gait. Jack lined up the gun for another shot. The mobile statue moved swiftly. He couldn't get a decent shot but he held his position, determined to blind the thing while he had the chance.

Just before the clanking monstrosity reached him, Samson tackled Elliot, propelling them out of the robot's path. The takedown surprised Jack, knocking the gun out of his hand. It went sliding across the floor.

The robot slowed after it passed the two, but not fast enough. The giant construct struck a wall, rebounding from it, staggering and toppling onto its back on the floor with a loud crash.

"Cursed machinery," Mother said. "I don't—"

"Put the receptors against your limbs like so," a man said through the robot's mouth, his voice fainter than Mother's.

"Oh," Mother said. "That's what you were talking about before. Yes. Excellent."

The robot spun around on the floor, pushing up, climbing to its feet in a smoother manner than it had run moments before.

Jack scrambled to his feet, searching the darkness for his gun. He couldn't see it. "Shine your light around," he hissed. "I have to find my gun."

Samson swept the light in various directions.

"There!" Selene shouted. "I see it. It's to your left about fifteen feet away."

Jack saw it, too. He raced for the gun. The robot followed with its dreadful clangs. He had to shoot out the last eye-port, blind Mother from using the ancient technology against them.

Jack tried to scoop up the gun on the run.

"Look out, Jack! It's right behind you."

He didn't look. He was concentrating too hard on getting his gun. He reached down, grabbed it—and cold, golden, outsized hands gripped his wrists. The robot lifted him off the metal floor, raising him so his boots dangled several feet in the air.

"I am going to tear your arms off, Agent Elliot," Mother said. "I am going to watch you scream in agony. Then, I shall do likewise to Samson. You have angered me with your persistence, my boy."

The robot turned, pushing Jack forward in the air as she kept him dangling. "What do you think, Dr. Khan? Are you impressed yet?"

Jack strained in the robot's grasp. He had no chance of breaking free. Yet, he had to think of something else... What if—

"Selene," he said.

The doctor's horrified gaze switched from the jackal-head to him.

"Use your tuning fork!" Jack shouted. "Maybe it can shark this thing."

"Quiet," Mother said, as the robot shook him. "I can prolong your agony if you desire."

"Who are you?" Jack said. "What is your goal?"

"Always the efficient D17 agent," Mother said. "The—"

A vibrating hum cut off her speech.

Samson's flashlight beam caught Selene. She stood with the tuning fork in her hands. The fork part vibrated wildly, making Selene's hands tremble.

"Quick, Jack," Selene said in a shaky voice. "Pry yourself free."

Jack squirmed, but he couldn't break the robot's hold. "Get out of here," he told them. "Escape while you can."

"No," Selene said. "I'm going to try other buttons."

"Listen to me," Jack told her.

Deliberately, Selene pressed another button on the tuning fork's control pad. The vibrating sound changed pitch.

Jack felt the robot vibrate. "It's doing something to it!" he shouted.

Selene stepped closer, aiming the tuning fork at the golden robot.

The vibrating worsened, although Jack felt the robot's fingers tighten. He endured the grinding together of his wrists bones. Suddenly, parts inside the robot ground against each other. There were electrical pops and sizzling sounds. The

305

smell of electrical smoke made Jack cough. The metal hands no longer tightened. In fact, the left opened enough for him to rip his wrist free.

Jack gritted his teeth as he dangled from one arm. He looked down. It was at least a three-foot drop to the floor.

More popping and sizzling sounds came from the ancient construct. The other golden hand loosened its hold.

Jack fell. He braced himself, striking the metal floor, rolling to absorb the shock.

The last glowing eye winked out. The jackal mouth had opened. Flashes of light emitted from it. Then, dark smoke billowed out of it. The statue leaned forward.

"Get out of the way!" Selene shouted.

Jack scrambled across the floor, barely getting out of the path, as the golden monstrosity banged against the metal tiles.

A gush of flames spewed from the mouth. Afterward, an interior explosion dampened the fire. Showers of sparks emitted like a Fourth of July firework. Abruptly, that ceased as well.

As it did, Selene clicked off the tuning fork. The vibrating sounds in the chamber quit. A few soft buzzing noises emitted from the robot. Otherwise, silence filled the smoky chamber.

Mother did not speak from the robot again.

"Where did you get that?" Samson asked.

"From an underwater station in the Indian Ocean," Selene said softly. "Why, does it matter?"

"It's a hummer," Samson said.

"Okay."

"I think we can use it."

"To do what?" Selene asked.

"To get into a chamber that might tell us why Station Eight went offline."

-67-

SUB-ROAD 112
IRAN

The air-conditioner roared at full power as the SUV raced for Alamut Mountain. It was blistering hot outside, had been like that at the tiny airport where they'd landed. Marcus sat behind the wheel, taking the mountain road much too fast. He trusted his reflexes. The heated tires squealed constantly as each of them swayed from side to side.

"Monsieur," Ney said. "Your tablet is buzzing."

"Press the bottom switch," Marcus said, refusing to tear his gaze from the road. "Then hold it up so I can glance at the screen."

"*Wei*, monsieur," Ney said, obediently following the instructions.

"My boy," a robotic voice said from the tablet. "I have grave news. Samson Mark Three is inside Station Eight with Jack Elliot and Selene Khan."

"Samson Mark Three?" Marcus asked.

"Just a minute," the robotic voice said. "I see. You're not rated for that revelation yet. Samson carries modified genetic material in him. He's fast and strong—like you."

"He's one of your children?" Marcus asked.

"Precisely," the robotic voice said.

"Does he possess advanced weaponry?" Marcus asked.

"It's quite possible. You must handle the situation with extreme prejudice."

Marcus frowned. The three subjects were in Station Eight. Was it possible Mother lacked information concerning their present actions? He'd always assumed she had security data on everything going on inside a station. By her words, it seemed his assumption was faulty.

"What about Dr. Khan?" Marcus asked. "Do you still desire her capture?"

"More than ever," the robotic voice said. "Her resourcefulness impresses me. I want her captured with minimal damage. I plan to use her. The other two are highly dangerous. I cannot risk their continued existence. I'm too close…"

"Yes?" Marcus asked.

"Hurry, my boy," the robotic voice said. "In this instance, you may use a Level II weapon and security arrangement."

Marcus raised his eyebrows. A Level II weapon and field— this was unprecedented.

"Dr. Khan has acquired a hummer, by the way. It seems she stole it from Station Thirteen. If I had been informed earlier…"

Marcus kept his features deadpan. Mother had dropped several amazing hints tonight. Could it be possible the nearness of The Day caused her anxiety? Normally, Mother acted as cold as ice. He would have to remember that she was human after all.

"I should be at Alamut Castle in fifteen minutes," he said.

"That should be sufficient. Show me your mettle, my boy, and I will bump you into the next rank once you reach headquarters. The things I can show you…You will marvel at what I am about to achieve. Your wildest dreams cannot conceive of it, dearest Marcus. That means your highest concentration is needed tonight."

"I hear and obey," he said.

Mother cut the connection.

With a scowl, Marcus ordered Ney to lower the tablet. Then, the big man put a little more pressure on the accelerator. The SUV's tires squealed as they took the next turn faster than ever.

STATION EIGHT
IRAN

Selene felt strung-out, her nerves exhausted. The golden Anubis robot had severely shaken her. The stone object with its hideous needles—it truly gave longevity treatments?

This was too strange, too unbelievable. Why had the instructions been written in ancient Egyptian hieroglyphics? Could Samson's theories be correct? Had Souk touched upon the truth? Did a few select women throughout history live incredibly long lives? Had they been the genius behind a vast conspiracy stretching throughout time?

"I just realized something," Samson said.

Selene remained mute.

"What's that?" Jack asked.

"The golden robot..." Samson said. "It brings to mind a story from ancient Crete. Legend holds that a giant man made of bronze patrolled the shoreline three times a day. Its name was Talos. Some stories say the bronze man hurled rocks at passing ships to scare them away."

"You're suggesting the robot used to do that?" Jack asked.

"Many myths and legends contain hints of truth," Samson said. "Maybe the legend of Talos is an old memory of golden robots."

309

Selene shook her head. It felt as if her world tilted toward madness. The man couldn't be serious, could he?

"We must hurry," Samson said. "Mother will not rest until she's stopped us."

The big man marched them through Station Eight. With the hummer, as he called it, he opened hatches that had resisted his best efforts previously. They moved along a gleaming steel corridor, the diffuse glow in the ceiling lighting their way.

Jack kept touching his right wrist. It had already purpled from the robot's treatment. The D17 agent looked more worn than ever. He never complained, though. The man had a will of iron, refusing to succumb. What had made him like that? He'd shouted at them to run away at the end. Selene hadn't expected such gallantry from him. Jack Elliot seemed too grim for such gestures.

Samson opened yet another hatch. It felt as if they'd been tramping underground for hours already. How deep had they gone?

Selene looked around at this new, large chamber. It was vast with colored lights pulsating slowly along the walls. The ceiling brightened with the diffuse glow.

Samson turned in a circle. Finally, he pointed at a large screen. "That's it, I believe."

"What is it?" Selene asked.

"You've heard of a ship's log?" he asked.

She nodded.

"I think that's the station's log, done with video, or what passed as video back then."

"You're talking about the original builders?" Selene asked.

"That's what I'm hoping for," the big man said.

Jack moved to a chair, slumping into it. He set his purpled wrist on his lap. Then he massaged his eyes. When Jack saw her watching him, he nodded as if to encourage her.

"If you'll give me a few minutes," Samson said, "I should be able to get this operational."

Selene went to another chair, sitting down. The strung-out feeling grew. She remembered the toughest year in college, studying for finals. Hour after hour, day after day, cramming data into her brain had left her feeling thinned out. Danny

Ferguson had suggested she ingest speed to keep her awake for the last final.

She'd followed his advice. In those days, she had done whatever he suggested. After the week of study and then in the test hall, trembling from the speed—that's how she felt now. She was exhausted, but she was wired and excited. The mystery of all this had built to an incredible degree. She yearned to know the reason for the stations.

It was frustrating watching Samson at the controls. He tapped screens, pressed buttons and adjusted dials. The dials more than anything else told her this wasn't present-day control systems.

"Hmm," Samson said. He tapped an area. The lights in the room began to flicker.

Selene looked up, terrified he was going to destroy the place or wipe data banks of their records.

Samson continued to turn dials, press buttons—the flickering quit. Now, colored lights began to blink along the walls in new sequences. A soft hum told Selene he'd done something to the machines.

"Ah," the big man said. "I'm beginning to understand."

Samson didn't elaborate. He kept experimenting. Selene wondered what he'd done before Mother had banished him to this place? When had he learned to operate this kind of machinery?

Selene thought about getting up and comparing notes with Jack to see what he thought about all this. She simply didn't have the energy.

Time passed. Selene wondered if she dozed with her eyes open. Jack slouched in his seat with his eyes closed, snoring from time to time. Maybe the D17 agent knew how to catnap when he had the chance.

"I've found it," Samson said, "the beginning process, at least."

Selene sat up, the excitement bubbling within her. Words in a foreign language spoke solemnly from wall speakers. Selene found herself walking toward Samson. The big man sat hunched at his controls, absorbed with the video on the screen at his panel.

Selene saw a woman, tall, statuesque with flowing dark hair almost to her rear. She wore a gown that hid her feet. Could that be Mother? Others worked in the background. It looked like this exact chamber.

The woman spoke, her gesture taking in the chamber and the people in it. Most of them looked Asian.

"What's she saying?" Selene whispered.

Samson didn't acknowledge the question, but he said, "After all these years, we are about to begin the process."

"You understand her?"

Selene turned, seeing Jack standing on the other side of Samson. Elliot had asked the question.

"I do," the big man said.

The woman on the screen spoke again. Samson interpreted her words: "This is a trial run to see how much energy the capacitors still have. Their technology is amazing. After a millennium, the stations still function. I cannot believe it has taken me so long to find them. The wasted centuries…it is mind-numbing."

Selene and Jack traded glances.

"Can Mother be the only woman to have taken the longevity treatments?" Selene whispered.

"It's impossible to tell," Samson said. "We need more data."

"If—" Jack said.

"Shhh," Samson said. "This looks important."

Selene edged closer to get a better view of the screen. It must have jumped time. The statuesque woman wore a Victorian gown. She faced the camera or faced whatever recorded the event. A shimmering field blocked her features from view.

"Is that some kind of mask?" Selene asked.

"What do you mean?" Samson asked.

"Is Mother human or some kind of energy being masquerading as human?"

"Notice her hands," Jack said. "She's wearing gloves."

"The gloves must be an affectation," Samson said. "I can see her throat. It's skin of a brownish hue. She's human all right."

Selene leaned closer, examining the woman in the screen. Dr. Khan nodded after a moment, exhaling with relief. She could believe Mother was human wearing some kind of energy mask. She was relieved they weren't dealing with aliens. That would be too freaky.

The woman on the screen spoke rapidly now.

"She's giving commands," Samson explained. "The others look busy. Can you hear the background noise?"

"I do," Selene said. "It sounds like giant generators."

The next moment, the scene altered dramatically. Everything shook in the old recording. Sparks flew from the walls. Smoke billowed and several Asians screamed, tottering around the room as they turned into electric torches. Their hair stood on end as a blue glow engulfed them. One by one, the harmed personnel melted, their charred corpses thudding onto the steel floor.

The survivors ran from the chamber. Only Mother remained. A blue nimbus shone around her, possibly some sort of personal force-screen.

After a time, the nimbus snapped off. The woman Selene believed was Mother slowly approached a panel. Her gloved hands turned dials and pressed controls.

Samson leaned forward. So did Selene and Jack.

"What is that?" Selene whispered. The screen no longer showed the underground chamber but a flattened forest with every tree lying on the ground in the same direction.

"I'm not sure," Samson said. "It looks vaguely familiar, though."

"Those are pine trees," Jack noted.

"Yes," Samson said. "I remember where I've seen such a sight. It looks like the Tunguska Event."

"What's that mean in English?" Jack asked.

Selene shuddered as she stared at the devastation on the screen. The entire forest as far as she could see had been flattened against the ground. Had some kind of bomb done that?

"The Tunguska River is in Siberia," Samson said.

Mother spoke on the screen again. She spoke slowly, quietly. Samson strained to hear what she said.

313

"Well?" Selene asked.

"She's overwhelmed," Samson said. "Station Eight...is destroyed. It had an overload. The capacitors are empty. The other stations—emergency procedures saved them. She's wondering how many years—centuries maybe—it will take to repair the damage from the single botched test."

"Does she say anything about Tunguska?" Selene whispered. "Are we sure that's what we saw?"

Samson continued to listen to Mother. He nodded shortly. "Yes indeed," the big man said. "Gravitational forces slipped from the proper magnetic controls. Before the override systems saved the other stations, a magnetic energy pod flattened the pine trees with an explosive air burst."

Samson turned around, staring at Selene. "There's one mystery solved. We know now why no one ever found any meteor remains at Tunguska. Mother destroyed the Siberian Forest, not debris from space."

"What's the Tunguska Event?" Jack asked. "How about someone explain it to me? Why haven't I ever heard of it before?"

Samson faced Elliot. "Maybe because it happened in 1908," the big man said.

STATION EIGHT
IRAN

"1908?" Jack asked. "I don't understand. I've been listening to what you have been saying. It sounds to me like...*Mother* just discovered the station. She ran a test, correct?"

Samson nodded.

"That means she found the station or stations around 1908, maybe a little earlier," Jack said.

"Yes. I'd agree with that."

"Yet, she or her clones or whoever those women were have been around since...the dawn of time? Is that right?"

"No," Samson said. "The dawn of time, who can say when that happened for humanity? The Book suggests one date. Modern science gives another."

"Oh, please," Selene said. "Let's not get into *that*."

Jack glanced at Selene, surprised at her sudden anger.

"I believe that Mother or those like her have been around since the oracle of Ammon," Samson said. "I find it suggestive we found a robot of Anubis and hieroglyphics on the stone object. The legend of Talos belongs to Minoan Crete, which was around during the time of the pharaohs."

"Why is any of that important?" Jack asked. "Are you saying the ancient Egyptians built all this?"

"Not at all," Samson said. "If you study the ancient Egyptians, however, you find they claim to have gained their knowledge elsewhere. The god Thoth was supposed to have taught them their advanced sciences and medicines, and he was supposed to have lived for ten thousand years."

"You actually believe that?" Selene asked angrily.

"I've studied the ancient myths and religions," Samson said. "As I suggested earlier, I believe they contain particles of truth. Clearly, someone built the stations. Just as clearly, the ancient Egyptians did not possess these marvels. Still, they built the pyramids and practiced advanced medicine far in advance of the other ancient peoples around them."

"So what's your conclusion?" Selene asked.

Samson studied his thick hands. "I'm not sure yet. I desire more data."

"No!" Selene said. "You believe more than you're saying. I'd like to hear your theories."

"First, tell me this," Jack said. Why was Dr. Khan so angry? What was Samson saying that had upset her?

"Tell you what?" the Assyrian asked.

"What is the Tunguska Event? What happened when Mother turned on the station? Maybe if we know more about the event, it can help us understand what she's trying to do now."

"That's an excellent point," Samson said. "The event has puzzled scientists for some time. Theorists have suggested that an air burst from a small asteroid or comet exploded with ten to fifteen megatons of force. That would make it one thousand times greater than the Hiroshima atomic bomb. The blast knocked down an estimated eighty million trees in an 830 square mile area. The shock wave would have measured 5.0 on the Richter scale."

"And Mother caused this with her test?" Jack asked.

"Exactly," Samson said. "She did it with an explosive magnetic pod and gravity waves, apparently."

Jack shook his head. "What could she have possibly been trying to do?"

"Yes…" Samson said. "That is the question. Do you have any ideas, Doctor?"

Selene uncrossed her arms. "Yes. I have an idea. Magnetics...I find that interesting. Some birds can sense magnetic fields. It's said to help them during long flights so they know which direction to travel. Could a bizarre magnetic field have upset the birds at Angkor Wat?"

"What does the ancient Cambodian temple have to do with any of this?" Samson asked.

Selene told him the story about the suicidal birds.

"As you say," Samson murmured, "interesting. Could magnetics have anything to do with the hotter temperatures across the planet?"

"I don't see how," Selene said.

"The scale of what we're seeing is..." Jack shook his head. "I find it hard to wrap my mind around it. If all these stations had to coordinate, what does that imply? Why build the stations and why leave them on autopilot for most of human history? Where did the builders go? Did aliens make the stations or was there a technologically advanced society before...before recorded history? "

"It's too bad you're never going to find out," a deep-voiced man said from behind.

Jack whirled around, drawing the semiautomatic from his waistband as he did. He saw the big man from the D'erlon Plant stride into the chamber. He'd never forget the soldier. Two others flanked him, each of them with a drawn weapon.

Jack fired without thinking, putting two bullets into the leftward man. As that person pitched to the floor, he recognized David Carter.

The massive soldier aimed a device at Samson. Jack's shots didn't seem to upset or worry him. The Assyrian's chest burst open with a spray of blood and gore. Samson toppled backward with a groan, striking a panel and crashing onto the floor with blood gushing from his mouth.

Jack pumped three shots out as fast as he could pull the trigger, having targeted the huge soldier. A blue nimbus glowed around the soldier, startling Jack. Each bullet slowed down and then stopped altogether as it struck the field. It was as if time slowed down in the energy field. The bullets began to tumble downward in slow motion. Each one struck the floor, rolling away from the soldier. Once they left the energy field, they rolled at regular speed.

The soldier laughed. "Oh, you're good, faster than a striking cobra. I would even say you're exceptional for a regular man. It's too bad you're so badly outclassed. Good-bye Agent Elliot."

The soldier aimed the flat black device at him. Jack fired again. He didn't know what else to do.

Heat bloomed against his chest. Then, Jack cried out as something intensely hot burned through him. The last thing Jack knew was falling…falling…falling…

-70-

HIDDEN RUNWAY
IRAN

Selene woke up to the Frenchman shaking her.

"It is time, mademoiselle. You must use your own two feet. I for one am tired of carrying you. As pretty as you are, you weigh too much."

She stared at the face in front of her, trying to comprehend what was going on. The last thing she remembered—

Selene groaned, flinching from the Frenchman. They'd killed Jack Elliot and Samson. The soldier had done it so effortlessly, so easily. It was the same giant man she'd shot in the throat under the Temple of Ammon. How could he be up and around like this? His throat was smooth without any scar or wound. Right there at the end in the control chamber, it seemed as if the soldier had used a personal force field, just as Mother had used in the video. Jack had never had a chance against the soldier.

"Dr. Khan," Ney said. "Can you hear me?" He snapped his fingers near her face.

Selene blinked. The soldier had approached her after murdering Jack. She'd wondered if he'd wanted revenge for the throat-shot. He'd put a cloth over her mouth. That was the last thing she remembered.

They kidnapped me. Why would they do that? What am I to them?

"She is resistant," Ney complained.

"Help her," the deep-voiced but unseen soldier said. "We don't have time for games. This blasted heat—"

Selene didn't hear anymore. She felt the heat, though. It was like a wall slamming her in the face. She found it difficult to breathe. What was happening to the world?

The Frenchman put his hands behind her back, forcing her to sit up. He pushed harder. Selene bumped her head against the SUV's back seat.

"Careful," the deep-voiced soldier said. "If you injure her, I'll take it out on you."

"*Wei*, monsieur, I understand."

Ney pinched her hard in the side. Selene moaned, and she woke up a little more.

"Move your pretty tush," Ney hissed into her ear. "If he takes it out on me, I will take it out on you."

Selene found herself walking across a blistering hot tarmac. Stars glittered overhead. A plane, a business plane by the looks of it, loomed before her. Where were they taking her?

Then the reality of the situation slammed home. The shadowy people had caught her again. She tried to move her lips in order to ask questions. Her mouth was numb. Why didn't her mind work right?

"P-Please," she whispered.

"Please, cup my breast for me?" Ney asked in a humorous tone. "Please kiss me? I do not know what you want, mademoiselle. You must be specific."

Selene faded out...

An engine roared with life. She felt motion. Then, blessedly, a gush of cool air pulled back some of the veil over her mind. She sat by a window. The ground rushed under her. Then, the ground began to recede, gaining speed until a dark forest spread out below her.

I'm in the plane.

She looked around. The soldier and Ney were in the seats, and that was it. She was all alone with these monsters.

"Where..." Her voice was faint. Her throat felt raw. She swallowed several times, finally asking a little more loudly, "Where are we going?"

320

The soldier looked up. He had a notebook in his hands. It was Souk's notebook. The hummer was in the seat beside him.

"What did you say?" the soldier asked.

"Where are you taking me?"

"Mother wants you," he said.

"Why?"

The soldier nodded thoughtfully. "I don't know, but I'd like to."

"Why is it so hot outside?" Selene asked.

"Questions, questions," he said. "You can ask Mother when we reach Libya."

Selene looked down, frightened of him. She felt naked when he stared at her like that. He'd murdered Jack Elliot and Samson. They had been so close to uncovering the truth, too.

What is the truth? Will I ever know? Selene wanted to weep. She'd never felt more defeated in her life.

-71-

STATION EIGHT
IRAN

With exhausting effort as he lay on the chamber floor, Samson managed to slip a pill into his bloody mouth. The capsule was bitter to his taste buds. He had known it would be. His tongue felt so weak. It was difficult to breathe. Carefully, with great effort, he positioned the pill between his teeth.

Then, he waited. It had taken everything he had left to bring the pill this far. He was not sure he had anything left. He silently prayed one of the mighty prayers as told in the Book. Mentally, he begged God to give him the strength to do this. He pleaded, pleaded...

His teeth crunched the pill, breaking it. The bitterness almost made him spew out the substance. His was mouth was so dry, which was odd. He had blood in it.

Swallow the pieces of the pill. Do this last deed.

Convulsively, Samson swallowed the debris of the pill. At the end of the ordeal, he waited. He had no idea how long it took.

A lifetime later, strength flooded into his ruined body. He'd lost far too much blood and chest substance. Despite that, the power of the pill numbed the pain, allowing him to think again.

From that point, Samson began his greatest feat. He crawled across the floor, coming to the body of Jack Elliot. Samson couldn't tell if he was breathing, but it didn't matter anymore. He must do this thing as his last act of defiance against Mother.

Samson dragged the inert body of Jack Elliot through the steel corridors. It must have been a gruesome sight, the two of them. Time no longer had meaning. This was his final act of existence, dragging the inert form just a little farther.

An eon later, Samson realized he shined a flashlight in a dark chamber. The air tasted awful here. It didn't matter. In a few more minutes, he could allow himself to die. He would have done what he could.

Setting the flashlight on the ground, Samson dug in a pocket. He had a piece of folded paper at the bottom. He put the folded paper in front of the shining flashlight. That would have to do.

Afterward, Samson concentrated as he prayed again, summoning every article of faith. With one of his last breaths of life, Samson struggled to his feet.

He grabbed one of Jack's limp arms and hand over hand hauled the inert man to his feet. With agonizing effort, he lifted Elliot, staggering to the stone object. He laid Jack's body into the cavity. With his last surge of strength, Samson closed the stone lid and heard it latch.

At that moment, life departed Samson Mark Three. He toppled backward onto the steel floor, dead.

-72-

THE STONE OBJECT

Jack didn't hear the soft whirring sounds or the strange snick-like noises around him.

If he could have heard, he might have squirmed and thrashed. Instead, he did nothing. Half-moon bracelets slid out of the stone and circled his motionless arms, legs and chest-ruined torso. They clamped down, cinching him into place. Other restraints held his inert head in check.

Jack's eyelids didn't open. Therefore, he didn't see the dim red light bathing him or the silver needles inching nearer and nearer his flesh from every side. No hands moved the needles, but they seemed driven by a dark intelligence.

A mist jetted against his face. Maybe the numbing agent did its task. Maybe it didn't. In either case, at that moment, the needles stabbed into his flesh, but Jack's body didn't twist or flinch.

The needles bored mercilessly through his flesh and muscles into his bones as Samson had surmised they would do. Liquids in slender containers behind the needles waited. Then, a stopper in each needle pushed the liquids, forcing them through the needles and into Jack's bones so they soaked the marrow.

Soon, the needles slid out of his bones and then out of his skin, disappearing into the stone niches. The red light vanished, leaving Jack's body in stygian darkness.

Even more time passed. A biological acceleration must have occurred because Jack's body became hot. The process devoured the reserves of fat and some muscle tissue. Incredibly, the ruin of his chest, even the bones, reknit at a fantastic rate. Throughout his body, wounds disappeared as the internal heat continued. Finally, the process slowed and then quit, and his body temperature returned to normal.

Suddenly, Jack gasped. His eyes flew open, staring into darkness. He made a surge—the restraints had already slid out of sight. He found himself trapped and fell back exhausted. Mercifully, he passed out.

***

Jack awoke later, feeling different. It took several seconds for him to realize he felt no pain, no discomfort. In fact, he felt better, healthier than he ever had. A new vigor gave him hope.

He recalled the soldier. The big man had shot him with an invisible beam. Jack had fallen. He couldn't fathom anything after that.

I must be in the stone object. Someone must have put me in here. The needles—

Jack heaved against the lid. Slowly, it raised a fraction higher. He gained a better advantage because of that and heaved again. The lid opened a little more. Jack saw the light from the flashlight, and it gave him hope. He shoved harder still, opening the lid high enough to slither out.

Afterward, Jack stood panting against the stone object. He was ravenous and lightheaded. After a moments, he checked his skin. There were tiny pink dots all over. His chest was very pink, lacking hair. His shirt was charred in front while his pants and sleeves had tears and holes in them. That meant—

That meant the needles had sunk into his bones. The flesh had already begun to heal. The shirt confirmed the heat of the invisible beam. The pinkness of his chest showed he'd healed a massive amount. Maybe that's why he felt so hungry and thirsty. What else did this mean for him? Had the solution changed him?

Jack shook his head. He could theorize later. Right now, he had to think carefully. The soldier and his squad were in the facility. David Carter might be dead.

I killed David. I shot my friend.

Guilt billowed, a gnawing, accusing beast. With an effort of will, Jack forced that aside. He would accept the guilt later. Right now, he had a mission. He had to concentrate...

"What the," he said, seeing the folded note in front of the flashlight. He saw the dead Assyrian, realizing the man had saved his life. Samson's corpse told him the others—the enemy and Selene—must have left the station. Otherwise, they would have stopped Samson from coming here.

Jack took the note and unfolded it. He read what was written there. This was incredible, and it might even have been logical given the stone object. A new sense of purpose hardened in him. He knew what he had to do next. Now was as good a time to start as any. Thus, he picked up the flashlight, heading for the exit.

PART FOUR:
THE PYRAMID

-73-

LEARJET 85
EASTERN MEDITERRANEAN

The Learjet shook as it struck more turbulence. Selene hung onto her armrests with the seatbelt already cinched tight. The stars blazed through the window. Whenever she looked down outside, all she saw was the top of the thick cloud cover.

Despair ate at her. She'd struggled so hard for days on end, and it all meant defeat. The one hundred mile swim had all been for nothing. Her escape from the mind machine in the Siwa Oasis, the flight to Tehran—Mother won in the end. Who could defeat the ancient woman? Who could understand her resources? Who had built the stations?

The jet lurched upward, and so did Selene's stomach. She just wanted the ordeal to end. She wanted to go home, pull the covers over her head and sleep for a year, maybe never get up again. If only she could hold Danny one final time—

"What's wrong?" Marcus demanded.

Selene turned in her seat, peering across the aisle at the big man. He looked angry as he spoke through the plane's intercom.

"It's gotten worse," the pilot said. "It's hotter outside—"

"How much hotter?" Marcus demanded.

"It's one hundred and twenty-three outside the plane," the pilot said. "The number of superheated air pockets has grown, too. Worse, they've gotten more dangerous for us as they're even hotter than earlier."

Selene frowned. Clearly, the underground stations did something to the weather. They'd blasted a forest in Siberia to the ground in 1908. What caused the stations to uniformly heat the Earth now?

The fuselage's shaking lessened, allowing Selene's stomach to unclench. She found that her hands trembled. She still felt groggy, although no longer nauseous. Was that how Elliot had felt in Cairo and Tehran? The man had done fantastically given that.

"Hey," Marcus said.

Selene looked up at him.

The big man pitched her a water bottle. She fumbled the bottle but finally managed to grab it.

"Drink that," he said.

She studied the bottle, noticing the blue-tinted water. "Maybe later," she said.

"Look, if I wanted to drug you more, I would do it. Drinking that will help you feel better. I don't want any sick people on my plane."

She could see his logic. So she twisted off the cap, raised the bottle and glanced at him. He stared at her too intently. She lowered the blue water, suspicious again.

"Do I have to call Ney?" Marcus asked. "He'll pour the drink down your throat while I hold your mouth open."

Selene gauged the big man. He seemed tougher than Samson had been. Marcus seemed denser, his muscles longer, heavier, more compact. There was something off in his eyes. They were deadly, as if he was on the verge of going berserk. Frankly, he terrified her.

She sipped the water. It had a tang like orange juice.

"Drink all of it, sister."

Selene frowned, staring at him again. "Why do you call me that?"

Marcus's smile grew.

"If—"

"Drink it," he said. "Then I'll tell you. Then, you'll be in a condition to understand."

With a growing sense of fatalism, she put the mouth of the bottle to her lips and began to guzzle.

The drink was refreshing. She hadn't realized how thirsty she was until now. With a gasp, she pulled the empty bottle away. An immediate sense of lightheadedness struck. She closed her eyes and lowered her head until the top bumped against the seat in front of her.

"You lied to me," she slurred.

"Wait a few minutes," he rumbled. "You'll feel better soon. I don't have any reason to lie to you, sister."

"Stop calling me that. I'm not your sister."

"But you are," Marcus said. "You're one of us. That's easy to see up close. It must be why Mother wants you."

"What are you talking about?" Selene asked, with her eyes closed.

"Wait a bit. You should start to feel better soon."

She did wait, hating him as the minutes passed. He sat in his seat, watching her in his arrogant way.

Then, to her disgust, she did begin to feel better. She'd been unbelievably groggy before. He must have used chloroform on her.

Selene raised her head.

"Catch," Marcus said.

She turned just in time. He pitched her a basket. She caught it neatly this time, no longer fumbling things.

Selene tore off the plastic wrap. She was ravenous and hadn't realized it until now. The basket held two ham and cheese sandwiches. In short order, she devoured both.

Marcus tossed her another water bottle. This one contained normal liquid.

"Starting to feel human again?" he asked.

She avoided looking at or answering him.

"You're going home," he said. "Are you excited?"

"I don't know what you're talking about."

"Fair enough," Marcus said. "So if I were you, I'd be nicer to me so I could learn what's what."

"You're not me," she said.

"Are you still upset I killed your friends?"

330

"Yes!" she said. It struck her that some of her terror of him had evaporated. That didn't make sense...unless it had something to do with the blue water.

"Don't be upset," he told her. "I did them a favor killing them."

Selene glared at the grinning man. Soon, she looked away. The idea she had anything in common with him was preposterous.

"Do you realize that you're smarter than most people?" Marcus asked.

Selene shook her head.

"Substantially smarter," he added. "You're a better physical specimen as well. How do you think you managed the Indian Ocean swim without becoming a physical wreck? Good genes, of course."

"That's not true."

"It's nothing to be ashamed of," he said. "I know I have excellent genes. It's one of the things that makes me the best."

"The best at what?" she snapped.

"Ah," Marcus said, nodding. "That's a critical question. I'm not the best in the brains department. That would be Hela and Fredrick. It's one of the reasons they're Mothers' favorites."

Selene finally realized her position. She was talking to someone who knew the secrets she desperately wanted to know.

"Who is Mother exactly?" she asked.

"Yeah," Marcus said. "That's a damn shrewd question. I'd love to know myself. What did your little movie show you anyway?"

"I'm sure you already know."

"Nope," he said. "The nearest I've been to a regular station was outside under the Siwa temple. I've just been to headquarters, where you're going now."

"I suppose you're going to tell me that you don't know the reason for that, either."

"That's right," Marcus said.

Selene blinked several times. She believed him. He didn't know. In fact, she realized it was obvious he didn't know in the way he breathed, the radius of his pupils—

Selene groaned, lowering her head, massaging the upper bridge of her nose.

"You're finally feeling it," he said. "Does it tingle? I hear it tingles?"

"What are you talking about?" she whispered.

"Reason it out. You should be able to do that now."

Selene frowned, rubbing the bridge of her nose harder. Why should she know? He didn't make sense. He...

She sat up with a start. She felt a tingling sensation all over. It was worst in her fingertips. She shook her hands, looking up at him.

"Well?" he asked.

"What's happening to me?"

The big man shook his head. "That's not how it's going to work. You're going to tell me all kinds of things. You're a little Brainiac, aren't you? You're so smart, creating new gadgets. Yeah. I know about the TR-1010. I hear Hela created stuff, too. Frederick was more theoretical, not as hands-on, if you get my drift."

Selene closed her eyes. She could almost feel the wheels turning at hyper-speed in her head.

"You gave me a brain enhancer," she said.

"Sure did," he agreed.

"I suspect it must have been difficult for you to acquire it."

"You're right on target, little sister."

She clutched her head, squeezing. "You overdosed me. My thoughts can't slow down."

"We're short on time, as you can well expect. I gave you a double dose. It's a risk, but hey, I have to know a few things before—"

"Before we land and you make your great decision," Selene said. "You're in the dark about Mother, too, aren't you?"

"Not as much as most people are, but it's true I'm curious about a few things. The Day is almost here."

"The Day?"

"Think about it," Marcus said.

Selene's eyes grew wide. "The Day," she said. "The Day Mother turns all the stations on full blast to do whatever it is they do."

"There you go," Marcus said. "You're shifting into high gear. What did you see on the screen? That was Mother on it, wasn't it?"

"Why did you kill the others?"

"Had no choice, "Marcus said. "I don't want to guess wrong, you can understand. Mother won't approve if I fall out on the wrong side of her."

"Are you going to kill me once you're done with the questions?"

Marcus stared at her coldly.

Selene realized her life depended on what she could figure out in time. If Mother were too dangerous...would he try to kill her or be too afraid to try? Did he have truth-hearing ears as Samson claimed he'd possessed? Selene realized she could tell now if someone told the truth or not.

If I can't figure out Mother's game in time, or if it's something Marcus can't fight, he's going to kill me in order to cover his tracks of giving me the blue solution.

-74-

STATION EIGHT
IRAN

Jack staggered through the deep corridors of abandoned Station Eight. The air was foul down here. It was hot, too, making breathing questionable. He was also stuffed, having eaten and drunk far too much. It was crazy but he still felt ravenous.

He refrained from popping more almonds into his mouth. His pockets bulged with them, taken from Samson's hidden food stash.

The flashlight didn't shine as brightly as it used to. The batteries must be running low. He didn't relish the idea of trying to find his way back to the surface in the dark. He had to hurry and get this done.

With his hand before his mouth, Jack doggedly increased his pace. His skin shone with sweat and his hair was plastered to his scalp.

It was true he'd almost died. It was also true he felt stronger than at any time in his life. The serum in the needles had already begun their transformative work. He felt strength surging through his muscles. It was a heady experience. Nonetheless, the ordeal worsened the lower he traveled through the deep corridors.

What had begun some time ago as a low hum had become louder and steadier. It was a throb, a giant, mechanical heartbeat. It didn't soothe him in the slightest. It was the sound of approaching death, the heavy tick-tocks of a doomsday clock he didn't understand.

Samson's dying note spurred him on. The man had given his life to bring him to the stone object. The possibility the note was true...

Jack's eyes burned intensely. He marched with the same finality as the day the speed freak had slain his mom and dad. This was his task. This was why he lived right now. Nothing else mattered.

He kept seeing in his mind's eye the Victorian-dressed woman on the screen. He recalled the shimmering mask hiding her features. It had been highly advanced tech, greater than anything in human possession. This place—he couldn't fathom anyone having built it. The deepness of the shafts, the corridors, it had taken technology no one had ever possessed in the present age.

Logically, that meant no one in previous centuries had constructed these steel corridors either.

Samson had said Atlanteans might have made it or the Antediluvian people. The Assyrian had even suggested ancient astronauts.

Does it matter right now who built this place?

Jack staggered, coughing explosively. He breathed a pocket of bad air. Increasing speed, he staggered through the area, soon able to taste the air without gagging.

He shivered from exhaustion. The stone object had healed his concussion. Sheer tiredness was doing him in now. The D'erlon soldier had killed Samson. It made sense that the man had taken Selene. Why did the others want her?

"Focus on your mission," Jack whispered.

The flashlight's beam weakened, growing dimmer over time. The throb surrounded him now. The steel walls sweated. He put his hand on a section of metal, jerking it off a moment later, shaking his hand. The walls were *hot*. They also vibrated.

Jack did not like it down here. "Just a little farther, Elliot," he told himself.

After a span of time—he didn't know how long—he came to a hatch. This one looked old. It had a round device on it.

Jack shined the light on the glass. A needle was in the dark area. A little more to the left and the needle would be in the red.

This was the place all right. The note had led him here. Samson's last plan might actually work. He couldn't believe it.

"Enough," Jack said, sounding angry. He didn't like this excessive thinking. It was time to act, to do. If he failed—

"Screw that," he said.

He pressed the buttons on a panel in an exact sequence. After pressing the last one, he waited. Had he done it wrong? Had—

A loud *clack* sounded from the door. It cracked open, and wisps of frost trickled from it.

This is going to be cold.

Jack grabbed the handle and pulled. The hatch was heavy. He continued to pull, opening a thick door, allowing freezing cold to billow out.

Jack shined the beam into a frost-covered chamber. Cyclers pumped loudly. He walked into the freezing cubicle, immediately beginning to shiver.

He didn't have a shirt, only pants and boots. His body was slick with sweat. He shivered uncontrollably and his teeth chattered.

Jack shined his light on frosty, ice-coated machines. There was a long central tube in the center of the room. Staggering there, he tried to figure out the controls on the cryogenic cycler.

Jack shined the light around until he spied a panel. His teeth chattered nonstop. He went to the panel, using his fingernails to scrape off frost. Finally, he recognized a control pad, each button with a weird hieroglyphic on it. He began to push stiff buttons in a special sequence. He had to stop, pulling out the paper to look at it. His hand shook too much for him to read the note.

Jack retraced his steps, exiting the freezing cubicle. He shined the beam on the paper in the hot area, reading the hieroglyphic sequence. Once he was sure that he could remember it thirty seconds from now, Jack steeled himself and hurried back into the cold to finish typing the sequence.

336

A cycler speeded up. Steam and frost billowed from various machines. A hammering sound grew deafening. Finally, that dwindled to a pumping sound.

Jack just stood there, shivering like a fool, waiting. He rubbed his body and arms. This wasn't going to work, was it?

"What else should I have done?" he asked aloud.

A loud creak caused him to spin around and face the metal casket. The top made a snapping sound. Slowly, with rusty hinges creaking, the cover began to rise like the dead coming to life.

Jack stopped breathing. Had he done it?

The lid halted as steam billowed. After enough steam poured out, Jack could see a body down there. It began to tremble as the fingers and toes twitched. The person in the cryogenic tube had apparently survived the ordeal of time and its disease. Now, could it survive revival? And if it did, was he an imbecile because the machines hadn't worked right or would he remember enough to help Jack take the next step?

337

-75-

LEARJET 85
CENTRAL MEDITERRANEAN

Selene stared at Marcus, her brother in some fashion. Her mind still spun at high speed. "You're a genetic experiment just as Samson said he was."

The big man nodded encouragingly. "Mother called him Samson Mark Three."

"The third model of the Samson series?" Selene asked.

Marcus shrugged.

"What happened to the other Samsons?"

"I have no idea," he said.

"Are there other 'models' in your series, men exactly like you?"

The soldier's eyes narrowed. It appeared he didn't like the idea.

"If there are more like you," Selene said, "it doesn't sound like you've met them."

"No. There are none like me, although there are more of *us.*"

Selene thought about that. She'd been an orphan. Had Mother put her in the orphanage, or had someone escaped Mother's shadowy service and put her in an orphanage for safekeeping?

Marcus made an impatient gesture. "Let's stick to the issue. We're going to be in Libya soon enough. I have to know..."

"Know what?" Selene asked.

Marcus watched her. It seemed to Selene that he gauged what he could tell her. He was gambling with his life, with his status in Mother's organization. What would cause him to gamble? What did he fear?

She felt it would be unwise asking him that last question. Marcus exuded confidence, power—*ambition*. Maybe that was the key. Marcus didn't like second place, or whatever place he did have. This man wanted to rule. He was born to rule. Mother must realize that. Surely, she wouldn't have survived the ages without understanding human behavior. Mother must have safeguards in place.

"If you're quiet," Marcus said, "it means you're thinking. If you're thinking without talking, I take it to mean you're plotting against me. That is unwise. It's time to talk. Tell me about Mother."

"The shoe should be on the other foot," Selene said. "I hardly know anything."

"Which is why I gave you a double-dose of the Brainiac solution," Marcus rumbled. "You have no idea how difficult that was to achieve."

"I know this much. Mother will have safeguards against you."

"Now you're stalling," Marcus said. "That implies you know something you're trying to hide. That's what I want to hear."

Selene smiled bleakly. Thoughts roared in her head. She was making one intuitive leap after another. It bewildered her. It was frightening. The things she understood in this moment—

"I should be recording my thoughts," Selene said. "I don't want to forget any of this."

"What do you surmise about Mother from the video?" Marcus asked, leaning toward her.

Selene made a vague gesture. "Back then Mother was surprised by the stations. She spoke of centuries of wasted effort. That implies several things. First, that she hadn't known about the stations until quite recently. I mean back then in 1908."

"How can you know the precise date?"

Selene told Marcus about the Tunguska Event.

"Got it," he said. "What else did the video imply?"

"That Mother was old even then. Do you have any idea how old she might be?"

"I've guessed centuries," Marcus said, "three or four hundred years, at least."

"Could she be four thousand years old?"

Marcus turned away, staring out a window. "I can't accept that. Such vast age would have made her inhuman, made her vastly different in outlook from the rest of us. She's never struck me as fundamentally different, just diabolically clever."

"That's an interesting point," Selene conceded. "Let's go with that for now. Mother is...less than nine hundred years old."

"Why did you pick that number?"

"Methuselah is supposed to have been the oldest person in legend. He apparently lived 969 years."

"Fine, fine," Marcus said.

"If that's the case—that Mother isn't older than 900 years—it would imply one Mother after another taught her understudy. What did the older Mothers teach the younger ones? Have they been searching for the stations all this time? If so, why didn't they find them until around 1908? From what I watched, it seemed the present Mother didn't know everything there was to know about Station Eight."

"Ah," Marcus said, rubbing his hands. "This is interesting. Keep going, little sister. You're doing fine."

Selene exhaled raggedly. Her mind whirled but her body felt as if she'd run a long race. The drug speeded thought process was taking a physical toll.

Could it be killing me? The idea was chilling. Selene had no doubt Marcus could do that to her. It's possible he didn't know of the aftereffects. Surely, there were some.

"Let me ask you something," Selene said.

Marcus made to object.

"I need data if I'm going to give you the answers you seek."

He thought about that, finally nodding. "Ask away," he said.

340

"What have you been doing for Mother? What's your job?"

"I run various departments," he said, "killing now and again when it needs doing."

Selene rubbed her forehead. "It seems odd to me you'd be running department stores."

"Plants," he said. "I've run various plants that came under different departmental headings."

"Oh. Do you mean manufacturing plants?"

"Exactly," he said. "They've produced antimatter, magnetic seals, magnetic containers, high-energy stabilizers, gravitational coils and other...unique components."

"These plants made things beyond modern science as the rest of the world conceives of it?"

"Yeah," Marcus said. "That's right. Is that significant?"

Selene laughed, which made him scowl.

"None of that. I've had a lifetime of... Never mind," he finished.

Selene ingested that as more data. It would seem Marcus suffered from an inferiority complex. Yes, Hela and Frederick, he envied those two. Mother treated them better than she treated him. Is that what this was all about or was her first estimate correct: that of soaring ambition?

"When you get that faraway look in your eyes," Marcus said, "it means you're plotting about me. I know. I've seen it all my life. So, stop it or I'll stop it for you."

"I'm going to make a guess," Selene said. "I'm combining your information and Mother's hints in the video. She broke Station Eight in 1908. In some fashion, she harmed the other stations as well. For the last one hundred years, Mother has been repairing the damage to the other stations. She wants to turn them on again and do whatever they were built to do."

"Yes, obviously," Marcus said. "What is it they're going to do? That's what I want to know."

Selene rubbed her chin. It felt like she was missing something. The something hovered just beyond her consciousness. "Give me a second. I mean, don't get angry because I'm quiet. You have to let me sort this out and make intuitive leaps. If you're going to get paranoid each time, I don't think I can do this."

Marcus grumbled under his breath, but after a moment, he nodded. "Go ahead, brainstorm."

Selene rested the back of her head against her seat. She closed her eyes. It felt as if she could see her inner eyelids. Flashes of light popped here, there—

"Oh," she said. Selene regarded the anxious soldier. "We're missing the easiest point."

"Yeah?" he asked in an excited voice.

She cataloged the thought that everyone wanted to understand what Mother's grand purpose was. The need to know what she was trying to do was like an intoxicant.

"Someone built the stations," Selene said. "The fact of their existence obviously proves the builders. The historical records don't tell of them. Well, that's not exactly right, is it? Maybe history does record them, but it only does so through myths and legends. What does that tell us? A lot, I'd say."

"Yeah?" Marcus asked.

"You might think this is mere conjecture, but I think it's very clear given the facts. It means a catastrophe or cataclysm took out the original builders. This catastrophe clearly destroyed the knowledge of their technology. I mean, no one knew about these stations for countless centuries. That's a critical point. The present Mother only found out about them a little over one hundred years ago."

"Right, right," Marcus said. "That makes sense."

"There are legends of a worldwide cataclysm in nearly every culture," Selene said. "The legend of Atlantis tells of devastating destruction. There are universal Flood myths from almost every ancient society. Might those stories have a basis in fact? Let us suggest yes—" Selene stopped abruptly.

"What is it?" Marcus asked.

She felt hot all over, although her face felt numb. She blinked repeatedly. The full impact of the possibility of her idea frightened Selene. She regarded the soldier.

"Don't you see?" she asked.

"No! Tell me. I want to understand."

"It's so straightforward..." Selene said. She took a deep breath. "Whoever built the stations used them. The action brought a mighty catastrophe to the planet. That's what

342

destroyed the advanced civilization. I mean, it wiped it out—gone. There were a few survivors. Samson told me the ancient Egyptians believed their knowledge of mathematics and medicine came from Thoth, who was said to have come from an advanced civilization. The ancient Egyptians held him in such awe they thought of him as a god.

"Mother tested the stations in 1908. What happened then? Well, she created a mini-catastrophe, the Tunguska Event in Siberia. Before more disasters happened, override systems took over, shutting down the other stations. Unfortunately for her, the Tunguska Event caused the effective end of Station Eight."

"So you're saying…what exactly?" Marcus asked.

"What happens when The Day arrives?" Selene asked. "Maybe it's already happening. Look outside. I bet the stations working in unison is causing the temperature to rise so dramatically. In other words, it could be more than possible that Mother is unleashing another worldwide cataclysm. She hopes to do something amazing, but she's making the same or similar mistakes as the original builders did. Mother could be bringing about the end of human civilization."

Marcus's mouth opened. "If that's true…we'd have to stop her."

"Yes," Selene whispered.

There was a commotion from the front of the aisle as the cockpit door swung open. A lean man wearing a pilot's uniform and badly needing a shave stepped out. He strode toward them with an intense look on his face.

After several strides, a gun went off in rapid succession. Three bullet holes appeared in the pilot's chest, each spaced in the area around his heart. The unshaven pilot staggered backward as shock transformed his features. Bumping up against a seat, he stopped and slowly examined his chest. Blood began to trickle from the wounds. He frowned, coughed and sank to his knees.

Another shot rang out. He fell onto the aisle.

Selene turned. Marcus remained in his seat, shocked. She looked back another row. Ney leaned out into the aisle with a gun in his hand. Smoke trickled from the end of the barrel.

343

Ney stood with wide staring eyes. It seemed that he was finding it difficult to speak. Finally, he managed in a husky voice, "I am sorry to inform you, monsieur, mademoiselle, but you are badly in need of a pilot to fly the plane."

CRYOGENIC CHAMBER
STATION EIGHT

Jack helped an ailing, bald, skeletal man out of the cryogenic tube. The man coughed every time he sucked air. His breath smelled horrible and his eyes were bloodshot, leaking a yellow fluid.

"Wrap this around your shoulders," Jack said, throwing a dusty quilt around the man's neck. He'd found it in a chest in the corner.

The man nodded as he raised skeletal arms. He looked wasted, which made sense. According to Samson's note, the man had an incurable disease. It's why they'd put him in a cryogenic tube.

"Let me help you up," Jack said.

The man must have understood English. He allowed Jack to help him. The man was cold and shivering. Together, they moved into the hot corridor.

"Maybe you should lie down," Jack suggested.

"Let… me lean…against a wall," the man said, coughing afterward.

"Can't do that," Jack said. "The walls are too hot here."

The man turned his bloodshot eyes on Jack.

"The station's running after a fashion," Jack told him.

The tall, stooped man kept staring at him. It was an uncomfortable sensation. "You're not one of hers," the man finally said.

"If you mean Mother, no, I'm not. I belong to D17."

"I've never heard of it," the man whispered.

"We're a ghostly American Intelligence organization. We haven't known it, but I think we've been battling Mother for the last few years."

"Ah," the man said. He sat on the floor, careful to keep on the quilt.

"Do you want food, water, anything?" Jack asked.

The man nodded.

"Name it. I'll see what I can do."

"First tell me. Why…why are you here?"

"Have you ever heard of someone named Samson?"

"Of course," the man said. "That's my name. Oh. Do you mean Samson Mark Three?"

"Maybe," Jack said. Yes, he could see the resemblance now that he searched for it. Without any facial hair and lacking more than one hundred extra pounds…this could be what, a clone?

I guess it's possible.

"I am Samson Mark Two, an earlier model. We met, though. Mother has always striven to avoid that happening. I told Mark Three…" The skeletal man frowned, suddenly hesitant. "Why should I tell you anything?"

Jack began to explain the situation. About a third of the way through, the skeletal Samson asked for water. Jack hurried to the chest, bringing the man dusty water bottles and old packages of concentrates.

For the moment, Samson Mark Two was content to guzzle water.

"Go ahead," he told Jack. "Finish your story. It's fascinating."

Agent Elliot did just that, leaving little out. Before he finished, Samson Mark Two tore open a food packet, eating the crunchy substance. Finally, Jack told him the latest, including the long journey down here to the cryogenic chamber.

"I'm beginning to perceive that my brother desired me to help you. He must believe we're in the final stages. You do realize that waking me like this dooms me to die?"

Jack found it impossible then to meet the man's gaze. Too many people had died lately instead of him. He was building a heavy blood debt.

"It's all right," the withered Samson said, patting Jack on the shoulder. "I forgive you because I accept my brother's judgment. He was a good man, a wise man, if possessed of too few of the critical facts. I felt it better to keep them to myself. I was never as trusting as he was. If I told him all that I knew, I wondered if he would ever thaw me out. Maybe I misjudged him."

"You actually know what's going on?" Jack asked.

The man endured another coughing fit and drank a long swallow of water before he could answer.

"By 'know what's going on...' I assume you mean the nature of the stations?" Samson asked.

"Sure," Jack said.

"I have a good idea, yes. I was one of Mother's original thinkers. I was part of the experimental brain team she created to help her solve what she couldn't."

"I'm not sure I understand that," Jack said.

"No, of course not," Samson said. "To be precise, Mother was too much of a primitive to know how to fix what she broke in 1908. Although, to be fair to her, many of the components had already been damaged before the Tunguska Event. She was born during the Black Death, sometime in the fourteen hundreds, sometime in the 1350s, I believe."

"She's over seven hundred years old?" Jack asked.

"Sounds strange to say it out loud," Samson said. "The modern mind recoils at the idea. But the answer is yes. You should understand that the Mother before her trained our present Mother. I think the age limit with the serum is close to nine hundred years at the most. The various Mothers didn't know about the stations then, although they had a few amazing devices. I suspect they used the various devices more like magical artifacts than simple tools. The point is this: Mother was raised and lived most of her life in a pre-technological age.

Of course, one could argue there were technological revolutions in the Middle Ages with the windmill and—"

"Excuse me for interrupting," Jack said. "But you don't need to get all technical with me. I'll believe you. Mother thinks like a primitive. In other words, you can't teach an old dog new tricks."

"That's a colloquial way to say it, but it's apt nonetheless. Yet, sometimes you can teach the old dog something new. It gets harder the older the person becomes, though. Mother thought of a brilliant solution. It involved some startling new discoveries and modern technologies."

Jack nodded impatiently. This was taking too long. Just like Samson Mark Three, this one liked to talk. If they were going to do something, the sooner they started the better.

"Ancient legends have something of the truth in them," Samson said. "That's critical to how I discovered Mother's method to solving her problem."

"Great," Jack said.

Samson coughed weakly. He had gained some strength since leaving the cryogenic tube. The water seemed to have helped the most. Now, though, the skeletal man began to tremble.

"Are you too hot?" Jack asked.

"No. I-I feel faint. C-cold all of a sudden," the man stammered.

"Stay with me. You can't pass out now."

Samson Mark Two nodded. The weak coughing didn't stop, though. He continued one cough after another. It got worse, and the man began to lose color.

"Drink this," Jack said, shoving a water bottle at him.

"Shock," Samson gasped. "I'm going—*cough, cough, cough*—through post-recovery shock. I'm—" The man's eyes closed as if on their own accord. A second later, he collapsed, falling, striking his head as he began to thrash on the floor.

-77-

LEARJET 85
CENTRAL MEDITERRANEAN

Selene couldn't believe it. Ney had just shot the pilot dead. The wide-eyed, French DGSE agent stepped into the aisle, passing the big man and Selene before turning toward them. The Frenchman aimed his gun at the soldier's chest.

"I will admit that I feel strange, monsieur, mademoiselle. I ask you to excuse my odd behavior."

"Put down the gun," Marcus ordered in a stern voice.

Ney's eyes widened and the staring, hypnotic quality became even more pronounced. "I went under the mind machine, monsieur. You know that, yes?"

"Why did you shoot Sten?" Marcus demanded.

Ney grinned so widely that it revealed his back molars. "You do not understand yet, monsieur. You lack the final pieces to see clearly. But I, Ney Blanc, I see. I belong to the DGSE. I serve France and in doing this I have served humanity."

"You serve Mother," Marcus said.

"Yes, yes, I did. The mind machine turned me as it has so many others. But I am a cunning man, monsieur, the greatest agent France ever possessed. I have learned and studied you people. Piece by piece, I regained my native wits. Mother never suspected because I am the best of the best."

A frown touched the agent's features. "I have killed many innocent people and many not so innocent. I have remained undercover all this time. I have come back to who and what I am, monsieur. That is what I am telling you."

"Why did you shoot the pilot?" Marcus snarled. "By killing him, you aided Mother. Haven't you been listening to her?" He indicated Selene. "Bah! The mind machine scrambled your thoughts. You're confused. Put down the gun."

Ney shook his head. "*You* are confused, monsieur."

Marcus stared at the Frenchman. Selene had the impression the big man wanted to launch out of his seat and rend the smug Ney in two. Finally, the soldier leashed his visible anger.

"What do you know?" Marcus asked in a strained voice.

Ney straightened his jacket as if preening. He seemed inordinately proud of himself. Still, Selene noticed he remained alert enough to keep his gun trained on Marcus.

"The pilot was Mother's watchdog," Ney said. "He was coming to kill you, monsieur. I have just saved your murderous life. You are in my debt."

"The Hell you say!"

"I will prove it." Ney head gestured to Selene. "Go to the pilot. Check his pockets. Bring what you find there."

Selene glanced at Marcus.

"Do it," the big man growled. "Let's see if this imbecile knows what he's talking about."

Ney stepped back into a seat row, giving her space to pass. Selene eyed him as she approached. Ney's eyes were glazed, fixed on Marcus. He didn't even seem to be aware of her.

With a growing sense of surrealism, Selene hurried to the pilot. She knelt by his cooling corpse, and she saw it. There was no need to check the pockets. Near one of the pilot's hands was a small, black flat device with a tiny opening for a beam.

"You see something," Marcus said.

"I do," Selene said.

"Of course she does," Ney said. "Bring me the item."

Selene licked her lips, uncertain what she should do. Could Ney have spoken the truth? Why did he seem so...odd then?

She picked up the device, showing it to Marcus. Then, she walked back.

"Lift it up again," Ney said, as he kept watching the soldier. Selene did as told.

From where he sat, Marcus studied the flat device. "Sten had a heater," the soldier said, sounding surprised. "How did he acquire it?" he asked Ney.

"I must presume that Mother gave it to him in case he ever needed to kill you, monsieur."

"Why would he want to kill me? Do you have any idea?"

"*Wei.* It is obvious. Sten heard your conversation with this dark-haired beauty, listening in by a bug. I would assume that Mother had given him orders. Sten either reported in to Mother and she just instructed him to kill you or the pilot felt the circumstances warranted your death."

"What would cause Sten to act on his own?" Marcus asked.

Ney stood silently as if he hadn't heard the question. Abruptly, he said, "We are no longer in communication with anyone, monsieur. I have a tracker… I know when Sten contacts Mother."

Marcus scowled fiercely.

"Mother doesn't trust you," Selene told the big man. "The pilot and navigator—"

"No," Ney said. "He is just a navigator."

"You're part of the watchdog team, too, aren't you?" Selene asked Ney. He couldn't have figured all this out otherwise. That was why he was behaving so strangely all of a sudden.

The DGSE agent regarded her, nodding slowly.

"Why haven't you shot me then?" Marcus asked.

"Oh, I want to, monsieur, most assuredly, I do. I feel the order in my mind, struggling to overcome my resistance. You see, it is only through my valiant effort to think my own thoughts that keeps my trigger finger from twitching and destroying you. I have broken the conditioning…because I am the best. It was the reason I was given this assignment by France."

"Lower your gun," Marcus ordered.

"Alas, I cannot."

"You haven't completely broken the conditioning, have you?" Selene asked.

351

Ney hesitated before saying, "You are correct, mademoiselle. Yet, there is more to my reluctance to lower the gun. Monsieur Marcus is a distrustful and arrogant individual. He will suppose I could revert once again to Mother's authority. Thus, he will believe that his wisest decision would be to kill me the moment he has the opportunity."

"Why don't you simply kill him then?" Selene asked.

Ney smiled sadly. "Because I believe the world needs his talents. I frankly admit that I need his assistance."

"In order to stop Mother?" Selene asked.

"Precisely," Ney said. "Yet, despite my need for aid, I dare not trust him. It is a dilemma, no?"

As Selene considered the dilemma, her knees lost strength. She sat down in the row in front and on the other side of the aisle as Marcus. "Even if we work together, how can the three of us possibly stop Mother?"

"Our chances are minimal," Ney said. "Nevertheless, we must proceed in the attempt. I have been listening to your theories, mademoiselle. I believe you are correct. In the past, the station builders must have almost destroyed humanity. Mother must be on a similar path."

"Let's call for help," Selene suggested. "Let's ask Washington for D17 agents."

"There is no help," Ney said. "We are alone. Our radio no longer works."

"How do you know that?" Marcus asked.

Ney reached inside his jacket, pulling out a small radio. He pitched it to Marcus. The big man used his thumb to turn it on. A loud hissing noise emitted from the box. The soldier tried various frequencies. The same noises continued.

"Mother must be doing that," Selene said. "Or to be more precise, the stations are causing it."

"How?" Marcus asked her.

"I'd have to know what the stations do," Selene said. "What is their primary function?"

Marcus shook his head.

"You must have some idea," Selene said. "Jack Elliot told me you produced antimatter. Why does Mother need antimatter?"

"I have no idea," Marcus said. "Look at Ney, consider his hidden task to watchdog me. Mother trusts no one. She has a hundred backup plans, each more secretive than the other. One of her wisest security arrangements is the need-to-know principle. Mother believes few of us need to know anything more than the most basic facts."

Selene nodded. "Well—"

The Learjet lurched to the left before it began to plummet straight down. Selene lifted off her feet, floating in place. Several second later, her feet struck the floor. The engines roared and then quit altogether. The front edged lower, titling more sharply by the second.

Ney's gun slid away from him. He'd lifted and fallen just like Selene, dropping his weapon. He climbed to his feet. "Monsieur!" he shouted at Marcus. "Can you fly the plane?"

Marcus didn't bother to answer. He grabbed the back of a seat, hauling himself into the aisle. Then, the soldier charged down the rug-way, racing for the cockpit as the plane began to dive.

-78-

CRYOGENIC CHAMBER
STATION EIGHT

Jack sealed the cryogenic tube with Samson Mark Two inside. He was hoping that closing the lid would restart the—

Yes, the machines began to clack. The small window in the tube frosted over as a glass refrigerator door in a supermarket would after someone had opened it.

Jack gave the tube fifteen minutes. He couldn't afford longer. He was hoping the process would help to stabilize the sick man. After the time limit, Agent Elliot repeated the thawing out procedure. He didn't know if this would help or not, but he hadn't been able to think of anything else. Soon enough, he helped a weary and trembling Samson Mark Two back into the corridor.

For a time, the skeletal man didn't say a thing. He wheezed with his throat rattling. Finally, he peered up at Jack.

"I don't have much time left," Samson whispered.

Jack didn't say anything to that. He didn't like the idea of using the dying, trying to squeeze the last particles of utility out of them. His code of honor was conflicted on this. But he didn't know what else he could do if he was going to have a chance of stopping Mother.

"I was going to tell you before..." Samson whispered. "Mother found an ancient underwater chamber. It was deep in the Persian Gulf. Back in the 60s...the 1960s, some of her

354

people opened the chamber. Inside was an ancient DNA stamper. It was a complex machine, able to take embryonic cells and modify them to specific aspects. There were various patterns preset in the machine…"

"What do you mean patterns?" Jack asked.

Samson gave him a ghastly smile. "Have you ever heard of Hercules?"

"Of course," Jack said.

"The legends say Hercules was a demigod," Samson whispered, "the son of Zeus and a mortal woman. It was the same with Gilgamesh among the ancient Sumerians. In the Book, it mentions the Nephilim, the heroes of old who came about through a comingling of humans with fallen angels. How did the *bene elohim*, as the text calls them, the sons of God, do this comingling? Could it have been with advanced genetic machines?"

"Wait just a moment," Jack said, incredulous. "I hope you're not suggesting the stations have a supernatural origin."

Samson looked away, wheezing horribly. When he regarded Jack again, the withered man said, "It's a definite possibility."

Jack frowned.

"Hear me out," Samson whispered, and there was a new intensity in him.

"Sure," Jack said.

"Have you ever heard of the Book of Enoch?"

Jack shook his head.

"It tells of two hundred fallen angels that appeared on Earth before the Great Cataclysm. According to the ancient text, they taught humanity new and wonderful technologies. In the Book of Enoch, they called some of those techs sorceries."

"I went to Sunday school as a child and I never heard anything like that," Jack said.

"Don't be so quick to discount what the ancients wrote."

"Come on," Jack said. "You're saying fallen angels, guys with wings and—"

"No," Samson said. "Firstly, no account in the Book speaks about angels with wings. That is a medieval convention and has nothing to do with the actual text. Secondly, what does

355

fallen angel mean in a strict sense? It means a being from another place quite distinct from Earth. Wouldn't such beings have access to fantastic technology? Why do we presume they would use archaic tools?"

Jack frowned.

"The indications are these fallen angels before the Great Cataclysm no longer had access to their supernatural heritage," Samson said. "In some manner, they had fully entered our physical sphere of existence and could no longer access the spiritual sphere. Yet, they still presumably had knowledge of deep mysteries. Therein is the origin of the ancient stations."

Jack stared at the man, shocked Samson could expound such ridiculous ideas. He could accept ancient aliens, the old Chariots of the Gods thesis. Real fallen angels struck him as too...*wild*.

"You're unconvinced," Samson whispered. "I can see it in your eyes. If it helps, a fallen angel or *bene elohim* is by definition an alien, a being from somewhere other than Earth."

"Okay. So what about the gods and goddess in Egyptian, Greek and other ancient religions? Are you going to tell me you think those accounts are true, too?"

Samson's eyes burned intently. "How would the ancients have viewed beings with fantastic powers and advanced technologies? They could easily view them as gods. Stories can become garbled over time. It would make sense that some of the ancient books are more accurate than others. We know that all the ancients speak about a mighty disaster that overtook the world, and they each indicate it had something to do with the higher gods or God being angry with what was happening on Earth."

"Or...it could have been a power struggle between the aliens on Earth against those not on Earth," Jack said. "Or maybe the aliens used their stations wrong just as Mother did when she caused the Tunguska Event."

Samson was quiet for a time, finally saying, "You're suggesting that Arthur C. Clarke's quote is correct."

"What quote," Jack asked, "and who is he?"

"Clarke was a famous science fiction writer. He said that 'any sufficiently advanced technology is indistinguishable from magic.'"

"Right," Jack said. "That makes more sense to me than this other stuff. Why do we have to get all metaphysical about this?"

"We do know this for sure," Samson said quietly. "The ancient beings used the stations they built at the dawn of history. In some manner that brought about their downfall, wiping out the first civilization so our only memories of them came from the Book and from the tales in Egyptian, Greek and other religions. It appears these beings made super humans for reasons we can't know now. Mother used a DNA stamper her people found in the Persian Gulf in present time to make me and others just like me, those she calls her children and my brothers and sisters."

Jack thought about the soldier he'd first seen in the D'erlon Plant. The big man had been quite real. Here was something concrete, not...

"Why did Mother use the DNA stamper," Jack asked, "in order to create a conquering army of supermen?"

"That is clearly not the case," Samson whispered. "Mother possesses superior agents, but that wasn't the main reason for our birth. She needed superior technology, stronger brains and bodies than ordinary humans possess. She wanted to understand the ancient technology and duplicate it where she could."

"In order to repair the broken stations," Jack said.

"That is correct."

"And you're saying that you're one of those hyper-intelligent supermen?"

"Yes."

"But you had a falling out with Mother."

Samson began to cough weakly again, nodding as he did.

Jack turned away. The ideas were fantastic, difficult to accept. What did the stations do anyway? What could the ancient beings—the aliens one way or another—have hoped to achieve on the ancient Earth with the stations? What did Mother hope to achieve in the here and now with them?

"You have to stop her," Samson said in a fading voice.

Jack faced the trembling man, noticing the bulging eyes staring at him.

Samson Mark Three had carried him to the stone object. He had a second chance because of that. Otherwise, Jack knew he would be dead.

"Why don't I put you in the stone object?" Jack asked. "Let the needles pump you full of the healing substance like they did to me."

"The ancient needles won't work for me. Mother saw to that at my birth. She didn't want any of us living as long as she did. To give us long life would only be her discretion."

"What do you mean?" Jack asked.

Feebly, Samson waved the question aside. "I know of potent weapons I never showed my clone. I'm dying, and I don't want to go back into the cyro-tube. It's time to attack. From what you've said—"

"What kind of weapons?" Jack asked. "And where do I go and how do I get there? I have the feeling time is running out for us."

"You're going to have to help me get there."

"You got it," Jack said.

***

Jack found that Samson was heavier than he looked. He mentioned that. The man informed him that his muscles had greater mass and his bones were three times as dense.

"My predecessors were heroes once," Samson whispered.

Jack saved his breath instead of commenting, staggering as Samson gave him directions. They hurried through hot corridors with the floor plates vibrating under them.

"I thought this station didn't work," Jack said.

"The repellers are offline here, if that's what you mean."

"What are repellers?"

Samson began coughing, leaning more of his considerable weight against Jack. When the man finally wheezed, he was too tired to comment. After several more turns in the corridors, they came to closed doors.

358

Samson's lips moved. Jack had to reposition the man so he could put his ear near the man's mouth.

"Now it gets interesting," Samson whispered.

Soon enough, Jack typed in a sequence of hieroglyphic symbols. The doors opened, revealing a large elevator. They entered, and Samson typed in a code.

The elevator doors closed and the box dropped, picking up speed the deeper it went. Jack expected the elevator to stop at any moment. It did not, but kept on plunging faster into the Earth.

"How far are we going?" Jack asked.

"Several kilometers down," Samson whispered.

"What? Are you kidding me? How is that possible?"

"Magic," Samson wheezed.

Jack realized that was an Arthur C. Clarke joke.

It grew hotter inside the box the farther they traveled. Sweat slicked each of them and began to drip off their noses and fingers.

"What powers the stations?" Jack shouted. The elevator had gotten considerably louder, too.

Agent Elliot had put his ear beside the man's mouth again. Jack thought he heard, "Thermal vents." But that couldn't be right. Did the super-genius mean magma heat? How was that possible under any kind of high-tech?

Finally, the elevator slowed and then stopped. The doors opened.

Billowing hot air shoved the two of them against the back of the elevator. Samson recovered first. It was as if he'd been saving his strength all this time. He pulled Jack to his feet, propelling the two of them down a trembling, groaning corridor.

"This station is broken," Samson shouted. "The protective shields aren't in place anymore. That's not going to matter soon."

"This place is going to explode?" Jack shouted.

"Hot magma will gush up into it."

"When is that going to happen?"

"I'm not sure. Soon enough, I imagine."

"Then what are we doing down here?"

359

"Before I went into the cryogenic tube, I rigged Station Eight to respond to the other stations. It's running like this as a warning."

"Okay..." Jack said.

"Everything works on magnetics and concentrated gravitational forces," Samson said, appearing to be weakening again. "The stations are linked to each other. It wasn't like that in the beginning. The ancient beings made tunnels in the deep rocks through magnetic and gravitational drilling. Likely, it's getting desperate on the surface."

"What do you mean?"

"I no longer have time to explain everything. You'll find out later if you're successful. If you're not, it's not going to matter anyway. The stations are linked. That's the important point. You're going to go from here to the underground pyramid using gravitational acceleration."

"What underground pyramid?"

"The one in the Libyan Desert," Samson said. "It's the first pyramid ever built on Earth. They constructed it as a control center. The pyramids in Egypt are poor copies of the original."

"Go on," Jack said.

"I don't know if gravitational acceleration will work now."

"You mean it's dangerous?"

"Yes," Samson said.

Jack nodded. He should have known nothing was going to be easy.

"I'll show you how to use the pads. I'll also give you a force-field suit. It's good against bullets but won't stop heaters."

"What do heaters shoot?" Jack asked.

"Lasers. I'll give you one."

"Got it," Jack said.

"Your task is to reach the underground pyramid and kill Mother. Then, you have to shut down the stations. If you can't convince any of my brothers and sisters to help you, kill them and start destroying control panels. That might or might not work. It's all a gamble. I'm sure if you fail Mother is going to destroy the Earth, if nothing else by accident. If I'm right about everything, though, she's going to bring another judgment from God against us."

Jack discounted the latter, but after watching the Tunguska Event, he felt the former to be more than likely.

"We're at an acceleration pad," Samson announced.

The corridor widened here with a silver disc on the floor beside a panel of flickering, colored controls. Instead of a steel corridor, a rocky tube went horizontally into the Earth. After several hundred feet was a sizzling, shimmering energy field of some sort. Heat radiated from the exposed rock.

"I left weapons and a suit around here somewhere," Samson said. "Ah. Now, I remember. We have to move fast, my friend. If we're going to stop Mother, now is the time to act."

-79-

LEARJET 85
LIBYA

Selene had a pounding headache. She was sure it was the brain enhancer wearing out her mind, making it spin too fast all the time. How long could she keep going like this?

Marcus piloted the Learjet. The navigator said little. All his instruments were dead. The engines kept the jet going, but little else worked on the plane. Every time they tried the radio, harsh static sounded. It had become intensely hot in the jet, the air conditioner barely humming and sometimes sputtering.

Ney still had his gun, although Marcus had taken the flat, heater device. Had the DGSE agent forgotten about the force field that had snapped on around Marcus when Jack Elliot had shot the soldier? Was the hidden force field the reason why Marcus hadn't disarmed the Frenchman yet?

Marcus glanced at Selene. "We have to stop Mother," he said.

"You really believe we can?" Selene asked.

"The Tunguska Event proves your thesis that the ancients misjudged the power of the stations. Why will Mother do any better now? I've begun to wonder, though, whether we're too late."

"If that's true—that you doubt we can make it to headquarters in time—why did Mother send you after me and then tell you to bring me in?"

362

Marcus nodded. "I would suggest Mother wanted to keep me busy so I wasn't at headquarters with her."

"Why order you to come in then? That doesn't make sense."

Marcus shrugged. "I don't have all the answers. Only Mother knows all. Maybe in giving me orders others listened to what she said. Mother has or had to keep them off guard, too. Remember, Mother is exceptionally cunning when it comes to wielding and keeping power. The fact of her extended existence says it all."

"If Mother is so intelligent," Selene said, "why does she persist in an endeavor that threatens human civilization?"

"My guess is that she doesn't care about mass death or our puny civilization. Her great age assists her in this. She has watched everyone come and go. She has seen ideas bloom and wither away. Her goal must be paramount to her. It is the only stable thing in her long existence. That is why it must be easy to sacrifice whatever she must to achieve her dream."

That made sense. Yet—

"You must secure yourself," Marcus said. "The weather— it's too turbulent up here. We must go lower."

Selene hurried from the cockpit, selecting a seat in the first row. She snapped a seatbelt into place.

The jet shook worse than before. The nose lowered and air howled outside. Wouldn't it be worse lower down with the desert sands buffeting against them?

There was no more time to ponder the idea. The plane began to shake and rattle, while the howling noises became deafening. Every few seconds a terrible thud caused Selene's head to snap up.

She didn't want to stare outside anymore. It was too frightening. Why had it become so hot? The extreme heat must be causing these great weather shifts. What could the stations possibly do that made it this much hotter?

Selene groaned as she bent her head. The throbbing in her mind faded away. That was a relief. The noise around her grew so loud it drowned out everything else. She felt as if she was in a womb.

The flashes in her mind continued. New thoughts popped into existence. She mulled them over and then a new idea bumped an old one aside, and she sped along a new train of thought.

I have to get control of myself. What good is a heightened intellect if it's uncontrollable?

Selene fought for self-mastery. She wanted to order her thinking, making one logical step after another. The stations...heat...hums...magnetics...ancient technology... Selene found herself panting with her mouth dry. Slowly, she realized that she heard individual sounds again.

She raised her head. The shaking had lessened. Marcus must have found one of the quieter air zones. Selene dared to unbuckle the seatbelt and totter on unsteady legs into the cabin.

"I have an idea," she shouted.

Marcus focused on flying the plane. He had a reason for that. Outside the window, the desert flashed before them. They were barely flying one hundred feet above a sea of sand dunes.

"It's not so windy down here on the deck," Marcus said.

The navigator looked sick and frightened. He had curled into a corner, as if didn't want any more to do with this. Ney had removed himself, buckling down in the passenger area.

"You should go sit down," Marcus said. "It could get dangerous at any moment."

"I've thought of something," Selene said.

Marcus nodded without tearing his gaze from the window.

"In some fashion, the stations are causing this unnatural heat. Have the stations been idling do you think?"

"Why does it matter?"

"Global warming," Selene said. "It's hot now, probably because the stations are working up to full power. Maybe Mother has been testing the stations the last decade or so. That's what caused the melting ice, hotter weather and the reason why the global warming was always so spotty. You know, every time they had a global warming conference it would be freezing there. The stations might have slowed down, and that allowed normal weather to proceed."

"You may have something there," Marcus said. "Now, please, go buckle up."

364

"Listen," Selene said, trying to tell him while she focused on the idea. Already, other interesting puzzles buzzed for her attention.

"There's more?" he asked.

"If I'm right about this, the reason for global warming, that means Mother has been testing the stations for some time. I'd really like to know why you needed antimatter."

"You have another idea?"

"I'm not sure," Selene said. "It depends if I'm right about—"

A loud explosion aboard the plane made the jet sink fast. A second later, engine silence told them the worst.

"Buckle up!" Marcus shouted. "We've lost the engines."

"Where's Ney?" Selene asked.

"Buckle up!" the big man shouted. "We're going down. I can't glide far, and we're still too far away from headquarters."

The jet sank again, making Selene stumble. She caught the door before it swung shut. Then, she staggered for the nearest seat to buckle in before the plane crashed into the desert.

-80-

GRAVITATIONAL LAUNCH PAD
STATION EIGHT

Jack couldn't believe he was actually going to try this madness.

Samson Mark Two had finished explaining the propulsion system. By the implications, it meant he was far down inside the Earth's crust, as in many miles down. They were supposedly as low as the ocean crust. The elevator had taken them down much deeper than he had suspected.

Magnetic tubes bored ages ago by gravitational drills linked the various stations, at least the deeper shafts. It would appear Mother knew less about the intricacies of the stations than some of her children. It was like a racecar driver not knowing everything about the engine, hard to believe but possible.

"It's either that," Samson had explained, "or she's not worried about anyone trying this."

Jack could believe that. He wore a force field suit. The field would deploy briefly to deflect high-speed objects that neared him. If it stayed on at all times, he wouldn't be able to breathe. The force field suit didn't sense lasers, so a heater could kill just as dead.

Jack had two fully charged laser pistols—heaters. He wore goggles, a heat jacket and rebreather over his mouth and nose. Samson said he was going to need those while flitting between stations.

"I still don't see why I won't be burned to death," Jack said.

"Magnetic force screens," Samson whispered.

"You mean force screens like on science fictions shows?"

"That's close enough," the skeletal man said.

"Maybe I should head back up, use a plane to get there."

"It's too late for that. Besides, this is the fastest way to Libya from here. There's another thing. Everyone should be too busy inside the pyramid to notice you slinking through the corridors. As the saying goes, they'll never expect this."

"There's a reason they'll never expect this," Jack said. "I'm supposed to fly underground through a tube no one has ever used before?"

"The ancients might have used it."

"Great," Jack said.

"That's the wrong attitude," Samson chided him. "I wish I could go with you."

Jack nodded, feeling guilty about Samson's nearness to death. He was actually going to have a chance to change the outcome—if this ancient transportation system actually worked. The problem was that Jack had always hated the rides at amusement parks. Spinning like a top or going up and down on roller coasters...it had always made him sick, which was weird in a way, because he did okay jumping from a plane or doing an underwater insertion.

Samson turned his head, coughing. The man trembled all the time now. His sweat had a dank, sick odor to it.

The man was dying on his feet. Yet, Samson fought death in order to keep giving Agent Elliot further instructions. Jack's heart went out to the man.

"This is it," Jack said. He stuck out his hand. "It's been an honor knowing you and your brother. Thank you, my friend. I'll never forget you."

The two men clasped hands. Samson had a fierce grip. After letting go, the skeletal man began coughing harder than ever.

He took out a rag and wiped blood from his lips. "I'll watch from this end," he whispered.

367

Jack nodded, wishing there was something he could for the man. He knew there wasn't, so he put the rebreathing nozzle back over his mouth and nose. He put the googles over his eyes and zipped up the heat jacket. Putting on the gloves, he realized he couldn't hesitate any longer.

For a moment, Jack stared at the pad before him. It was a silver disc, large enough to hold three men comfortably. Around the disc were colored-light controls. The disc was the end of the line, or the beginning, depending on one's vantage, into the hot rock tunnel. He could hear the shimmering force screen. What happened once he passed through it?

Taking a deep breath, Jack decided he might as well get this over with. It was time to pay his dues for living. He boldly stepped onto the silver pad.

Nothing happened, not a damn thing.

The two men stared at each other.

Samson glanced around, picking a small silver tube with a button on it. "You forgot this," he whispered. He reached out, giving the tube to Jack.

Agent Elliot gripped it with his gloved thumb hovering over the button. He nodded once to Samson. Then, Jack faced the shimmering force screen down the tunnel. With a decisive motion, he pressed the button.

***

Jack lifted off the silver disc, falling forward headfirst. It was a horrible sensation. In the wink of an eye, he plunged through the shimmering force field. Heat slammed against him, and it got dark except for the light behind the shimmering field. The light faded in seconds as he continued to plunge headfirst, falling...falling...falling...

At first, Jack held the shout inside him. He continued to fall, though, and he flailed now, trying to grab something to steady himself. It didn't help in the slightest. He found that it wasn't perfectly dark. He could see the rock tunnel flashing past him in a blur.

He shouted, and scalding air leaked past his rebreather mask. He stopped shouting, concentrating on breathing the cooler air.

The heat jacket helped a little, but he sweated fiercely. What had Samson said? The tunnel had a magnetic sheathing, helping to keep out the worst of the heat. It didn't help enough though.

Jack continued to tumble through a tunnel deep under the Earth, deeper than any human drill had ever reached. He fell forward due to a change in the gravitational direction. It propelled him at faster and faster speeds until he reached terminal velocity.

This was clearly beyond human science. This was alien, alien to Earth, at least.

Jack slowly worked himself around, putting his feet in front so he fell feet first. It felt safer, but what did that really mean? Maybe the builders had figured out how to shoot someone down a tunnel, or along a tunnel, but they had no idea how to give the rider a safe landing. They had destroyed the first civilization. Heck, they had destroyed themselves. So just how smart were these ancients anyway?

Jack kept falling forward, working now to keep from heaving inside the rebreather mask. He doubted he would be able to successfully breathe the hot air if he lost his rebreather. He was supposed to go from Iran to Libya. Just how long would that take?

Get your mind in gear, Elliot. Once you land it will be go time. You have to know what you're going to do.

Samson had droned on and on about the underground pyramid, the first one, he'd called it. The thing was huge, and it supposedly controlled the other stations. How had it survived the great disaster of long ago?

Focus on the mission parameters.

Yeah. This was his show. He'd been given a second chance to make everything right. That's why he'd survived the night his parents had died. The speed freak—

Jack's eyes narrowed. The night boiled up in his chest. He remembered sitting frozen on the Lazy-Boy chair. The freak had surprised him. The human monster had surprised his dad, too. If they'd known—

Jack shook his head. That day didn't matter. He had survived because he had concentrated on one thing: killing the speed demon unleashed on his family. The killer had come disguised as a junkie. This time, the killer was an ancient woman who called herself Mother, and she was threatening humanity's very existence.

It didn't seem right that Jack's mission was to put down Mother, but it was. Samson said she had been born during the Black Death. She was old and she was the most dangerous person in the world. No one compared to her. How many mysteries and conspiracies went back to Mother or the Mothers before her?

If one could yank back the curtain of history, how many Mothers would one find pulling the strings? It came down to now, didn't it. Jack could stop the giant conspiracy that had begun before the start of human history. That was a crazy idea. Who was he? He was just one man with two heaters in his pocket and a force field to snap on to stop bullets. That was pretty good.

Get in the zone. Get pumped.

Jack closed his eyes and snapped them open a second later. He didn't like falling forward with his eyes closed. It made his stomach turn.

Silver light flashed before his eyes. He held his tongue. More silver flashes stuck his eyes as loud whooshing noises assaulted his hearing.

Something weird happened. He looked at the walls. He still couldn't see much, and the flashes and whooshes had stopped. Even so, he had the feeling of traveling at a tremendous speed. He was sure that he moved faster than terminal velocity, driven faster by some kind of magnetic propulsion.

Was he like some bullet underground? *Look at me. I'm superman.*

A feeling of claustrophobia struck then. Jack began sucking air and blinking like mad.

Calm down, Jack. You're fine. This is no big deal.

In Jack Elliot's life, when he said it was no big deal he meant that he was close to blowing a fuse and going berserk. Once, in college, a freeloader in another dorm had snuck into Jack's room and taken his pickup's key. The man had used Jack's painfully earned Chevy to make a burger run, almost getting in a wreck because the guy always blew through stop signs. Jack had found out about it. Even then, he always did in the end. He remembered going to the guy's dorm room and knocking on the door. The guy had opened up, giving him a nod. Jack had just stared at the guy, his anger building.

"Hey," Jack had said in a winded voice. "It's no big deal, but did you break into my room and swipe my truck key?"

"Who told you that?" the guy had asked.

Jack had blinked at the freeloader, wanting to hit him in the face. Jack didn't like others just taking his stuff. He was very territorial that way.

"Is it true?"

"I guess so," the guy had said. "I was starving, you know? I needed a Big Mac."

Jack had nodded, even managing to smile. "Don't ever do it again," he said. Something in his eyes must have bothered the guy, because he looked down, no longer able to meet Jack's gaze.

"Okay," the guy had said.

"Great," Jack said. "Thanks."

And that had been that, no big deal, just like this sledding through the bottom of the Earth was a piece of...of...

Jack slowed his breathing, wondering when the hell-ride was going to end and where in the underground pyramid the gravitational tube would deposit him.

-81-

SAHARA DESERT

The beast grew wary as it peered around the latest dune. The Land Rover tracks in the sand led to a large flat area and disappeared abruptly. The tracks were barely visible as it was. Sand hissed through the heated air, swirling fine particles everywhere.

The beast shook itself. Sand flew from its shaggy fur. It hated this place: the lack of water, large game and the oppressive heat. Its tongue lolled as moisture dripped from it. Why couldn't it have escaped in the forest? Why had it succeeded in this forbidden territory? The beast couldn't conceive anyone coming here on their own volition. The masters—

The beast whined. Why did it still think of them as masters? It was free. It must change its thinking on this. They were not masters. They were the oppressors, tormentors...its enemies.

Maybe the better plan would have been to leave the desert. No, no, it had made its decision. It must not fear. It must not whine like a defeated dog.

Even as it thought that, the beast whimpered. A fierce hum came from out of the ground. The noise hurt its sensitive ears. Lying down on the shaded sand, the beast attempted to cover its ears with its paws. That did not stop the pain. In fact, the sonic hum worsened.

The beast jumped up and fought the urge to bark wildly. It had to stop the noise. It had to attack, but nothing was here, just the eerie sounds. Barking...that was a primitive, instinctive reaction. It could think. It could—

The huge beast found itself racing toward the hum. A savage desire to destroy, to kill, to shake the hum by its throat and lick its blood—

The beast reached the end of the faint tracks. It began to dig wildly in the heated sand. Its paws moved faster and faster as they sank deeper into the surface. The hum drove it wild. It panted, winded, thirsty, hungry—

Its claws scraped against metal. It dug more, exposing the metal, a sheet of it, to the hot air.

Ah. The beast believed it understood. This was—

A clack of noise and movement of the metal told the beast it had found an underground opening. A section of the metal was moving.

Maybe the tormentors did not like its exposing the hidden entrance like this. They must have sensed it and were on the way to investigate.

Warily, the beast trotted away.

The clacking noises increased.

The beast raced back to the dune, running into the shadows. It lay down, and then it froze, panting on the cooler sand.

The clacking noises ceased. It heard engines revving. The beast knew those sounds. It was like the Land Rover sounds, but whinier, two-wheeler sounds.

Yes, the beast saw a motorcycle with a silver-clad rider roar up out of the ground. Two more followed. The three vehicles had larger than normal tires. They raced around in a circle as helmeted men studied the ground. One of them pointed at the sand.

The men pointed out its tracks.

Each of the riders drew a long-barreled dart gun.

The beast growled, slowly slinking backward. It knew it could not outrun the two-wheelers. No. This was going to be a death game around the dune. He had to kill all three if he hoped to survive and wreck vengeance against the rest of the tormentors.

Two of the men had lifted their visors. They spoke to each other. The beast could hear the murmur of their words, but not the meaning.

One of them shut a visor. The other reached for his, and stopped.

The beast raised its head. It heard a new sound.

The three riders peered behind them, looking up into the sky.

The beast scanned the sky as well. It had watched birds before. Normally, it did not worry about the—

The beast saw a speck in the air. It was a flying machine. It made stuttering noises and it was heading toward them. Even better, it caused the motorcycle riders to pause. The beast did not think they liked the flying machine.

What did the approaching plane mean? Sometimes, for reasons the beast did not yet understand, humans fought against each other. Was there a way to use that for its advantage?

The plane sputtered as it came, growing larger by the moment.

-82-

LEARJET 85
LIBYA

Thick, billowing smoke poured into the passenger area of the plane. No flashing lights went off, but oxygen masks had dropped. Selene put one over her face, breathing the pure air as her eyes stung from the smoke.

A roar and lifting power told her the engines had resumed enough to give them more motive power. Then, they cut out again. The plane sank, and the engines began once more, giving another lift.

Selene's stomach lurched. How long could this go on? The plane's air-conditioning systems had stopped, and the heat in the cabin quickly became unbearable.

Selene sweated. It had to be over one fifteen in here already.

Marcus nursed the stalling, starting plane. The smoke didn't quit either. Without the oxygen mask, Selene didn't believe she would have remained conscious.

Marcus gained height by slow degrees. Selene could tell by leaning against a window and looking outside. The sand dunes had gotten smaller. She looked up. There wasn't a cloud in the sky.

Ten minutes later, the engines cut out again. The Learjet glided, the ground rushing closer much too fast. Still, it seemed like a controlled descent after a fashion. Selene wondered why

375

Marcus hadn't used the engines when he'd had them to land. Maybe getting nearer headquarters was more important.

The intercom system didn't work anymore. Sometime during the ordeal, Marcus or the navigator had shut the cockpit door.

Selene became aware the smoke was thinning. Then it was definitely dissipating. A howling sound caused her to glance back. Someone had opened a door to the outside. The smoke had fled through it. She saw Ney wave to her. He was buckled into a seat near the open door. Had he done that?

Selene looked out the window. They were a mere one hundred feet above the dunes. She cinched her seatbelt and assumed the crash position with her head between her knees.

Marcus could get them down. He was—

The underbelly of the Learjet struck the desert, and everything became a sliding, screeching hodge-podge of noise and motion. Selene was jerked forward, backward and side-to-side. She clutched the armrests, sucking air, waiting for the final crash to end everything. Instead, the infernal screeching lessened and the motion was no longer quite so violent. All of a sudden, the motion came to a jerking halt! Selene slammed against the seatbelt, moaning. Then, the screeching also stopped. They were down, stopped and it appeared that Selene was still in once piece.

Now what should I do? What was that smell?

The cockpit door flew open. Marcus charged out, shouting, "Hurry up! We have to get out of here. The plane is going to explode!"

Selene must not have moved fast enough for his tastes. The soldier plucked her from the aisle as she stood. He carried her as easily as an adult might a three-year-old. Clasped against Marcus's chest, Selene felt his strength and had a better understanding of his speed.

Marcus leaped from the open door, thudding onto the blistering hot sand.

"Put me down," Selene said.

The soldier did not listen. He charged across the sand. Ney struggled ahead of them, dust and sand exploding from his thrusting feet.

376

"Go!" Marcus shouted at Ney.

Selene struggled to free herself. The soldier simply tightened his hold. He had muscles like steel. There was no way short of knifing him that she could tear herself loose.

The soldier sprinted across the sand. He closed the gap between Ney and him.

"Wait for me," the navigator shouted.

Selene saw the man jump from the plane. At that moment, she heard whining engines. Three motorcycles appeared around the front of the Learjet.

"Look!" she shouted.

"I saw them before we crash-landed," Marcus panted.

The motorcyclists must have seen them. One raised a long-barreled gun before lowering it. The distance must be too great for a good shot.

"Get ready," Marcus said. He threw her from him before she'd realized what he'd meant. The next moment, the soldier dove onto the sand.

Selene plowed against the hot particles. She tumbled end over end. She had been aware of something in Marcus's fist. What could he have—?

Selene figured it out a second before it happened. She pressed herself against the burning sand and covered the back of her head with her arms. An instant later, a terrific explosion rent the air as the Learjet burst apart.

It would seem that Marcus had rigged the jet fuel to ignite.

The blast reached them, lifting Selene and rolling her across the sand. Metal shards hissed past. Heat billowed across her. Then, Selene gasped as she landed on the sand again.

She seemed to be in once piece. Groggily, she dared to peek up. There was no sign of the navigator. He must have been too close to the explosion to survive it. All three of the motorcyclists lay unmoving on the sand.

Had Marcus timed that?

Before Selene could decide, she noticed the soldier striding back toward the burning wreckage.

A secondary explosion caused Marcus to hit the deck. Selene whimpered, trying to make herself a smaller object.

After more blast and heat washed over them, Marcus shouted at her. Selene didn't understand what he was saying.

"Get up!" Marcus shouted. "We have to use this while we have a chance."

She stared at him, still stunned from the blast.

"The cyclists don't matter anymore," Marcus shouted. "They're dead. We have to get into the pyramid."

"It's near?"

The soldier laughed grimly as he ran toward her.

-83-

SAHARA DESERT

The beast cowered as an explosion sent debris spinning through the air. Big sheets of metal tumbled through the heat. One sped this way, *clanging* against the metal hatch buried in the sand. A long shard like a javelin hissed into the dune the beast hid behind.

The explosion was amazing and exciting. Could anything survive such a blast? The beast wasn't sure. The drivers of the two-wheelers had been circling the grounded flying machine at the time of the blast. The beast doubted they had survived the explosion.

The beast waited just to be sure. A good hunter knew when to attack and when to hide and watch. This was one of the watching times.

Nothing changed except for a few more explosions. The beast wondered if it could—

Ahhh… the beast saw an old enemy, the soldier. The man walked widely around the burning, grounded machine. A woman walked with the man and a lesser man brought up the rear. Two of them possessed weapons, the soldier with his monstrous gun.

The beast whined in anticipation of ripping out the soldier's throat. He would kill the other two as a matter of course. They walked with the tormenter. Thus, they would die with him. It was obvious the soldier belonged to the two-wheeler drivers. They must have gone out to greet the soldier.

The huge hound raised its hindquarters the slightest bit. No doubt, the soldier planned to enter the hidden entrance. The beast would attack them once they began their descent with their backs to it. This would be good. This would—

The metal clacked, sliding open again. Something popped out of the opening. A sizzling object flew into the air.

Among the others, the soldier saw it first. He shouted, turning, beginning to run from the thing. Was he afraid of the sizzling ball? It would appear so. That made no sense to the beast.

A blue electrical explosion sent sizzling lines in all directions. One of the lines struck the lesser man and the woman. The line hissed and knocked them onto the ground.

It was different with the soldier. A blue nimbus shone around him preventing the sizzling line from reaching his skin. It didn't seem to matter, though. The soldier stood frozen with his mouth agape. The line sizzled stronger. With a cry of despair, and his hair standing on end, the soldier staggered first one way and then another. Finally, he collapsed onto the sand, shivering and gasping before going limp. At that point, the nimbus quit and so did the sizzling line.

The beast wagged its tail, having enjoyed the spectacle. Afterward, it waited again. This wait was shorter lived.

Three individuals in bulky, crinkly suits with large helmets emerged from the hidden place. They tromped across the sand toward the stilled tormentor and his allies.

The beast thought furiously. It would seem the tormentors had disagreements among themselves. Those underground did not seem to like the ones from the flying machine.

That was interesting.

In those moments, the beast reasoned out an ancient human thought: *the enemy of my enemy is my friend.*

As it watched the three suited people approach those lying on the sand, the beast decided to gamble. It would never re-cross the desert on its own. It had come to kill, was that not so? What else was left to it? This was the great opportunity.

While keeping its shaggy body close to the ground, the beast began to slink toward the opening in the sand. As it did so, inspiration struck. As much as it could, the beast put its paws in its previous tracks. It was a difficult process, because it kept watch of the suited ones and the paw-prints back and forth.

Finally, the beast reached the opening. Cool air blew up out of the ground. It saw a ramp leading down. The cool air decided it for the beast. The beast kept itself from racing there. Instead, it slunk to the entrance. Then, its claws rattled against a ramp as it descended into the desert underground.

-84-

GRAVITATIONAL TUBE

Jack passed another set of flashing lights. He grunted as a force struck him. He no longer felt as if he was falling forward. His sense of direction had distorted. He was sure he fell straight down, maybe heading for Hell. It was hot enough, and getting even hotter.

That would be a lousy trick, getting a fast ticket to the Lake of Fire. That wasn't real, right? It was just a thing preachers told people back in the day to scare them straight. Maybe that's why he discounted Samson's fallen angel thesis. Wouldn't their existence mean that Hell was real?

Jack glanced around, deciding he wasn't going to think about it. How everything had come about wasn't as important as stopping Mother in the here and now.

The blur around him didn't seem as fast. Had the flashes of light back there and the bumps slowed him down? Did that mean he was nearing the end of his fantastic journey? He hoped so, and he hoped he was still on Earth. The bizarre tech and the weird things that had been happening to him...he just wanted to go back to being an ordinary D17 agent, stopping regular high-tech enemy advantages like superior anti-tank missiles or a new kind of IED no one could detect. Gravitational tubes, kilometer-deep stations built in ancient times...no thank you. He'd had enough of this to last the rest of his life.

382

How long was it going to last, anyway? Elliot would just be happy to quit falling. He wondered if he set a world record for falling. Did it count if it was falling sideways instead of down?

Whoa! He squinted as a light nearly blinded him. The light brightened and he expected the worse. It rushed closer, closer, and he burst through a shimmering field. Light poured at him now. It made his eyes water. He felt himself slowing, and then he slammed down onto a silver disc, the wind knocked out of him.

Jack groaned, twisting on the disc. He still held the tube with the button, and he came very near to pressing the button. Would that have sent him zipping back to the station in Iran? Maybe magma had already flooded the place. Was Samson Mark Two still alive?

Jack dropped the tube and crawled off the silver disc. His lungs unlocked as he began to suck air. Soon, he breathed normally.

This place has light. I don't see anyone, though. I don't see any flashing warnings.

Jack used a wall, leaning against it as he climbed to his feet. Gingerly, he removed the rebreather mask. The air was cool down here. Just as good, he couldn't feel any vibrations on the wall or floor.

Jack shed the rebreather tank and took off the heat jacket. He must stink like a basketball player. His clothes were soaked with sweat. There was no help for that now.

Taking out a heater, Jack checked it. A tiny light shined green. The thing had a full charge. A tight smile played on Jack's lips. He'd reached...

What station is this anyway? Have I reached the underground pyramid? How can I tell?

He realized Samson should have briefed him about the op for several days, at least. There was far too much too know. He needed a partner. He needed a map.

Jack nodded, determined. It was time to gather intelligence on the enemy. That meant he had to find someone to question.

Jack took a deep breath before carefully scanning the chamber. A second later, he looked down at his feet. This place must have security cameras. He had to operate on that assumption, which meant he needed to look like one of the bad guys, not gawk like an intruder.

There was no more time to think. He was going to have to act on his instincts. He must be deep underground and likely had to get a lot higher to reach Mother.

Jack straightened his garments, kept the heater hidden in his hand and put his hand against his leg. In a regular but crisp gait, he headed for the hatch. Here was the first big test.

Jack clutched the latch, hesitating for just a second. Would it open? Was he locked in here as a simple precaution?

Trying to twist the handle, Jack found that it wouldn't budge. He couldn't believe it. He'd fallen here all the way from Iran in a gravitational tube, and now a locked door had stopped him.

-85-

CELL
UNDERGROUND PYRAMID

Selene groaned as she blinked groggily. Someone spoke to her but she couldn't understand a thing. A sharp smell made her cry out. Selene raised her head, blinking, trying to bring things into focus. Her head hurt. She tried to touch it, and found that she couldn't move her hands.

Concentrating, Selene tried to understand. By slow degrees, she realized that she lay on an articulated frame. Her arms and legs were stretched out and all she wore were her panties. That wasn't the worst. Buzzing, electrical lines circled her wrists and her ankles. They must have done something, because she couldn't feel a thing.

"Comfortable?" a woman asked.

Selene realized that she could feel her head and itchy nose. She looked up, straining, and saw the arrogant woman in the white lab coat, the one from the Siwa Oasis and mind machine.

"Are you Hela?" Selene asked, finding that her mouth was dry.

"That answers many of my questions," the woman said. She had severely pulled back blonde hair. "Marcus told you things he should have kept to himself."

"I know that's what you think," Selene said. Her thoughts were fuzzy and disordered. She wanted to time to think this

385

through. Flashes appeared in her mind, making it difficult to see.

Hela stepped closer, taking a penlight from one of her lab coat pockets. She clicked it on and shined a bright light into Selene's left eye.

"Hmmm," Hela said. She examined the right eye, shaking her head afterward.

"What's wrong?"

"Marcus gave you the solution. I'm guessing he made it a double dose. He always was too anxious. He may have permanently damaged your mind. Mother is going to be angry. This time he has gone too far."

"For some reason you don't realize it, do you?" Selene said. "We're all in danger."

Hela smiled sternly. "Is that what Marcus told you? The man loves dramatics. His model is brutish, given to acts of strength and physical daring. I won't say he doesn't have his place in the Old Order of existence. In the New, though, we're not going to need him anymore."

Suddenly, Selene didn't care about any of that. She wanted to know one thing. "What do the stations do? Why can't anyone tell me?"

"It doesn't matter to you what they do," Hela said. "We have to stabilize your mind before you reach a critical impasse. Mother won't be able to accelerate you if you're impaired."

"Please, tell me what this is about. It's driving me crazy not knowing."

Hela took a step back, slipping the penlight into a pocket. "I know. You think we're monsters. The primitives never understand in time. You belong to the old way of pitchforks and fire. Burn and kill what you don't understand. Does it matter that you're throwing away paradise? No. You don't realize the gift Mother yearns to give humanity. We're about to bring universal peace and order to the Earth and you act as if that's a terrible sin. Mother is trying to save the human race. We've worked so hard against so much ignorance for so long…"

Hela sighed. "It's almost laughable."

Selene shook her head. Maybe she should play along. She couldn't do that, though, as her emotions burst forth.

"I don't know why you're trying to trick me, but it's not going to work. You planned to put me under the mind machine back in the Siwa Oasis, screw with my brain and turn me into a mental zombie."

Hela sneered. "I see Marcus has rubbed off on you."

"You screwed with Ney Blanc's mind, didn't you?"

"Of course I reordered his thinking," Hela said. "The French Intelligence services wanted to infiltrate our organization. We had to protect ourselves. Mother has been on the run her entire life. Only her incredible genius has kept the dream alive. Now, we're approaching the moment of truth."

"And destroying the Earth at the same time," Selene said passionately. "Haven't you been outside? Don't you realize the stations are driving the world's temperatures up?"

"Of course I know that," Hela said. "The world has been heating up for some time. We're one of the key reasons people haven't taken global warming seriously. We doctored the data to make the so-called alarmists look foolish."

"What? Why?"

"The stations needed running time as we ironed out the kinks. That created the various hums, which began to make people like you curious. It also meant warmer periods for the planet. If everyone believed in global warming and had acted accordingly, and quickly realized nothing they did affected the worldwide temperature, in time, they might have looked for us harder. This way, with the world embroiled in its usual quarrels, it gave us time to calibrate the stations. Now, everything is ready for the final push."

"No! You must help us stop the insanity."

Hela smiled, shaking her head.

"You're all so smug!" Selene shouted. "It's maddening."

"Don't work yourself into a frenzy. Mother wants to talk to you. After she's broken through—"

"You have to stop her," Selene said. "You're smart. Surely, you must realize that the last time Mother used the stations it brought about the Tunguska Event."

"I know that, of course. That's why I exist, to help fix the problem."

Selene didn't understand the last comment, so she ignored it, pressing on with her key argument. "Before the Tunguska Event, the ancients almost destroyed the world."

"No!"

"Yes!" Selene cried. "It's self-evident. Why did everything go wrong in the distant past?"

"You know nothing," Hela said. "It was blackest sabotage that ruined the original attempt. Mother has taken every precaution this time."

"I don't believe you."

Hela shrugged. "No matter, it's still the truth."

"How do the stations raise the Earth's temperature?"

Hela stared at Selene, and it seemed as if pity stirred in the woman's blue eyes. "Oh, this is ridiculous. If you want to know that badly I suppose I can tell you. The stations are giant repellers, magnetic repellers, as I'm sure you've already surmised."

"I knew they did something magnetic. What do they repel?"

"Ah," Hela said. "That is the interesting part. Did you know that the inner core of the Earth is made of iron?"

"I'm a geologist," Selene said. "Of course I know."

Hela spoke as if she hadn't heard the answer. "The core of the Earth has the same temperature as the surface of the Sun. One would presume it would be a seething cauldron of liquid metal down there. But that is not the case. The intense gravity in the center of the Earth keeps the inner core as solid as a piece of iron."

"Are you saying the repellers do something to the Earth's core?" Selene asked.

Hela smiled in a superior way. "The inner core lies in a larger molten sea of nickel, iron and small quantities of other metals. The gravity isn't as intense there so it can remain in its liquid state. The outer core is two thousand kilometers thick, as I'm sure you know."

Selene watched the woman.

"Differences in temperature, pressure and composition within the outer core cause convection currents in the molten metal as cool, dense matter sinks while the warm, less dense matter rises. The flow of liquid iron generates electric currents, which in turn produce magnetic fields. The Van Allen Belt protecting the Earth is the result."

"The stations—"

"The stations force the solid inner core to spin faster and faster, creating a greater electric current, which in turn produces a stronger magnetic field."

"But..." Selene said.

"I understand. You are famous in your field. You must realize that the technology needed to do this is of an incredibly high order."

"It's unbelievable, light years ahead of us. The energy needed to do this...I don't understand. Does antimatter power the stations?"

"Heavens no," Hela said. "We needed the antimatter to clear several critical areas deep under the Earth. We tried nuclear bombs before, but the components melted before they could reach the impasse points. Mother finished the controlled, antimatter explosions several hours ago. Now, everything is ready."

Selene stared at the woman.

"The stations are a marvel of technology," Hela said, "built ages ago when humanity was young. Our benefactors wanted to—"

"Wait a minute," Selene said. "The repellers are driving the solid core faster. That's what you said, right?"

Hela nodded.

"The Earth's surface temperature is heating up," Selene said, trying to piece this together. "That can't be the only danger to a stronger magnetic field. If the gauss levels rise too high, it will have civilization wrecking effects. Distance power lines will fail because of increased impedance. In fact, most electronics will fail in time. The Earth's magnetic field will swamp most generators and electrical motors." Her eyes widened with understanding. "Of course," she whispered.

389

"Radio noise will jam most frequencies. It's why we couldn't call anyone on the Learjet."

"The effects won't last forever."

Selene laughed wildly. "What I've outlined would only be the beginning problems. With increased magnetics, the poles will draw certain asteroids to it so they'll bombard the Earth, heating up the atmosphere even more. Volcanism will also rise dramatically. Don't you see? That's what must have happened the first time. A great cataclysm destroyed the ancient invaders and almost took humanity with them. You have to shut down the repellers. First, use the stations to slow the inner core back to its normal speed."

"Mother needs the strengthened magnetic field."

"Why? What is she going to do with it? I don't understand why the ancient invaders built the stations in the first place." Selene frowned. "Maybe that's not even the great danger."

Hela smirked.

"Have you ever heard of Nikola Tesla?"

"Of course," Hela said.

"Maybe these repellers will start a great vibration in the crust. Tesla once said, 'In a few weeks, I could set the Earth's crust into such a state of vibration that it would rise and fall hundreds of feet, throwing rivers out of their beds, wrecking buildings, and practically destroying civilization.'"

"Bah," Hela said. "You're overreacting."

"I wonder," Selene said. "I'm beginning to think that must be what happened in the past. The Earth had a...a Tesla Event. The crust went up and down possibly just as he suggested. By spinning the core too fast, you may be bringing about another such event through the buildup of the vibrations over time. Surely, a fast spinning core will wobble. The effects to the planet..."

Hela opened her mouth. Before she could speak, an intercom buzzed. "Just a moment," she told Selene. Hela stepped to the intercom, pressing a button. "Yes?"

"Mother wants the applicant to see the grand finale."

"I haven't stabilized her mind yet."

"The Day has arrived, dear sister. Mother is insistent. You can repair Marcus's damage later. Bring the applicant to the main chamber."

"I hear and obey," Hela said. She turned from the intercom.

"What does she mean calling me an applicant?" Selene asked.

"It should be obvious. The solution is making your mind race, putting seemingly unrelated events together, helping you make intuitive connections."

Selene frowned.

"There's only one job opening left," Hela said.

"I'm to be the next Mother?" Selene asked.

Hela clapped her hands. "Yes! Mother has allowed you a normal childhood and life. It will give you the right perspectives when the time comes for you to make the ascension into Motherhood."

"But...The Day has arrived. The New Order is about to begin. Do you need a new Mother after this?"

"That is a shrewd question," Hela said. "One of Mother's key attributes is to always prepare for the worst. The Day hasn't happened yet, although we're less than an hour away, I would think."

"What is going to happen exactly?" Selene asked.

Hela pressed a control. The electric lines no longer snaked over Selene's ankles and wrists. The numb feeling immediately switched to pinpricks of sensation.

"Your clothes are under the frame," Hela said. "We must hurry. This is the greatest moment in human history."

Selene sat up, feeling woozy. She kept blinking, waiting for more feeling in her limbs.

"Come," Hela said, with her hand on the latch.

Selene slid down to the floor. It was warm.

Hela turned the latch, opened the door and gasped with astonishment.

-86-

GRAVITATIONAL TUBE CHAMBER
UNDERGROUND PYRAMID

Jack took his thumb off the heater switch as foul-smelling smoke curled before him. He looked around, saw a bundle of wires and picked them up. With the plastic-coated wires acting as insulation, he grabbed the hot latch, yanking open the hatch.

He had burned out the locking mechanism with his heater. It had cost him an appreciable portion of its charge. Fortunately, he had two heaters.

He tossed the wires into the chamber and kicked the hatch shut behind him. He was outside in a corridor. He noticed something different right away. This corridor wasn't metal like Station Eight. No. The walls around him were fashioned out of stone.

Am I inside the underground pyramid? Does that make sense?

Could the gravitational rock tube have angled upward from its original depth at Station Eight? It was possible, he supposed, more than possible given the fantastic technology he'd been seeing so far.

Jack listened. He could hear a hum but he didn't hear any voices or footfalls. Was this the right place? The rock corridor made him think so.

He advanced with the heater ready. He'd made it. At least, he would work off that assumption until proven otherwise. All the deaths, the pain and sacrifices to get him here at this place at this time—Agent Elliot planned to make it count.

His heart didn't pound. He did not grip the heater with a shaking hand. He moved cautiously but loosely. His eyes burned with desire and intensity. This was his Superbowl appearance. This was why he'd trained all these years. A group of super-humans wanted to screw with his world. An old witch figured she could outmaneuver everyone. Jack was sure Mother had ordered an attack upon Secretary King and caused David Carter's mind to betray him. Because of that, Jack had shot his friend. It was payback time now. It was time to stop the conspiracy from destroying everything Agent Elliot held sacred.

For the next few minutes, Jack prowled through the stone corridors. He passed locked hatches, a heat vent and peered into a room with screens and hieroglyphic symbols. It struck him then. He recalled the sniper he'd caused to plummet to his death from the helicopter in Siwa. The shooter had had a hieroglyphic on the sole of his foot. Now, Jack knew why. The man had belonged to Mother.

Finally, he came to closed doors reminiscent of those in Station Eight. He typed in the same commands Samson Mark Two had shown him on an outer pad.

The doors opened. Jack stepped into a metal elevator. He pressed a button, wondering if he was making a mistake. The doors closed, and nothing happened for a moment. Jack dreaded hearing someone chuckle at him through a speaker. Had this been a trap?

Then, the elevator began to rise. Jack let out his breath. Until then, he hadn't known he'd been holding it. The ride went smoothly enough. He had no idea how many floors he passed.

With a lurch, the elevator stopped. The doors opened and three big men, each the size of the D'erlon soldier, stared at him.

Before they could respond, Jack pressed the heater stud. He burnt a neat little hole in the first man's chest, drilling the heart. He did the same thing to the second man. The third swung at him. Jack swayed back. The fist grazed his chin. It wasn't enough, though. Jack still pressed the stud, burning through the man's neck. The giant of a man staggered backward. Jack shot him in the chest now, causing the man to crash onto the floor.

Agent Elliot panted. He was in overdrive, a human wrecking ball meant to stop Mother's brood any way he could.

He checked each dead man, lifted a heater off one and a small control unit from another. As he stepped to the third, he heard a terrified scream from down the corridor. A second later, his mind cataloged the noise. That was Selene. She was in the underground pyramid, nearby and in danger.

-87-

CELL
UNDERGROUND PYRAMID

The beast had been waiting patiently, having sniffed out the trail of one of the plane people. That one was behind the door, a barrier the beast hadn't been able to open. It had slunk into an alcove as one of Mother's tormenters had hurried past a little while ago. She had opened the door before it could react, slipping inside and closing the barrier behind her.

The beast had recognized the woman and remembered her scent. She had been the worst tormentor of all, the woman in the white lab coat with her hair pulled back on her head. The beast had bitter reason to remember her. She had watched him many, many times, as she'd practiced one foul experiment after another on him in his puppyhood.

With the scent of her still strong in its snout—the hound lay down, forgetting its other plans. It wanted revenge upon the chief tormentor. The beast's hackles rose even as it controlled itself from squirting urine in recollected fear.

The beast panted, blinking, thinking of the joy of sinking its fangs into her flesh. He would taste her blood, killing her for the evil of her experimentation.

Finally, the latch moved.

With a low growl, the beast rushed out of the alcove. The door opened. The tormentor saw him. She gasped. It was a lovely sound. Terror filled her eyes, but also a pitiless resolve to live. A hand sank into one of her lab coat pockets. At the same time, she began to close the door.

No! The beast would not lose her now. The shaggy hound leaped, hitting the hatch a micro-moment before it would have latched shut. The hatch slammed open at its weight, crashing against the tormentor, hurling her backward.

The seconds seemed like hours to the beast. It was in an altered state. Everything moved in slow motion. Its paws descended toward the floor. The woman continued to backpedal, gaining control of her feet. A red welt rose on her face. How she kept her balance, the beast didn't know, but she did. Worse, her hand pulled out of a lab coat pocket, holding onto a heater.

The beast landed on the floor.

The woman's thumb jabbed down on a button. A red light on the end of the heater blinked on. The tormentor's hand swung upward. The beast realized she was trying to align the red light with its body. The beast remembered heaters and their invisible beams. It had a great respect for invisible dangers. The tormentors had taught it that. The hound ran, moving away from the alignment. It strained to reach the enemy. She sought to regain bodily control. She was fantastically coordinated and deadly. The race seemed to take an agonizingly long time. Her hand came closer, closer, the beast strove to move and then its fur began to singe from a dreadful invisible heat.

The beast leaped, opened it jaws as a vicious growl emanated from deep in its throat.

At the same time, another woman began to scream. She stood beside a board in the room. Her scream was piercing and went on and on.

The beast flew through the air. The hand with the red-lit heater strove to align with it. Then, the beast reached the tormentor and time flowed back into its proper stream.

The beast bore the tormentor to the floor. It bit the hand with the heater, crushing flesh, hearing bones snap, breaking the weapon. The tormentor squirmed and thrust a knee against it. The beast snarled with spittle flying, whipping its head about. For an instant, they stared into each other's eyes. The beast recalled those eyes watching it many, many painful times

396

from behind a glass partition. There was no partition now. Its fangs sank into soft throat-flesh. The tormentor tried to fight back.

Savagely, it shook the tormenter and bit down harder.

"Stop it!" the other woman shouted. "You're killing her. You're—"

The beast released the tormentor, snarling, staring up at the woman leaning against a frame.

She stared into its eyes. Her words stilled from her slack mouth. The beast could sense her fear and helplessness. She had been in the plane, however. That had been significant a little while ago. Now, with the blood of a tormenter in its mouth—

"Selene!" a man said from behind.

"Jack?"

The beast whirled around. With a start, it realized he recognized the intruder. The beast had faced and fought this man before in the forest. The man had cut it with a knife. The beast had slain his friend in an attempt to escape the invisible barrier. If only that little box had worked to allow it freedom from the dish-shaped fences.

"Look at its braincase," Selene said, who was hurriedly fastening her bra.

"I see it," Jack said, who aimed a heater at the hound.

"It's smart and it just killed Hela."

"I heard your scream," Jack said. "I think everyone in the pyramid heard it. People are going to show up soon. We have to find Mother before that happens."

The beast perked up as a fierce desire washed through it. The beast trembled with desire. Mother, it had heard the tormentors speak of her many times. Mother was the author of all its woes, this it had come to realize. As much as it wanted to kill the man with the weapon in front of it, the beast wondered if the man was the enemy of his enemy.

"Do you see how the dog is listening to us?" Selene asked.

"Yeah," Jack said. "I wonder if Mother's people messed with its DNA, using the stamper on its embryonic cells. They made it smart."

397

Selene nodded as if that made sense to her. "Do you understand me?" she asked the hound.

The beast cocked its head. It had learned in the past that the tormentors enjoyed when it did that.

"You *do* understand me," Selene said. "Do you like Mother?"

The beast growled.

Selene looked up at Jack. "Did you see that? It hates Mother just as we do."

"That's an awfully big leap," Jack said. "Maybe it just hates us talking to it."

"Help us," Selene told the hound. "Help us and we'll help you later."

The beast understood her words. It didn't trust her, though. It certainly didn't trust the man with the weapon aimed at it.

"Maybe I should just kill it," Jack said. "This is the creature that killed my partner back in the Ardennes Forest."

The beast grew tense, ready to whirl around and charge the man. The trick would be to catch him by surprise.

"None of its past actions matter," Selene said. "The hound is here. It killed Hela. Why did it do that?"

"Because it's a crazed beast," Jack said.

"Agent Elliot, what matters more than anything else right now?"

Jack glanced at Selene. She was beautiful, distracting him in her bra and panties. Then, he regarded the hound again. "I don't like you because you killed my friend," he told the beast. "But I'm willing to work together in order to stop Mother. Are you smart because the ancient beings played with animal DNA as if they were gods?"

The beast deliberately scratched its front paw on the floor. That had always impressed the tormentors in the old days when they had tested its intelligence.

"It understands you," Selene said in wonder.

"I don't know…" Jack said slowly.

"Mother is accelerating the inner core of the Earth," Selene said in a rush. "That's making the magnetic field stronger. That's what's playing havoc with the world's temperature and electronics."

398

"How is she doing that?" Jack asked.

"The stations are giant repellers, using magnetics to spin the inner core faster. Haven't you noticed how hot it is everywhere?"

"Actually," Jack said. "I haven't been outside lately. I reached this place by using a gravitational tube."

"We're running out of time," Selene said. "We have to get to the control room and stop the process before our technological civilization is demolished by high gauss levels."

Jack didn't know about gauss levels, but he agreed about stopping Mother. "What are we going to do about the dog?" he asked.

"If you're willing to help us," Selene told the hound, "rub your front paw on the floor again."

The beast understood her words and rubbed its paw on the floor.

"What do you say, Jack?" Selene asked. "Should we join forces with the intelligent dog? We're going to need all the help we can get."

Agent Elliot kept his weapon aimed at the hound. Finally, he lowered his arm. "I must be crazy, but okay. Do you have any idea how to get to the control room?"

"I don't," Selene said.

The beast glanced back and forth between the two humans. Then, it trotted toward the man. For a moment, it seemed as if the man was going to aim the heater at it again. Instead, he stepped aside.

A wild, instinctive impulse to attack the man nearly overcame the beast's desire to kill tormenters first. By reason alone, the hound refrained from attacking the man. Instead, it trotted out of the cell. It had understood the last question. It believed it knew the way to the place they wanted to go. There was a peculiar odor in the air. It would follow the smell and see what happened.

-88-

STONE CORRIDOR
UNDERGROUND PYRAMID

Selene's mind seethed in turmoil. New thoughts flashed for her attention, trying to bind seemingly irrational propositions into intuitive insights. It gave her a headache and made it difficult to concentrate.

"Wait," she said.

Jack halted. They'd barely gone twenty feet from the cell.

The beast didn't listen to her, holding its snout in the air, testing scents, she supposed, as it trotted along.

Jack whistled softly. The beast looked back, perhaps noticing they'd stopped, as it finally did likewise.

"Is there a problem?" Jack asked her.

"Yes. It's just the three of us against Mother's horde. Marcus—"

"Who's that?" Jack asked.

"The soldier you shot in Station Eight," Selene said. "After taking me to his plane, we talked. I was able to convince him to help me against Mother."

"You're kidding?"

Selene gave Jack a quick rundown of what had happened in the Learjet. "Marcus must be nearby," she said at the end. "It stands to reason that if they held me in this area, he should be in one of these cells, too. We could use Ney Blanc, as well."

"The French traitor?" asked Jack.

400

"I don't have time to explain." Selene glanced around the corridor. Then, she turned to the hound. "Is anyone behind these hatches?"

The beast examined her. The braincase was too large for it to be a normal hound. It also watched her with too much intelligence. What had Mother done to make it so smart? And why?

Finally, the beast put its nose to the floor. It seemingly followed a scent, halted, sniffed in a new spot and then trotted past them. The beast went to the hatch beside Selene's former cell. The beast whined in an odd manner. It suddenly seemed eager.

"We need the man behind the hatch," Selene said.

The beast cocked its head.

"What's going on?" Jack asked her, sounding perplexed.

Selene explained to him about the brain enhancer injection. "My mind's racing at hyper-speed. I can put things together faster than ever. I'm thinking the hound hates these people. There has to be a reason for that. I'm thinking it hates Marcus."

"The hound was an outer sentry at the D'erlon Plant in the Ardennes," Jack said. "How much can it hate them?"

"It's intelligent and sensitive, but I bet they still treated it like an animal."

The beast stared at her as if listening to every word.

"Can you break into this room?" Selene asked Jack.

Agent Elliot approached the hatch while the beast watched him carefully.

"We're allies," Jack muttered to the thing. "You'd better not forget that."

The beast didn't step aside.

"Talk to him in a friendly way," Selene suggested.

Jack gave her a look.

"Talk to him like you'd want to be talked to," she said.

"You're laying down the Golden Rule on me, huh?" Jack asked.

Selene nodded.

Jack cleared his throat as he regarded the hound. "We were enemies once. Now, we're friends. I'm going to trust you..." He looked up at Selene.

401

"You're doing well," she said. "He's smart and sensitive. He can understand you. Don't ever forget that."

Jack regarded the hound again. He nodded a second later. "The past is the past. We're both fighting for our world. I'll cover your back and I hope you'll cover mine."

The beast peered at Agent Elliot. Slowly, the shaggy creature stepped out of the way.

Jack heaved a sigh of relief. Then he stepped to the hatch, testing the handle. It moved. "Ready?" he asked Selene.

"Go," she said.

Jack opened the hatch, jumping through with his heater ready. "Jackpot," he said a moment later.

The beast followed and stood stock still, staring at the sight.

Selene saw why a second later. A nude Marcus lay on an articulated frame. The big man didn't move nor did his eyes open. An electrical arc surrounded his ankles, wrists and neck.

"What's under the frame?" Jack asked.

"Probably his weapons and clothes," Selene said.

The beast growled deep in its throat. It was a frightening sound, putting an atavistic dread in Selene's stomach. She'd guessed right a moment ago about the beast hating Mother's people. She gathered her resolve, turning toward the thing and going down onto one knee.

It regarded her.

"Marcus is our ally," she told the hound. "I don't like him, but he's against Mother now. I think he always has been. I understand that you hate him, but we have to work together to defeat Mother. Do you understand me?"

The beast glanced from her to Marcus. Slowly, its hackles lowered and then it turned away, sitting down, waiting.

"What do you think?" Selene asked Jack.

He shrugged.

Standing, massaging her forehead, Selene approached the frame's controls. She tried to remember what Hela had done earlier. It wasn't clear from looking at the panel.

"I'm going to have guess," she said.

"Whatever you're going to do," Jack told her, "do it quickly. We're probably out of time as it is."

Selene touched a control. Sizzling sounds grew louder as Marcus's body arched as if in pain. Frantic that she'd injured him, Selene manipulated controls faster. Marcus thrashed on the frame. The stink of burned flesh heralded wisps of smoke from his ankles and wrists. The unconscious man groaned.

Selene stepped back from the controls.

"You can't do that!" Jack shouted. "Finish what you started."

She tried different buttons and switches. Several seconds later, the electric arcs around his throat, wrists and ankles disappeared.

"You did it," Jack said.

Marcus's eyes flew open. He jerked upright to a sitting position, twisting his head to stare at them. Convulsively, the big man tried to roll off the articulated frame and crashed face-first onto the floor.

The beast found that irresistible. It lunged at the prone man.

"No!" Jack shouted.

The beast growled at Agent Elliot.

"Please, we have a greater objective," Selene told the hound. "You have to control your baser desires if we're going to defeat Mother."

The beast regarded her with wonder, deliberately sitting down a moment later.

"Well done," Jack said. "We averted one disaster." As he finished speaking, a klaxon began to blare outside in the corridor.

-89-

STONE CORRIDOR
UNDERGROUND PYRAMID

Marcus felt the hound's scrutiny. He knew the experimental hound didn't trust him. He couldn't say he blamed the creature. It was amazing to him the hound was free inside the pyramid. Yet, it made sense now why the motorcycle riders had been armed with dart pistols instead of guns. They must have been tracking the hound. The beast must have slipped into the pyramid during the Learjet's explosion. He'd always felt that Mother had underestimated the thing's cunning.

Marcus gripped his .55 Knocker. He didn't like seeing the D17 agent here, didn't like the idea of working with the man. He was Marcus. He could do this on his own. Still, he would use what fate had given him.

Marcus understood the others needed him to do this. He'd woken up to their fright concerning the klaxon. It had stopped sounding. The klaxon hadn't had anything to do with them. Instead, it had announced the beginning of The Day. The final countdown was here, and he still didn't know what the stations were ultimately supposed to achieve.

The geologist had told him they repelled the iron core of the planet, creating a stronger magnetic field. She'd wanted to know if that gave him any hints as to the grand purpose.

Frederick and Hela might have known. Marcus didn't have a clue. He would have soon, though.

Marcus hadn't been to any of the other stations. Station Eight had been the first after all these years, and it had been abandoned. Although apparently not completely so, not given the D17 agent's fantastic story of gravitational tube transfer.

The point, though, was that Marcus knew his way inside the underground pyramid. He kept them hidden as they advanced toward the great central chamber. Mother would be in there, doing whatever it was she'd planned these last seven hundred years.

Marcus grinned intently. This was it. Finally, he was going to face a worthy opponent. There wasn't anyone like Mother. She would have her lackeys at the controls around the room. Marcus hefted his Knocker. He knew what was going to happen to Mother's favorite children. Hopefully, smug Frederick would be in there. Amazingly, Hela was already dead.

Marcus led the way with Jack, Selene, the hound and Ney behind him. They'd found the former DGSE agent in the next cell, secured to another articulated frame.

Maybe he would need allies to cover his back. His siblings were dangerous just like him. How many would be in the central chamber?

Marcus had been doing some hard soul-searching for many years. It had crystalized on the plane ride back to Libya. The stations were dangerous to the Earth. Selene had told him about Hela's comment: that Mother wouldn't need him in the New Order. He felt betrayed by that, but he understood. The smart ones always thought to use the fighters, the champions.

He was going to kill Mother, shut down the stations and pick up the reigns of Mother's hidden kingdom. It was time to do things his way. He'd been the subordinate long enough. That meant he had to kill everyone in the pyramid, including those marching behind him. Treachery was wrong, especially as the others had freed him from the frame. But, to gain control of Mother's apparatus, it was worth backstabbing his allies this one time.

405

To defeat Mother in her lair, Marcus would need every advantage. Thus, he would fight with his allies one hundred percent.

Marcus was going to trust his instinctive judgment to know when to turn on them. At that point, he wouldn't hesitate, coming out on top with Mother's empire ready to obey him.

Marcus paused, glancing back at the D17 agent. The man watched him. Marcus didn't like that.

"We take an elevator up several floors," Marcus whispered. "When the door opens—we're going to have to kill everyone in the chamber."

The D17 agent nodded curtly.

"Mother won't show us mercy," Marcus said.

"Got it," the man said.

"We, therefore, must be equally ruthless."

The D17 agent became blank-faced.

It was then Marcus had a glimpse of the real Jack Elliot, the man's deadliness. It caused Marcus's features to harden. That in turn made the agent's eyebrows lift fractionally. Both men's gun hands tensed.

Marcus forced a smile. He'd almost raised his Knocker to obliterate the dangerous agent. At the last second, he recognized the slight, telltale signs of a force field suit. His .55 caliber bullets would not reach Agent Elliot. He was going to need a heater to slay the man.

The soldier also realized the agent recognized his desire to shoot him. Jack had barely restrained himself.

Instead of making Marcus afraid, he felt a wild elation sing through his body and mind. This was why he had been born, to fight worthy foes. First, he would take down Mother. Then, he would rid himself of the second most dangerous person on Earth, Jack Elliot. That would prove that Marcus was the champion of the world.

"Are you ready?" the soldier asked in a low voice.

"Let's do it," Jack said, hoarsely.

"Yes," Marcus said, "let's."

-90-

ELEVATOR
UNDERGROUND PYRAMID

Jack checked the fully charged heater, slipping it inside a front pocket. He stood before Marcus with his back to the soldier. The five of them including the hound rode a lift upward.

"How big is the pyramid?" Selene asked from the back.

"Five times the Giza pyramid," Marcus rumbled.

"It's huge then," Selene said.

"Yes."

"Who built it?"

Jack heard Marcus's jacket rustle. The soldier must be shrugging.

"You don't know?" Selene asked.

"No," Marcus said, flatly.

"Aren't you curious?"

"Does it matter who?" the soldier asked.

"I should think it matters considerably," Selene said.

Jack cleared his throat. "Samson told me two hundred fallen angels started the mess."

"What?" Selene asked.

"Samson said it's all recorded in the Book of Enoch," Jack said, quickly explaining some of what Samson had told him.

"What does any of what you just said have to do with the stations?" Selene asked.

"I didn't think so earlier," Jack said, "but now I think the fallen angels built them."

"Ah...I have news for you, Jack. The stations use high technology."

"I got that," Jack said.

"Angels don't use high tech," Selene told him.

"How do you know that? If they understand great mysteries, why wouldn't they be able to make high tech stations, lasers and gravitational tubes?"

No one spoke for a moment. Jack turned around. Selene stared at him in disbelief. Marcus was stone-faced. Ney seemed uninterested.

"Let's use our reason," Selene finally said.

"I'm all for that," Jack said. "I'm just telling you what Samson Mark Two told me. He was pretty certain about it, too."

"Madmen usually are certain," Selene said. "It's one of the signs of their madness. Clearly, the stations are wrecking the Earth just as they did last time. That doesn't take God. It just takes meddling aliens who unleashed powers they couldn't control."

"But—"

"Listen," Selene said, "Tesla once said, 'what one man calls God, another calls the laws of physics.' If you want to call these aliens fallen angels..." Selene shrugged.

Jack blinked several times. "Whatever the stations are supposed to do," he said, "it must be critically important to Mother."

"Hela spoke about bringing universal peace to the planet," Selene said. "The use today is supposed to usher in a new order of existence."

"We have another two floors to go," Marcus announced. He drew the Knocker, the huge barrel looking murderous this close.

Jack pulled out the heater he'd filched from one of the soldiers he'd slain earlier. It was fully charged. He put that in a different pocket. Then, he took out a flat, palm-sized control unit with several buttons on it. He debated asking Marcus what it was supposed to do. He hesitated, though.

408

Jack didn't trust Marcus. He had a nose for these things. In the secretive world of espionage and commando raids, one had to rely on one's instincts if one was going to come out of the ops alive. The man behind him was a killer, had attacked them in Station Eight at Mother's orders. The soldier had switched sides because the Learjet pilot had turned on him—Selene had whispered the story to Jack while walking down a corridor.

What did Marcus desire most of all? That was the key to understanding the soldier. So far, Jack had felt smug superiority from the man. Marcus walked, talked and acted like a superman, looking down his nose at them. Would such a man be content to live an ordinary life? Marcus hadn't even buckled under Mother's rule. What did that tell him?

Elliot snorted to himself. He recalled a lesson from Sunday school. This was a crazy time to think about it. It must have been Samson's tales getting to him. What had caused the Devil's fall from grace? It had been pride, overweening ambition to replace God with himself. That had started the war in Heaven.

Why should it be any different down here? A man like Marcus didn't want to take second place to anyone. Maybe it had galled Marcus all these years taking orders from Mother. Wasn't the soldier supposed to be a superman? Sure. Why did Mother trust some of her supermen and not the others? Surely, the world's most cunning person could recognize whom she should keep at arm's length.

What did that mean for them? It meant that Marcus was a temporary ally. He would have ulterior motives. The soldier's arrogance screamed that to be true.

Should I turn around and fry him? Is he more dangerous at our back or is he worth more fighting with us against Mother?

Jack inhaled as he set himself. They were almost to the control chamber. The ultimate objective today was stopping Mother. That meant they badly needed Marcus's help. Once they shut down the stations, if that was possible, then it would be time to worry about the aftermath.

This was like Russia and America uniting in World War II to take down Germany. Once the fighting ended, then round two started.

The beast growled from deep in its throat.

Jack's neck prickled with anticipation. It was too bad Mother or her scientists hadn't given the hound the ability to speak.

We have to stop Mother.

Jack squeezed his eyes shut and opened them wide. Unlike normal ops, he was nervous today. His heart pounded and his palms had become sweaty.

Jack transferred a heater to his left hand, wiping his right palm on his pants. Then he re-gripped the heater with the right.

Marcus chuckled low under his breath.

That made Jack's gut twist. The soldier yearned for this. He was going into battle with two DNA-freaks. What had it been like in the world before the Great Cataclysm? Had there really been heroes of old, supermen?

The elevator slowed.

Jack used the back of his right hand to wipe his mouth.

The elevator stopped. The doors began to open. As they did, Jack felt the soldier's left hand on his back just below his neck. The doors slid open faster. Marcus shoved Jack, propelling Agent Elliot into a vast chamber the shape of an inner pyramid.

People stood at controls everywhere. Some sat on seats halfway up the slanted walls. There were giant screens in various places. What seemed like computers whirled with colored displays. It was like NORAD, only in an underground pyramid built before human history had started.

Jack kept stumbling, working to catch himself, doing his best to keep from tripping onto his face.

In the middle of the vast chamber that was bigger than three football fields stood a person in a cloak and hood with her back to Jack. Before the person was a giant circular object maybe thirty feet high and as far across. Blue lights pulsed along the circular disc. There was nothing in the center of the disc. Jack could see through it onto the other side of the pyramidal-shaped chamber.

There had to be two hundred people at the controls. Jack hadn't expected so many. He wondered if Marcus had.

Finally, stopping, glancing over his shoulder, Jack saw Marcus. The big man raised his Knocker with preternatural speed. He aimed at the person in the center of the chamber and began to squeeze his trigger finger.

Jack whipped around to see what would happen to the person he assumed must be Mother.

-91-

CONTROL CHAMBER
UNDERGROUND PYRAMID

Selene saw Marcus shove Jack out of the elevator. It seemed like a treacherous thing to do. Agent Elliot was good on his feet, though, managing to remain upright as he stumbled into the chamber.

The soldier bounded out, raised his gun and aimed at the woman in the center of the vast room. Marcus pulled the trigger several times. The .55 Knocker went *click, click, click,* the hammer rising and falling to absolutely no effect but for the noise.

Jack moved almost as fast, aiming a heater with his thumb pressed against the firing button. His silent weapon had even less effect.

Marcus reacted faster, turning, aiming the gun at a nearby operator. He pulled the trigger again, producing another useless *click.*

Many operators glanced at them. Selene noticed they reacted badly to sight of the hound. The beast watched tensely with its hackles raised.

Marcus roared with frustration, shaking his Knocker. He glared at the assembled operators. "Follow me!" he shouted, holstering the big gun and breaking into a sprint for the cloaked person in the center.

That one had turned. She wore a shimmering mask just like the one she'd worn in the video from 1908. It was Mother. Selene knew because goosebumps rose on her arms and thighs.

Marcus moved like an out-of-control semi, his features flushed and his lips pulled back in a fierce snarl. The hound lunged after him, streaking past Jack. That must have finally penetrated Agent Elliot's thinking. He ran after the other two. Selene saw a gleaming knife in Marcus's right fist.

"Hold," Mother said, her voice loud, maybe amplified. She raised something metallic in her right hand. It flashed blue, sending a wide blue beam that caught Marcus, the beast and Jack within its ray.

All three of them slowed and then stopped, standing rigidly still as if they couldn't move.

"We are undone, mademoiselle," Ney whispered to Selene. The DGSE agent hadn't charged with the others. He now holstered his gun with a minimum of fanfare, no doubt hoping to remain unnoticed.

"Marcus," Mother said. "You're interrupting my moment of glory. That is unseemly of you."

Marcus didn't respond. It was quite possible he could not.

"You brought friends," Mother said. "Look. There is the experimental hound. I consider its presence a monument to my genius. I have bested the ancients in that field, whose greatest creature was the untamable Minotaur. I believe the next few moments will show another of my triumphs as I excel beyond anything they achieved."

As Mother spoke, Selene glanced at the giant screens. They showed frightful images. There was a city somewhere. It had masses of palm trees and other tropical plants. Hordes of people madly pedaled their bicycles. Something shimmering appeared above them. A second later, a mighty explosion filled the air. Buildings burst apart. Trees flattened themselves just like in the Tunguska Event and people went flying.

A similar event happened in the Artic or Antarctic Ocean. The sky-flash sent ice and snow hurdling into the disturbed sea.

Other screens showed howling winds sweeping everything before them. Cars, parts of houses, trees, cows, dogs, people and fences flew through the air at terrific speeds. In another

413

screen, electrical discharges flashed upward into the roiling sky. It hurt Selene's eyes the bolts were so intensely white. Charred corpses lay scattered everywhere there.

Selene glanced from screen to screen. Mountains shook. Lava spewed out of prairies. Cities crumpled from devastating earthquakes. Massive tsunamis sped at coastlines.

She's destroying the Earth, Selene realized. *Is this what happened last time thousands of years ago?*

"We're ready to begin the countdown," a lean man said at one of the control panels. "I'm not sure how long we can funnel the energies," he added.

"What are you hoping to achieve with this madness?" Selene shouted at Mother.

The woman with the shimmering mask turned toward her. "Ah. Selene, my child, you always strike to the heart of the matter. You are a pleasure to me. You have surmounted many obstacles to reach this place. I am well pleased with you."

Selene took courage at that. She raised an arm, indicating the various screens. "You're destroying the planet. Nikola Tesla predicted such a thing."

"Tesla," Mother said. "He aided my research for a time. He had a brilliant mind, but he did not truly understand vibrations."

"What?"

Mother laughed. "What you're seeing is an illusion, sweet girl. The worthless ones die by their millions, but it doesn't matter in the end. We will rebuild paradise on Earth. Later, we shall expand throughout the galaxy with the noblest civilization in existence."

"Do you see the screens?" Selene shouted. "It's a mass disaster just like last time."

"Last time," Mother said, "the ancients lost control at the end. They unleashed uncontained energies due to their attempt to breach the Citadel. That produced a disaster, as you say. It did not destroy the world machine, though. I will search for different outposts, connecting with them and reaping the benefit of their greater wisdom and technology."

Selene shook her head. "What does the world-machine do? I don't understand."

"The great ones came here from afar," Mother said. "They were banished, I believe. They did not travel by spaceship, but through a doorway, through interdimensional travel. That is as good a word as any for what this is." Mother indicated the circular object rising from the floor behind her. "The great ones had been left adrift on our mud-ball planet. They did not accept the verdict, however. They used their wisdom and craft, deciding to build a world machine so they could return home."

Selene frowned.

"The Citadel's protective devices must have overloaded through the doorway," Mother said. "That unleashed a surge of uncontained energies onto the Earth, bringing about what many refer to as the Great Cataclysm."

"You're about to do that again," Selene protested.

"No, no, dear child," Mother said. "You are either not listening or failing to perceive. I am not attempting to breach the Citadel. I am trying for a different location, somewhere we may link up with the others."

"What others?" Selene asked.

"The ones that surely must exist in the vast cosmos," Mother said.

"We're ready," the lean man shouted.

"Excellent, dear Frederick," Mother said. "Let us begin the search."

Selene glanced at Frederick and realized she'd seen him before at the Siwa Oasis. He had left in the caravan of Land Rovers. He now sat at intricate controls with a screen before him.

"I'm engaging the dimensional scanner," Frederick said.

His screen buzzed fuzzily before coalescing into a sea of bubbling lava. A strange stone ship appeared to float through the steaming red, sluggish substance. In the background, stars blazed in profusion.

Frederick manipulated the controls.

The screen turned fuzzy again, this time coalescing into gently rolling granite hills that glittered with millions of gems. Above the millions of green, red, white and yellow stones slid a gray barge fifty feet above the ground. Tubes snaked down from the barge, vacuuming the gems from the hills.

415

"I have a possibility," Frederick said.

Mother examined a larger screen nearer her showing the same image. "No. That reality strikes me as too mechanistic."

Once again, Frederick adjusted his controls. After a time, the screen showed a nighttime world with several cratered moons hanging in the otherwise dark sky. A sluggish sea appeared in the background.

Selene squinted, looking closer. It appeared that a giant tentacle slid out of the mucky sea to grasp at something skimming the surface.

"That's too primitive," Mother complained.

"The coordinates are difficult the farther afield I try," Frederick said.

"Try something nearer our reality then," Mother suggested.

Once more, Frederick manipulated the controls.

Selene was beginning to understand what he was doing. The solution Marcus had given her still stimulated her brain to furious and fast connections.

This time, the screen showed a meadow with a brook. There were tall green fronds that waved gently in a breeze. Red spines grew elsewhere with purple pods hanging near the fifty-foot spikes. A strange, purple-feathered bird flittered through the scene.

"Do you see that spire?" Mother asked. "Zoom into the background to the left."

Frederick did so.

Selene gasped. Others in the room murmured.

On the screen rose a slender silver tower. It was beautiful. An equally silver air-car slid toward the spire.

"There," Mother said. "We have found an outpost. I am sure of it. Open the way. It is time Earth reconnected with the universal civilization."

Selene glanced at other screens. The devastation throughout the world had worsened. Would opening the dimensional portal take more power? Would that strain the Earth even more as the world machine did whatever the ancient beings had designed it to do?

Oh, this was terrible.

-92-

CONTROL CHAMBER
UNDERGROUND PYRAMID

Jack strained to move his right hand. He'd been straining ever since Mother had hit him with the paralysis beam.

He could hear just fine, but he couldn't move his head, although he could move his eyes back and forth. What he saw on the nearby screens sickened him. The world machine as Mother called it—the stations and whatever else she had—caused vast destruction. He had no doubt this had happened in the past. Maybe the portal let in worse energies.

What had Mother said before? The ancient beings had tried to breach the Citadel. Could that have been another word for Heaven? There had been war in Heaven with a third of the angels thrown out.

Jack's jaw muscles bunched as he strained to move his right hand. The beam had exhausted him, made it so none of his limbs obeyed his will. He had a feeling that he would have succumbed to total numbness as well, but every time he rested from straining, his energy to try returned almost right away. Could the substance in the needles from the stone object have already changed him? He suspected that was it. He recovered faster than he ever had in his life. It gave him the resolve to keep doing this.

Jack willed his fingers to twitch. One did the slightest bit. He could do this if he kept struggling.

417

The inner war occupied everything in him. He heard the voices going back and forth, Mother and Selene, but he didn't pay attention to the words anymore. His world zeroed down to his titanic effort. Marcus had frozen. The smart hound couldn't do a damn thing. It was all up to Jack Elliot. He had been in this situation before. He knew how these things should go.

Total focus was the answer. Absolute concentration took over as Jack strained, strained, and moved his right hand just a fraction toward his pocket.

He had two more heaters, as he'd dropped the first one. They were all useless now. Mother must have some kind of dampening field in place.

He had to reach the tiny gadget he'd stolen from one of the supermen he'd killed in front of the elevator. Could it do anything?

I have no idea. There's only one way to find out, now isn't there?

Jack's fingertips touched the top of his pocket. He'd gotten this far, he could go farther. He struggled and nearly blacked out from effort.

He stopped for a moment, recouping. The blood pounded in his ears and made his eyes blurry. Faster than he could believe, though, he felt good again.

Jack strained, pushed, focused and slid his fingers into his pocket. They touched the gadget, sliding over the front. With infinite patience and furious trying, he pressed a button.

Of course, nothing happened.

Jack struggled again, pressing another button. Again, he struck out and remained frozen. Then…

Wait a sec. He felt tingling throughout his body. His head twisted to the left. He was nearly frozen but thawing.

"Stay in one spot," he whispered to the others. "I have a buzzer. It's negating her beam. Let's wait until we can attack at full coordination."

Marcus grunted.

On the other side of Jack, the beast whined.

Seconds passed. Jack slowly moved his head. What he saw frightened him.

Down the slightly slanted floor in the middle of the chamber, the circular object blazed with a bright light. Jack could no longer look through the middle. It was like the surface of a vertical, shimmering pond, creating ripples. Then the ripples vanished and Jack peered into the most beautiful meadow in the world. What's more, he heard birds chirp. It was simply fantastic. He spied the silver tower in the distance. What was that place?

Mother approached the shining circular object in the middle of the chamber. She appeared to be looking into the new world, searching for something.

At that moment, claws scratched against the tiles of the floor. To Jack's left, the beast broke into a run. The beast darted for Mother, straining to reach the cloaked woman.

Did the hound attempt to reach her before she turned to see her danger?

"Mother!" a man shouted. "Behind you! The hound has broken free. It's attacking."

Jack leaped forward and began to run at Mother, too. So did Marcus. The soldier quickly pulled ahead of him. Marcus truly was a superman in strength, maybe in daring too.

The beast was already halfway to Mother when she turned around.

-93-

CONTROL CHAMBER
UNDERGROUND PYRAMID

Selene nudged Ney. The Frenchman glanced at her.

"You have a gun," she whispered.

"It doesn't fire in this chamber," he whispered back.

"You can still use it as a club, can't you?"

"*Wei*," he said.

"Then get ready to use it."

"Against whom?" Ney whispered.

"Frederick," Selene said, starting toward his spot along the wall.

She had a plan. It was a wild one, workable because Jack Elliot had found a way to break the freezing blue beam. She had thought of it because the flashes kept snapping in her mind, seeing connections and putting two and two together faster than she had ever been able to do in her life.

Selene believed she knew how to operate Frederick's board. It was incredible to her, but it controlled some sort of dimensional portal. That meant Mother had opened a path to a place far from Earth in space, possibly time and maybe even in a different dimension. Clearly, such a transfer was very difficult. Otherwise, wouldn't aliens have used such a method to come to Earth more often? Mother attempted to reach the extraterrestrials that had arrived on the planet in the distant past. If the ancient memories of that time were correct, the aliens had set themselves up as gods, toying with human lives and producing monstrosities to terrorize the primitives. Why would the extraterrestrials be any better this time? It was up to her to cut the tenuous connection, to make sure the arrogant aliens stayed far away from this world.

Frederick glanced at Selene. He scowled, and he glanced past her at Mother.

"Turn off the damper!" Mother shouted.

"Yes," Selene told Frederick. "Do that and we can shoot Mother down like a wild beast. Please press whatever switch you have to so we can gun down the lot of you."

Frederick glanced at a particular switch on his board. Selene noted the look.

Frederick scowled at her. Maybe he understood she'd just tricked him. He reached under the panel and came up with a knife. "First things first," Frederick said. The man lunged at her.

Selene barely twisted aside. Danny had always told her to run from a knife. A few cuts and a person bled into unconsciousness. This time—

Ney shouted and swung. He came from around Selene. Frederick was one of Mother's supermen, however. He had impossible reflexes. The man shifted his swipe and managed to thrust. The knife went into Ney's chest. The DGSE agent still completed the swing, though, clubbing Frederick on the side of the head with the gun handle. That staggered Frederick. The lean man tripped over his feet and went down onto the floor.

Ney groaned, releasing his gun and crumpling.

Selene hardly thought. She reached the console and pressed the button Frederick had glanced at, the dampener switch hopefully. After it clicked, she picked up Ney's fallen gun. At the same moment, Frederick clutched her left ankle as he lay on the floor.

Selene shot him twice. His grip slackened and she kicked his hand away.

A moment later, Selene sat down at the controls. Yes, here was the selector switch and here was the one that cycled through the various coordinates. She could put this on a timer, opening and closing pathways. That was very interesting. This was the final key to ridding the Earth of Mother. Selene had to play this just right, though. It would be tricky.

She began to manipulate the panel. Movement at the corner of her vision caused Selene to turn. Two of Mother's people rushed her. Selene grabbed the gun and shot them.

More of the operators were getting up. Too many whispered together as if they were going to rush en masse at her.

Backpedalling to Ney, Selene dug in his pockets, finding more magazines. The DGSE agent was coughing up blood, dying.

Selene steeled herself to the necessity of shooting people. If she didn't do this, the Earth could find itself under an alien heel ten times worse than last time. Mother had talked about peace, but she meant extraterrestrial domination over a supine human race. Freedom meant she had to do this.

Aiming at the nearest operators, Selene began firing, killing Mother's children. She found it sickening, her stomach turning over and squeezing. Her hand began to shake.

"You have to do this," Selene told herself. "Saving the planet has become your responsibility."

Wheezing from the effort of will, Selene used her thumb, letting the empty magazine clatter onto the floor. She shoved in another, continuing the grim task.

Many of the operators ran away. It seemed none of them had brought a gun. Mother would have likely forbidden such a thing.

Selene noticed that Mother ran through the interdimensional portal. It was an interesting decision on her part. Mother became blurry. Then, her feet sank onto the green meadow on the other side. Mother had crossed to the beautiful place, likely to get alien help.

Selene whirled around to the control panel. This could actually work. She had to time everything just so. Manipulating controls, she activated the cycler.

The beast raced for the portal. It was closer to Mother than anyone else was. The beast howled its bloodlust. The giant hound leaped, blurring as it passed through the portal. Then its paws sank onto the green substance. After a moment, it looked around, spied Mother and gave chase again. The beast neared its prey. Mother spun around, and there was a gleaming thing in her hand. She wasn't going to go down easily. Mother aimed the object at the beast—

Marcus sprinted for the portal, blocking the view. He ran with bitter determination. Then, the portal became fuzzy. Would he guess the significance of that? Yes. The soldier slid to a halt. He did not enter the pathway.

Selene believed he would have transferred into oblivion if he had. She had cut the connection between realms, places, planets, however one preferred to say it. Presently, no pathway linked the two different spots.

Marcus looked at Mother's operators, the majority of whom stared at Selene.

Dr. Khan felt their combined gazes. It was like a weight against her soul. Did they realize the significance of what she had just done? Selene believed they did. Many of them seemed horrified. Unless someone reconnected the pathway, Mother was trapped on the other side, most likely forever. If aliens had easy access to Earth, they would have returned to rule. That meant they could not send Mother back, or if they could, they could not do so easily.

Now came the hard part. Now, Selene had to make sure no one ever reopened the pathway to the meadow world from this side. That meant she had to destroy the underground pyramid, which should destroy humanity's ability to open a dimensional pathway.

Selene took a deep breath and broke into a sprint for the portal. She had to time this just right with the cycler or none of this was going to work. If she failed, Mother's children could potentially reactivate the portal.

-94-

CONTROL CHAMBER
UNDERGROUND PYRAMID

Jack had run after Mother. Then, he'd heard gunfire behind him. He'd stopped and seen Selene kill some of Mother's people. He'd realized that her gun worked, which meant the dampening field must no longer have been on. Agent Elliot had drawn a heater. He'd begun burning those charging Selene, giving her more time to use the controls.

A short time later, Selene dashed for him.

Jack glanced at the large screens. The devastation continued on the Earth. They had to stop the process. They had to turn off the stations spinning the planet's core faster.

Marcus shouted in dismay.

Jack looked where the soldier pointed. The portal had become fuzzy.

"They're gone!" Marcus shouted. "Your woman switched dimensions."

It took Jack a moment to realize what the soldier said. Mother was gone. She was trapped somewhere else with the hound chasing her. She'd turned to face the beast at the last minute. Who would win that battle?

"Get ready!" Selene shouted as she sprinted for the portal.

Get ready for what? Jack wondered. Dr. Khan ran smoothly, her long legs eating up the distance.

Many of Mother's people had already slipped out of the control chamber. There was more than one exit. Jack was sure they raced to get guns or heaters. They had to get out of here. They would be sitting ducks in the center of the chamber.

"Don't let anyone reach Frederick's panel!" Selene shouted. "If they do, Earth loses forever."

Jack looked over there. He saw people trying to reach it. He beamed two women. With the roaring Knocker, Marcus put down a huge man trying to do the same thing.

"Get ready, Jack," Selene panted. She was almost to him.

"Get ready for what?" he asked.

"To run through the portal," Selene yelled. "I set it for Earth. Look! A path is connected again."

Jack glanced at the portal. He saw sand and palm trees. A camel ran like mad with a turban-wearing man whipping it. What was going on out there? A gust of wind blew sand into the chamber through the portal.

"Go, go, go!" Selene shouted. "Run through the portal. We only have a few seconds if we're going to do this."

Jack blinked, trying to figure things out.

Marcus shouted, sprinting for the portal. The soldier seemed to have divined Selene's plan. That was good enough for Jack. He sprinted after the soldier.

Marcus ran through first. Jack was next. For a moment, it felt as if he ran through jelly. A cold sensation hit him. He staggered a moment later, stumbling across sand. The coolness vanished as heat slammed against him.

Marcus surged across the sand, attempting to gain distance. Was there a reason for that?

"Jack!"

Agent Elliot spun around, catching Selene as she stumbled against him.

"Move to the side of the opening," she said. "Get out of their line of sight."

He stared at the opening. It just hung there with nothing supporting it, at least nothing he could see. Through the portal, he saw the underground pyramid's control chamber. Selene tugged him, pulling him to the side. Farther away, Marcus did likewise.

425

Seconds later, bullets flashed through the portal, striking sand where they had been. Some of Mother's children had found weapons to fight back.

The portal began to close in on itself. Suddenly, it closed faster, making a sucking sound. Then it was a pinpoint of color that simply disappeared from existence.

Selene clung to him, laughing wildly as her fingers dug into his flesh.

"Now what?" Jack asked, bewildered. The closing portal had been a weird sight.

"We wait to see if I did it right," Selene whispered.

"Why did we run away? They'll take control of the world machine again. They'll go help Mother against the hound."

"Maybe not," Selene said, cryptically.

Marcus crunched across sand as he walked toward them. He seemed like a gorilla wearing clothes and clutching a hand cannon.

Selene checked her watch.

"Are you waiting for something?" Jack asked her.

"Yes," she whispered.

"We escaped," Marcus said. "But—"

At that moment, in the far distance, maybe forty miles away, a column blew up into the sky. The column grew and grew before expanding into a vast mushroom cloud.

"Get down," Jack shouted.

In time, howling winds shrieked over them. Great heat billowed against them and sand blew in heaving gusts. Eventually, the winds died down and it became simply blistering again.

Selene, Jack and Marcus emerged from the sand that had covered them.

"We did it," Selene said triumphantly, brushing sand out of her hair. "The Earth is safe from Mother and safe from the arrogant aliens she was trying to reach."

Jack and Marcus glanced at her questioningly.

"Do you know what happened?" the soldier asked.

"I do," Selene said. "It's what I planned to do. You see, with the timer and cycler, I reconnected the portal to the lava

426

world. The coordinates were already in place. Frederick had already done all the hard work."

"I don't get it," Jack said.

"You saw what happened when I linked the portal to here. Sand blew into the underground pyramid."

"Right," Jack said. "I do remember that."

"Well," Selene said. "Instead of sand blowing through, lava poured into the underground pyramid. The explosion we just witnessed was the result. Gentlemen, I have destroyed the controls to the world machine. Without the controls, the dimensional portal won't work. That means no one can make a pathway to the alien world where Mother fled."

"That...that means she's trapped on the other side," Jack said.

"Exactly," Selene said.

"Maybe the experimental hound has already killed her," Marcus said.

"That's a possibility too," Selene said.

"You've trapped the hound over there," Marcus said.

"True," Selene said. "But that seems like a world the hound would like."

"I agree," Jack said. "It's a better place for the hound than the Sahara Desert."

"Maybe the aliens will just send Mother back to Earth," Marcus said.

Selene shook her head. She told them her theory about such travel.

"You call them aliens," Jack said. "I think they were fallen angels. I think Samson Mark Two was right."

"Whatever they were or are," Selene said, "we've cut the link between them and us. By destroying the critical underground pyramid, the Earth is rid of Mother for good."

The three of them grew thoughtful.

"I have a question," Jack said.

Selene nodded.

"Is the Earth's core still spinning too fast?" Jack asked. "If it is, how do we slow it down with the control pyramid destroyed?"

427

Selene nodded. "That is the question, isn't it? No doubt, it's going to be a matter of time before we find out about the core."

Jack blinked several times, as he seemed to mull that over.

Selene thought the agent might actually smile for once. He had been so serious every moment they had been together, which had been good, of course. The world needed saving. Could he relax now that they had—?

Before she could complete the thought, Agent Elliot whirled around to face Marcus, aiming a heater at the soldier.

-95-

LIBYAN DESERT

Jack had felt his nape hairs stir. He had a good idea what that meant. Stepping away from Selene and from Marcus, he drew a heater, pivoted and pointed it at the soldier.

Marcus froze with a hand on the butt of his holstered Knocker. The big man hadn't drawn the .55 yet. Marcus's features switched several times. First, he showed shock seeing a heater aimed at him. Then, anger flashed across his face. Finally, the soldier smiled in a good-natured manner. He took his hand from the .55 and spread them both in a gesture of good will.

"What's the meaning of this?" Marcus asked. "We're friends, and we've just won a great victory. We should be celebrating."

"I'd like to know what you're doing, too," Selene told Jack.

Agent Elliot didn't say a word. His nostrils flared as he studied Marcus. So much had happened so quickly. Mrs. King was likely dead. Heck, the world as he knew it might have already vanished. Jack recalled the screens, the fantastic disasters everywhere. There had been Tunguska Events all over the planet. Given enough of them, it would be as if the Earth had gone through a nuclear war.

"We have a decision to make," Jack told Marcus.

"That may be," the soldier said. "First, I'd like to know why you're practicing treachery at a time like this."

"It's called a first strike attack," Jack said.

"I fail to understand your meaning."

"Really?" Jack asked. "Mother's premier hitman doesn't understand what I'm driving at."

Marcus's eyes burned intently. His neck muscles tightened. A moment later, he turned to Selene. "Perhaps you can reason with your murderous friend. Despite our success, we are still in a grim predicament. I suggest we can still benefit from each other's help."

Jack's thumb almost depressed against the firing switch. He knew the soldier's kind. He had a good idea Marcus intended to murder them when the soldier felt the time was right. Yet, there was a tiny particle of doubt and Jack's code of conduct demanded that he be sure when it came to dealing death.

"I have to admit I think Marcus is right," Selene told Jack. "We—the world has changed. Our sides might not even be there anymore."

"Whose side do you think he was on this whole time?" Jack asked. "I'll tell you whose. He was on his own side and no one else's."

"My actions prove otherwise," Marcus said.

Jack snorted with disbelief. "You kidnapped Selene, remember? You did it—"

"If I had not done so," Marcus said. "Mother would still be in the control chamber, enacting her seven hundred year old plan. We have won. Mother is gone with no way to return. She may even be dead by now. The Earth is safe. Let's celebrate our great victory by staying united. We're in the middle of a desert in a blistering heat wave. Our chances of living are slender. Together, we have a much better chance of doing so."

"We might need Marcus's help in turning off the stations around the Earth," Selene added. "What if they're still working and continuing to spin the Earth's core, making the magnetic field stronger and stronger?"

Jack nodded slowly. He felt ninety-eight percent certain that he should burn down the soldier. Selene had valid points, though. Even more importantly, Marcus had knowledge D17 needed. Could Selene and he stay alive if the soldier remained?

"Toss your gun onto the sand," Jack said.

"That is no way to continue our partnership," Marcus told him.

"You're right, but staying alive the next few hours is my primary objective. Therefore, toss the gun or I'll be forced to kill you."

"Cold-blooded murder?" Marcus asked.

"Yeah," Jack said. "It's not my first choice, but neither is dying at your hand. I don't trust you."

The soldier smiled coldly, glancing at Selene and raising an eyebrow as if to say, "Are you seeing this? Are you listening?" Then, he lifted the .55 from its holster and tossed it at Jack's feet.

Jack stepped back from the gun. "Dr. Khan, do you mind carrying it for a time?"

"Please, Jack. I trust your judgment. I want you to keep calling me Selene."

Jack glanced at her. Her hair was tousled, her face smudged with dirt and her eyes ringed with exhaustion. But she looked like the most beautiful woman in the world just then.

Jack's lips twitched as the right corner trembled as if using muscles long out of practice. Slowly, the right corner lifted upward in the slightest of grins. It was the most he'd smiled since…

"Selene," Jack said, with a catch in his throat, "do you mind carrying Marcus's gun for a while?"

"Not at all," she said.

"Am I supposed to be your prisoner?" the soldier rumbled.

Jack shook his head. "I'm grateful for your help."

"This is an odd way of showing it," Marcus said.

"True, but you're more dangerous than me. I recognize that, and I know you have ulterior motives."

"As do you," Marcus said.

"True," Jack said. "I want to protect my country. What do you want?"

Marcus turned away, silent for a time. Finally, he said, "I want to know the state of our world, whether we're going to have one or not. We won't find out staying here."

"I'd like to trust you," Jack told Marcus. "I have to trust my instincts more, though."

The soldier didn't reply.

"Let's get started," Selene suggested.

Jack agreed.

"Where should we head?" she asked.

"For the coast," Jack said.

"What direction is that?"

Jack glanced at Marcus. The soldier still wasn't speaking. "That way," Agent Elliot said, "north."

-96-

38 HOURS LATER
LIBYAN COAST

Alone at night Marcus slipped into a dark coastal village. After secretly slipping away from Jack Elliot, he had left the other two far behind in the desert.

Agent Elliot had proved adept, getting the drop on him and remaining alert every minute afterward. Well, except for the last several minutes that had allowed Marcus to run far enough away so the heater couldn't reach him. After that, it had simply been a matter of keeping ahead of the weaker couple.

Jack had been so watchful otherwise that the D17 agent had even seemed to sleep while remaining awake. That had been a neat trick, well worth learning someday. Marcus's subtle efforts to turn Selene against Jack had failed. He'd had two options after that. Attempt to kill Jack Elliot or escape from the man's vigilance. Remaining with them as second fiddle hadn't been conceivable to his pride.

A dog snarled in the darkness as Marcus crunched across gravel. He ignored the nervous creature. It would not dare to close with him.

Above, a fantastic Aurora Borealis lit the night sky, making it difficult to see the stars and showing that the Earth's magnetic field was still many times stronger than before to shine so brightly this far south. In normal times, people would

433

only have seen the so-called Northern Lights up north where they belonged.

No electric lights burned in the homes of this village because likely the long-distance power lines no longer carried electricity. The world had changed and maybe was still changing.

Did any of the underground or underwater stations remain? Did they continue to spin the Earth's core faster or keep it going at this higher speed? Marcus planned to find out as quickly as possible. He needed to contact whoever remained in Mother's organization. Then, he would have to answer Jack's infernal question.

What do I want? That would depend on many things.

Another hound began to howl. That brought a chorus of barking directed at him.

Marcus picked up a stone. He would shut them up.

A moment later, a truck roared into life ahead of him. The headlights snapped on, blinding him with their brightness.

That told Marcus several important things. Engines and electronics still worked. Wires could carry electrical power for short distances even though the long-distance lines didn't work right now.

Behind the headlights, a man shouted at him.

Marcus understood the language. He raised his hands in the air.

A man with a cloth wrapped around his head stepped into view. He cradled an AK-47. He shouted instructions.

Marcus lay on his stomach, putting his hands behind his head.

Soon, three men stood nearby. Each likely aimed his assault rifle at him. Marcus didn't believe these three were villagers. They had a rough edge to them and they seemed nervous that he had friends.

One of them poked the back of Marcus's head with the barrel of an assault rifle.

"Who are you?" the man demanded.

"I'm a Frenchman," Marcus said. "I'm here to help restore the electricity."

"What happened?" the man demanded. "Why doesn't the power work anymore?"

"The Americans have a new weapon," Marcus said.

"That is a lie!"

"It is true," Marcus said. "The French government has sent aid—"

"Why are you alone?" the man demanded.

"An American drone shot up our convoy," Marcus said.

The three men whispered among themselves. Marcus could hear every word with his keen hearing. They debated the idea among themselves. Two believed Marcus. The leader did not. The leader suspected this was a French trick, come to rescue the villagers.

That's when Marcus realized he was right. These were bandits or terrorists, taking advantage of the chaos. It gave him the direction he would take with these men.

"Can you fix radios?" the leader asked.

"I can, indeed," Marcus said.

"Then get up. You will fix mine. Then...then we shall see."

Marcus climbed to his feet, marching ahead of the three. Someone ground truck gears. The vehicle paced him, lighting the way to the biggest building. It might have been a post office. Several other trucks were parked in the small lot.

The running truck stopped, keeping its headlights on as the motor idled.

"The radio is inside," the leader said, poking Marcus in the back.

Marcus turned around and plucked the weapon out of the man's hands. It astounded the leader. Marcus knew how to move fast. He shot the leader through the heart. He shot the other two as well for good measure.

The lesser men had such dulled reflexes, nothing like Jack Elliot.

Moving fast, Marcus fired above the headlights. When he reached the truck, the driver was slumped over dead at the wheel. The corpse had a bullet in the brain.

If there were other bandits or terrorists in the village, they must have been asleep. Marcus threw the dead man onto the street, climbed into the truck and put it in reverse. He had almost a full tank of gas. That was good.

Marcus braked, put the truck into first gear and roared out of the village. No one gave chase. He hadn't expected they would.

At that moment, he decided to head for Tripoli in order to pick up more gear. Once he had what he needed, he planned to head to the nearest underground station. Speed could be critical. Whatever had happened to the world, he planned to take advantage of it. For that, he needed a disciplined organization and high tech. The stations could well contain both.

Marcus tightened his grip of the steering wheel. Later, he could capture Selene. She might be the smartest person on the planet now. She would help him figure out his next step. And Agent Elliot—

Marcus scowled. He had a score to settle with Jack. Mother, Frederick and Hela had all learned what it meant to make him an enemy. Jack Elliot was going to learn that soon enough, too. On that, Marcus vowed.

-97-

The Libyan coast fell away to the south as the dhow headed for Italy. The boat was of an ancient design, propelled by sail alone.

Jack stood at the prow, watching the waves. He had seen the Northern Lights in the Libyan night sky. Selene had explained their significance to him. Every night the lights had seemed a little brighter and the stars dimmer. What did that mean for humanity? Was there a way to reverse what Mother had started with the Earth's core?

Jack sighed.

Marcus had escaped. That troubled him. He had a feeling they hadn't seen the last of the supposed superman. It was good to know Mother wasn't coming back. There was no dimensional portal, not until someone built something like the underground pyramid again. Jack hoped the hound had won the fight between them.

As Jack stood at the prow, his eyes grew heavy. He hadn't been able to sleep well ever since the soldier had slunk away. He had expected Marcus's return and had been extra vigilant because of that. Under those conditions, Jack had slept like a wild creature, jerking awake frequently, aiming a heater at the slightest stir of air.

We should be safe out here, at least.

437

Jack closed his eyes, and jerked awake some time later. He turned. One of the crew was several feet from him. The Libyan smiled, although the man had one hand behind his back.

Here we go. Jack stared at the man.

That made the Libyan nervous. The man finally asked, "I wish to know if everything is satisfactory?"

Jack didn't answer. He just watched the man. What did the Libyan hold behind his back?

A clunk sounded. The man shuffled his feet, kicking a rope over something, a knife, a sap, something.

"That's a good start," Jack said. "Now, back up."

The Libyan bowed his head, smiling wider than ever. The other two Libyans in the dhow watched, one at the tiller, the other patching sail with a needle and thread.

"Did you spot anything out there in the sea?" the Libyan asked.

"I said back up."

The man hesitated too long.

A heater appeared in Jack's hand. The thumb hovered over the switch.

"You understand that these are troubled times," the Libyan said, licking his lips. "The world…is changing. I must feed my family. I must—"

Jack moved toward the man.

The sailor at the tiller pushed. The dhow moved sharply. Jack staggered because of that and went down to one knee.

The Libyan standing before him must have been waiting for that. He scooped his hand low, coming up with a knife, a wicked little blade. He rushed Jack.

Jack sighed inwardly. He'd had enough of death, of killing. The world likely needed everyone who was left. He let the Libyan close, and judged the knife thrust a practiced one. The man obviously knew how to wield a blade.

It didn't prove to be good enough, however. The knife and hand thrust forward. Jack shifted just enough to avoid the weapon and struck the man's wrist. The knife fell a second time. The man stared at Jack, his eyes growing larger every second. Agent Elliot hit him in the face, catapulting the man backward.

438

The crazy thing about all this was that Selene slept soundly throughout. She was exhausted just like Jack.

Five minutes later, Jack had the three Libyan crewmembers backed up against a gunwale. The Libyan coast was still visible. It seemed that while he'd been sleeping, the crew had shifted course.

"I should kill the lot of you," Jack said.

"Please," the youngest of them begged. "We are—"

"Shut up," Jack told him.

The young Libyan did. The other two watched with bitter eyes.

"I'm not going to kill you," Jack said.

"Oh thank you, merciful—"

The Libyan shut up a second time as Jack raised an eyebrow.

"You're going to swim, though," he told them. "See the shoreline out there."

"It's too far," the oldest Libyan said, the one who had shifted the tiller.

Jack shook his head, jerking a thumb at Selene. "She swam over one hundred miles just a few days ago. This—"

"It is too far. We will drown. If you wish to kill us…" the oldest Libyan shrugged.

Jack studied the trio, the three who would have killed him without compunction.

"Okay," Jack said. "I'll strike a deal. Show me how your dhow works and I'll allow you to go near shore. Then, you're going to swim the rest of the way."

The young one nodded happily. The other two watched Jack even more carefully.

"Otherwise," Jack said. "I'll burn you down here and now, and push your corpses overboard."

Sullenly, the older two agreed. They showed Jack the tricks to the dhow and then headed back toward the coast.

-98-

CENTRAL MEDITERRANEAN

Selene stirred at the sound of splashing. She thought she'd heard shouts. They dwindled as the dhow creaked in its ancient rhythm.

Later, her eyes opened. She yawned, moving her limbs. It felt good to have slept so peacefully. She sat up, sipped some water and finally looked around.

Jack was at the tiller. The wind made the triangular sail billow.

"This is better than marching through the desert," she said.

"Yes," Jack agreed.

Selene sighed, laying back, putting her hands behind her head. The flashes no longer made her mind feel like an out-of-control top. She was woozy at times. But if she remained still, the feeling went away.

Sitting up again, stretching, she had the feeling that something was off. That was too bad. She had—

"Hey," she said. "Where are the others?"

"They left some time ago," Jack said.

"What? Why? How did they leave?"

"Who can know why they jumped overboard and began to swim for shore?" Jack said.

"Agent Elliot," Selene said. "I demand you tell me what happened."

He did.

"And you never woke me up?" Selene asked.

"You looked so peaceful," he said. "I didn't have the heart."

She thought about that. After a time, she looked away. It had started for her on the high seas. Now, it looked like it was ending on the water. All the people she'd called friends were gone. Many others she'd just known as acquaintances might be…dead.

Selene shivered. What a dreadful word that was. There had been too much death these past few days. It was incredible so much had happened in so short a time.

"What do we do if…?" she left the question unasked.

"We're headed for Rome," Jack said. "If the lights are going out of civilization, we'll have to make our choices then. If not, I need to contact D17. They have to know what happened. Then, we have to see if any of the stations are left and go from there."

"That makes sense," Selene said.

For the next hour, Jack steered the dhow north. Selene got up and helped with the sail. She knew the sea and she knew boats.

They ate later, and Selene became very thoughtful.

"What are thinking?" Jack asked her.

"The explosion," she said.

"Which one?"

"The big one at the end," she said, "the one that sent the underground pyramid into the sky. The destruction that made sure Mother was never coming back."

"What about it?"

"Why did it go nuclear like that?" Selene asked. "I mean the giant mushroom cloud at the end."

"You said because of the lava world gushing into it," Jack replied.

"The more I think about it, the more I'm not sure that makes sense."

"What else could it be?"

"That's what's troubling me," Selene said. "What if…"

"Yes?" Jack asked.

441

"What if I let something alien onto the Earth? What if the alien thing was smart and it did something to the pyramid that blew it sky-high?"

"I'd call that problem solved," Jack said.

"Or maybe just begun," Selene said.

Jack spit over the side of the boat, shrugging afterward. "Maybe, maybe, maybe," he said. "Right now, I know that we're alive. We beat Mother, got rid of her and stopped her from destroying everything at a blow. Maybe the stations are still spinning the core faster, but we're going to stop that if we can. Therefore, now isn't the time to worry about it. Now, it's time to enjoy a few moments of peace and congratulate ourselves that we won this round."

Selene realized this was the longest speech she'd ever heard Jack make. "You're right. Let's enjoy these moments of peace."

Jack nodded.

Selene had found a bottle of wine, which surprised her. Maybe the Libyans had drunk while out at sea. She now grabbed it by the neck and approached Agent Elliot at the tiller. She raised the bottle, swinging it suggestively from side to side.

"How about joining me for some sips as we swap tall stories?" she said. "Then, we can see what happens afterward."

The slight grin appeared at the corner of Jack's mouth again, and he nodded once more to let her know he understood her meaning. Afterward, he tied the tiller into place and went to join her for some well-deserved wine.

-Epilogue-

It took Jack and Selene longer to reach Rome than Agent Elliot had expected. It was chaotic in the city, although a few homes had lights. The Italian military supplied whatever order there was.

Surprisingly, Americans still worked at the U.S. Embassy. Jack spoke to the CIA liaison there. The woman instructed him and Selene to wait.

Three days later, Marine guards drove Jack and Selene to the airport. A U.S. Air Force bomber waited for them on the runway.

"This doesn't make sense," Jack told the CIA liaison.

She shrugged. Maybe it didn't make sense to her, either. It appeared, though, that she had her orders.

Jack and Selene shook her hand and boarded the jet. Soon, they were airborne, heading for America.

"Sir," a Marine sergeant said. "If you would both come with me please."

The Marine guided them into a plush compartment. It had a wet bar with a man sitting on a tall stool, his back to them. Quietly, the Marine took his leave.

"Secretary Smith?" Jack asked in surprise.

The man swiveled around. He wore a black suit and tie with the sleeves a little too short. He had shaved away any hint of a mustache. He still had the same doughy face and pudgy hands, though.

"Can I get you something to drink?" Smith asked.

Jack ushered Selene to the bar.

She sat, saying, "I'd like a Bloody Mary, please."

Smith got up, went behind the bar and began to make the drink. After he set it on the bar, he looked at Jack.

"A brandy will do just fine," Jack said.

Smith poured him one.

Jack sipped, sighing afterward. It was good. "I don't understand why you're here, Mr. Secretary."

"Really?" Smith said. "You have no idea?"

"I think I do," Selene said.

"It's a pleasure to finally meet you," Smith said. "I'm looking forward to hearing exactly what happened. I've only heard the briefing Jack gave the CIA liaison."

"What is this about?" Jack asked.

"This," Smith said, waving a hand, "is an indication of just how important you two have become. Just to let you know, we've stormed two underground stations so far. We took incredible losses doing so."

"Are you talking about D17?" Jack asked.

"No," Smith said, "the U.S. Army. We won in the end because compared to the station personnel we had an unlimited number of bodies. Some of the country's top scientists have begun working on the enemy's weaponry. We want to mass produce them for ourselves."

"Civilization is still hanging on?" Selene asked.

"That's an astute question," Smith said. "The short answer is yes. The Earth has taken terrible damage, no doubt about that. Many countries are mere shells of what they were. Disease and starvation are running rampant just about everywhere. That's the bad news."

"There's good news?" Jack asked.

"Oh, yes," Smith said. "We discovered something incredibly important. The underground pyramid—"

"You know about that?" Jack asked.

"We learned about it several days ago," Smith said. "That was after the army overpowered the personnel in Station Five. When the pyramid exploded, it began an automatic reaction in the various stations. They immediately began slowing the Earth's core instead of repelling it."

"Ah," Selene said, "interesting."

"Yes," Smith said. "The magnetic field is already decaying from its intense setting. That means given enough time, we can rebuild what we lost. We know Mother almost destroyed civilization. If the spin had continued any longer…"

"How do you know Mother's name?" Jack asked.

"I told you. We interrogated captured station personnel. They told us many interesting things."

Selene sipped her drink, staring at a bulkhead.

"Maybe we can use their advanced technology to help rebuild faster," Smith said.

"We did it then," Jack said. "We won."

"Well," Smith said, "that depends on what exactly happened to Mother. We haven't learned anything concerning her fate."

Selene told him the details.

"Excellent," Smith said after she was finished. "I think I should call Secretary King and tell her the good news."

"What?" Jack said. "You said King had a heart attack."

For the first time, Smith looked embarrassed. "We called it a heart attack. That's what I told you over the satellite phone. In reality, Mother sent a special assassin to kill Mrs. King. The assassin simulated a heart attack in King but it cost him his life. King shot him before the simulated heart attack incapacitated her. Then, she immediately called me. We barely got her to the hospital in time."

Jack nodded in appreciation.

"You just said something interesting," Selene told Smith. "You claimed you can call the Secretary as in with a radio?"

"It isn't through a radio," Smith said, "but we can communicate long distance again, at least if we're flying high enough and are in direct line of sight. It's one of the new technologies we picked up. Are you ready?"

"I am," Jack said.

"I believe so is the Secretary," Smith said. "She has a new assignment for you. It involves the stations."

Jack and Selene traded glances.

Smith raised his eyebrows. Then, he pulled a small device from an inner coat pocket, clicking it. A screen lowered. He pressed another button. Several seconds later, Secretary King of D17 smiled at them from her office in Washington D.C.

Jack Elliot allowed himself another of his rare grins. They had won. Earth was intact. Mother was gone forever. The core was slowing down and humanity had begun to rebuild from the terrible damage. Maybe just as important, America knew their hidden enemy now, the ones who had pulled the strings behind the scenes for so long.

Maybe this time, they could rebuild the world into something better than before. Jack reached across the bar and took hold of Selene's left hand. Then, he listened to what Secretary King had to tell him.

The End

Made in the USA
Middletown, DE
04 April 2020